every thing will be okay

every
thing
will be
okay

every
thing
will be
okay

DARK ROOM
PRESS

Sean J.
Gebhardt

First published in 2025 by Dark Room Press
Copyright © Sean J Gebhardt 2025
The moral right of the author has been asserted.

ISBN: 979-8-9918732-0-8 (paperback)
ISBN: 979-8-9918732-9-1 (ebook)

Cover design by Duncan Blachford
Text design and typesetting by Typography Studio

for all of us when we were younger,
and all the ones we left behind

HF: How are you feeling today?

NW: Fine.

HF: Always fine with you, isn't it?

NW: Always.

HF: Nicholas—

NW: It's Nick, you know this.

HF: Nick—

NW: Look, doc, save it. Can I just be honest with you?

HF: Please.

NW: This whole thing is a joke.

HF: Which thing?

NW: The whole thing.

. . .

HF: I'm listening, please, go on.

NW: *I'm listening, please, go on.* This shit. First off, don't give me
that clinical treatment. I'm not trying to be an asshole, but
I'm not an idiot, okay? The easiest way to act like we're friends
is to act like we're friends. I know we're not friends. I know
you don't give a shit. But if you really want me to believe that
you give a shit, then you're going to have to act like you give
a shit. And if you don't? Then don't. Just stamp my form and
let me go home because this is a joke. I've been here for six
weeks. I'm not threatening you or myself or anyone else. I'm
lucid and coherent and in possession of all my faculties. I can
stand on one foot and do the alphabet backwards if you want.
I don't know what else you hope to accomplish by asking me
how I'm *feeeeling* all day. In fact, I don't know much at all, but I
know enough to know that this whole god damn thing is a big
fucking joke. I want to go home.

HF: Hah. Alright, alright, that's fair. I suppose you're right, we're not friends. I am not your friend. And yet, your life is not a joke to me and so here we are. Is life a joke to you?

NW: Yeah, I'm laughing alright. Can't you tell? Jesus, what is wrong with you? Did you actually go to school for this shit?

HF: Believe it or not. So am I the joke?

NW: Look man, I don't really know you and I don't want to. I don't want to sit here and attack your life's work, but you really suck at it. You don't know shit about me and every time we talk you just keep asking me "How do you feel? How did you sleep? How is the food?" like you're a nerd on a blind date with a supermodel. Bring something to the table, man, or she's never going to reciprocate.

HF: And *you* are the supermodel in this analogy?

NW: Zing. Good one. Fuck you, you know what i mean.

HF: Forgive me, I just want to be clear I understand. As you were.

NW: God dammit doc, we almost had a moment there and you just went and fucked it off again. I'm trying to tell you I hate this and that I just need you to listen to me and fuck off, so will you please just stamp the form and fuck yourself out of my life?

HF: I am listening, and we can discuss my fucking off if you tell me what I want to hear.

NW: What do you want to hear? That I'm sorry? That I'm so grateful I'm alive? That it'll never happen again? That my daddy wasn't around and my mommy loved me too much and that's why I want to— Ugh. Never mind. I mean really, man. What is it? What is the point of this shit? Six weeks, man. Six. I'm fine. I'm not crazy. I'm not psychotic. I'm not hurting anyone. I just want to be a warm fuckin' ray of sunshine on everyone I meet. What do you want? Jesus.

HF: What do *you* want?

NW: I want you to stamp my form and let me leave.

HF: Nick. Do you want to die?

NW: I want to go home.

MONDAY

1

"Oh fuck, not again."
　　　　　　—DR. HENRY FOSTER, every single day

Decades brought different cities, different beds, different faces on adjacent pillows, periods of waking up alone. Different birdsongs, the sunlight encroaching from different angles. Different neighbors with different habits. Lawnmowers, leaf blowers, power washers, motorcycles. The years in apartment complexes: feet stomping overhead, bad music in the walls, punctuated bass drums. Each morning a minor trauma. Body consciousness never came quietly. The aches, the hunger, dry mouth, damp shirts. The quiet and the cold winter-grey mornings. Rainfall. Cemetery silence. A mattress on the floor in college with three roommates and no hot water. Waking up in someone else's bed. A coffee habit short only of the bedside IV. Those misguided months of marriage to early-morning exercise. The perpetually hungover twenties. Career-driven thirties. And now, trudging through mid-life.

The changing conditions made no difference to the fresh, waking mind of Henry Foster. Rotary alarm clocks to digital clock-radios to the eight or nine successive cell phones, each bringing subsequent technological advancements to the act of waking up. So many bells, chimes, and ringtones. Once he had briefly owned an ambient-noise clock, which gave him the option of waking to waves crashing or the sounds of a tropical rainforest at dawn, and despite all of this, for sixteen thousand three hundred and thirty-six consecutive days, it felt like the first sound he discerned upon waking always came from somewhere in his skull rooted deeper and older than his active cognition saying,
　　　　　　"Oh fuck. Not again."

Every morning was the same. In all of human history, there had never been a more daunting task than his rising to meet another day. In his first waking moments, the shock became anxiety became despair, and he would often spend the earliest hours of his day grappling with his own will to live. He had spent time indeterminable with eyes closed in denial, attempting to reconstruct some sense of self from an incoherent mosaic of excerpted ideas or memories.

In his most lucid moments—usually later in the day, when he could reflect with some humor on himself—he was certain that this was a pathological disorder worthy of diagnosis. It couldn't just be simple laziness, or the reluctance of inertia. Honestly, the days were not often even so daunting at all. He had written his own schedule for ten years and had been secure in his career for even longer. He scoffed at ideas of clinical depression or an anxiety disorder; the intervals of despair were so predictable and fleeting that his life was met with no ostensible dysfunction at the hands of these morning tantrums. And furthermore, he was not depressed. He could take inventory of his life, his accomplishments, his trajectory, and congratulate himself on all he had seen, done, and possessed. Life had bestowed upon him a series of heartaches and hassles, sure, but that wasn't depression.

He had seen depressed people. Worked with them. Studied them. He was an expert in psychological and emotional disorders and disturbances of all kinds. The irony of moving through life as an expert on depression with undiagnosed depression was too great for him to accept, and so he did not accept it. This was just the price of waking up each day. And every morning, the price felt too high.

Henry was mostly fair in his assessment of his own accomplishments. He had lived a remarkably productive life, after all. If productivity was the measure of well-being, then Henry Foster was doing just fine, *god dammit*. He had survived childhood and the war of adolescence and had come out clean on the other side. He had completed grad school, earned his doctorate, and been successful in his career, eventually building a lucrative practice of his own. His name was on titles and deeds, his savings flush, his schedule full, his history rich, and he was still young enough to believe there was much more to come.

But these things did not matter when the alarm tones interrupted his sleep without warning, and in hypnagogia, a collision of reverie and consciousness presented an irreconcilable reality fraught with disappointment, tragedy, uncertainty, the dull ache of an aging back, the smell of sleep thick in the air, the sense that something great and significant had been lost along the way, and the certainty that if it could not be identified it could not be regained. It was a panic; it was a puzzle.

Every morning, it was the same. The first breath like the gasp of someone trapped under ice emerging just prior to meeting God and her devils. Was it a rescue or a robbery? The minutes that followed demanded a rapid inventory of all objective truths. *It is Monday. It is 6:15am. The date is December 5, 2022. This is my home. I am alone. This is my life.*

Fuck me.

Moments passed, the mind raced, eventually the body followed suit, and he got at least from the bed to the bathroom to make room in himself for the coffee that was to follow.

I am okay.

Thank god for the coffee-pot timer.

Pour a cup. First sip black. *Everything is okay.* He added milk and sugar to soften the edges. "Life is bitter enough," he would say when his ex-wife teased him about his preference for sweet coffee. She had known better than to cajole him before he had signaled his readiness. Ever since she moved out, the time to readiness had only extended.

Too nauseous for food already. The acids from the coffee swirled with those in his stomach and only made the idea of breakfast that much more undesirable.

He looked around his house, eyeing his belongings in search for an anchor to reality. The antique grandfather clock which haunted his living room, a relic from childhood that had been handed down from some order of great or great-great-grandpeople. In his youth he sat beneath the clock waiting for it to strike on the hour to watch the pendulum swing in measured melancholy while the dutiful chimes sang a requiem to the honor and glory of another moment gone, never to return. A song of time lost to time. Life lost to life. Sixteen bells of "Jowett's Jig" reminded him of a longing to live, or at least a healthy fear of dying. This remembrance would come to be a welcome gift in the anguish of the mornings when neither was anywhere to be found.

I am alone. We all are. Each of us and all together—alone. His greatest fear was that the morning was the only time the thoughts came clear, uninhibited, unobstructed, unadulterated by the myriad distractions of waking life. *Is this delusion or is this clarity?*

The doubt always lingered. He could never be quite sure which was which when it came to matters of personal experience, and it troubled him. Even late in the day, when the panic was gone and his wits were about him, he remained skeptical. He had been traumatized by his career, perhaps. Hours spent with individuals unable to reconcile their emotions with their positions in life. He knew just how far a mind could mislead its owner from objective reality; the idea itself was unnerving.

In the delusory transience of emotion, he had found not just incessant doubt, but also a touchstone of salvation, and the only absolute Truth he knew: *All things pass.* Of course, sometimes it all felt so heavy he thought he might collapse beneath it. Sometimes it felt like none of it mattered at all. Sometimes he was sure that everything would be okay, and still the internal dialogue would remind him not to get carried away on the whim of emotion. *It will pass*, a mantra which repeated in his head like a prayer and a plea and a patronizing little slogan, a commercial jingle of relief.

This morning he stared silently, searching. Through the rising steam of the second cup of coffee, through the glass of the kitchen window, through the still space of his backyard, through the wet leaves of the sentry of trees in the oversized yard of the house across the fence, through the frosted blue skyline backlighting the neighborhood just down the hill from his view, through the vapors and the clouds, past the remnant quarter-moon dying with pride before the awe of the dawn, through light years of indecipherable transmissions from the stars and the dust clouds and the progenitors of all of history, he looked for reprieve from this plague of self-doubt.

He couldn't remember a time when he was able to move from sleep to waking without the pain of the transition, though in recent months—maybe a year or more, but he wasn't counting—the grief had been compounded by a hangover that seemed to get worse with each morning that he woke up alone in the bed he once shared with his wife.

What are you looking for? He winced. *She isn't out there.*

He told himself it wasn't about her. The drinking, well, maybe that was. But who hadn't used an extra drink or two to cope with loss, to adjust to change, to process grief and stress?

Suck it up. You're an adult, for Christ's sake. Get dressed. Let's go.

The panic always settled, but the weight of doubt, regret, and fear lingered on and haunted his days. More and more he would repeat to himself, *I am okay. Everything is okay. It's going to pass.*

By midday, what demons had greeted his waking mind would return to the nightmares they inhabited, and any remaining sense of significance therein would be compartmentalized for safekeeping, while those tormentors who did not go so quietly would be subject to drowning by drink and the occasional pharmaceutical-grade sedative. These days, they never went quietly.

Every night he drank himself to sleep, and every morning was the same.

‡

Session transcript from patient files of Dr. Henry Foster
Patient: Wagner, Nicholas
10/10/22, continued

HF: I need to know that you aren't going to hurt yourself.

NW: *Do you?* Do you *need* to know? Will you just lose so much sleep tonight wondering if little Nicky is safe out there in the big bad world if I don't promise you I'll be okay? Come on, man, you've got to be smarter than me, *doctor*. You've done just fine here. You play dumb but I see that stupid watch. What was that, fifteen k? You know what else you can buy for fifteen k? A god damn car. And guess what? That motherfucker'll tell you the time just as well. You don't give a shit. You couldn't possibly. But you've got to be smart enough to understand that I'm not an idiot. I'll just say what you want to hear and you can stamp your form and we can both go about our happy little lives, alright?

HF: Right again, Nicholas.

NW: It's *Nick*—

HF: Quiet. Listen to me. You talk a lot for someone who doesn't want to talk, you know that? You're right, Nick. I don't care. And I'm certainly not going to care more than you do, because I am a sane person with the ability to discern between battles worth fighting and those from which it is wise to walk away. I don't want to fight with you. I know this has been painful for you, and I can only imagine what you're going through. But this hasn't exactly been pleasant for me either. At this point, I want to shuffle you out of here as quickly as you want to leave. I have better things to do than try to help someone who doesn't want to be helped. And yet, tragically for us both, I am bound by law and ethics to assure the State of California's Medical Board that I did everything in my power and professional judgment to determine that you are not at risk of harming yourself or someone else before I can "*stamp my form.*" You were released from jail into our custody, and if you would like to remain out of theirs, then I'm going to need to hear you say it. I can recommend another hold and the judge will sign it and you can stay here another month if you'd like. I hear you're teaching Jerry how to play the piano. How fulfilling that must be for you. Perhaps it is time well spent for you, beating your head against the wall, trying to get an eighty-nine-year-old with severe Alzheimer's and shit in his pants to remember a four-chord progression from breakfast until dinner. So you might actually understand what it's like for me trying to hold a conversation with you for the last six weeks. Maybe you can make good use of your time here after all? Is that what you would prefer?

...

NW: What. The hell?

HF: Do you remember the events that led you here?

...

NW: Yes.

HF: Are you having any suicidal thoughts today?

NW: No.

HF: Do you have any plans to hurt yourself or anyone else?

NW: No.

HF: Excellent.

NW: Can I go home now?

HF: I'll sign for your release to be executed today. But Nick, I need to see you back here. I'm going to order that you come back and see me weekly until further notice. Understood?

NW: What? Why? You just said you don't give a shit.

HF: And yet, I'm ethically obligated to, so we're both fucked.

NW: Wow. You are a real asshole, aren't you?

HF: Nick, listen. This is going to catch up with you. You might not believe me, but going home won't be as easy as you think.

NW: Catch up to me. Right. And if it doesn't? I'll be gone. What then?

HF: If I don't see you next Monday, or if you miss any scheduled appointment, then I will call the police myself.

NW: And tell them what?

HF: I'll send them out on a medically ordered welfare check. They'll have to patrol until they find you and bring you in for evaluation. If I'm not here, they'll have to keep you in custody until they get hold of me. Could be another little stretch for you, and then you'd be back here with me all over again.

NW: Fuck you, man. You love this shit. You're sicker than I am.

HF: So, I'll see you Monday?

NW: Uh huh. Sure. Thanks a ton, doc.
HF: It's what I'm here for.

‡

Henry arrived at his office fifteen minutes before his first session of the day. He needed the fifteen minutes to acclimate to the office, to disrobe himself of the man whose mornings could dissolve him into a puddle of panic and uncertainty, and to appropriate the air of a calming and expert source of solace. It was all in the presentation. These people didn't care who he was; they only cared what he presented as in the time they spent together. He supposed this was true of all human interactions, but he knew it was in poor taste to share such a thought, and so he did not. He committed to playing the role that was expected of him, dutifully and always. And most of them were only here for drugs, anyway.

Henry's office was a spacious second-floor room in a two-story building just on the edge of the walkable downtown district in the mid-sized California suburb of Santa Lucia. He had no lobby, no front desk, no receptionist, and no real colleagues, apart from the other building tenants. Parking was plentiful, overheads were low, the elevators were modern, and the architecture was generous with window coverage and blinds which ran from floor to ceiling and wall to wall, allowing for a perfect tailoring of sunlight to fit the mood of the moment.

From the beginning of his private practice, he had prioritized presentation. As a young doctor going into business on his own, it had been difficult to convince himself that his fees were not exorbitant—that he would be able to justify his price to his patients. He had combatted this insecurity by investing in an office that looked like it was worth the money. His ex-wife, Gretchen, had helped him design a space that felt more like a chic and cozy den than a doctor's office. They had replaced the cold white-and-black-speckled tile that lined the rest of the building with dark woodgrain laminate flooring and a large area rug with long swaths of greys, greens, and deep blues. She insisted he use floor lamps and natural sunlight instead of the overhead fluorescents. She hung earth-toned floral prints on the wall instead of the abstract art or landscapes he had always seen in hospitals and other doctors' offices.

Even the furniture she had picked felt inviting. Pillowy and low to the ground, featuring soft, neutral brown fabric on a matching loveseat and armchair-ottoman combo. A low wooden coffee table sat in the center of the arrangement, upon which sat a small self-contained stone fountain trickling an endless stream of natural ambient noise. Opposite the recliner was Henry's chair—the absurdly expensive reclining brown-leather lounge chair and matching ottoman that Gretchen had bought him as a surprise at the end of the remodel. In the corner opposite the window, behind his lounge chair, sat a modest wooden desk. A light finish, four legs, and enough depth for a single drawer. On the desk was a laptop computer, a lamp, a notepad, and a pen. In the drawer was a prescription pad and a bottle of 2mg Alprazolam bars. The former was a relic from a time before the Information Age gave us instantly transmissible prescriptions, and the latter was to treat the occasional side effects of living in such an age.

It was Monday, and his first patient would be Bobbie Mills. Bobbie had been coming to see him every other Monday at 9am for four years and he didn't know why. Originally she had come to see him on a referral because she was experiencing a renaissance of curiosity about her child-hood, brought on by some trouble she had been having with depression after a particularly bad breakup. After a prescription for a general anti-depressant and the passing of time balanced her moods, her curiosity abated and the sessions became routine check-ins more akin to gossip of the week than any constructive self-exploration.

Henry didn't mind and neither, it seemed, did Bobbie. Every now and then he would gently remind her that if she wanted to save some money, she could check in on a less frequent basis and he would continue to manage her prescription. But she trusted him and seemed to appreciate the opportunity to vent or process the goings-on of her week, and though he couldn't have been less interested in the petty dramatics of her dating life and squabbles with her sister and mother, she was pleasant enough, carried the bulk of the conversation, and never balked at a bill, so he appreciated the easy and reliable start to his Monday.

Henry sat in his lounge, drinking coffee from his thermos, semi-engaged in the content on his phone. He scrolled through news articles, reading the headlines to absorb the general mood of the world-at-large today. If one particularly piqued his interest, he would skim the opening paragraphs before moving on to the next.

Chair of Senate Ethics Committee Indicted on Charges of Corruption

Never trust the guy in charge of the Ethics Committee.

Top Scientists Plead with World Governments to Heed Climate Warnings

Pipe down, nerds. We're busy destroying everything. When we need your help, we'll ask for it, and then we will also ignore it.

"Voice of God" Nebula Continues to Perplex Astronomers with Complex Radio Transmissions, Prompting People Around the World to Ask, Have We Found Evidence of God in the Stars?

Hold on, let me guess ... Nope. Next.

These 27 Photos of People Acting Like Embarrassing Fucking Morons in Public will Literally Make You So Uncomfortable You Will Want to Murder Your Neighbors and then Swallow a Live Hand Grenade and Run Screaming into Traffic

12

He clicked the last one and was halfway down the list when he heard Bobbie's hurried footsteps echoing in the hall. It was 9:06 when she appeared in his doorway. She paused there for a moment before walking in.

"Oh my god, Dr. Foster, I'm so sorry. Is it alright if I come in still?" she said, using her neck and shoulders to make herself smaller. With a sheepish look, she gestured toward the loveseat with the sunglasses in her hand.

"Of course, of course. I hadn't even noticed the time. Come on in." Henry motioned with his hand, welcoming her into his office. "Forgive me, I just have to finish this one thing and then we'll get started. Have a seat, have a seat." He held his phone upright in his hand, careful not to expose the screen, and scrolled through the remainder of the list.

When he was finished, he put down his phone, affected a pensive expression, and apologized again for keeping her waiting.

"Oh no, I'm the one who should be apologizing! I know you're a busy man!" she said, still coming down from the stress that tardiness imposes on a person.

"It's alright, it's alright. It all worked out and here we are now. Not to worry," he said, waving his hand. "So, tell me, how are things? What's been happening? How are you feeling today?" Then he sat back in his chair, confident that it would be some time before he had to speak again.

His 10:30 was a monthly med consult with a patient named Alex, whom Henry suspected was selling his prescription stimulants on the streets. Alex had come to Henry over a year ago, adamant that he suffered from ADHD. He had even brought a collection of infographics he had found on the internet to corroborate his claims. Alex insisted that amphetamine treatment was the only thing that would help.

Alex was not the first or even among the first several dozen people to have made some version of this presentation during Henry's time practicing medicine. Most people sought out a psychiatrist with a diagnosis already in mind, it seemed. *Majority of people are just here for quick relief. It's the drugs they're after.* (Except for Bobbie Mills and select other bizarre exceptions—those who preferred psychotherapy from their prescriber, and could afford it.)

Through his career, Henry had come to believe that, when held to any real scrutiny, diagnosis and treatment of mental-health issues were ultimately more art than science. It was a guessing game, a wheel of fortune that could land a result anywhere from placebo-progress to suicidal ideation to miracle cure, depending on how good the guess.

But who was he to judge the faith in which people came to him for assistance? He was not the police; he was just a doctor doing what he could to help. So, besides his intuition, he had no real evidence or compunction about Alex's dealings either way, and he was happy to continue writing the script. What happened after that was up to Alex; it was not Henry's responsibility. *You can lead them to water, but you can't stop them from taking the water back home and selling it to their friends.*

The eleven o'clock hour would bring would bring a man named Chuck, who had been on an SSRI for several months and was not in need of routine follow-ups. But a week prior, Henry had received an email from Chuck at close to midnight on a Saturday:

> Hey Dr. Foster just checking in. I would like to come for an in person appointment ASAP, I have a question about my medication. Everything is going well, don't worry. Just need to talk.
> Please schedule as soon as you can.
> Thanks,
> Chuck

Henry had read the email the following morning and tittered to himself. The timestamp and deliberate vagueness of the email were telling. *Someone's Saturday night was a little ... soft.* What Chuck did not know was that Henry would have called in a prescription to combat SSRI-induced erectile dysfunction at no cost, with no consultation needed, had Chuck only been brave enough to discuss his problem directly via email.

But men struggle to talk about their penises, at least in any way that matters, so Henry acted surprised when Chuck told him his situation, offered reassurances without overdoing it—lest Chuck feel his masculinity to be in jeopardy—and happily collected the $175 fifteen-minute med-consult fee before calling in a prescription for ED meds to Chuck's pharmacy.

Once Chuck was satisfied that his situation was common and that there was nothing to worry about, he stood and gave the doctor an ebullient handshake with many *thank yous* to match. *Another happy customer.* The thought amused Henry and disgusted him all at once.

After ordering the prescriptions from the morning's sessions, Henry left his office and made for the building's communal kitchen. His last scheduled patient of the day had canceled and, though Henry wasn't hungry, he was hoping someone had left coffee in the pot. He was still tired, maybe more so after several hours of performing for his patients. And despite being finished at the office, he was not done working for the day.

On Monday afternoons, Henry worked as the attending psychiatrist at Willow View, the city's psychiatric hospital. It was a job that only paid a meager stipend when compared to his private billables, but Henry had done his clinical hours there during med school and had remained on staff in some capacity ever since. After almost twenty years, it was more of a hobby than a job. Although it could be more taxing interacting with patients committed to hospitalization than the type of patients his private practice brought in, he enjoyed the low time commitment and the pride of working in the trenches where he had started.

There was no coffee in the kitchen. Unfortunate, but not devastating. He would make more before leaving. As he reached into the cupboard to retrieve the can of ground coffee, a voice boomed without warning from the hallway behind him.

"Hands up, motherfu—"

"Jesus Christ, Will," Henry started, cutting off the man who had appeared in the doorway. Henry slammed the coffee can onto the dark marble countertop and then hung his head, one hand on the counter and the other pinching the bridge of his nose.

"A little tense today, are we, doc?" Will said, unperturbed by Henry's reaction.

Will Henderson was a CPA at Morgan and Sons Accounting, the firm which neighbored Henry's office on the second floor. Though he was neither a Morgan nor a son, Will had been at the firm for several years, and in that time had managed to weasel his way from a co-tenant of Henry's, to acquaintance, to something like a friend. Will chuckled softly as he sauntered into the kitchen and toward the far end of the counter where Henry was making coffee. There he found a jar of trail mix and picked it up, inspecting it for a name or some sign that it wasn't to be shared before opening the jar and rummaging for the candied chocolate pieces. He gathered a small handful quickly, set down the jar, and began popping the candies into mouth from hand one at a time.

"I don't know. It's been a rough morning, I guess. " Henry turned to face his friend as he leaned back against the counter in surrender. "How do you manage to sneak around this building like that anyway? I feel like you can hear every footstep from downstairs in this building."

"Light feet. It's a superpower, I guess. Just one of my many powers, if you know what I mean." Will smirked and rapidly fluttered his eyebrows up and down several times in cartoonish suggestion.

"What are you, hitting on me now? Thanks, but not interested," Henry said and turned back to resume the coffee preparation.

"Oh, come on now, a little company could do you some good. You've been a wreck since . . . you know." Will's jest abruptly halted and he turned his face downward and shrugged.

"I'm fine. Jesus, what, are you scared all of a sudden? You think I can't handle it if you say the D word? Don't be a child." Henry didn't look up from the pot he held beneath the running faucet. His posture was stiff and his tone was sharper than he had intended.

"Nah, Foss, it's not like that. You know what I mean. I just hate seeing you like this. How long are you gonna just drift around here like a fuckin'

16

ghost? It's hard to watch, man. I'm sorry, I didn't mean—"

"Stop it. I'm fine. You're fine. It's fine. It's just been a rough morning. I slept like shit and woke up like shit and I haven't shaken it off, I guess. Did you come in here for something, Will?" Henry's attempt at an apology fell short but his effort was noticed, and Will was relieved at the chance to move on.

"Yeah, actually I did. Look, Tyler and his brother are doing this birthday thing for Maddie on Wednesday and I think you should come along."

"Awwwww, Will, come on, you—" Henry started to whine before Will cut him off.

"Shut up. Foss. Shut up shut up shut up," Will said, emphasizing his words with his hands in front of his face, pinching his index finger and thumb together on each hand as if he were gesturing at holding Henry's mouth closed. Will was naturally charismatic; his voice filled rooms and he had a way of commanding attention without effort. He had a confidence about him that was pleasant, infectious. Persuasive.

"Listen to me." Will clapped his hands as he spoke. "It's just gonna be a dumb little thing with Tyler and Todd and Ashleigh and a few of their friends and I don't want to go either, but I have to. It's a free dinner. We'll run up a tab at the bar."

"I'm sorry, but I actually quit drinking this week," Henry said, closing his eyes in feigned disappointment and holding his fingers to his forehead as though he had just remembered something he had previously forgotten.

"Yeah, right. When, just now? Mister Fiending-over-the-coffee-pot-still-nursing-a-hangover-at-noon-on-a-Monday. Maybe drinking with a friend for once will be good for you. Your ass probably hasn't been anywhere but work or the bottom of a bottle in months. Come on," Will said.

"All I wanted was a cup of coffee, Will," Henry said as he turned to the pot percolating on the counter and stared wistfully into it, waiting.

"We'll drive together. Pick me up at seven. Wednesday night. Don't forget." Will strolled out of the room victoriously as he said this, then paused, turned around, walked back to the counter, and picked a few more chocolates from the jar. He winked at Henry, walked back out of the kitchen and disappeared into the hall without a word or a single sound from his footsteps.

Light feet.

God dammit.

The coffee finished. Henry filled his thermos. He added powdered cream and sugar from the cabinet, walked back down the hall to lock his office door, and left the building.

‡

Session transcript from patient files of Dr. Henry Foster

Patient: Wagner, Nicholas

10/17/22

HF: You made it back. I wasn't sure I'd see you again.

NW: Yeah. Well, you did say if I didn't come you would call the cops on me.

HF: Hah, I suppose I did, didn't I?

NW: Uh huh.

HF: So.

NW: So.

HF/NW: How are you feeling?

NW: Jinx. See how predictable you are?

HF: I guess I am. It's a habit. You know, you'd be surprised how much time most people I see can kill just talking about how they feel. It's usually a good way to start things off.

NW: Well, that's what it's all about, isn't it, doc? Feelings?

HF: Is it?

NW: You know, that's really annoying.

HF: What's that?

NW: The like ... vague, leading-question thing. Always responding to everything that way. Feels like you're trying to trap me, like you're a cop or something.

HF: I'm not trying to trap you. Are you always this paranoid?

NW: I'm not *paranoid*. Just regular annoyed. I don't like wasting time with all this pretense and bullshit. I don't even know what I'm doing here and I sit down and you start acting cagey and grilling me all vague and weird and it feels condescending and like a waste of my time. *You* told me to be here, man. You told me I needed it. But I'm only here because you literally said you'd *call the fucking cops* on me if I didn't come. So I'm not gonna sit here and spill my guts to you. I don't need to. Now, did you even have something you wanted to talk about or are you just trying to fuck with me to clear your own conscience?

HF: Why would my conscience need clearing, Nick?

NW: Oooh I swear to god, if you answer another question with a question I'm going to snap.

HF: I'm sorry—last one. Why do you think I'm fucking with you? Let's start there. Obviously this won't work if you and I can't get at least close to the same page as one another.

NW: I don't know. The cops brought me here and said you needed to evaluate me and then I could go. I waited all weekend for you to show up and then when you got here you decided to keep me and then it was almost two god damn months before you let me go.

HF: Yeah, and I guess I am sorry about that. But I did and still do believe it was necessary.

NW: Do you? Don't you have better things to do? Some of those people in there could use a doctor a lot more than me, man.

HF: Nick, do you remember coming here?

NW: Obviously.

HF: Do you remember what you said?

NW: I said a lot of shit. I was pissed off.

HF: I remember you were saying you needed it to end.

NW: Yeah. So? I wanted to go home.

HF: Nicholas—

NW: —*Nick.*

HF: I'm sorry. Nick, do you remember saying that you didn't want to do it anymore? Begging us to just leave you alone and let you go?

NW: Yeah. I didn't want to be here anymore. I was losing my mind. I wanted to go home. What's your point?

HF: Sure ... alright.

NW: What? Why are you saying it like that?

...

NW: What? Don't fuck with me. If you want us to get on the same page then stop talking to me like that.

...

NW: *What?*

HF: I'm sorry ... Okay ... Look, you're right. Let's just dispense with pretense. I'm just not sure that you were talking about leaving here. The intake staff noted suicidal ideation in your intake interview and quoted you as expressing sincere wishes to end your life. Now, I know that you were in shock and acute distress when you arrived here, and in the several weeks that followed you seemed to shift in and out of that shock. Eventually you seemed plenty lucid and we were able to talk, you remember, and you assured me that you didn't feel that way anymore, but I think it's important that we talk about it anyway. These kinds of feelings don't tend to resolve on their own, you know?

NW: They didn't. I had six fucking weeks in the psych ward to help me resolve it. Which, by the way, you were only a part of for a few minutes each week. You weren't here for all the therapy and the groups and the rest of the shit I had to do while I was here. And you weren't there when I got here either. I had to wait days for you to even show up the first time. So go talk to your staff or whoever because they are wrong. I'm fine. I had a bad night, and anyone in my position would have had a bad fucking night too. It's not crazy to think that I might have been a little upset, you know? Jesus.

20

HF: No, it's not crazy. Do you want to talk about that night? About what happened before you came here?

NW: No need. It's done. I'm fine.

HF: Right. Sure. That's fine. But Nichol— Nick. Like I said, these things don't just resolve and go away on their own. I think there is still work to do. Whether you think it or not, this will catch up with you, and when it does, I want you to know that you're not alone. I don't know what your support system is like out there, and so I want you to have the best possible chance to heal and move on from this.

NW: *Support system.* Hah. Yeah. I got support, don't worry.

2   HB: No, it's not crazy. Do you want to talk about that night? About

2

Nick Wagner sat on the roof outside his bedroom window, the hood of his sweatshirt pulled over his head, and lit a cigarette. It was nearly midnight on a Monday in late August, and the neighborhood was still, silent, lit only by scattered street lamps. From the eave where he sat, he could see the rooftops of houses for several blocks, a sea of shingles breached by trees and light poles, dozens of units all clustered together and still so discrete in their collective isolation. The great paradox of suburban sprawl before him.

He pulled on his cigarette and mused many righteous excoriations from the perch atop his mother's house. It had been several months since he had last been home and so the same view with which he had grown up now inspired a fresh sense of intrigue in him.

In his childhood the neighborhood had seemed a suburban idyll, safe and colorful, intimate and friendly. But he had come to loathe the neighborhood with age. To him the whole block looked like it could have been made of cardboard, replicated and stamped in little squares over and over in a grid that stretched across the green earth like a rash. There was no community that he could see. It was all handshakes and side-eyes. Welcome mats and tall fences. Curtains drawn tight. Houses crammed together for their fear of being alone; doors locked and deadbolted for fear of one another.

He drew deeply on the cigarette and blew the smoke out his nose with a self-satisfied chortle. *Idiots.* Nick was twenty years old, and from his perch he felt elevated beyond it all in every way. Exempt. Ascended. Enlightened.

He drew again on his cigarette and his phone buzzed one short pulse from the pocket of his sweatpants. He checked the phone; it was a text from his mother.

I smell cigarettes.
You had better not be
smoking in your room.

He sneered slightly and texted her back.

No mom I'm outside, go to sleep

…

The bubbled ellipses indicated she was texting back and would not be going away that easily.

Nicky please get off the
roof. You know I hate
when you go out there

I'm not on the roof, don't
worry. Go to sleep.

You better not be lying to me.

I would never.

Now I know you're lying.

😂 Go to sleep mom.

Please be safe. I just got you
back. I don't know what i'd do
if something happened to you

Nothing is gonna happen. I'm
home and I'm fine. I promise

Okay … I love you Nicholas.
I'm glad you're home.

I love you too mom. Good night

Good night

…

Another bubble with the dots appeared. Nick held his phone in his hand, waiting for the message.

And quit smoking.

> I'm working on it. Now
> go to sleep and stop
> worrying about me.

It's my job to worry about you.

Nick put down the phone and took a final long drag from his cigarette before flicking it off the roof. It hit the driveway below him in a splash of sparks. He watched the ember slowly diminish and flicker back to life several times as it gasped at the passing breeze and fought for life. He thought of wildfires. Little accidents, big tragedies. All the quick decisions that stack up to build enduring and unendurable consequences. He thought of all the times in history that humanity must have gotten wrong if it led to living in these little clustered neighborhoods, full of malice and discontent. Confused about our very natures. He wondered if wildfires would be the worst thing that could happen.

He wondered if it was really as bad as it felt. He wondered why he couldn't seem to enjoy the fruits of it all the way others seemed to. He wondered if they were just putting on a show. He wondered if he was just putting on a show. He felt his phone buzz again in his pocket and he forgot all about what he had been wondering. He checked his phone and saw a notification from Alison. His heart rate increased in simultaneous excitement and frustration.

Wtf Wagner? Why didn't you
tell me you were home? 😠

The corners of his mouth turned up and his eyes glittered in the dark night for only a moment. He picked up the phone in both hands to text her back.

I didn't know you'd care

Ew byee

don't be dramatic

Okay Mr. "I didn't know
you'd care" LOL please
you are the worst

fuck you lol

you wishhh 😛

He stared at this last message for a moment. He pursed his lips tightly and screwed up his face into a pained sort of contemplation, picked up his pack of smokes with his phone hand, and pulled a cigarette to his mouth with his teeth. With his free hand he retrieved the lighter from his other pocket. He drew in, puffed out his cheeks, then exhaled loudly.

He did wish. He had wished it for years, and he spent a great deal of time in a great deal of certainty that she did too. But it just didn't happen. Ever. Not yet, anyway. Over the years they had veered close enough to be maddening, but at this point he had to accept that it could never happen. He told himself he was okay with it and had told her the same, but neither of them believed it.

Nick and Alison had met in high school, where they shared an art class in their senior year. He had needed an additional credit, which the school allowed him to fulfill by taking a creative art class. He had no artistic talent or even any interest in art to speak of, but it seemed the easiest path to making it out of school with a diploma in hand, so he took the class.

Alison had been an art student through all of high school. She possessed an impeccable eye for depth and light. She drew the female form with pencils and charcoal and painted it with oils and watercolors, always different and always sublime. Her girls stretched, sprawled, contorted, and curled, sometimes tragic and sometimes triumphant; they each seemed so much more than lines on paper, renditions of something more profound and more human than anatomy. They suffered, they rejoiced, they cried. They spoke.

Nick would scrawl vulgar shapes across his canvas, chaotic scenes of cartoon-looking buildings on fire and weird forests of leafless trees, toppled and blackened under raining ash and clouded skies. He would watch Alison sit before her canvas with headphones in, drawing from images inside her mind and bringing another girl to life with shading and contours, rendering something he could never do even with a million models, a million canvases, and a million art classes.

He would watch carefully, when he could, as she held her face so calm and poised, her mouth open slightly, her features soft and stoic. She would tilt her head smoothly this way and that, everything about her countenance fixed in repose, except for her eyes. Her eyes would dart across the page with intense focus, leading her hand. They sparkled as though they were full of gathered stars projecting the sights of her mind onto the canvas, while her hands traced the lights.

She had approached him first, several weeks into the start of class. Had she not, they probably never would have spoken. Nick would have never dared speak to her. He would have cited high-school hierarchy and the obvious differences in social strata that marked the two of them, but she always got upset when he referred to such things.

"You're so full of shit, none of that cliquey stuff is real. You guys just want it to be so you can feel outcast and edgy," she would say, or some version of it whenever this type of talk came up, to which he would respond, "Yeah, you only feel that way because you've never been outcast anywhere in your life. You have pretty-girl privilege and you don't even know it." The truth, of course, was either somewhere in the middle or something large enough to encompass both points at once.

Nick did fancy himself an outcast, and he did his best to dress the part. He had always worn his troubles outwardly as though they were a mark of identity. His clothes were dark and his face was stern, unwelcoming. He sulked and brooded around the other kids who felt they were different: the punk rockers, the drug crowd, the ones who had been bullied and tormented for their differences until they found the acceptance of the misfits, and all the others who rejected the trends of their time and instead embraced the varied uniforms of the counterculture.

Alison, on the other hand, had never worn her troubles conspicuously. Instead of donning the black clothes, facial piercings, and whatever other quirky fashion statements Nick's cohorts were partial to, she hid her troubles in plain sight. The fit of her clothes, the time and attention to detail in her morning makeup routine, the obsession with so many numbers to measure one small figure—waist size, bra size, and the reading on the scale in her bathroom every morning and every night. With her shoulder-length blonde hair and her radiant blue eyes, her carefully assembled outfits and her calculated speech, she could only hope to pass some impossible test that was sure to have started without warning and would never really end, a test that was being administered by everyone and no one and some voice in her head all together at all times without reprieve. A test that every day she appeared to pass without difficulty. A test she only ever felt she was failing.

"I like your shirt, Wagner."

The five words that would change his life forever.

Nick was walking into art class late on a gray and dreary October morning. He had been in the park behind the school getting high with his friends. He felt the weed helped him tap into his creativity so he could perform better in art class. Never mind that Nick and his friends did this every day, before almost every class—that was not the story he told himself, and so it was not the story at all.

On his way to class, Nick had spent so long in the bathroom trying to wash the scent of smoke off in a haze of paranoia and dreamy dissociation that it took the chime of the second bell to alert him to his tardiness. By the time he walked into class, everyone had already taken up their tools and begun working. The room was silent. He felt everyone's eyes on him as he shuffled quickly to his station, his head hung low and eyes on the floor. He set his pack down near his work stool, then took off his hoodie and draped it over his backpack. When he looked up, everyone else had returned to work except Alison, who was staring directly at him. The room was silent, save for the sounds of the scraping and brushing and scribbling of students at work. And there she stared, softly smiling. She broke the silence without reservation.

"I like your shirt, Wagner," she said casually.

"I uh—" Nick stammered.

There were several issues preventing him from completing a coherent sentence:

1. The weed
2. The shock of being spoken to by anyone in this class, which was so often as quiet as a library or a crypt that he hadn't been sure if anyone was even allowed to talk
3. The shock of that person being someone like Alison
4. The fact she had known *and* addressed him by his last name
5. He could not remember what shirt he was wearing (possibly due to #1, but not for certain)

He remedied what he could and tabled the rest. He looked down at his shirt to remind himself what he had put on this morning. It was a black tee shirt with a flock of white cartoon sheep and one black sheep separated from the pack running the opposite direction, the words "Minor Threat" scribbled at the top. He looked up at her and laughed.

"Hah. I forgot what I was wearing. Yeah, yeah. Thanks," he said flatly through his awkward muted chuckle. He opened the drawer of his work bench and pulled out some charcoal and a pencil, readying his station to work.

"Didn't they start the whole drug-free thing?" Alison asked him through a knowing smile that had stretched across her face. She tilted her head down and looked up at him, chastising him with her eyes but never breaking that smile.

"There's no rules in punk rock, Alison," Nick said. "Besides, straight-edge kids are nerds, but they do make the best music."

"I'd drink to that," said Alison and she laughed at her own joke.

"Alright, now, that's enough. I know he's cute, but this is a classroom, not CBGB. Eyes on our papers, mouths zipped tight, eh, kids?" Mr. Alistair, the art teacher, chided playfully from the corner of the room. "And Mr. Wagner, I don't know if you know this thanks to the artsy vibe I like to keep in here, but this *is* actually a real class and we begin *at* eleven. Try to remember that going forward, alright? Alright."

Nick and Alison looked at each other a moment longer. She rolled her eyes up high in their sockets, cocked her head to the side, and hung her tongue out the side of her mouth, fashioning an exaggerated face of the hanged. He laughed silently and shrugged his shoulders.

Starting that day, the two developed a somewhat clandestine friendship. Outside of art class, they never spoke at school. They rarely socialized publicly and they both enjoyed the privacy of their relationship. It was odd, marked by sporadic text messages and long conversations late into the night or early morning, in which they traded music suggestions or gossiped about their respective friend groups—which did not often mix—commiserating with each other on the unfortunate circumstances of their days. They had become fixtures in each other's lives, and only a few apart from the two of them ever knew it.

Nick deleted several potential replies until finally he settled on one that wouldn't betray him irreparably. He put his cigarette between his lips and held it there, using both hands to type.

> you're pretty but at least
> you're not conceited

Aww you think i'm pretty?

> Pretty annoying

Har har.

When did you get home?

> Today. I was gonna call you I
> just didn't know if it was cool

Why wouldn't it be cool?

Because James?

James doesn't go on my
phone. besides he knows
you're my friend it's fine.

uh huh. since when

He's over it. Besides, he
just acts like that, he's like
you — all bark no bite. I have
a thing for softies i guess

Nick wasn't sure which he hated more, being called soft or being compared to the guy she was dating. He opted to ignore both and play it off.

Aww you have a thing for me?

Lol shut up — you
know what i mean

Remind me again why i'm
still friends with you?

Because you love me and
none of your other friends are
anywhere near as cool as i am.

Mhmm, right. i knew it was
something like that.

So, what the hell are you doing
Wagner? Are you going to
come pick me up or what?

Right now?

Duh.

He paused before responding. Mostly for effect, but also because he hadn't planned on going out at all and was, in fact, quite high and had to check in with himself. He quickly determined that he was in plenty good condition to drive, but that was irrelevant; he would have been en route to see her regardless, and he knew it from the moment she had told him to come.

Okay, gimme 20

His phone buzzed one more time as a pink heart icon appeared over his last message, Alison's punctuation mark on the conversation. Nick gathered his cigarettes and his lighter and put them back in his pockets along with his phone. The cigarette in his mouth had burned to the butt. He pulled it from his lips and flicked it off the roof onto the concrete below where it quickly died.

As he turned to crawl back through his window, he thought nothing of wildfires.

3

Nick pulled up to Alison's house at 11:55pm and texted her to say he was outside. He parked across the street from her house, locked the doors, turned off the lights but not the motor, and watched for her front door to open. He checked again to be sure he had locked the doors.

Alison's neighborhood never rested. Addicts and derelicts wandered at all hours of the night. Malnourished waifs walked bicycles, wide-eyed and lock-jawed, haunting, haunted. The houses here were at least a half-century older than the rest of the town, most with cracked and sun-bleached paint. Patinated cars half disassembled in driveways. Short chain-link fences lined unkempt and weeded lawns. Concrete multi-unit buildings horseshoed small parking lots where people congregated and smoked cigarettes, just barely out of sight from the street.

Tangles of power lines hung low overhead and spread out in every direction. Nick always noted these. From his window eave at home he could see houses for a mile and there was not a power line in sight, as if an unobstructed view of the sky out one's window was a privilege only people of a certain class could enjoy.

Without warning there was a loud banging on the passenger window and Nick jolted upright and felt all of the blood in his body turn white hot with fear. He looked to his right and Alison was standing on the other side of the window with her hand over her mouth, laughing quietly. He thought for a moment about just leaving her there to laugh all by herself. *Fuck her, god dammit.* But he knew he wouldn't do it. He glared at her and gathered himself, slowly.

"You gonna let me in or what?" she said through the window, still laughing and so pleased with herself. His eyes fixed on hers, he mustered his most menacing expression, slowly moved his hand toward the power lock switch, and finally unlocked the doors. Immediately she opened the door and was in the car with the door shut behind her.

"Let's roll, nerd!" she said with glee. He turned on the lights and shifted into drive, pulling away from the curb and up the street out of her neighborhood, not saying a word.

"Aw, Nicky, did I scare you?" she asked, her tone somewhere between sweet and mocking.

"I don't know, a little. I thought I was getting jumped or something. You shouldn't do that, you could get yourself killed."

"Oh no—were you going to shoot me?" she said and then laughed again.

"It's not funny, Ali! You don't know, maybe I would! It's like midnight in your shitty neighborhood, maybe I would!" he said, his eyes on the road and his voice stern.

"I forgot you're such a tough guy," she said. Then, before allowing the condescension to sink in and risk embarrassing him further, she leaned across the center console and put her arms around him, pressing her head into his chest. "I'm sorry, I'm sorry. I'm just so excited you're back. You idiot—stop doing dumb shit. I need you; don't you know that?"

"You need a psychiatrist," he said, pretending to be unmoved by her display of affection.

"Eh, there's a million psychiatrists. Only one Wagner." She unwound her arms from his neck, but instead of resuming her position in the passenger seat, she pulled her feet all the way onto the seat, turned her body toward the front of the car, and rested her head on his shoulder. He could feel her full weight sinking onto him now and nothing else. The adrenaline from the shock had passed. The subsequent embarrassment was forgotten. All that was left in the world was the friction from the road dampened through rubber and steel, the headlights on the yellow lines before him, and her head on his shoulder.

They drove in silence for some time. Maybe it was moments, maybe it was much longer. The houses and apartment buildings of Alison's neighborhood passed by the windows of his pickup truck and faded from its mirrors. Nick followed a route they often took on these midnight drives which cut out through the west side of town and into the rural districts. He drove until the street lamps became sparse and eventually disappeared. The sidewalks became dirt shoulders and the road narrowed and began to wind.

"So what was it like?" Alison asked, breaking the silence but not moving.

"What was what like?"

"Prison. Were you scared?" she asked softly and with sincerity.

"I wasn't in prison," Nick said.

"Or jail, whatever. I don't know the difference, I'm not a criminal like you," she said with a sardonic smile.

"Yeah, right, and you're a perfect angel. Was I *scared*?" He scoffed in disbelief.

In truth, Nick *had* been scared. Almost the entire experience from arrest to eventual release had been characterized by fear, frustration, and boredom. Just days into his time in the county jail, he had determined that incarceration was far more devastating to one's psyche than could be presumed without experience. On its face it seemed no more than a time-out for grown-ups, but as the minutes and hours dragged into painfully long days, each of which seemed to last the span of weeks in civilian time, he came to realize the price he would pay for his sins was greater than just the time itself.

First it was the swelling anxiety of uncertainty that consumed him. When would he be free to go home? Was it to be days, or years? How would his mother take the news? How would he survive in here? For days there were no answers. Overwhelmed by all of these questions, he moved blindly from one moment to the next, his autonomy surrendered to armed thugs and locked doors, pushing him through some rigid routine he didn't understand.

He had called his mother collect from the module payphone and asked her for bail, but she would not oblige, though she offered sympathy and consolation as best she could. "I'm sorry, love, you're just going to have to do this on your own. You got yourself in there, now you have to wait until they let you out."

34

He had known before he tried that his father wouldn't accept the call, but he tried anyway.

The correctional officers were brutish and deliberately withheld information, especially information that had been requested of them. Simple questions of when food would be served or when he could use the phone or bathe were dismissed with a *"When I say so"* at best, or, from the less helpful officers, met with a simple *"Shut the fuck up."*

Periodically the lock on the door to his cell would release with a loud pop, sometimes waking him in the dead of night, sometimes in the middle of the day, and he would be permitted to move about the rest of the module for a short while. Over time he determined that the timing of his releases was not entirely random. There were a dozen or so other inmates locked in the same module, and only one was allowed out at a time. They were each to be released twice a day for short spells, the length and time of which were at the will of the officer on duty, thus they were heavily dependent on the mood and measure of sadism present in each.

Even at his arraignment, the public defender assigned to him was brief and remarkably unhelpful, telling him only that his charges *could* carry a sentence of up to five years and that today he should plead not guilty and they would request a bail reduction. When the judge called his name, the public defender repeated the plea and the request, which was promptly denied, and then a new court date was set for two weeks from that day.

The next two weeks spanned the life of some smaller stars. He lay in bed and read books he took from the small library cart in the module. He slept. Three times a day, a steel slot in his door would open and a pair of hands would slide in a tray of monochromatic goo and browning leaves that had once been green, which he ate in fevered haste without critique or reservation. He would sleep. He would dream of being somewhere else where he would cry tears of joy at the sight of the sun. Then the door would pop so loud he would be jolted awake to lament his reality. The cruel irony of losing the freedom in his dreams to the perverse "freedom" of his mod time never escaped him.

He had obsessed nearly every day over the potential outcomes of that next court date. His mind was locked in a heated battle with itself, vacillating between the hope of release and the fear of the maximum sentence. It didn't matter which side was winning, as they both incited an overwhelming sense of impotence which he knew was the only reality. His own powerlessness was all he could rely on; everything else was fear and fantasy. And still he rolled both possibilities over and over again in his mind until they were ground together into dust and he couldn't tell them apart any longer.

After his sentencing, there were at least answers. *Six months in the county jail.* An apparent break, since he was a first-time offender. If he continued his time without incident, he would earn a reduction of one third of his sentence. Four months. He could be home before summer was over. There was some comfort just in knowing.

Still, he had to contend with the time itself. He didn't know how people could serve years in state prisons. He hadn't seen the sky in mere weeks and was already feeling disoriented and claustrophobic. He had never before felt such a deep longing in his life as his longing to breathe fresh air, to eat real food, to see a face he recognized. At night he dreamed of cigarettes and sex, of taking drugs with friends, of drowning beneath the crashing waves of an apocalyptic tide. He woke in a sweat to the pop of the door and he grew to hate his mod time. His dreams were the only place where he wasn't locked up somewhere. Anywhere his subconscious took him was a welcome respite from the jail.

No matter how many days passed, it always felt as though the ones that remained were insurmountable. Ninety or sixty or twenty-five or fifteen: like an infant he could only measure time in terms of *right now* or *not at all*. He became unwell with worry. He became terrified that it would never end, that somehow he wouldn't make it. That they would revoke his credits and impose the full sentence on him, or that they would find a mistake in his file or find some reason to delay his release. Some nights, he couldn't loose himself from the grip of his anxieties enough to sleep at all. He feared he would become undone before he would be released.

Nick came to a stop sign at a four-way intersection far from town, thought for a moment, and then turned right toward a trailhead parking lot he knew would be vacant and likely unpatrolled all night.

"Nah, it wasn't really scary. Annoying, mostly. Boring. Everyone in there was an absolute moron. The cops and the other inmates. Just morons everywhere," he said, the word *moron* dripping with disdain every time he uttered it.

"Checks out. You think everyone is a moron," said Alison, looking up at him from where her head still rested on his shoulder, and without looking down Nick could hear her eyes rolling in the tone of her voice.

"That's because everyone *is* a moron. How'd you know I was home, anyway? I *just* got out this afternoon."

Nick felt her fidget and her voice got smaller. "Oh, uh. Connor told me," she said.

"Speaking of morons," he said, then continued with a start, "Ali, tell me you're not buying shit off that guy!"

Alison pulled away and sat upright in the passenger seat. "Nothing crazy—just some addies here and there. Just to keep up with my classes."

"You're killing me, dude. You're too smart for that shit. What are you doing? You're a college student, not a crackhead." Nick spoke in an exaggerated tone; he wasn't exactly angry but he wasn't exactly joking either.

"Calm down. It's community college, it's not a big deal," she said.

"But it's a big enough deal that you have to take *speed* to make it through? That makes no sense. Don't fuck around, Ali. You're gonna fuck up your whole life and you're gonna get me killed in the process."

Nick pulled off the road into a dirt clearing hidden from sight that served as a parking lot for a local hiking trail.

"My life's already fucked-up. Yours is too. Maybe we'll both get killed, eh, Nicky? Whaddya say?" She leaned back toward him, raising her eyebrows and putting the full size of her pleading eyes prominently on display before him. "Let's just wreck it all. Who cares?"

"You've lost your mind. You need to get out of this town before it *does* kill you."

"Yeah, maybe. Besides, you wanna tell me how you had been home for hours and I couldn't even get a call from you, but Connor had not only heard from you already, but said he had *seen* you earlier today?" She pursed her lips and held one eyebrow higher than the other.

Nick thought of lying, but then thought better of it, or simply realized he didn't care enough to commit. "I just got out. It's been a long couple of months. Give me a break," he said, more pitifully than he had intended.

"Mhmm. And here I've been thinking you'd come back to me all rehabilitated and shit."

"I need a fuckin' smoke. Come on." He opened the driver's door, turning to her and nodding his chin toward her door, suggesting she follow. Alison climbed out of the cab and Nick reached into the backseat to retrieve an oversized comforter he had kept since the first time they had been out late into the night. He walked around to the back of the truck with the blanket. He opened the tailgate and laid the blanket down on the bed of the truck.

They climbed inside and lay down on their backs, side by side in the bed of the truck beneath the sky. He could smell the perfume she wore. He could feel her press closer to him; whether it was for warmth or affection didn't matter. Sometimes he felt the two of them were separate parts of one whole; sometimes he felt closer to the stars than he did to her.

"I'm glad you're home, Wagner. It sucks around here without you."

"Yeah. I bet it does," he said and lit a cigarette.

"So, come on, tell me what it was like."

"Eh, it's not interesting. Like I said, it's mostly boring. It's like being locked in a box with all of the worst things about being alive and nothing else."

"What do you mean?"

"I mean all of it . . . It's like holding a magnifying glass up to the shittiest parts of life. The loneliness. The dark, intrusive thoughts. Hopeless feelings. The inability to control anything. The forced interactions with people you can't stand. The fantasies that are so far from your reality, and how bad it hurts to even try to dream. The feeling like you should be doing so much more but still knowing that you're not going to do anything other than what you're doing. All the shame and regret playing in an endless loop in your head, like watching the same tragedies on repeat all day and night. Never wanting to be awake, not being able to sleep. The way time just wears on you, never at the pace you need it, never at the pace you want. It's all of it, and you're just locked there with all of that, alone and without any real distraction from it. Just shitty books donated from people's reject piles to the special cases in county who couldn't spell 'literacy' if their lives depended on it."

"So ... it's just like regular life, but without a phone?"

"Hah. Uh ... " Nick said, stammering, uncertain as to whether or not she had been joking. "I want to say no, but ... yeah, kind of. I mean, none of your friends are there and the drug situation in there is fucked so there's that but, yeah, basically. Regular life without a phone, I guess, but Jesus, that's kind of dark."

"Says Mister Everything Sucks himself," Alison said.

"Fuuuuck you. Like you're Miss Mary Sunshine all the time."

"It's why we get along, I guess," she said, then pulled something from her pocket and held it to her mouth, drew from it, and blew out a cloud of smoke that smelled like cotton candy with a hint of chemical solution.

"What the fuck is that, Ali? I leave for a few months and you start vaping?"

"Oh my god, you are *not* going to give me shit about this, you chain-smoke like an old TV villain," said Alison.

"Yeah, chain-*smoke*. Like an adult. That shit you're smoking smells awful and it's probably going to collapse your lungs or something," Nick said, lighting another cigarette.

"I can't even talk to you right now. You sound insane. It smells like *candy* instead of flaming dog shit and battery acid. And cigarettes *will* kill you, it's a fact. Vapes just *might* kill you. Plus my hands don't stink, see?" Alison's grin was rich with mischief and she held her knuckles up to Nick's face and rested the back of her hand just beneath his nose and on his mouth.

"Smell like shit to me," said Nick, working hard to hold a straight face.

"Fuck you! They do not!" Alison jerked her hand back from his face and continued, "You always do this shit. You take drugs and it's fine. I take the same drugs and suddenly it's *so* problematic. You smoke cigarettes all day long and it's no problem at all, but when I pull out my own vape, all of a sudden I'm a criminal! You're a hypocrite, Wagner. And a misogynist. You're a hypocrite and a misogynist *and* you're an asshole." Alison punctuated her words with her chin cocked upwards and took a long, self-satisfied pull from her vape, then turned her head toward Nick and blew the cloud of vapor hard into his face.

"Fine, fine fine fine. I'm an asshole. Fuck me for caring about your health and safety and your life," Nick said.

"And what about your life, huh, asshole?" Alison said, turning onto her side to face him.

Nick drew on his cigarette and said nothing for a moment. He looked at the sky and thought about the unimaginable violence in each burning star and marveled at how perspective alone could render them stalwart beacons of serenity and wonder instead of the impossibly vicious galactic hellscapes that they were. He thought of this paradox often, and though he never found comfort in it, he believed that it too was only a matter of perspective—that with enough effort and focus, there had to be some meaning to be found in such a thought. It all had to matter, somehow, but he could never figure out exactly how it should.

"I guess *that's* why we get along," he said after several moments. Alison had closed her eyes during the silence but opened them lazily and looked up at him.

"Hmm? Why?"

"Neither of us can be bothered to care about our own lives, but we never stop worrying about each other," Nick said and looked down from all the burning stars into his friend's eyes, which glimmered in the dark and looked into his. He wondered what violence burned within those eyes, and whether the hope he read in them was also only a trick of perspective.

"Yeah, well. Another big joke on us, isn't it?" Alison let out a feigned laugh, muted by sleep.

"Yeah, and ain't life just one big fuckin' joke?"

"And at last, we come to the difference between us," Alison said, her eyes closed and her voice softening.

"What, you don't think it's all a joke?"

"No, it's not that. It's just that you get so angry about it. And I . . . well, I guess I think the joke is funny." She tilted her head up and kissed him on the cheek and laughed again before burrowing her face into his chest for warmth. Her breaths grew deep and slowed as she fell asleep against him. He smoked and stared at the sky. He wouldn't sleep yet.

Nick had waited those seemingly endless months to see the stars outside of his dreams. To share the air with the trees again. To see her. He had thought that maybe she would be single by the time he was released, ready to reconsider their relationship once more. But he had not been so lucky. Still, she was here with him after everything, and James was somewhere else. This could not mean nothing.

He had been high earlier on his roof, before Alison had texted, but hours had passed and the pills had left him only tired as he tried to fight sleep. He listened to her breathing and lazily let the smoke from his cigarette swirl upwards from his mouth and into the still, pre-dawn darkness. He felt the time passing rapidly. He knew the sun would rise and Alison would wake up and they would each return to their homes. She would see James, and Nick would wait until the next time she had a free evening. He wanted to breathe in every moment of the night, to stay still and here as long as he could. But time passes at her own pace.

Last week, from his jail cell, he would have bowed down before the moon and offered his head in sacrifice to end the long and sleepless night. Tonight, in the bed of this truck, he would have taken up arms to fight against the rising sun itself. With heavy eyes he thought of time, the greatest trickster of all.

We can't just trade lifetimes for moments. There has to be more than this. But there isn't. And we do. Is it worth it?

That's how it gets us. That's why we stay. Foolish, desperate, hopeless romantics, all of us. "Maybe it'll all be worth it," we say. And maybe it is. We'll see, eventually.

What other choice do we have?

They slept through the final hours of the night and well past sunrise. They used each other and the oversized blanket to shield their faces from the sunlight while the wet morning air found rest on their skin. Hikers arrived after dawn, but the two were undisturbed by the arrival of their cars. No one noticed the young couple sleeping in the bed of the old pickup truck.

Nick dreamed nothing of consequence.

TUESDAY

4

Henry walked quickly from his car to the sidewalk. The morning was cold and the clouds hung low, threatening rain. He looked left and right, then across the street, trying to locate a parking meter. There must have been one of those centralized multi-space kiosks around because there was no traditional meter near his space, but he couldn't see any kiosk through the people crowding the block. He was almost twenty minutes late to his appointment. Henry was rarely late.

Panic was bubbling up inside of him like bile, and he couldn't focus. He knew he was overreacting, but he couldn't control it. He considered leaving without paying. *How much can a parking ticket really cost?* He decided to risk the ticket and abandon his search for the kiosk. He looked around at the buildings on the block and couldn't discern their addresses. They all had names in gold trim lining the doorways, but none of the names matched the one he was looking for.

He took a step back toward the edge of the sidewalk to escape the buzzing throng of pedestrians and looked for some other clue as to which building was the one he was looking for. He was sure he had been here before, but apparently he had overestimated his familiarity with the area.

The buildings on the block were tall; some stretched up into the gray morning and disappeared in the clouds. The city was so much bigger than he remembered it, and though he tried, he couldn't recall the last time he had been here. He tried to focus, but the sounds from the street were overwhelming. A cacophony of passing cars, indiscernible murmurs of passing conversations, periodic horns, and shouts from workers and passersby. Somewhere on the block a car alarm was sounding, the shrill siren's repeating giving a voice to Henry's anxiety as if it were the soundtrack of his inner monologue.

He scanned the face of each building, looking for something he could recognize. He would know the right one when he saw it. He stood in front of one building with a short staircase leading up to a heavily tinted wall of windows and a single door with a brass handle. A man was sitting on the steps, wearing a filthy hooded sweatshirt under an old windbreaker. His hair was greasy and his face was dirty and weathered.

Henry noticed with some discomfort that the man was staring at him. His mouth was pulled tight and his eyes were fixed on Henry. Through him. Into him. Henry felt fear, and then shame, and then with some remorse he decided to look away without acknowledging the man or the feelings he had experienced in that moment.

The ground level of the building next door had tall floor-to-ceiling windows, and inside he could see people standing in a line in front of what looked to be a counter for ordering food. Beyond the line, people were seated at small tables, drinking from mugs or paper cups. A woman sat alone with her laptop open and headphones in, one hand on her keyboard and the other holding a mug just in front of her face, barely below her mouth, suspended somewhere between sips while she fixated on her work.

At the next table sat a man and a woman. The man was speaking and the woman was smiling. He noted her large, picturesque smile and the way she held her fingers loosely over her mouth as if she were trying to cover it, and he thought to himself, *Don't you cover that beautiful smile.* His ex-wife, Gretchen, had the same habit when they were younger, and every time she held her hand to her mouth when she laughed, he said those words to her.

The girl turned slightly and they made eye contact. His stomach turned and for a moment he thought his legs would fail and he felt the scene around him turn sideways or upside down and he thought he was falling. Gretchen was looking back at him through the cafe window. When she saw him, her smile froze while her eyes first took on a look of confusion, then cold animosity.

He wanted to know who the man was. What they were doing. What he could possibly be saying to make her smile that way. But the way Gretchen stared at him made it difficult to focus on the man at all. She looked through him. Into him. The clouds had begun to expel the rain they carried; in torrents the water fell, and streaks distorted his view into the cafe. All the people from the sidewalk seemed to have run for cover, except the man on the steps of the building in front of him who emitted a mad and screeching cackle as the rain splashed on the steps around him.

Gretchen stared through the window without blinking, two fingers over her mouth, and through them he could see she was speaking, or mouthing words, but he couldn't make out what she was saying through the water running down the glass. The man on the steps began shrieking as the water from the gutters pooled up over the sidewalk in a flash flood that was soon rushing past Henry's ankles.

Henry tried to move toward the cafe to take cover, or to confront his ex-wife and her companion, but he struggled to wade through the flood. The rushing water, the cackling vagrant, the rain and the wind, the car alarms blaring—the sounds overwhelmed him and he was frozen in fear.

He looked up again and Gretchen was sitting on the lap of the vagrant, straddling him and grinding her body into his. They were kissing deeply, their mouths open and their tongues entwined. Henry opened his mouth to shout at them but he choked on his effort, then stood paralyzed while rain filled his mouth. Gretchen was undoing the pants of the man on the steps and her face shined in rapture. He watched them while the rain washed down his throat and filled his stomach and his lungs. The car alarm rang out from up the street and everything turned black.

5

Henry groped frantically at the alarm clock for the **Off** switch and then lay on his side with his eyes closed in defiance. His throat was dry and irritated and his bladder screamed for relief, but his stomach was in knots and he felt like he would vomit if he moved. Still reeling from the visions of his dream and not yet acclimated to his surroundings, he felt as if the floor beneath him might give way and the entire world would collapse in on itself and crush him and everything else. He prayed for it. *I can't do it anymore. Every fucking day is worse than the last and I'm not doing it again. I'm not fucking doing it anymore.*

He thought of canceling his appointments for the day. Canceling his lease on the office. Canceling his cell-phone plan and staying inside alone, taking pills in bed until he could sleep again. He thought of canceling the idea of ever waking up again.

The heavy drinking from the night before was testing the limits of his bladder and he had no choice but to acquiesce. With much reluctance, he made the arduous migration from bed to bathroom where he sat on the toilet with his face in his hands and all the sorrows of the Virgin Mother and the weeping Christ upon him.

It was 6:15 on a Tuesday morning, and she was not there.

Henry was alone in his house. *This is my life*, he thought, lifting his head to see the pristine white marble that lined his bathroom. *Fuck me.* He swallowed down the feeling that he might vomit. He knew it too would pass if he breathed just right and kept his head just so.

He finished in the bathroom and walked to the kitchen, but not before holding his middle finger to the man he saw in the mirror over the vanity as he passed. The man returned the sentiment and they each avoided the other's gaze. Henry walked to the steaming pot of coffee, retrieved a mug from the cabinet overhead, poured a cup, took a sip, then added a spoonful of sugar from a small jar on the counter and moved to the refrigerator for milk.

He leaned against the counter, holding his coffee in his hand. His body and his eyes stayed fixed in place while the rest of him went somewhere else. He stood a vacant body while his mind recounted every horrific scene he had ever witnessed and he tried to find the courage to ever set foot outside again. He saw the faces of old patients at the hospital, ghastly and haunted by visions no one else could see. He saw his father on his deathbed, delirious, jaundiced, and angry, cursing at Henry and choking on phlegm. He saw his wedding band sitting loose in the change dish in his car, Gretchen standing alone in the kitchen, and a girl he barely knew smiling at him in a hotel bar.

He saw Gretchen's face in ecstasy as she pressed her body into the man from his dream and he winced. He saw that giant smile spread across her face, her eyes and attention fixed on someone else. He saw her walk away for the last time, and the dreadful loneliness that filled him then filled him again now as he stood alone in the kitchen.

Once, they had shared this house and, as with his office, most everything had been by her design. What items of his remained had only been done with her approval. Henry had changed almost nothing since she had moved out, except for the few pictures of her he had removed from shelves, windowsills, and the walls in the hallway. The house plants and small trees and ferns she used to tend died quickly after she left, and they had all been thrown out as well, likely never to be replaced.

Her influence and his memories of her inhabited every corner of every room, and still he could only feel her absence. Henry tried to breathe life into his memories, to sense even a ghost of her presence, but she had left nothing of herself besides furniture and a box of trinkets for which she would never come back. The house was always silent now, hollow—a model of a house where once a home had been. Henry felt like a captive, like an exhibit of a man in a superficial habitat created for him to eat and sleep and bathe in and eventually die. But he had no audience; no one was watching him. He was alone under glass and no one would notice if he was gone. Once, he had someone, and now he had only the furniture she had picked out, the walls she had painted green, the wooden butcher-block countertops where she used to cook because he could not, and a cardboard box of items she had left in a drawer.

The box. Henry snapped back into his body at the memory of the box and turned his head toward the hallway. After taking down the photos of Gretchen from around the house, he had stowed them in a box of her belongings that she had forgotten in her nightstand when she moved, but he had never taken the time to inventory its contents. Suddenly compelled by loneliness or an instinct for penance, he moved out of the kitchen, down the hall, and into the second bedroom where he stored the box in a closet.

He hadn't been in the guest room in weeks, maybe longer. The bed in the center of the room was made up to welcome no one and the shelves held more dust than anything else. He stood before the open closet and stared at the box on the floor for a moment. Just an ordinary box, the top panels folded over each other haphazardly to keep it closed. It was inanimate and unassuming, but his heart still raced at the sight of it. Perhaps it was the anticipation of seeing some part of her again, or a sense of guilt at violating her privacy. She had not been back in months, and likely would never return, and there could be nothing of value to her or to anyone else inside the box. Still, it was foreboding. For a moment he felt an icy fear like that of death in his bones and he considered throwing the box out or leaving it on her porch and driving off without a word.

Why are you like this? It's a box of bullshit. Calm down.

All of Henry's basest instincts were skilled at impersonating intuition, a fact he knew about himself and believed to be true of all people. Thus he reasoned that intuition was a treacherous guide and one not to be trusted. Insecurities, fears, desires, and emotional reactions could disguise themselves as good reasoning or survival instincts and mount campaigns of misinformation that could lead a person astray, so he was careful to dismiss anything he felt when it contradicted the things he believed to be true. How he could tell the difference between his intuition, his emotional responses, and his good reasoning was a process only he could explain.

Shame and remorse were no doubt playing tricks on him, but he knew that he would open the box, despite his anxiety and hesitation, just as he knew there was no risk of harm or death in doing so. *Enough with the dramatics—this is embarrassing. Just admit it, you want to see her. You want to see her face and it's okay. It's fine. You're fine.*

He kneeled down and took a deep breath in through his nose and opened the flaps of the box. The walls did not shake. The sky didn't open. He didn't turn to dust. *See? You're worse than the loonies they send you at the Willows and you're not getting any better, chief. Wake up, you're a fucking mess.*

At the top of the box were the several framed pictures he had discarded when Gretchen moved out. He pulled them out one by one and looked at them. Some dated back to the days before their marriage—moments they had both wanted to capture and immortalize. Over time, the sentiment of the moments was lost and the photos became common artifacts for decoration. When she left they became sentient—taunting little spies watching his every move, reminding him of his follies and his failures, observing him as he toiled in the consequences of his actions and mocking him as he went. Now, seeing them again after all this time, he saw they were lifeless, all melancholy and distant, an open line, silent without anyone on the other end. He stacked the photos on the floor next to the box.

Beneath the photos was a small stack of books that were vaguely familiar. Self-help books and a pulp novel that had sat on her nightstand for years. There was a pewter jewelry dish engraved to look like a turtle on its back, with four legs, a head, and a tail that extended upward. A small pair of headphones, the wire neatly coiled up and tied off. At the bottom of the box was another book. Henry reached in and pulled it out.

The book was bound with burgundy and metallic gold floral brocade, and had no text on the cover or spine. He opened the book and let the pages flip rapidly across his thumb, revealing a journal full of handwritten pages. If he had come looking for an actual trace of his ex-wife, he knew he may have found more than he had wished for.

Without thinking, he closed the book again, stood up, stepped backwards, and slowly sat down on the edge of the guest bed. His heart was beating hard in his throat and again he was nauseated. He felt as he might have if he had stumbled across the open window of a disrobing woman: tempted and ashamed. Possessed by curiosity more than reason, he opened the book.

The first page was ruled with dark lines, and near the center in small, elegant, and clean letters was written:

This is not for you.

Henry turned to the next page, found weird doodles of birds or something, and turned the page again. Another page with indecipherable scribbles, a phone number, nothing of interest. He turned several pages at once, settling at random on a page that was filled with writing. All of his guilt and indecision had gone silent behind the blind drive to know what these pages held. Without pause, he read:

8/5

You were always a risk worth taking.

    Even if you never learned, never changed, were never quite
strong enough to carry what weighed you down, you were
enough, the way you were. It's everything you try to be that is
your cause for suffering. And mine.

    But there are some things you cannot fake.

    You can't fake the way you love me.

    A fierce protector, determined to provide.

    You love me as if I were a child.

    You praise my beauty, my loyalty, my fidelity.

    You love me like a dog.

    It is love, after all.

    It's not your fault you suffer, but it's not mine either.

    I've suffered too, you know. I've struggled, like you, to make peace with the way my ideals hold no water in the world, carry no influence, change almost nothing. My frustrations themselves work in futile spats and sporadic little fits and the only option day after day is to surrender them and accept the freedom that comes with letting go.

My anger is inconvenient. Unproductive. Maybe even irrational.

Your anger colors the world for you and fills the space we share.

It's okay to be angry. It's okay to be afraid. It's okay to feel over-whelmed and hopeless and unsure of what to do about it all.

I want to tell you all of this. I want you to tell me too.

But we don't hear each other anymore.

We don't speak the same tongue.

And through it all, I love you too, you know.

I carry your heart like it's my cross to bear.

I hold this space and keep it open for you, like the steward of your kingdom while you quest in search of something worth the fight. Worth bringing home. Worth waking up for, again and again. Something that could fulfill all your dreaming.

I know you suffer, and I know why.

Maybe you never will. Maybe you will always be this way.

I once was sure that you were worth the risk.

But I'm not sure you've been worth the cost.

Breathless, lifeless, he sat still. His heart trudged on like footsteps in deep mud, all struggling and stopping and sucking and sinking lower with each beat. Whatever it was that had encumbered him, enslaved him, and dragged him into this room, sat him at this bed, and commanded him to dig into the past had retreated and was now nowhere to be found. In the face of her words, he felt more alone than he had ever been.

What? Are you going to cry? What good will that do you?

He wasn't sure if the thought was his or his father's. He wasn't even sure what he felt. Had he the same awareness of himself that he had for his patients, he might have felt somber, remorseful, even ashamed, but he only knew he felt like crying, and that spurred in him a great conflict. Gretchen had always been so much more expressive than him. Untrammeled by inhibition or shame or repression, she would often shed tears and sob as though it were an exercise of routine bodily expulsion. He had never been quite so liberated. To him, tears should be reserved for only the greatest of life's tragedies and triumphs. Births, deaths, and little in-between.

In his guest room in the early morning, he felt stripped naked and exposed before himself for the first time. From the page she cried out to be heard, but he was so late to hear her. He had loved her the only way he knew how, but what had he really known of love? He had fought to provide; he had done all he could to reciprocate her bids for intimacy. But *had* he? Now he saw himself in his memory, cowering and snarling from behind walls of self-defense, fighting her every step of the way. Stifling her. Suffocating her. Had he listened to a word she'd been saying?

Where he thought he had been her foundation and frame—stalwart and resilient, supportive and strong—had she been carrying the stubborn weight of him all along? Where he had sought to be the solution to the problem of her myriad uncomfortable emotions, had she wanted only a partner with whom to explore them instead? He had only ever called her irrational so as to help her see the objective truth of the thing, but now he was having doubts about his own grasp on the truth.

Births, deaths, and perhaps divorces counted. It's possible that the loneliness he felt in his home at six-something in the morning with the ghostscribe of his true love gasping forsaken truths from his lap might constitute an exception to the no-tears rule. He thought three simple words, *I fucked up.* His eyes were hot and pooling with water, but before any escaped to adorn his cheeks, that old reservation reached up through his throat from the dark of his belly and force-stopped the whole process at once.

By the time they separated, Henry and Gretchen had been together for nearly fifteen years, married for half that time. In the years preceding their marriage, the primary source of discord between them was on the merit of marriage itself. In the years following, it was the topic of having children. Regardless of the subject, there were fundamental differences in each of them that underlay all of their marital tensions. Henry found Gretchen to be overly idealistic, even naive in her optimism, and in turn, Gretchen found Henry to be curmudgeonly and obtuse in matters of romance and the heart.

Both of them were indeed happy to forgive each other their differences, because the intensity of their connection for so long dwarfed any conflict that arose between them. It wasn't until the hard cost of years gone by was realized that either of them began to understand the breadth of the chasm between them, and how greatly such a rift had affected the potential course of their lives.

Henry had been in his late twenties when he met Gretchen. Henry's then-girlfriend, Megan, had insisted that Henry go with her to Gretchen's birthday party. At the time, Megan and Gretchen had not been close for some years, but they had been roommates in college and had stayed in touch in the years since graduation. Henry dutifully accompanied Megan to the party, but upon arrival, he was quick to find a drink and a seat outside, away from the bulk of the congregation.

The seat he found was in a courtyard that was shared with three other condos neighboring the one where the party was taking place. The late-January evening cold had shepherded most of the visitors inside to find the warmth of other bodies sheltered in heated rooms, and only one other person was sitting outside.

Henry sat on the low wall of the flower box and took great pains to give the illusion that he did not notice the young woman sitting in one of the folding chairs near him. But he had noticed her. The way her face was poised, perfectly still behind her dark hair with her eyes cast down at the paperback in her hand, afforded him the opportunity to study her for a moment, almost naturally as he had walked from the door into the courtyard. For a moment he had probably been ogling, but he restrained himself to something closer to admiration, before finally looking away and returning to her the privacy he had taken.

People talk of chemistry, of gravity between people, and of destiny, things that Henry abhorred and dismissed. Still, in the moments following his first sight of the woman in the chair, he felt a maelstrom of grief and desire swirl and rage within him. As a young man in his twenties, it was always exciting to see a pretty girl, but from the ledge in the back of the party he was avoiding, near the woman in the chair with her oversized honey brown eyes shining out from behind her long, dark hair, he felt the call of a tyrant impelling him to invade her space, to possess her beauty, to make every part of the person she was, or might be, his own.

He had no explanation and a healthy sense of guilt for his reaction, considering both the young woman and his own girlfriend, whom he had abandoned inside the party. The conflict caused visceral tension in him, and it was all he could manage to sit and stare at the gray clouded sky and quietly drink from his bottle of beer. He fashioned himself into a perfect picture of solitary disinterest, and he was proud of himself for his self-awareness and his restraint.

"Excuse me. Do you have a cigarette by chance?" the woman said, negating all of Henry's efforts to leave her be.

"No, sorry, I, uh ... don't smoke," he said and patted his pockets and then shrugged, immediately second-guessing himself, wondering if his choice of gestures was appropriate for the situation or if he had just dismissed her the way one dismisses a panhandler in the street.

"Right. Me neither, actually," she said.

"Ah, of course. Explains why neither of us have any cigarettes then, I suppose," he said, as though making a Holmes-worthy deduction. "Glad we cleared that up."

The woman gave a quick laugh and said, "I don't *usually* smoke, I mean. Sometimes it helps with the nerves in social situations and stuff though, you know? Like, all of my friends are in that house right now because I invited them here to celebrate my birthday, and now that we're all here, I wish I had just stayed inside and celebrated my birthday with one or two people eating Thai food and watching a movie or something. Like, why did I think I needed a whole party to celebrate me, you know? I don't even like parties!"

"Well, I wasn't going to say anything, but since you mention it, after twenty-one, no adult should throw themselves a birthday party except for maybe on the decades. Thirty, forty, fifty, you know? Those are probably still okay. Otherwise, it's like, what is the actual point? I get why kids do it, I guess, but adults—what are you even celebrating?"

She was holding a hand over her mouth, three fingers hiding the smile that had swept across her face, her large eyes soft and forgiving, a hint of condescension on her brows. "You don't celebrate birthdays?" she said.

"I mean, anniversaries are a bizarre cause for celebration in the first place, if you really think about it. 'Oh hey, it's been three hundred and sixty-five days since this thing last happened, let's celebrate it again'? Why? It's arbitrary. But treating the anniversary of the day you were born like it is some historic event to be canonized and commemorated annually by you and everyone you know is just *delusional*. I think if it weren't a part of the social contract, or if you were just . . . an alien looking down on Earth or a visitor from some other culture where birthdays didn't exist or something like that, you would probably think it's the most masturbatory thing, a birthday party," Henry said. He was looking down as he spoke, eyes fixed on the ground, but his attention was not anywhere near the place they sat, like he was looking somewhere far away or reading a script off a teleprompter inside of his skull.

The woman held her mouth agape in shock, her large sarcastic smile now fully exposed, and said, "Wow, well . . . remind me not to come to you for reassurance again any time soon."

"Oh, I'm sorry, were you looking for reassurance? I thought we were just talking about our mutual disdain for birthday parties," he said, dripping with performative sympathy, deliberately disingenuous, mocking himself and her at the same time.

"Sir, you are not allowed to tell the guest of honor how you truly feel about being invited to her birthday party. It's in the social contract—fine print," she said. "Why are you here anyway? Who even are you?" She was laughing heartily as she spoke, one hand over her mouth and the other pointing toward Henry, palm to the sky in inquisition.

"Oh, I'm Henry. People call me Foss, but Henry is fine. For now. We'll work our way to nicknames."

"Oh, will we? Great then, Henry, good to meet you. I'm Gretchen," she said and held out her hand.

"Oh, and we're shaking hands, how formal!" he said and clasped her hand in his. They held the handshake for just a moment longer than one would expect while maintaining eye contact, as if they were challenging the other or sizing each other up.

"So, Mr. Henry, how did you wind up at this awful event?"

And dammit, she ruined it.

"Oh, I came with, uh . . . Megan, a girl I'm dating," he said.

Henry tried to read her face, looking for any kind of sign—evidence of disappointment or condemnation. He didn't know how close she and Megan were, and he wasn't sure if their interaction so far had been perceptibly as scandalized by flirtation as it was in his mind. He wasn't sure if his initial thoughts of her were displayed in his speech and mannerisms. He saw nothing to indicate either with any certainty. To his disappointment, he found that she seemed altogether unfazed.

"Oh, of course," she said. "I love Megan. You know, we were in school together and we've lived in the same town ever since and almost never manage to see each other. I'm glad she made it. God, am I an asshole, hiding out here like this? How many people were in there when you walked out?"

"You might be an asshole, but they'll live. The house was pretty full; everyone seemed to be having a good time and no one seemed concerned with your whereabouts that I could see."

"I'm not sure if that makes me feel better or worse, actually," she said, again laughing a composed and measured laugh with her hand covering the center of her wild caricature of a smile. She turned her head slightly away from him and watched him out of the side of her large brown eyes and squinted, raising her soft chin as the hair fell again from behind her ear and into her face.

"Should we go back in?" she asked.

"It's your party, isn't it? I think you're allowed to do as you please," said Henry. The veil between his words and his intentions was dangerously thin, but tangible enough to offer him the comfort of plausible deniability should she not like what she saw on the other side. Though he could not be certain she was interested in continuing to speak with him in private, he could not deny that the air between them seemed to carry a weight that made it palpable. It dragged space and time to the center of the line from his body to hers and threatened to fold in the space around them and with it draw them both to meet in the middle of everything. The context of their meeting had become secondary, the reason and the situations that drew him to the courtyard were not relevant to the moment. The noise from inside was muted and distant. The courtyard and the building complex were a stage in a vacant hall.

Gretchen sat silent, maybe only for a moment, and she cast her eyes back down to the book in her hand. Henry wondered how great his delusions were; he could have convinced himself that he was being overly grandiose if not for what she said next.

"Then I guess I'd like to stay out here a while longer, please," Gretchen said and looked back up, right through Henry's poorly veiled intentions and into the naked and optimistic invitation of his blue eyes.

Henry remembered the way they looked at each other in the yard outside the condo of some friend whose name he could not remember at Gretchen's twenty-fifth birthday party while his girlfriend was inside dancing or mingling or sitting alone waiting for him to return. He remembered how familiar Gretchen's gaze had seemed, how intense the need to stay had felt. He remembered how after weeks of flirtation his willingness to remain in denial had been drained from him completely and he told Megan that he was sorry and wished her all the best.

He remembered how she spat in his face and turned to leave without another word. He remembered the ecstasy of relief he felt in that moment, and he remembered wondering if he should have felt more.

He felt something similar now, sitting on the edge of the bed in the guest room of the house that he and Gretchen once shared, holding her ugly red-and-gold diary in his lap and cursing her name silently with his jaw clenched so tightly he felt pain in his gums. He no longer noticed the beat of his heart or the sweet, metallic taste of adrenaline in the back of his throat. He didn't notice the sun shining through the blinds, illuminating the layer of dust like glitter across the windowsill and the wooden footboard of the bed on which he sat. He didn't remember the look of pleasure on Gretchen's face in his dream, or how he woke up feeling like he could vomit at any moment.

Amid all the complicated and uncomfortable feelings and his fundamental inability to make sense of them, his body reacted in his stead and did what it knew how to do: resort to anger. He wasn't worried about the day before him, his patients, Will's stupid fucking dinner party, or anything that had ever happened prior to this moment or even anything that would ever happen again. He just wanted a drink, some coffee, and to get started with his day.

Henry closed the book and stood up. He walked with purpose back to the kitchen and laughed to himself as he muttered incomprehensible curses. He opened a cabinet above the refrigerator and pulled down a bottle of scotch, pouring a shot into his mouth and then two more into his thermos. He filled the thermos with the remaining coffee from the pot and topped it off with half and half. Then, he returned to his bathroom, taking the journal with him, and began to prepare for work.

‡

HF: Alright. So, moving on then to today. Do you want to tell me how things are going, Nick?

NW: They're fuckin' going, man.

HF: Yeah, I suppose they are.

NW: Yup.

. . .

NW: Aren't you supposed to, like, ask me something else, or something?

HF: What's the point? You're not ready to talk yet, are you?

NW: What's the *point*? That's what I've been asking *you*, dude.

HF: What's it going to take to get you to participate here?

NW: Hey, you know what, forgive me if you met me at literally the worst fucking time in my whole life and I'm not super keen on sitting around and chopping it up with one of the dickheads who is holding me hostage.

HF: I'm not holding you hostage, Nick.

NW: No, you literally are. First I couldn't leave until you said. And now you've blackmailed me into coming back every week.

HF: I wish you wouldn't see it that way.

NW: Yeah, well, I wish there was another way to see it.

HF: You could try to see what I'm trying to do for you.

NW: You're not trying to do anything for me, you're covering your own ass and treating your own guilt.

HF: I told you before, I don't feel any guilt with you. I know you don't see it, but I think everything I've done so far has been in your best interest. That's the thing about youth, I guess. It's hard to think of the big picture, to really appreciate the scope of time ahead of you and how the things you do will impact a future that you can't even conceive of yet.

NW: It's not about what I can and can't conceive of, doc. It's about the point of the thing.

HF: The point of the thing?

NW: What's the point of conceiving of the future? Why would it matter? Look around, today is already fucked and it's abundantly clear that the future isn't getting any better. It's not even guaranteed. Planning for it is not a priority. Why should it be?

HF: Well, because it's coming. Whether you like it or not.

NW: Is it though? How can you be so sure? And should that even really affect what I do today? Life is for the living, doc. Not the "maybe later."

HF: Hah. All of a sudden you have a lust for life, do you?

NW: No, it's not even that. It's just . . . I guess I would rather live every day without reservation than walk around on eggshells all scared of how it *might* all turn out someday. Because, spoiler alert: It ends. Usually badly. So, would you rather live a life regretting what you did do or regretting what you *didn't* do?

HF: Well. I guess it's not that simple. That's the thing about choices, Nick. Whatever you choose to do or not to do, it's still the very choice that you will live to revere or regret. And it's all just a trick of words, anyway. For every thing we choose to do, there is something we choose to *not* do, and in either case, only the result of the decision will guide whether or not we regret it at all.

NW: I can't tell if what you're saying is wise or just bullshit.

HF: You sound like my wife—well, ex-wife.

NW: Oh, you're divorced.

HF: Yes, I am.

NW: So you know a thing or two about regret then, dontcha, doc?

HF: Indeed, I do. So listen up once in a while, would you?

NW: Why am I gonna listen to a guy who fucked it all up?

HF: Because who knows better than someone who has learned the hard lessons already?

NW: Okay. So then what you're saying essentially is that it's all a roll of the dice, right?

HF: I don't think I said that, exactly.

NW: You did, you said all we have are choices and it's only the outcome that justifies the choice. So, you're really making *my* point. We do what we're going to do because it isn't going to matter anyway. It's either gonna work out or it's not. It's celebration or regret, and I don't get to choose which because how it all works out isn't really up to me. Isn't that what you're saying?

HF: Well, no—not exactly. What I'm saying is that there are consequences for every decision we make, regardless of our intentions, and what I am trying to get at is that it is in our best interest to consider the possible consequences *of* those actions prior to making decisions in order to give ourselves the best possible opportunity to enjoy the fruits of our choices rather than labor in regret and misery over the consequences of reckless, impulsive actions.

NW: And if we work really hard to consider the consequences, and we make the best possible choices, and life shows up and does what it does and pulls some shit we didn't see coming and knocks us off our pedestal of righteous action, then what? What do we do then? Just say, "Aw shucks, I gave it my best shot" and end up suffering anyway? You're saying, play it safe, and maybe everything will be okay someday. And I'm saying, no fuckin' dice. I'm not going to spend my time hoping that someday it'll all work out. Because it doesn't work out. For anyone. Ever. Best you can hope to do is delay the inevitable. It'll never be okay. It'll just be . . . whatever it's gonna be. And most of the time, it's gonna be fucked.

HF: And how's that working out for you so far?

NW: Fuck you. How's yours working out for you?

6

It was shortly after noon when Nick could no longer ignore the numerous intrusions on his sleep. For months, he had awoken at 4am to merciless fluorescent lights switching on outside the window of his cell and the banging of doors and stomping of feet and so many other sounds from sources he couldn't see through the gray brick walls that contained his whole world. Today he buried his head under pillows to deaden the sound of the birds crying for the passing of the day and the cars of the people with purposes and places to be. The heat from the high August sun radiated through the second-story window of his mother's house and baked his room where he lay twisted in his bedsheets, a mess of sweat and the heavy haze of a sedative sleep.

In county, he rarely saw sunlight, though he did have the option to venture outside during his free time to a small enclosure with high walls where he could catch a glimpse of open sky through a cage-like ceiling of barbed wire and netting. The window in his cell had been a thick, multi-paned, and heavily fogged plexiglass that let just enough light through that he could determine whether or not the sun was out. He hadn't realized how much he would miss the warmth of sunlight on his skin until he no longer had the pleasure.

But on this day, so far he had been doing his best to ignore that same sun, despite its relentless persistence. The light, the heat, the sweat, the sounds. Still he slept. It wasn't until the knocking at his bedroom door that he finally surrendered to the day and opened his eyes.

"Yeah, yeah, yeah. What's up?" he said, probably just loud enough to be heard by his mother on the other side of the door. She pushed open the door, timidly at first, and then, after assessing that he was decent enough, she opened it all the way and let herself in. She stopped just inside the doorway and released a near-imperceptible exhale, whether of relief or resignation couldn't be discerned. Nevertheless, she smiled softly as she looked at the young man in his bed while the sunlight from the window gathered in her blue eyes and soaked into the skin of her face, which, despite being well-preserved for her age, was beginning to show signs of the years it had experienced. She wore a matching set of scrubs the color of rose-pink amethyst and plain white sneakers. Her lion-golden hair was parted off-center, pulled back tightly and held in place by a large cream-colored butterfly clip.

"Come on, Nicholas, it's almost one o'clock, what on earth are you doing in bed?" she said, imploring with more concern than condemnation, as was her nature.

"Mom, I was out late. I didn't even come home until this morning. You were already gone when I got here," Nick said. He struggled to kick the sheets from the tight coil in which he had wrapped himself in his sleep. He rolled onto his back and held his hands to his head, pushing his hair back and using his palms to apply pressure to his temples as he attempted to adjust his drowsy and sensitive eyes to the light and the unyielding woman in his room.

"Don't think I didn't notice, and . . . Christ, Nick, it's hot in here." She walked across the room to the window on the opposite wall and slid it open. She clicked her tongue against her teeth and looked at the open window frame. "One night home and your screen is gone again, I see. I told you I don't want you smoking out there, how hard is it to just go downstairs and use the door like everyone else?"

"Mom—" he started, but she was not finished yet.

"Save it. I know you're not gonna listen so I don't wanna hear it. Where were you last night, anyway? Please tell me you weren't out with those friends of yours again. Nicholas, you *just* got home. Do you *want* to go back?" She stood now at the foot of his bed, facing him with her pink scrubs and her blonde hair catching the light from the sun and bringing so much more brightness to a room that was already too well-lit for Nick's liking.

"Mom, I wasn't—" he started again.

"Oh, like you'd even tell me. Nicholas, what are you going to do? You're twenty years old, honey. You can't keep living like this. Oh, I'd hoped that whole thing would be a wake-up call for you. Has it been? What are you going to do? I can't let you just be out all night and sleep all day until you get yourself arrested again or even killed! Oh god, Nicholas, don't do that to me!"

"*Mommm!* Calm down. I wasn't doing anything, I was out with Alison. We fell asleep in my truck in the park while we were just catching up, I wasn't doing anything. I'm not going back. And Jesus, Mom, I'm not gonna fucking die!"

"Nicholas!" She bent down and whipped his bare foot with the tips of her fingers, hard enough to make her displeasure with his language known.

"Sorry, Mom, sorry. Jeez, knock it off, would you? It's too early for this shit." His tone sounded annoyed but they both knew he was putting it on for effect.

"It's *one o'clock* in the afternoon you . . . lazy little sh—potato! Some of us have already worked half a day." She gestured out the window to the rest of the wakeful and working world as Nick erupted in laughter.

"Lazy little shpotato?" he said, amused. Whatever agitation he had felt at waking up and being thrust immediately into the frazzled inquiries of his sweet but stressed-out mother now dissolved into something like glee, only somewhat dampened by the remnants of the drugs he had taken the night before.

Nick's mother turned and sat at the foot of his bed, watching her son laugh. "Too early. My god, how did you end up this way?"

"Ask yourself. You raised me," he said.

"Touché. Guess it's all my fault then, isn't it?"

"Guess so." Nick shrugged and laughed again. "Now, don't you have to go back to work or something?"

"Oh, I'm sorry. Did you have some pressing matters to tend to? Some urgent appointments to keep, do you?" She stood quickly and held up her hands in surrender as she walked backwards to the door, apologizing with her mouth and mocking him with her eyes. "Please, don't let me keep you from your busy, busy day, young man. I know you'll be showered, dressed, *and looking for a job* before I know it." She dropped her hands and her chin at the same time, raising her eyebrows and delivering a steely-eyed transmission with unmistakable meaning that only women who have raised children could convey.

Nick said nothing but returned her gaze with a wink and raised two fingers to his eyebrow in a half-hearted salute.

"Good. And don't do anything stupid, I'd like to keep you home for a while," she said.

"Uh huh. I love you too, Mom."

She winked and saluted back, pulled the door closed, and walked away. Nick listened to her footsteps move down the hall, away from him toward the stairs. He heard each step get quieter as they moved down the staircase. He heard the sound of her keys as she picked them up off the small table by the door, then the creak of the hinges as the door opened and closed. Out the window he heard her steps on the driveway as she made her way to her car. Door open, door shut. Ignition. He waited—the hum of the motor beneath his bedroom window, the muffled sound of talking, probably a radio advertisement. *Who still listens to the radio?*

He closed his eyes and tried to breathe deeply into his chest. The moment of joviality had passed and his agitation returned. His lungs felt swollen, or maybe it was his ribcage that felt smaller than usual, cramping his chest and constricting his heart. His arteries pulsed behind his ears and sounded like a clock ticking away seconds he couldn't afford to spare. The soft *tick, tick, tick* in his ears became consuming, and he felt old. He sensed his mortality in each beat of his heart, and he was overcome with dread and regret. He wanted to rip his veins from beneath his skin. He wanted to make the feeling stop.

The clunking sound of the transmission shifting into reverse pulled his attention from his agonies, and he listened as the car backed out of the driveway and drove down the street until he could only hear the dull hum of the town and those obnoxious chirping birds. *Thank god.*

He lifted his head to locate his jeans, which lay on the floor beside the bed, and then lunged at them with the swiftness of a striking snake (though without the grace), reached into a pocket, and pulled out his cigarettes and lighter. He picked up his phone from beside his pillow and climbed out the window onto the eave. He sat disoriented in the sun, feeling like the only resting object in an intricate, buzzing system of activity and accomplishment. Out of place. Incongruent and surreal.

His neighborhood was still. Everyone was gone, well into their work days, classes, errands, or whatever else civilians do, he didn't know. It seemed everyone was always working or sleeping when he was on the roof. When they slept, he swelled with pride at his exemption from the mundane routines by which they were all enslaved. In the afternoon sun he felt less sure of himself. He felt like he was missing out on something. He felt like he had shown up late and been left behind by the whole world.

Through squinted eyes, he watched the flame from his lighter ignite the tip of his cigarette, and he breathed deeply as though the smoke were some remedy which would loosen his heart and lungs from the rigid clutches of his own ribs, and he thought for a moment that perhaps there was something wrong with his entire approach to everything. He wondered if the things he sought to relieve his suffering had only been causing him more trouble. Maybe everyone else was onto something. Maybe he had been wrong about it all. Everything, all along.

How do they do it? Alarm clocks and schedules. Sleep hygiene. Making plans and keeping commitments. Managing money. Building credit. Investments and properties and people all around. Close friends and loved ones. Intimacy and trust. Marriage. Children. Life-insurance policies.

Are they right, or are they brainwashed, or are they just too simple to see any other way?

They're happy. They're productive. And they aren't waking up at one o'clock on a Tuesday afternoon and smoking cigarettes alone, wondering if anything will ever matter enough to purchase an insurance policy on.

If ignorance is bliss, what does that make me? One of the smart ones? Because I'm anything but blissful right now.

Are they ignorant or ... have they just surrendered to it?

Sold their souls and made their peace?

Does it only work if you roll over and let it own you?

There has to be another way.

There has to be more.

Man, aren't you just so fuckin' glad to be home? This is what you've been waiting for.

Nick let out a small snort from his nose and he smiled with his eyes bright and bleary, laughing softly to himself at the irony of his circumstances.

Never can just be grateful for anything, can you, dickhead?

He picked up his phone and saw that he had several notifications. Sixteen missed calls and five text messages from Mom.

> 7:06am: Where are you?
>
> 8:15am: Are you up?
>
> 8:45am: Nicholas why aren't you answering the phone?
>
> 9:55am: Where are you?!
>
> 11:35am: CALL ME

Jesus Christ, Mom. Calm down.

Two text messages from Lia.

> 11am: You're home ... ?
>
> 11:45am: Fuck you nick

God dammit, who told you?

One text message from Connor.

> 12:02pm: Yo I saw Lia this morning heads up. i told her you were back lol my bad 😂

Look, my betrayer is here.

Fucking Judas.

Zero text messages from Alison.

He puffed his cheeks out and swished the air in his mouth from side to side, letting short bursts of air noisily escape the corners of his lips as he alternated left to right. He had not been prepared to talk to Lia in the first place, and now he found his position especially disadvantageous since she had found out that he was home before he called her himself. This position was nothing he wasn't used to with her (and nothing she wasn't used to either, for that matter), but that never made it easier.

His options were clear:

A. Text her back, fight, apologize, and see her
B. Ignore her until later, fight, apologize, and see her

He deliberated for a moment and then looked back down at his phone.

Thanks for the heads up, asshole.

My bad man, was she pissed?

Yeah. I'll deal with it later.

lmao. wyd?

just woke up. You home?

Yuuuup

Cool i'm gonna come thru in a minute

cool

Nick crawled back through the window and into his room. He considered showering, but decided that a clean shirt and deodorant would suffice for the time being. He pulled yesterday's jeans from the floor and clean socks and a black tee shirt from his dresser drawer. Grabbing cigarettes, lighter, phone, wallet, and keys, he left his bedroom, stopping in the bathroom to brush his teeth and push his hair around with his fingers until he was satisfied that he looked like someone who might have been awake for more than ten minutes. He found a pair of his mom's sunglasses on his way out of the house and put them on along with his shoes before opening the front door and walking to his truck.

He drove to Connor's house in silence with the windows up. He passed through intersections and traffic signals. He performed turns, yielded to vehicles and pedestrians, and navigated the route between his house and Connor's apartment, but upon parking in the visitor's space, he realized he couldn't recall a single moment of the drive. He wondered if he had run red lights or fallen asleep at any point. If he had, there didn't seem to have been any consequences. He felt something like remorse or fear bubble up from his spine, but chose to dismiss it as quickly as it came. He walked across the parking lot to Connor's apartment and knocked on the door.

The door opened and Connor stood with his arm extended in front of him and his palm forward, instructing Nick to stay where he stood. "Excuse me, sir, does your parole officer know you're here?"

"I don't have a parole officer, moron. That's not how it works," said Nick, pushing Connor's arm aside and walking past him into the apartment.

"I know, I know, I'm just fuckin' with you, buddy. What, are you pissed at me right now?" Connor said with an awkward and desperate cordiality.

"Why would I be pissed at you?" Nick didn't look up as he continued across the room to the sliding glass door that opened to a small, fenced-in concrete patio where Connor kept two white plastic chairs and a coffee can full of water and cigarette butts.

"About the Lia thing, you know, telling her you were out. Look, I didn't realize it was a secret or anything, I just mentioned that you had been by, you know, because I was stoked to see you and I figured she—"

"It's not a secret," Nick said, opening the sliding door and then turning around to face the room. He leaned against the door frame and pulled out a cigarette and lit it, exaggerating the effort to blow the smoke behind him and out the door, though it all rushed back into the room and swirled slowly. "I was gonna call her but something came up and I just hadn't got around to it yet."

"Still, man, I'm sorry, I just didn't know," Connor said.

"You didn't know," Nick affirmed, shrugging his shoulders with his hands hung low. "All good, man. She'll be fine. She just ... You know how she is, man, she's a hot one."

"Bro, you know who else is a fuckin' *hot one*? Your friend you brought over here before you got locked up. Alison? Dude. She's been coming by, and let me tell you, what I wouldn't give to throw one at her—"

"Jesus Christ, Connor," Nick said, interrupting his friend while trying not to let him see the jealousy which he suddenly carried heavy in his jaw and hot in his skin.

"What?" Connor said, retreating in shock while a Cheshire grin spread on his lips. "Don't tell me you're fucking her too? Wagner, you *dog!*"

"I'm not fucking anyone. Jesus. Lay off the uppers, you're so annoying right now," said Nick.

"I'm barely even on anything, man. I'm just saying, dude, if you're not hitting that, I'm going to, she's fuckin' unreal. She just shows up here in her little sundresses with her legs out and I'm like—" Connor made some obscene gesture with his mouth and his eyes wide and his hips jutting out, but Nick didn't understand exactly what he was pantomiming.

"Yup, a hot girl makes you act like an idiot. No surprise there," Nick said, trying again to stop him from talking.

"Say what you want. But if you don't do it, I'm going to." Connor raised his eyes and tilted his head, accenting the ultimatum he presented.

"How about this, if you touch her, I'll kill you?"

"Ooh, you're a real tough guy after a little time in prison, aren't ya, bud?" Connor jibed, adopting a boxer's stance: bending his knees, raising his fists in front of his face, and bouncing back and forth from foot to foot as if he were preparing to fight. "Come on, baby, fight me for her," he said, and he laughed while he threw some half-hearted punches at the air in front of him.

Nick blew smoke from his mouth and forced a laugh. He felt he had to emphasize that he was only joking, but he wasn't sure if he was. "Oh shit, okay, you're right, you're right. I don't want any of that," he said, and held his hands up at his shoulders in surrender. "Look, man, it's not even about fucking her or anything. It's all of it. I know she's on addies or whatever and she's experimenting and shit but she's not like us, man. You gotta take it easy with her."

"Not like us?"

"Yeah, she's not cut out for this shit. She's smart, she's going places. She doesn't belong here with us, doing all this shit," Nick said, his speech getting slower as his smile faded and he looked down at the floor.

"What are you talking about, dog? Like we're the fucking outsiders or something?"

"*The Outsiders*? What are you—I didn't even know you could read." Nick looked back up at Connor.

"Dick. They made us read it in school. Didn't you have to?"

"Have you been waiting since high school to try and draw that comparison, dude?" Nick was almost laughing again.

"I said we're *not* the outsiders, bro!"

"Yeah, well, we are, we aren't, I don't know what you're even talking about. The point is Alison is going places and I'm not letting your dumbass dirty dick fuck it up. Don't fuck her. Don't flirt with her. And don't sell her anything but addies."

"Are you joking me?"

"No, I'm serious. No percs, no xans, no coke, nothing you get your grubby little hands on except Adderall. And if you think she's getting out of hand with it, you let me know."

"She doesn't even ask for that shit," Connor said.

"Good." Nick dropped his burning cigarette butt into the coffee can and it hissed and spat when it hit the filthy rust-colored water and died. Nick thought of drowning. He thought of the moments in-between the last exhale and the loss of consciousness. He thought of a tidal wave of ineffable size blocking out the sun and pouring over some city. He wondered if he were there, would he run, hide, attempt to flee to higher ground? Or would he turn and face the tide? He pictured himself sitting cross-legged and calm before the flood. Resistance only contributes to stress and agitation. *Never get so attached to anything that you can't let it go when you have no other choice.* He knew he would run screaming, but he told himself he would welcome the wave.

"Speaking of which, give me ten of those boys from last night, them blue boys," Nick said, finally breaking his trance and looking up from the can as he spoke.

"Fucking Wagner. Right back to it like nothing at all." Connor shook his head and smiled with something that looked like pride. He sat down on the couch and pulled a black metal lockbox from underneath the coffee table, set it gently atop the glass, and opened it with a key that was already in the keyhole.

"What's the point of the lockbox if you don't lock the thing?" Nick said in a monotone and again looked down, watching the thin stream of smoke pour up from the coffee can.

"What's the point of locking a box that anyone can just walk away with?" Connor said.

"Huh."

"Besides, I'm always home, I'm never far from this box," Connor said, then he laughed his self-assured, maniacal little laugh again.

"You're a fuckin' drug addict, you know that?" Nick walked into the room and sat down on the couch next to Connor, who was counting out ten blue pills from a small Ziplock bag. Connor slid them across the table to his left where Nick sat.

"Nothing else I'd rather be," Connor said with pride.

"You really should consider going to rehab. Gimme some foil. I know you have some in your little box, you dope fiend, you."

Connor pulled a folded-up piece of tinfoil and a gutted ink-pen tube from his box and set them on the table.

Nick gathered his tools and prepared like a smith before the forge, every instrument in its right place, standing at the ready. The tin he sheared and shaped just so to receive the crowned jewel, the rock of the age, his dull and lifeless gem. The fire from his hands met the foil, and with all the delusive beauty of the siren, the hissing and snapping became her song. The sorcery of Circe enchanted the smoke in his lungs and he knew he would surrender any wisdom, ambition, or pride to the vulgar swinery that would set him free of his troubles and all his concern for worldly things, for romance and tragedy, for fear and for failure.

He would wallow in the filth of the faux-leather couch amid the smell of smoke and unshowered youth and remain transfixed on an apparition, an illusion, a fleeting promise without chance of fulfillment, and for a moment he thought that in the face of the Goddess herself he would kneel and ask to remain at her feet for a lifetime, at any cost, whatever her whim, be him man, dog, or insect, so long as she would have him.

But all things pass, and some quicker than others. Together Nick and Connor smoked and stayed quiet, focused. After some time and two pills shared between them, Nick again felt the weight of his worldly tethers and he sighed, despondent and grieving, and stood up. He opened the door to the patio and sat in one of the plastic chairs just outside, facing the room, and put a cigarette in his mouth. He patted his pockets in search of his lighter but realized it was still on the coffee table, maybe six feet from where he sat, though the distance felt insurmountable. In the dread of this realization, he accepted that in the event the great wave would come, he would die painfully and without dignity. There would be no graceful resignation, no cross-legged welcoming; he wouldn't have the concern for himself or even the wherewithal to run or fight. Instead he would freeze in fear and he would feebly cry, and every last bit of effort he could muster would be spent on regret and pitiful prayers that he might be spared by a miracle.

7

Henry sat in his office lounge chair and sipped from his thermos. The scotch was enough to warm his blood and taint the taste of his coffee, but not enough to be a problem in either case. He had second-guessed his impulsive morning drinking for a moment on his drive to the office, but he ultimately counted it as a luxury of writing his own code of conduct and chose pride instead. *I got myself here, I keep myself here. I'll do as I please.* If nothing else, it had cleared his mind enough to see beyond the dread of morning and helped him to somewhat recalibrate himself after the intensity of his initial reaction to Gretchen's words.

The recalibration did not come easily. The drive had been a tug-of-war between Henry's ideals and some part of himself that he could not identify or explain. A place inside where once-buried spiteful and malevolent things had disentombed themselves and now made awful sounds which disrupted his psyche and disturbed his thoughts. *She's so full of shit*, followed by, *What have I done, what did I do? So much I miss her* and *What if?* and *Where is she?*

This will all blow over in time, he thought before other shrill sounds consumed him and shrieked, *It isn't getting any easier and it's never going to, you're so full of shit*. He drank his coffee and let the taste of liquor rest in his gums and irritate his tongue. When he passed a police vehicle moving in the opposite direction, he felt a moment of fear and then spent several more in an intrusive daydream where he jerked his steering wheel to the left and struck the vehicle head-on. He wondered how bad it would hurt to be ejected through the windshield.

You're losing it, Foss, he thought as he drank from his thermos again. *We do this every day. Today is no different. So what, she thinks you're a piece of shit, maybe she always did. She left. There is no news here. You've lost touch with reality and you've given in to your feelings. Look at you. You're pathetic. This is pathetic. Drinking at eight in the morning over mean things a woman said about you? Just like that*, he revised his thinking. *You're a grown* man, *look at all you've built. No one in this world can stop you from having a drink whenever you feel like it. You're not some twelve-stepping alcoholic, for Christ's sake, you're a successful and respected doctor. It's her loss. Enjoy yourself. You could have a hundred more just like her if you wanted. But first, you need to get over this. It's not productive. It's not helping anything. You have a lot to do today. Get over it.*

He thought again about smashing into the police car and this time he only laughed.

That's the spirit, put those demons back in their cage and move on.

Now he sat in his lounge, his lips to his thermos and his phone in his hand, waiting for his first appointment of the day. He wondered if the mornings were getting worse; if it wasn't just the mornings anymore. If it was bleeding into the days. Into the nights. Waking up had never been easy. It was a quirk of existence, the toll he paid to live, his ante to play. But he had never before so frequently and so seriously considered the thing he considered daily now. All day, some days.

He blamed her for it all. He was fine before. He wondered if he would ever be okay again. How had she entrenched herself so deeply into his mind that now after a year or more he still couldn't fill the void she had left in him? He thought for a moment that he hated her. And then he wondered how she was doing. What she was doing.

He looked down at the phone in his lap to see the article he had only been partially reading—**Religious Groups and Scientists Rush to Lay Claim to Groundbreaking Discovery**—and decided there were more pressing matters at hand.

What is she doing?

He swiped his thumb across the screen to close the article, opened his phone's internet browser, and typed "Gretchen Foster California" in the search bar and pressed **GO.** The search engine returned myriad unrelated links, ads for background checks, irrelevant social-media accounts, and the bio page of some unknown actress. He scrolled past a number of misses until her face on his screen exposed how unprepared he had actually been to find her. A professional-looking headshot, black and white, that smile that seemed to become half of her face—unobstructed by her hand—and a soothing confidence in her eyes that could have cut him.

The photo was linked to a networking site for professionals. He also had an account with the site and he knew that its premium membership let users know who had viewed their page, so he paused out of fear that she would know he had been lurking. *What's she going to do about it? Call me and yell at me?* He would have been too ashamed to admit that the prospect of her calling him was the final thing that convinced him to click the link. The headline on her account page read:

Gretchen Foster
Professor of English, Creative Writing
Sacred Heart Community College

He read this and then stared at her photo, which was much larger and more prominent than the thumbnail in the search results. *Back to work. Good for you.* In his subconscious there was a great effort being made to restrict the frothing jealousy, resentment, hostility, and sorrow from boiling over and into the realm of superficial awareness. As a result, he believed his well-wishes to be sincere and not passive-aggressive, and he drank from his thermos with the long pull of a great thirst before swiping the browser away in dismissal. It was 9:29 and he could hear footsteps in the hall downstairs, which he presumed were the footsteps of a Ms. or Mrs. Bethany Cohen arriving for a consultation.

As expected, the footsteps grew louder until a young woman appeared in the hall just outside his open door. She paused there with her head hung in an awkward position, jutting out to one side, and she held her shoulders and arms tightly to her torso as though she were attempting to imitate a much smaller person, though she was already on the smaller end, as people go. Her lips stayed pursed together and formed a polite if uncomfortable smile, and even though she and Henry were making eye contact, she lifted one hand and knocked on the inside of the door frame. "Hi, I'm Bethany? We have an appointment? Um. Should I come in? Or do you want me to wait out here for a minute?" She drew her words out slowly and spoke in questions even when she meant to make statements.

"Of course, Bethany, come in, please have a seat," Henry said, gesturing toward the furniture across from him. "Anywhere you like, make yourself comfortable, please."

Bethany shuffled into the room, still holding her head at that awkward angle with her tight shoulders and arms pinned to her waist. Her posture seemed an apology for her very presence in the room. Beneath carefully layered monochromatic earth-toned attire, curled brown hair, and the powders and pens of her made-up face was an awkward and deeply uncomfortable girl of twenty-something. She sat in the large pillowy armchair across the coffee table from Henry and set her bag down on the ottoman in front of the chair. The way she sat upright in such a low and wide chair made Henry feel a sympathetic discomfort.

"Feel free to kick your feet up, if you'd like. There's no need for formality here, you're welcome to sit or lie or lounge as you please. Take off your shoes if you like, I don't care." He wondered if he had already overextended his welcome, if he was acting strangely. "No pressure, though—however you're comfortable is fine, of course."

Though he drank often, and more so in recent months than even he would be able to admit to himself or anyone else, he rarely drank at work. And though he felt he had only had enough to take the edge off, he considered the possibility that with the edge may also have gone some amount of his decorum, and so he decided to pay special attention to professionalism in this introduction. *First impressions.*

"So, I'm Dr. Foster, as I'm sure you know. It's good to meet you, Bethany. Welcome to my humble, uh, office, here. Let's see if we can't get you some help. Why don't you tell me a little bit about what brings you in?" He set his phone on the table in front of him and sat back in his chair, both hands now on the thermos in his lap.

"Oh, yeah, sure. I am, uh, Bethany, I guess I already said that, and you already know that anyway, but, hah, yeah, that's me. I am ... well ... I am ... umm. I'm not sure, really." She was massaging her left index finger with the finger and thumb of her right hand and looking everywhere in the room but at the doctor in front of her. "I just think there's something wrong with me, I guess. You know?"

"I can assure you, there's nothing *wrong* with you, though I understand how it can feel that way sometimes. It's alright, though, please, go on."

"Yeah yeah, no, yeah, of course. It definitely feels that way though sometimes, you know?" She laughed nervously. "Honestly it's not even a big deal, you know, I just ... Ugh. It sounds so stupid to talk about it. I just feel like maybe I'm depressed or something? Or maybe I'm bipolar, I don't know, you know what I mean?" Her wandering eyes had finally found Henry's and all at once she became still, firm. Her apologetic demeanor shifted to something more resolute. Henry saw the fear in her eyes become skepticism, then inquiry, and then they softened. Where before she had been wearing her posture like a shell or a shield, she now looked upward and loosened her shoulders and made like a cat, surveying a stranger for signs of danger before approaching. Unsure, but unafraid.

She continued, "I don't know what you'd call it, and I don't know what you do about it, but I know life isn't supposed to be this hard." She squinted and stared intently at Henry, who said nothing, but returned a patient look of intrigue and understanding. Apparently satisfied, Bethany looked down at the floor and took a pensive breath in through her nose with her mouth screwed up to the side. And again she spoke, again more self-assured than before.

"I feel like I am constantly at the whim of my mood, and I never know which version of myself I'm going to get. And I'm starting to realize that I will never be able to function this way and nothing I do seems to make a difference. I feel like I'm losing entire stretches of time in the blink of an eye. Whether I'm doing what I want to do or not, it's like it's always just ... over. And I'm looking back on it like '*Why* did I just do that?' And then before I know it I'm repeating the same thing again. Like my days are passing me by and I'm not even paying attention to what I'm doing at all. For example, I'll spend time with a friend, and then after we part I'll realize I spent the whole time on my phone or spacing out while they were talking to me, and then I'll feel like the worst person ever. And that shame keeps me from wanting to reach out to them again so I just get lonely and down on myself. But then I can't even count on myself to show up and be a better friend next time because, like, this is crazy, you know? I'll be so excited to make plans with someone and by the time we are supposed to meet up, I'm angry with myself for having made the plan in the first place and try to think of ways to cancel. And do I have anything better to do? No, I'm just going to order delivery and watch trash TV all night! And then if I *do* flake on the plans and stay in, I just end up feeling like a big piece of shit and I want to avoid my friends even more because now I feel bad about it. And it's weird, you know, because I miss my friends all the time. I see them on social media doing things without me and I feel left out. I wonder if they even care about me, if they all hate me or something. And then when they *do* call me, half the time I can't even bring myself to answer the phone. Like. What the hell is that?"

Henry wasn't sure whether or not this question was intended to be answered, so he lingered in the pause, feeling it was safer to move slowly, especially in his current state—maybe somewhat drunk, maybe only mildly lubricated, but either way, he was taking no risks. Once again the girl deflated; she sat back in the chair and she looked at the floor and said, "Haha, sorry, that was a lot."

"Is that all? Here I thought you were going to tell me you were harming small animals or something," Henry said, and then laughed at himself to dispel any possibility that she would mistake his levity for sincerity. Bethany looked up at him and scowled, dropping her mouth open in shock.

"Oh my god, I would never!" she said, starting to laugh with him. She leaned forward to pick up her bag, setting it down on the floor beside the chair and lifting her feet to rest where the bag had been.

"Well, that's great to hear, you're already better off than you think you are."

"I told you it's stupid. It feels one way and then when I try and explain it, it just sounds . . . I don't know, stupid. Like the words don't match the experience, even if I describe the experience exactly as it is."

"It always feels that way—don't worry so much about how it sounds. Whether it's stupid or not, it's your experience, and it's causing you grief, and I am only here to help. I assure you, there is probably nothing you could tell me that I haven't heard before. Whatever is in your head telling you it's stupid, let's put that voice to the side for now and see if we can't find out a little more about what's going on, shall we?"

"Okay, yeah. I can do that."

"Great. So, let's not worry about the details for just a minute. We'll get back to them. It can be so hard to translate our experiences, I know. Why don't we focus for a moment on the feelings themselves, would that be alright?"

Bethany let out a sigh and hung her tongue out of her mouth.

"Come on, now, it'll be fun."

"Will it, though?"

"You said something really interesting. 'I never know which version of myself I'm going to get.' I would like to hear more about this."

"Haha, yeah. Um. I just mean, like. Sometimes it feels like I don't have the gas in my tank to go anywhere. Like I should be going somewhere, but I just physically don't have the ability to get there. Sometimes I feel like I could *actually do* something, like I have the energy or whatever, and then I get so anxious and overwhelmed that I end up not going anywhere. Okay, it's like the stuff that I want and the stuff that I feel are not on the same page. It's like I'm moving in one direction and the whole force of the world is moving in the other, and we're never aligned. It's like I feel obstructed by something."

She sat still for a moment and looked at the ground, before her tight lips routed a heavy breath in and out of her nose. Finally, she continued. "I don't know if it's in my head or not, but I feel like I can't be bothered to do it sometimes. Any of it. This whole thing we're expected to do. Like I'm intrinsically resistant to doing it the way I'm told it's meant to be done. Or something. And I'm not a lazy person. I don't value laziness. But I feel like something inside of me is actively prohibiting me from functioning sometimes. And then I feel depressed about it. And then the depression adds a new layer of obstruction over the already existing layers of whatever other obstruction. Does this make sense?"

"Oh, yes, absolutely, it does."

"So? What is it?"

"Well, it could be a few things. We've really only just begun the process, and I wouldn't be willing to offer a diagnosis based on what I know, but there are definitely some immediate suspects. Could be so many different things I would hate to be so careless as to speak too soon."

"Can we, like. Fix it, though? With meds or something?"

"Probably."

"Probably?"

"With a high degree of probability, there is a medication or medications that would help to alleviate some of the symptoms you are experiencing and give you a better chance at living and enjoying your life the way *you* would intend to, rather than being at the *whim of your moods.*" Henry paused and took the last large drink from his thermos of whiskey-coffee before setting it down on the coffee table. "But it is important to note that whatever the case may be, while there are some instances where recovery and mental-health treatment are almost impossible without meds, there are never cases where mental health is *fixed* with *only* meds. You understand what I mean?"

"Yeah, like the drugs won't fix the problem?"

"That's right, yes, exactly."

"So, what else is there?"

"Oh, there are all sorts of options. There is psychotherapy or talk therapy; there are many methodologies we could explore. CBT, DBT, EMDR, life-skills coaching. There are clinical groups and a number of independent support groups that specialize in all sorts of issues, from addiction to grief to health concerns, and so on. There are also the often overlooked elements of diet, exercise, and lifestyle, which we can work to address, either together, or I can recommend people for all of these, really. You know, the body is a complex system, and we can never expect to treat just one part of the machine and see results everywhere, see? So, at some point we have to address the parts of ourselves that are in need of attention and nurturing, even if we are afraid of what we may find when we uncover them." Henry exchanged a long stare with Bethany, assessing her reception to all of this information before determining that she was prepared to move forward.

"So," he said with a charming grin, his placid eyes offering soothing invitation, "how does all that sound? Do you think you'd like to continue?"

Bethany's nose and mouth squished over to one side of her face as she pondered the ramifications of the commitment posed to her, her brows low and tight and her eyes focused intently on the doctor as though she were trying to look through him and into the quality of his intentions. One at a time the words seeped out; between clicks of her tongue against her teeth and several measured pauses she said, "I ... think ... that ... sounds ... great? Yeah. Great."

"Great. Then let's see if we can't narrow down the field of suspects a little bit and find the right place to start with your treatment. I'm going to ask you a series of questions, and I just want you to be as honest as you can in your answers and we'll take it from there."

The rest of the session proceeded as routinely as Henry could have expected. After ruling out a major personality disorder, Henry suspected Bethany was suffering from a more common emotional disturbance. Depression, anxiety, maybe even ADHD or a mood disorder, or some combination thereof. He suggested she try a low-risk antidepressant for a time, after which they would evaluate her progress and adjust as needed.

Everyone was different, and even then everyone was just the same. Sometimes the hard part was getting people to talk. Sometimes it was getting them to stop. Some came in desperation, unconcerned with cost or risk, starved for relief beyond the need for care. Some came with doubts, reaching down from ramparts of mistrust only long enough to express themselves in short and solemn bursts before retreating again behind their battlements. Even they, Henry knew, came for a reason. Some people just needed to perform their own little litmus tests on the doctor or the process before they could feel at ease. These people fancied themselves more expert than was warranted and often struggled to accept that they needed the help of someone better equipped to offer it. But he figured that most people were actually so unsure of themselves that even the idea of turning over their mental-health care to someone else put them in the position of making a critical life decision which they did not have the confidence to make.

This posed a problem that could manifest in a hundred different ways, depending on the person, but ultimately it all amounted to the same core need. From the defeated and sorrowful to the most hardened cynic, everyone who walked through his doors just needed to be heard, to feel understood, to be told there were solutions to their problems. They needed someone to tell them that everything would be okay.

Bethany Cohen was an easy case. He had been certain after five minutes with her that some friend of hers had been prescribed Zoloft or Prozac or some such drug and had sung to her the glories of the antidepressed renaissance they had undergone, and Bethany had only come to Henry in search of the same. She was unlikely to follow up with talk therapy, let alone be willing to address her nutrition or lifestyle.

It wasn't that he didn't have faith in Bethany the individual. It was his experience with the population at large. People almost never sat in the chair and said something like, "Hey, doc, look. Life is fucked, okay? If I have to live another year like this last one I might just fuckin' kill myself, ya understand? So look. I'm gonna need some of those happy pills you docs are always shillin' to people and I don't want to hear a fuckin' word about therapy or anything else. I just need a break. Can you help me out or not?"

It was never that.

It was always the song and dance. The sob story. The background. The context. The leading language and the buzzwords. Drop *anxiety* and *depression* and *I just can't focus* like a trail of breadcrumbs to lead the doctor to the diagnosis they were hoping for.

Occasionally, once they felt they had sufficiently laid the groundwork for a legitimate prescription, some would venture to name-drop a medication.

"Oh, my friend took something called … what was it … Ativan, maybe, and said it *really* helped them manage their stress."

Or they would become pharmacological hobbyists all of a sudden and say things like, "I've heard Wellbutrin doesn't have so many … you know … *side effects* … as other meds do?"

Henry understood why it was this way, but he still wished to dispense with the pretense, for everyone's sake, and to let those who wished to diagnose and treat themselves do as they please. So many of them wouldn't hear an alternative anyway. It seemed no one wanted to solve any real problems; they just wanted the pain to go away. The trouble to stop for a minute. They just wanted relief.

Such was the irony of his job. He had all the skills and resources necessary to affect positive change in the lives of everyone he talked to, and yet he was impotent in the face of the culture and the nature of people to resist any benefit that couldn't be realised in fifteen minutes or less with minimal sweat equity invested.

After some years, he had begun to believe that he was a doctor in name only. He had come to wonder what prestige the title even carried anymore. Once, doctors had been people who possessed knowledge that could seize life from the cold grip of death with only their hands and a few tools at their disposal. They were apothecaries who, with their grasp of chemistry and biology, could wage successful counterattacks against malevolent viruses. End plagues. Cure diseases. The promise of psychiatry had always been to move the miracle of medicine into the next frontier of whole body-and-mind treatment.

Henry reckoned that, for him, a doctor's license may just have meant the ability to sell drugs for his bosses in the shadowy boardrooms where titans of industry and government met. The diagnostic criteria for so many psychological and emotional disorders were so subjective, and the treatments were so experimental and dependent on the reactions of the individual—which themselves were wildly unpredictable—that he knew in his gut that it *didn't matter* if he only prescribed the patients whatever they asked for, barring obvious signs of fraud that might lead to legal liability. If the diagnosis eased their mind and the drugs helped them, then there was no conclusion to make other than that he had done his job well. And if in either case problems arose, they could be chalked up to trial-and-error nature of psychiatric treatment and he could move on to the next option. Again, this was the job.

Once, he had fantasized about being on the frontlines of ground-breaking medical practices that would forever alter the healthcare landscape and the collective mental health of the world. But enough time in any line of work will bleed one dry of such romantic notions.

He was twenty-two years old when he graduated with a bachelor's in clinical psychology. He and three roommates had been living in a three-bedroom apartment with a living room dissected by hanging drapes to annex a fourth sort-of-bedroom situation. Two of his roommates, Sam and Carl, had been colleagues in the psychology department. The third, David—the tenant of the living-room bedsheet annex—claimed to be an English major, though no one had seen any evidence of his matriculation, and while Henry, Sam, and Carl had been preparing for life post-graduation, David had been silent about his plans. He was not seen at the graduation ceremony. No one ever bothered to ask why.

The final year of college had felt like an endless loop of impassioned dialogues and debates between the three psych majors and David, the might-be English student. Henry was awaiting acceptance letters from medical schools while Carl and Sam argued almost daily about which psychological modalities offered the greatest benefit to society, and thus whose career path was more noble. The young men spoke as if they were holding court at the Agora, and countless circular conversations played out.

Carl believed that psychotherapy would become the gold standard of mental-health treatment. Sam argued that such treatment would exclude the bulk of the population due to cost alone. He contended that what segment of people could afford such treatment would be turned off by the sheer length of time and commitment necessary to yield any actual results. Sam was a believer in public service, crisis counseling, and behavior modification. He believed that catching people at their lowest was the most opportune time, when willingness met necessity, and that this was the most honorable path for someone who truly wanted to make a difference in the field.

Henry would listen to them argue, but knew in his heart that biological psychiatry was bringing about a revolution in western medicine that would change the entire landscape of mental-health care. From time to time, he would chime in: "You can spend a lifetime dredging up every tragic moment of a patient's childhood and still they will have learned nothing about how to live and enjoy their adult life. Soon we will be able to accomplish in a daily dose more than years of therapy could hope to achieve. We have pills for depression, for anxiety. Soon we'll have pills for anything you can think of. Pills to motivate, to placate, to invigorate. Pills to treat addiction, Sam, maybe even to cure it. The 21st century is the era of instant gratification. While you are pleading with junkies to *just say no*, or hand-holding somber adults through years of fruitless self-discovery, I will be in the business of providing people with immediate relief from life's greatest problem—the mind itself— and boys, business will be *good*."

Though some elements had not yet played out as he dreamed, he had not been entirely incorrect. Henry would see five more patients in person today. He would take two phone consultations and he would answer pharmacy requests for fourteen prescription refills. He would issue bills totaling $2850 for the day's work. Granted, with the monthly refills due, today was on the busier end of the spectrum, but the number was not staggering, nor did it merit much reaction at all from the doctor. The money would be transferred from online payment portals through some network of fiber-optic cables and satellite transmissions and into his checking account without so much as a thought from Henry. His bills were set to be paid automatically on their due dates, and fixed amounts were set to roll over monthly into his savings account and into a third cash account, from which his money manager would conduct market transactions on his behalf.

In the summer a year prior, Henry and Gretchen had audited their total assets and negotiated a divorce settlement which had cost Henry a fair amount of cash and a portion of their stock portfolio but allowed him to keep the house which now haunted him. Outside of those awful months, he had not given much attention or worry to money in many years. He had all but forgotten his time pursuing scholarships and financial aid, living on student loans and discount groceries, and the constant stomach pains brought on by his uncomfortably exiguous funds in the first years after earning his degree.

Now he drove a luxury electric vehicle, which maintained his preferred climate conditions even when it was not in use. He had a mail-order subscription to a clothing service that shipped him a wardrobe for every season for both professional and casual wear. Years prior he had purchased a small collection of designer watches, but had stopped after Gretchen teased him for investing such exorbitant amounts in lavish accessories when he struggled to grasp even the basic components of a fashionable outfit in the first place. In the time since their divorce, he had begun amassing Rolexes and Cartiers again without any reticence at the expense.

During the time they spent remodeling and decorating their home, they had returned time and again to a petty disagreement over budgeting. Gretchen was insistent that they buy secondhand wherever possible to minimize what she saw as wasteful spending. She often suggested that they try to do some of the labor themselves instead of contracting— even painting couldn't be that hard, she would say. Henry would hear no such thing, instead urging her at every turn to put aside her frugality and enjoy the fruits of their lot in life.

Henry would say, "Why should we, people who have the means, deprive other people of the jobs that allow them their lot in life as well? This is how it is all designed. You tell me what you want, I'll make sure it gets done, and everyone is happier for it."

So many petty disagreements that Henry was able to win with his logic and indisputable rationale. So many little arguments that Gretchen knew better than to fight. Such things, Henry would learn, were never about what was spoken, but always what was unsaid, or unclear, or in many cases simply unheard.

8

There is no light, it's all electric and dark.

Everything is soft. Intangible.

Overwhelming. Ecstatic.

Only darkness and nothing.

Naked and warm.

Blind and amazed.

Absent-minded and omnipresent.

Alone and unafraid.

From far off there is a sound. **NICK**.

That's my name.

I remember everything at once.

I remember ... a face. It's mine. And it hurts.

My face hurts and everything is so loud and so fucking bright.

"NICK. NICK, BRO, WAKE THE FUCK UP!"

Nick felt Connor's hand across his cheek and knew from the resonant sting on his skin and in his skull that it had not been the first time.

"NICK, FUCKING WAKE UP, GOD DAMMIT!"

Nick couldn't open his eyes. He noticed things in quick succession. First was the blinding light pouring through his closed lids and jarring his hearing and his equilibrium. Then the sweat pouring from his face and body, his shirt sticking to his skin. One cheek stung, hot and dull, through his jaw and into the orbital socket around his eye. His tongue hurt like he had been chewing on it. His other cheek was wet and resting heavy on the sticky surface of what must be the couch. His neck was stiff. As he came to understand the circumstances of his waking he felt the fleeting sorrow of something he had lost, something displaced by consciousness, and in his life he had never wanted something more.

"NICK—"

"Yeah yeah yeah yeah, stop it. Don't fucking hit me anymore, Jesus,"

Nick said without moving a single part of his body or face, the words sliding out vaguely through lips fixed in place.

"Don't hit you? You're lucky I don't beat the shit out of you." Connor was frantic, clearly not relieved by Nick's voice. "What the fuck was that? Get up, now. Drink some water."

"Gimme a smoke," Nick said, his face shining with sweat, yet his demeanour somehow tranquil, almost angelic.

"What?"

"Smoke me." Nick puckered his lips and made several sucking sounds that could have been mistaken for kisses but were almost certainly pantomimes of smoking a cigarette.

"Smoke yourself, man."

"No can do. Sleepy. You owe me at least the lighting of a smoke."

"Ex-fucking-scuse me? Owe you? You almost died on my fucking couch, Wagner."

Nick exhaled incredulously and sat up in one fluid motion like he had been spring-loaded at the hip. He opened his eyes for the first time, though heavily squinted, and through a scrunchy low brow he glared at Connor. His lips turned upward into a subtle grin and he lay his head against the back of the couch and closed his eyes again. "I wasn't dying. Stop being dramatic. You ruined the best high of my life by beating my face with your fat, grubby fuckin' palms and screaming at me. It sucked. You suck for that. More than you know. Now gimme a smoke, I can't move."

"Fuckin' Wagner, man. You scared the shit out of me." With a head that wouldn't stop shaking back and forth in disbelief, and without another word, Connor pulled a cigarette from the pack, put it in Nick's lips, and lit it for him.

Nick felt the blood moving in his body like hundreds of zippers being steadily pulled up and down his torso, arms, and legs. His breaths were deep and his skin was warm. Behind closed eyes and with a quiet mind he tried to capture what had been lost, but the sensations in his body were too tangible, loud, unignorable. He lamented what had been taken from him and he wondered at its significance.

The experience of losing all consciousness had stirred in him a great excitement and a thirst for more, but like everything else it had only ended in disappointment. He sat on Connor's couch, smoking and thinking of how many pills remained, how long they would last, and he wondered if he would ever feel so good again.

He thought for a moment about smoking them all at once.

The look he could see on his mother's face devastated him. He thought of smoking them all anyway.

He felt Alison's breath on his neck and he smelled her hair as she slept on him and he thought of what she might do.

It would probably be a load off of their minds. Lia's too, honestly.

Poor Connor would be in quite the pickle.

And it wouldn't be any of my concern.

"Don't fall asleep," Connor said, interrupting Nick's flagellations and jostling his ribs with one hand. "Do you want an Adderall or something?"

"Gross, no. Man. I hate that shit. It's hard enough to make it through the day, you think I'm trying to be up all night too? Sleep is the only break I get," Nick said.

"Whatever, man, just don't pass out again. You're gonna burn my couch."

"I won't, I won't, jeeeeez. When did you become such a little princess?"

"When did you become such a lightweight?"

"I've been back for two fuckin' days."

"Well, maybe you should take it slow then, huh, dumbfuck?"

"You sound like my mom." Nick's face was starting to animate as he spoke, the color returning to his cheeks.

"You get high with your mom?"

"Ha. Ha. You're an idiot."

Nick's phone buzzed on the table. He opened one eye and without moving his head he looked down and squinted to try to make out what was on his phone. He could not. He sat forward and hunched over the table, his every movement reminiscent of a man four times his age.

Text message from Lia. "Ugh." Nick lay back on the couch and returned his head to its resting place.

"Who's that?" Connor asked.

"Lia, again."

"Why don't you want to talk to her? I thought you guys were good?"

"We are, we're fine. We're good. Kind of. I just . . . Shit was weird before I got locked up and then she wrote me a couple letters and I only wrote back once, and then she wrote me this long-ass letter saying that she was sorry for everything and that if I didn't want to talk to her anymore to just tell her and all this shit, like basically giving me an ultimatum."

"What did you say?"

"I didn't say anything. I never wrote her back."

"Why not?"

"I didn't know what to say. It's just too much, you know? She's always so intense. It's like when she loves me she wants to talk about marriage and kids and our futures and our whole lives, and that's a whole thing on its own that's hard to deal with, you know what I mean? And then, like, when she's mad at me she says the most insane shit. Tells me I'm manipulating her, that I'm a liar and a gaslighter. That I use her and whatever, but then she still always wants to try and make it work. It's just too much sometimes. And I was in there and had my own shit to deal with and I just couldn't bring myself to write her a letter telling her I don't want to be with her. And then your ass told her I was out, so now she has the drop on me and I'm walking into this situation already in trouble so it's not gonna be any easier."

"Man, why are you always twisted up in so much drama, Wagner?"

"Shit gets more complicated when they aren't just using you for drugs. You'll learn that someday." Nick opened one eye again and pointed it at Connor, whose trickster smile returned.

"Man, I be using *them*—don't get it twisted, boy."

"Oh yeah, you're a real Iceberg Slim. Why are you talking like that?"

"Why are you such an asshole?"

"I don't know, buddy. Probably because I fucking hate myself."

"There he goes, Wagner Queen of Drama. So what are you gonna do, man?"

"About Lia?"

"No, right now. You can't just smoke cigarettes on my couch and be half-dead all day. And you owe me two hundred bucks."

"Damn, is this how you treat all the girls? Just get what you want and send me on my way?"

"Someone's coming over and I don't want to explain why I have a half-dead junkie on my couch."

"Harsh, but fair. Alright, alright. Give me a minute, I'll be on my way."

Nick took a deep breath in through his nose and exhaled. He opened his eyes and blinked several times while stretching all the muscles in his face this way and that. He sat upright and paused to assess his balance, then stood and did the same again. He walked to the slider and dropped his cigarette into the can with a splash and a sizzle that he heard in the base of his skull where his head met his neck, the sound reverberating like the sound of the pill burning as it slid down the foil.

"One for the road," he said, returning to the foil on the coffee table before leaving.

‡

Session transcript from patient files of Dr. Henry Foster
Patient: Wagner, Nicholas
10/17/22, continued

HF: What do you want to do, Nick?

NW: What do you mean, like in life?

HF: Yeah, like in life.

NW: I hate that question.

HF: Why?

NW: Everyone always asks it. But no one ever means, like, "What do you want to do in life?" like you would think based on the actual question. They mean, like, "What job do you want to have?" you know? "What do you want to do for work" is not the same thing as "What do you want to do with your life?" It's a bullshit question. Why would I base my entire life plan and my goals and my hopes and dreams around my fuckin' job? And it's so normal, people don't even think about it. Like everyone is just dreaming of careers and money and work. It's dumb.

HF: Well, careers can be fulfilling, and if nothing else they afford us the ability to live the lives we want to live.

NW: Yeah, exactly. It's like you have to pay to play. How is that the dream?

HF: I don't follow.

NW: Okay, they say money can't buy happiness, right? And then they literally design a system where you have to pay for your right to be happy. You have to earn your right to be happy. And now I'm not even dreaming of the life I want to live anymore. I'm supposed to be dreaming of the job I want to do to earn the life I want to live *when* I'm not busy working at my job. Now the dream is: Hopefully in my spare time I will have enough money to enjoy some of my life. *And* if I'm real lucky I can have a job that is tolerable enough that I can trick myself into believing I'm actually fulfilled by it. So now it's the job itself that is supposed to make me happy? Are you fucking kidding me? Like, are you fulfilled by this? Does this bring you joy?

. . .

NW: Does it?

HF: Sometimes.

NW: Sometimes. Great pitch.

HF: But the work *is* interesting. It's engaging. And when I am able to build rapport with people and am able to witness them make positive changes in their lives, then yes, it is quite fulfilling. And the life I have been able to build for myself because of this work is extraordinary. Plus, I would much rather be doing this than shoveling concrete or working some corporate job, and there are many people who do those jobs who would hate this work I do. And so, there seems to be something for everyone. It's the compromise of the system in which we live. There are costs and there are rewards. Again we return to this idea, don't we?

NW: Call it what you want. It's a scam, on all of us. It shouldn't cost anything to have what we need to survive and to be comfortable enough to enjoy life.

HF: And yet, it does.

NW: Yeah.

HF: Okay, let's indulge your idealism for a moment. Say money was no object—you could do anything in the world—then what would you do?

NW: You mean if money didn't exist or if I just had boatloads of it?

HF: Either way.

NW: No, not either way. They are completely different circumstances.

HF: What? How so?

NW: Well, think about it, doc, Jesus. If money didn't exist then the world would be completely unrecognizable from what we see today. The conditions of our days and our living arrangements and our communities and the way we interact with each other on a global level would be something totally different. It could be constant fuckin' war and bloodshed and tyrannical tribes enslaving populations to harvest resources, or it could be networking and mutual aid and some utopian existence where we all contribute and benefit and share with one another and barter across tribal borders and shit like that. I have no idea what I would do, it just depends on your view of human nature. Are we community-minded mammals looking for love or are we nasty, brutish, and selfish?

HF: Aha, okay, fair. Which do you think it is?

NW: Remains to be seen. Sometimes I feel like I'm both, depending on the day. How about you?

HF: I think I would agree. I think we each possess the potential to be either, and the circumstances of our lives determine which we become.

NW: Born into hostility and competition, become hostile and competitive. Exactly.

HF: I suppose so, yes. Alright, so then, that aside, what would you do if you had all the money you could dream of?

NW: I would probably do the same thing everyone else with money does.

HF: What's that?

NW: Spend it on bullshit and keep telling myself the next thing will make me happy.

HF: Well, now, there you go, you've contradicted yourself.

NW: How?

HF: You've twisted yourself up in these ideas of money and happiness. First it's the rejection that money can't buy happiness, and then you suggest that money is the means with which we are meant to buy our right to be happy, and now you've suggested that those with money are only living in a perpetual illusion of the pursuit of happiness. So it can't be bought, but it can't be obtained without money. This is a paradox.

NW: Haha. Yeah, exactly. That's exactly right.

HF: Nick, forget the money. Forget all of these other conditions. Forget the system, all of it. Let's go back to just the idea that money is not an object in *your* life, and there are no limiting factors. What would you do, if given the world to do as you wish? What would make Nick Wagner *happy*?

...

NW: Well, that's just it, man. That's just it. I'm just not sure it's going to work that way for me. There's no place where it stops. There's no place where it's just content. Where I feel like that's enough, you know? Never. I think if you gave me the whole world ... after a few minutes I'm just gonna want some more.

9

Nick sat in his truck in Connor's apartment-complex lot, parked in the shade with the sun visor pulled down and his mom's sunglasses on his face acting as the last line of defense against the terrible brightness which sought to sear his retinas and melt his eyes out from inside his head. His phone was in his hand and his thumbs were moving across the screen, making words out of letters, and his lungs made breath out of air, and his head made nothing from all the somethings in his day, but where he had expected peace of mind he found only the absence of mind, a severance that felt more uncanny than relieving.

Yet desires are never absent. Amid the vacancy he contended with the desire to avoid talking with Lia and the desire to avoid going home, and so he sat in the intrusive brightness and the emptiness of the moment and tried to see if he could feign a conversation of substance without saying anything substantial to a girl from whom he felt only distance.

Hey sorry, I slept in

Yeah I'm sure.

Where were you last night?

At home, why?

Bullshit. Why didn't you call me?

It's nice to talk to you, too. Jesus

Does it have to be like this?

It doesn't have to be
like anything

Okay ... ?

Should I leave you alone?

Do whatever you want Nick

I'm not gonna chase you

I'm not asking you to

Then what do you want?

I just wanted to talk

Now you want to talk?

That's what i said

Why

Because I'm out and we
haven't talked yet

Because you've been
ignoring me

I know. I'm sorry

Are you?

i said i'm fucking sorry.
what else do you want?

You don't seem sorry

How could I seem anything?
What does that even mean i
just texted you two fucking
words. I'm sorry What are you
a psychic now? Did you go
to psychic school? I'm sorry I
missed your graduation from
psychic school i bet it was
such a proud moment for you

You miss a lot of shit when you
just stop talking to a person

What do you want me to say?

I don't want you to say shit
You talk too much.
Just show me

Show you what.

That you miss me?
That you care?

100

That you're sorry for
ghosting me? Start there
and then we'll talk

                                    How?

Wyd now?

                             Waking up

At 2pm?
You're such a loser

                             Fuck you

Come over

                                   k.

Nick started the truck and made for Lia's apartment building, which was only a short drive from Connor's. He drove with the windows down and the wind blowing around him exposed the silence in the cab, making it feel more dead and more still and even more silent the faster he drove. He felt disconnected from the lively hum of the neighborhoods, the intrinsic sense of life in town, the people on the sidewalk, the cars on the road, the businesses in the full swing of the workday—all of it felt like it was behind glass, as observable as the world through the television screen, and he couldn't tell which side of the glass he was on because everything felt so unreal. He had to consider that maybe it was all just a program or a projection, or maybe it was someone else's dream.

He arrived at the apartment building earlier than he felt he should have, so he parked in the shade and waited for what seemed an appropriate amount of time. He had probably intended to smoke, but he didn't. He opened his phone and checked his social-media accounts, but his feed seemed to be transmitting from a place far away and in a language he barely remembered. Strange photos of familiar faces smiling on beaches. *Just how exactly did they get there, to an expensive beach like that?* A guy he had been in a fight with in junior high posing with his new motorcycle. *Checks out. How much ass-kissing and shit-shoveling does it cost to look like a rebel these days?* A video of a toddler and a cat engaged in what looked like some kind of sparring match. He wanted to hate it on the some principle about pacification, but he watched the whole thing and enjoyed it.

Enough was enough. He took a deep breath and tried to shake off his malaise. He looked in the mirror and made peace with what he saw, then made for her apartment.

As he turned into the courtyard of the complex, he could see that Lia was already standing outside, her skinny arms folded across her chest with her chin pointed down toward the phone in her hand. She was tall, nearly as tall as Nick, but she stood slouching into herself, her shoulders low and her spine and knees bending under the great weight of disinterest. As she lifted her face to meet him she revealed nothing, offered nothing. He thought he saw a snarl and a glimmer of malice in her cold green eyes, but if he had it had been so subtle and so brief that he wasn't sure he hadn't conjured it from his own fear of her.

She looked back down at her phone as he finished his approach and for that he was grateful; the walk across the lawn to her was already plenty tense without the added awkwardness of prolonged eye contact. He walked up to the porch where she stood and stopped, so unsure of what to say that he just put his hands in his pockets and looked down at the ground.

"You look like shit," Lia said, still looking at her phone, steadily scrolling with her thumb.

"Yeah, I know, I, uh . . . I slept all day and then just pretty much got out of bed and came here."

"You couldn't even wait a day to get high again?"

"Yeah, I mean, I just needed to clear my head. Shit's been fucked-up for a minute."

"But you could wait to talk to me." She broke character and looked up from her phone.

"Yeah, well, shit's been fucked-up with us too, you know."

"Yeah, I know."

"You look skinny. Are you eating?"

"Dude, that's literally so rude. What is wrong with you?"

"I'm sorry, I'm sorry—I just mean, like, you look good. You look great, really. I didn't mean like . . . You look great, just like you lost some weight. You know how you get, jeez."

"Don't talk to a woman like that. God, how long am I going to have to teach you how to be a decent fucking person?"

"I'm sorry, I'm sorry. Seriously, though, how are you? You okay? Connor says you've been coming by a lot."

"Oh, fuck Connor. God, that guy is such a little creep."

"Yeah, he's an idiot for sure."

"I'm fine."

"That's it?"

"I said I'm fine. What's *your* deal though? That's what I want to know."

"My deal—"

Nick was looking at the ground again, shuffling small pieces of gravel and concrete debris here and there with the toe of his shoe, contemplating every possible outcome of the situation at hand. He hadn't been lying when he told her she looked good; he had always thought she was beautiful—skinny or not, high or sober, healthy or haggard. She commanded his admiration with the force of her existence. She had an energy and an attitude unlike that of other girls he knew. Maybe it was that she didn't shy away from her anger, or that she didn't apologize for her feelings. She was opinionated and stubborn and aggressive, and though sometimes he feared her and sometimes he was exhausted by her, he never could manage to keep himself at a distance if she wanted him to be near.

"Speak, Nick. Quit acting like a little boy, it's not cute."

"Yeah, I don't know, I'm just thinking. Jesus."

"What is there to think about?"

He looked up and planted both feet on the ground. He didn't know what he was going to say, but he intended to say something that would satisfy her and progress things.

"Just . . . us. What we're doing. What we're going to do. What I'm going to do. I don't know what we're doing and I feel like you don't either. Except you act like you do, but you don't, and you just want me to be the one to do something, and I don't know what to do."

"You sound so dumb right now. What happened to you? You used to be so good with words."

"Yeah, well, there's no good words to use here. You drive me fucking crazy and I don't know what to do with you."

"Well, that's a start. At least I make you feel something. Come inside, you idiot. Take off your shoes."

"Yeah, yeah, I remember."

She went into the building and he kicked his sneakers off on the porch and followed her. Her apartment was immaculate, like it had been cleaned from top to bottom with great attention to detail. Her white carpets showed not a single speck of dirt or grime. In great contrast to where he had just come, the walls were adorned with framed artwork and photographs, and carefully arranged floating shelves housed books and incense holders and little porcelain animal figurines. Everything was in its right place and nothing was placed at random. A colorful tapestry of a tribal geometric pattern hung on a large wall and the furniture matched like the whole layout of the room had been planned in advance.

He had spent so many nights here that there had been times when it felt like it was partly *his* home, but today he felt like a guest in a foreign land. He moved silently, careful not to disturb anything or leave behind any impression of himself. Lia passed through the front room and down the hall to her bedroom and he followed.

"Looks nice in here," he said.

"Yeah, because you're not in here smoking all night and leaving your shit all over the place."

"Ahh, I knew something was different."

She sat down on the side of her bed and he sat across from her on a rope swing chair hanging from the ceiling.

"What are you, scared?"

104

"Can I smoke in here?"

"No, I don't do that anymore. Grow up." Lia paused, looking down at her toes, and took a deep breath before continuing. "Now, look. I'm sorry I came off like that, I just didn't know if you were fully ghosting me or what, so I got pissed off. I'm glad you're okay, and I'm glad you're here. I'm still pissed, but I'm willing to look past it if I like what you have to say."

She scrunched her nose up and this time did snarl at him, then softened her face into a smile and looked at him with either loving concern or condescension—he wasn't sure which one it was, but it didn't matter. Her smile was so welcoming and so intimate and, to him, so familiar among his feelings of alienation that it landed upon him and embraced him like a life preserver. He saw something in her eyes that reminded him of love. Maybe he had been denying it all along. Maybe his ridiculous and irrational crush on Alison had clouded his mind. Maybe their tumultuous history had tarnished his true feelings for Lia, and all they needed was a clean start. Maybe she was always going to be the one who saved him from himself. Maybe he was in love with her and still too scared to admit it.

He sank into the chair and felt relaxed for the first time since waking up. He was happy to be where he was, and he wasn't thinking of pills or floods or fires or the looks on people's faces when they heard the tragic news of his death. He thought he might be okay, if he could get her to let him stay.

"Well, I hope you will like what I have to say, then."

"Me too. So? Spill it. What happened to you, dude?"

"I don't know, Li, I don't know. Jail was really stressful and like . . . I just sort of broke down. It's embarrassing, you know? I hate talking about it because I feel like a little bitch, but it really took a toll on my head. I was just thinking about so much shit. Like how I got there, what I was going to do when I got out. You know they push twelve-step meetings and shit in there, and so when they let me go there were guys in there all talking about like being drug addicts and never being able to stop until shit gets so bad you just have no other choice, you know? And so I'm like twenty years old doing time already behind drug shit, and some days all I can think about is just getting out and getting high, and I was starting to worry that, like, maybe I'm a drug addict. And you're writing me letters talking about how you miss me and that you want to get together again and make it work, and I'm thinking I'm just gonna end up getting out and fucking it all up again. How am I gonna do that to you? Like, what's the point in trying to tell you everything will be better if I don't even know if I'm going to be able to pull it together myself, let alone for you or for us or whatever? It just started to feel like no matter what I do I'm going to fuck it up, and I couldn't lie to you and tell you everything would be okay. I was scared. I'm still scared. And you don't deserve that, any of it. You deserve so much better than me. I just don't want to bring you down with me. I don't want to fuck anything else up. And it was just easier to say nothing at all. I didn't want to tell you to fuck off or anything, because I don't want you to. But I couldn't tell you to stay either. So I said nothing, because I'm selfish. And stupid. And I'm a coward."

Lia sat, looking defeated. Her eyes were wide and slightly wet, and she shook her head somberly. She patted the bed beside her and said, "Come here, you idiot, why are you still so far away? Come here."

Nick didn't hesitate; he planted his feet and glided his body up and over the axis of his legs, turned around, and sat on the bed beside her. She pulled his head into her lap and hugged him and sort of cried but sort of laughed, and he surrendered completely to her consolation. They sat like that for a moment before he spoke again.

"So does that mean you liked it?"

"Liked what?"

"What I had to say?"

"No, I hated it. It was tragic and frustrating and I think you're the dumbest boy I've ever met. And you're lucky to have me, because you obviously can't take care of yourself. And you smell like sweat, and smoke. And neither one in a good way."

"That is literally so rude, you shouldn't talk to a woman like that," Nick said.

"Don't push it. Seriously, you stink. I've washed all the clothes you left here, why don't you go take a shower and change?" Then she added with a devilish grin, "I'll come with you."

Together they walked from bed to bathroom, in single file with her fingers in his hand. Mirrored, they removed their clothes and she turned to run the hot water while he stood silently and stared at her as she moved—the dimples from the discs of her spine on her back, the peaks of her hips and the soft valleys formed below. She stood up and pulled a hair tie from her wrist, and as she stretched her arms upward to tie back her hair, she made a shape with her body like a bow, extended and glorious, the arch of her body exposing her completely, and he saw no fear, no anger, no projection, no defense, no history, and no aggression—only a young woman, complete and raw before him, and he felt something like awe.

Hot water splashed and splattered and beaded and ran from body to body and into the drain. They bathed in water and steam; they shared their heat, their skin, their saliva. They traded touches and for a moment the two of them were pressed so close they moved like one, shedding skin cells in the friction between them. Lia had to insist that he wash his hair and his body, and he obliged with impatient mischief in his eyes. They resolved to move to the bedroom as Nick stole a glance at the cream-colored sundress blanketing the bathroom floor.

Long gone were Lia's days of wearing tall vinyl combat boots with black leggings, ripped jeans, chopped up tee shirts, long skirts, and tight dresses of satin and lace. Hair that had been a supernatural fiery red the day they met was now a deep brown that shone ochre in the afternoon sun.

They reached the bedroom and gave in to the eye contact, the subtle movements of hips, head, and hands. After all those years of give and take—all the life they had lived together and apart—they needed no rehearsal and no words, speaking a language of the body they both understood perfectly.

Five years prior, in the autumn of his sophomore year, Nick had overdosed on a cocktail of prescription pills he had cobbled together from his mom's medicine cabinet and a small bottle of liquor he shoplifted on the way to school. The major consequence of this incident was that he was sent to a juvenile drug treatment program for a few months that met daily in the afternoons at the hospital where his mom was a nurse. It was in this program that he met a girl named Ophelia—though later it would be only Lia.

After Lia's parents had found several bottles of prescription stimulants and sketchy diet pills in her room, they subjected her to an at-home urine test. She tested positive for every stimulant the test could verify, including cocaine and methamphetamine.

Lia and her parents found themselves at the intersection of her drug abuse and her self-destructive approach to her body dysmorphia, and her parents found it was more palatable, or perhaps more manageable, to send her to drug treatment and hope the rest would sort itself out.

She and Nick had gravitated toward one another the first day they met, and on the second day they left group early to share a joint in a remote corner of the vast hospital parking lot. They did not return to the group and no one in their lives mentioned it again.

Lia had been dating a twenty-eight-year-old unemployed but semi-successful weed dealer named Trevor, who provided her with cash, drugs, and more importantly a place to sleep that wasn't her parents' house. But she kissed Nick in the hospital parking lot that day after they got high together and Trevor never came calling for her when she stopped showing up at his house.

Lia was a senior in high school, seventeen at the time, and over the course of their relationship, she would often try to lord her advanced age over Nick to bully him into complying with her reasoning, though it rarely worked. Their first year together was the easiest. Nick's mother worked long and bizarre hours at the hospital, as she always had, leaving him free to spend his days and nights as he pleased and with little oversight.

Lia's parents were almost always home but were careful about where they would and would not direct their attention. The *woulds* being things like television, wine-tasting, vacations, and wandering about the house expressing to no one in particular sappy sympathies for the less fortunate. They assumed her drug episode had been an isolated incident, a stroke of bad luck, a youthful indiscretion resolved by her treatment, and was therefore of no further concern. They seemed to take everything Lia said at face value and rarely questioned her whereabouts or her goings-on, ensuring she had an abundance of privacy. This combination yielded two teenagers in love with each other and with no real accountability to anyone but themselves.

The two of them never separated. They would stay up late into the night together in her room with the door locked, smoking and drinking and taking whatever drugs they were able to obtain. They would sleep in late and missed school as frequently as they went. It was that year that Nick fell behind to such a degree that, had he not overcompensated in his senior year, he would not have graduated at all. Lia was already attending a more liberal high school with a relaxed curriculum and schedule, and so she was under even less pressure to be anywhere at any particular time.

Their first breakup came at the hands of a twenty-two-year-old skater named Darryl. In Nick and Lia's togetherness, each had plenty of opportunity to familiarize themselves with the friends and acquaintances of the other, both in the real world and on social media. When Nick noticed an increase in the frequency of an unfamiliar person, Darryl, engaging with Lia's social-media posts, he began to press her for explanation. As weeks went on, Darryl's engagement became more undeniable, his comments more personal, and Nick's jealousy more uncontrollable.

Though the actual sequence of events was always unclear to Nick, it was most likely a combination of the novelty of Darryl's attention and the intensity of Nick's desperation that worked to drive a rift between Nick and Lia that resulted, for a time, in her and Darryl dating. That was the reality until three months later, when Lia found Darryl was leaving nearly identical comments on the pages of other young girls in town and across the internet, and, in the pain of her betrayal and the lonely shame of her own fickleness, she showed up in Nick's driveway late one night and shouted up at him until he opened the window and beckoned her inside.

Nick was quick to forgive her and, having learned absolutely nothing from the situation, they bore ahead as though it had never happened. It was probably true that their relationship never recovered from that first breakup and, though they had moments that could compare with the best they had had before the Darryl incident, they would continue to find themselves repeating a cycle of enmeshment and distance; exuberant, rapturous highs and bitter, hostile lows.

Through all of this, they remained together more or less consistently, with some days marred by pettiness and spite and others colored with lust and a mutual, youthful yearning. They broke up and reunited sporadically over the course of two years, until his senior year, when Nick met Alison.

Suddenly and without warning or recourse, Alison invaded Nick's mind like a full-scale military siege under cover of darkness on Christmas Eve. Overnight, his every thought became of her; he couldn't shake loose his mind from her orbit and couldn't see beyond her horizon. He had been overtaken.

But Nick kept his predicament to himself. He became increasingly distant from Lia, and though they shared space and time and the sweat in their bedsheets, she could feel his attention was elsewhere. He was with her in the flesh, but he was so far away he didn't seem to hear anything she said to him. She confronted him several times and was met with non sequitur diversions and half-hearted attempts to dismiss and allay her concerns, which she tried to accept but knew in her heart were inadequate platitudes to assuage her doubts.

Nick had been out driving with Alison late one night when she shared with him that her relationship with her first love and longtime boyfriend, James, seemed to be deteriorating. The night ended with Nick and Alison crossing a boundary they had never broached; as they lay in the bed of Nick's truck under the sky and talked, they kissed each other so lightly it felt at the same time like their lips hadn't even touched and like two stars had collided in space and lit up the sky with the force of their impact. They fell asleep together for the first time that night, and though they didn't move any further or discuss the events of that night again, Nick could no longer afford the energy it took to feign a relationship with Lia. He texted her at 11:26 on a Sunday morning.

> Hey. We both know this isn't working out. I'm sorry, I hope you find someone who can actually make you happy.

Lia did not respond. They did not speak again until nearly a year later.

Through the rest of senior year and in the months after graduation, Nick and Alison began spending several nights a week together, talking late at night and occupying a space somewhere beyond the boundary of an appropriate friendship but not quite in the territory of an illicit affair. Needless to say, James would have been upset if he knew the scope of their intimacy, but neither Nick nor Alison felt as though any real boundaries had been crossed, save the one star-exploding non-kiss from that night a year prior. A moment diluted to nothingness by the countless moments before and since—insignificant, until it was not.

Nick was sitting outside Alison's house, smoking a cigarette and waiting for her to sneak out and meet him, when he got a DM on Instagram. It was from James Geddes, Alison's boyfriend.

> leave her alone u junky peace of shit. im not playing.

Before Nick could determine whether his heart rate had elevated from fear or in aggression, let alone ask himself if the two weren't actually one and the same, Alison was trotting across the street and letting herself into his truck.

"Let's gooo, buffalooo," she said and drummed her hands on the dash. Nick didn't drive. He didn't move. He sat with his phone in his hand and the message on the screen, silent but creating an unsettled and ominous air.

"What's wrong? What happened?" Alison looked at his face but he didn't look up. "Yooo, hello. Earth to Wagner. What's your deal?" She looked down at the phone in his hand and saw James's name illuminated and bold on the screen, and she reached across the cab and lifted Nick's phone from his hands.

"Oh my god, why is he like this?!" she said. "Nick, don't worry about him, he won't do any—"

"I'm not worried about him. I'll kill him if he comes near me."

"Okay, Mister Macho. Jeez, calm down."

"I'm not joking, Ali, I'll fuck him up. I want to fuck him up right now."

"You sound as dumb as he does. Why do guys always have to act like this?"

"Me?! I didn't do anything. Your illiterate ape of a boyfriend just threatened *me*."

"I *know he did*," she said in the put-on conciliatory voice one uses to talk to an infant. "And you'll *kill* him if he ever does it again. Jesus Christ, dude, you guys are babies. Just let it go. Can you drive, please? Let's get out of here."

"Fuck you, dude. Don't call me a baby," he snapped as he shifted the truck into gear and hit the accelerator sharply. The tires let out a short screech as he peeled away from the curb and began to speed down the neighborhood street.

"Ew. Back up. Don't talk to me like that. You sound like him."

The windows in the truck were fogging up and the air between them was charged, heavy with the threat of rising tensions.

"Don't compare me to that fucking dog of yours."

"What is your problem, dude? You're being so disrespectful right now. It's gross, Nick."

"Yeah, well, you should like it then. You let him disrespect you all the time and you still fuck him every day. Maybe it's time you switched up."

"Take me home."

Silence.

"What are you doing? Are you listening to me?" she said.

"You told me to drive, I'm driving," Nick said with an eerie calm, his voice measured and his syllables enunciated with precision. "I'm not the reason you're pissed off."

"Nick. Take. Me. Home."

But he only drove faster. He ran stop signs and his tires squealed as he hugged turns without braking. He had no intention of taking her home, but his angst had become an unbridled rage and he didn't know how to undo what had been done or how to get the animal back into the cage from which it had been released. An immediate remorse was already at work inside of him, but it was mixing with the hurt and the anger, and that produced a shame which bred reckless self-loathing and a complete disregard for the consequences of whatever was about to unfold.

"Nick, what the fuck are you doing? Take me home."

"Why?"

"Because you're acting insane and I don't deserve to be treated like this."

"Well, Alison, if I'm acting pissed off, it's because I am," he said.

"You're not acting pissed off. You're acting like a psycho and I don't want to be near you right now. Please take me home or stop the car and let me out."

He had no plan. He had no destination in mind. He had no idea how to reverse this chain of events, and everything in him that had been expanding and building pressure all at once deflated, and in defeat he pressed his foot on the brake, stopping the truck so fast that they both lurched forward and Alison had to brace herself on the dash. He turned the vehicle around and drove back toward her house in silence. His only redemption would be that he didn't leave her a mile from her house to walk home alone in the middle of the night. But it was a paltry consolation and he knew it. Still, he hoped it might be appreciated when the dust had settled and she could see beyond his viciousness again.

In the afterglow of a white-hot rage, he felt an impotent shame and the childlike urge to hide his face. He considered saying so many things.

You can't just run away whenever someone says something that you don't like. It's so childish that you're bailing. You should stay here to finish this.

or

I know I was an asshole back there and I didn't mean to say what I said but he just pissed me off so bad I couldn't think straight.

or

Every night since we kissed I've felt certain in my bones that you and I were meant for each other, and it's been building in me for so long because I don't ever know how to say that for fear that you don't feel the same and then I'll ruin our friendship and I'll never see you again.

or

I'm sorry. Please don't go, I fucked up and I'm sorry. I won't let that happen again.

But no words would make it beyond the genesis of thought, and so when he arrived at her house all he could do was grip the steering wheel tightly and stare out the windshield at nothing in particular while she climbed out of the truck and slammed the door.

Nick began to drive home, but there was a cacophonous swirl of thoughts and feelings that he couldn't decode, suppress, or satisfy, and from somewhere in that mess of untended desires and regrets rose a longing for comfort, for relief, and for love above all else. It was at that time, 12:42am on a Thursday night, that Nick sent his first text to Lia in nearly a year.

Li, I know I fucked up. Can
we talk? I can't stop thinking
about you and it's killing me.

Lia, who regularly eschewed sleep in favor of amphetamine pills and powdered cocaine, was awake and alone, and so she responded.

Yeah, asshole. you did
fuck up. come over.
no promises.

With some insincere words and a mutual need for comfortable distraction, that night the two of them resumed their labile romance once again—guaranteed to end but impossible to kill, the same as it had ever been.

‡

Session transcript from patient files of Dr. Henry Foster
Patient: Wagner, Nicholas
10/17/22, continued

HF: I'm going to ask you a question, and I think it would be beneficial for you to give it some consideration before moving to answer.

NW: You gonna ask me how I'm feeling again?

HF: Hah. No. I'm done with that for now—maybe next week. No, I think it's bigger than that. Maybe even more intriguing for you. I want to know what drives you.

NW: What drives me?

HF: Yeah. What is it? You have no goals for the future, and little hope, for that matter. You seem to have little faith in society, in yourself, in me, in anything, really. You say you don't value money, or a career, or even your own life. You've just suffered through a terrible ordeal ... and yet you persist. So, why? What drives you? What keeps you going? What is it that gets you out of bed in the morning?

NW: Jeez, when you put it like that . . . I don't know. I guess it's . . . I mean . . . Well. What's the alternative?

HF: There's always an alternative, Nick. You know that.

NW: Hold up. Aren't you supposed to be talking me *out* of killing myself? What is this, are you some fucked-up Kevorkian guy or something?

HF: Kevorkian got a bad rap.

NW: [laughter] Dude, are you joking?

HF: Yes, well, sort of. I mean, it's true, so no, but yes, I'm joking. No, Nick, I am not trying to push you to suicide. Just the opposite. Let's not ignore the elephant in the room, let's address him directly. Why do you keep going, given your particularly bleak outlook on life?

NW: My outlook isn't bleak.

HF: It's not?

NW: No. The world is bleak, and I'm not in any denial about that fact. And my life is especially bleak. Thank you for spelling it out in case I had forgotten, by the way. But my outlook is crystal clear and I already told you I'm not gonna fuckin' kill myself, so stop asking.

HF: That's great, but that's exactly it. Tell me *why*. What is it that drives you to face another day, knowing what you know, seeing what you've seen, believing what you believe? Why do it again every morning?

NW: I think you're mixing up ideas.

HF: How so?

NW: Well, the way you think about stuff is just all wrong, I think. It's always black and white. Like what you should do and what you shouldn't do. And things go well or they go bad. Things work out or they don't. Now you need to have a reason to live or you should probably just kill yourself. I don't see things that way at all. Nothing is ever as simple as yes or no. Good or bad. The way I see it, I only have this life. Mine. My life. The whole world

116

isn't my responsibility. The way everything turns out isn't up to me. I'm never gonna be in a position to, like, alter the course of history or change the trajectory of humankind or sit at the table and negotiate with the gods on the overall quality of our working conditions down here. It's not my fuckin' job, ya know? And I guess, like ... I'm gonna die. I have a one hundred percent chance of death. And probably sooner rather than later, if we're being honest. So what's the rush? There's plenty to do around here to keep things interesting.

HF: Huh. Okay, maybe you're right. Maybe I've been asking the wrong question all along. So then, what is it that interests you?

NW: Man ... Like ... I don't know. It's not, like, hobbies, or whatever. Or sports or shit like that. It's ... Okay. It's just ... It's the moments. You know? Like even in the worst of times there are still those moments where you just feel *okay*. Like. Have you ever been on just the exact right amount of drugs and then smoked a cigarette outside at night? Or slept with a girl you thought would never give you the time of day? Have you ever won a fist fight? Or, you know how there can be like a hundred different colors that the sky will turn at sunset depending on the weather or atmospheric conditions or whatever? And then one night the sunset just paints the whole sky this perfect blend of colors that speaks exactly to you on a personal level, and you feel like it was your turn, that this one was just for you to appreciate, and so you can't look away and you just stare at it in wonder? Or you find a song that feels like it could have been written by your own subconscious, if you were smart enough to have written it? And then you just listen to it on repeat over and over again until you actually start to cry? And then for however long, like the whole time that song is playing, you feel in your bones like you're not alone in this world. Or more than that, even, like you're actually connected to other people? Like you're sharing something special with someone you don't even know. It's those moments, those little perfect moments where you feel plugged into existence. Like you're undeniably alive, and . . . present. In tune with the world and everyone in it, and even though you'll never meet them and you'll never know their stories, that one fleeting feeling of tapping into a universal human experience makes you certain that through it all, we're all fighting and struggling together and we're all going down with this ship, together. We're all afraid. We're all alone and trying to reach out to one another, sometimes in the strangest ways, you know? And we're all in pain and we're all doing our best to capture these little victories, these little moments. And so you feel like you're a part of something for once. Those brief reprieves from this great experiment in suffering make the whole thing feel real. You know what I mean? Like. Look. Life is a fucking dumpster fire half the time and I don't see it getting any better. For all the hours and days that it feels like I'm just trying to keep my head above water and wondering if it's even worth it . . . When you catch one of those moments it's like . . . none of that is going to stop me from enjoying those moments. Nothing can. Because once I'm dead, it's curtains on everything. There's no coming back. There's no light on the other side of the eternal dark, you know? So I live my fuckin' life, because what else am I going to do? End it? Send it back? Fucking sit around and complain because nothing goes my way, or because people come and go, or because it fucking hurts sometimes? No fucking way. I'm going to live for every minute of peace and joy and every strange experience this world has to offer, and then when my time comes I'll go without a fight. But I'm in no hurry, alright?

HF: Huh.

10

I am a fraud. A charlatan. A sellout. I meant to disrupt the status quo, to push the envelope with my ambition and wit. Instead I surrendered to the tide of lethargy and apathy and now I sit on my ass and sell snake oil and shortcuts to the huddled masses of the tired and rich. I am a sheep in wolf's clothing and I fucking hate it.

Henry was home, lying on his couch with his shoes on, staring at the ceiling. He had not made it beyond the front room of his house before collapsing as though he had come home from traveling many miles by foot, instead of a six-hour work day spent mostly in an ergonomically tailored full-body lounge recliner.

Jesus fucking Christ you're a baby. Listen to yourself. You sound like an absolute tool. Do you understand me? Get your act together. This is embarrassing.

He contemplated the dilemma he was experiencing and how best to treat it. On the one hand, he could not deny that he was in turmoil. Some suffering was at work in him that caused the most mundane activities to feel like the apogee of hardship. Driving to and from work was proving potentially life-threatening. Piles of laundry in his closet represented behemoth nemeses ready for battles he was ill-prepared to fight. His dreams were laborious and his sleep was exhausting. Waking up to his own mind each morning was a recurring nightmare from which he could not escape.

On the other hand, the voice of reason in his head could not have been more accurate about his penchant for dwelling in obsessive self-pity. Countless trillions of galaxies had exploded into existence from nothingness or from infinity or from God itself, and through time and space and pressure a seed had borne life, had borne humanity, had borne him, and from the stone of life he had squeezed wealth and today, as yesterday, as tomorrow, the sun would rise and set and carry with it another day that he could seize or squander, and the choice was only his. And all of this could either make him feel triumphant or like that much more of a failure, and he could never predict which it would be each day.

So he lay flat on his back alone in his house with his memories of a time when his house hadn't been so lonely—on the couch that Gretchen had picked out from a store that he couldn't recall the name of because he hadn't been listening when she told him, and he waited for the voices in his head to come to some accord and direct him on where he should go from here.

He traded many rounds of deep breaths and disintegrations before the verdict came in that he would order Chinese delivery and watch television until bedtime, and he would grant himself another strong drink of scotch to finish the day as he had started it. Fine print in the agreement with himself ordered him to the whiskey first, and then, after standing in his kitchen drinking from the bottle with one hand and ordering his dinner on his phone with the other, he moved to the bedroom to clean up and change out of his work clothes and into his wallowing attire—the buttonless, zipperless sweatpants and soft shirt combination designed for long term lying down with minimal pinching and prodding.

He moved through the house without turning on lights, carrying the bottle of scotch in his hand and laughing at himself for what a mess he must look like. But self-awareness is a key component missing from the truly insane and he knew this to be true, so he was content to deem his late-afternoon drunken sweatpants affair as more an instance of transitory debauchery than a condition to be given too much consideration. *I'm fine, I just need a break. All people should be permitted reprieve without shame, after all.* Never mind that this instance of transitory debauchery was reminiscent of the week prior and the month, or months, prior to that. It was irrelevant in the moment, so he didn't feel the need to concern himself with so many dates and measurements, lengths of time, and bottles of liquor. There was nothing constructive to be learned in inventorying his drinking habit, and so he did his best not to do so.

It's been a rough stretch; I'm just doing what anyone would do. So what if I have a drink? I'm not some desperate drunken wretch. He stood in the bathroom and stared at himself absentmindedly, white marble framing his reflection in the mirror and the mirror itself, and both the marble and the mirror were flecked with dust but he paid no attention to any of it. Not the marble or the mirror or the dust gathering on the walls. The dour-faced man in the mirror stared back through Henry and paid him no more attention than Henry paid anything else, and everything in the room was silent. It is hard to say how long he had been standing there before he noticed the red-and-gold journal lying on the counter where he had left it this morning. He picked it up and went back to the living room to resume his position on the couch.

Henry could have considered any number of reasonable arguments against reading more of the journal. For instance, he and Gretchen were already divorced. The damage was done and could not be undone, and there would be nothing constructive to be learned from conducting a postmortem on their marriage in this manner. Or he could have reflected on his first foray into the journal that morning and considered the grief it had caused him and asked himself for what purpose he would subject himself to such unnecessary pain again. He could have considered the simple fact that it didn't belong to him and thus was none of his business, or the possibility that without context the words on the page could be misconstrued and blown out of proportion and so any significance he assigned to them would be misplaced. He could have considered any number of reasonable arguments, but he was not able to, because the moment he sat on the couch he opened the book and thumbed through the pages until he found a place to stop.

4/9
Anything you want, baby girl.

The world is in bloom and the honey bees gather nectar to bring home to their queens.

Sit tight, mama, and everything will be alright. I've got everything you need.

As promised, here I sit, plump and placated, and I should be
wanting for nothing
Yet I've starved and I starve and I'm starving for more.
I crave the sweetness from your tongue, but it finds me bitter
these days.
It's cold where I sit, alone in a closet the size of my childhood
bedroom
And I'm putting on all of your clothes to feel your warmth on
my skin, breathing deeply to remember your scent
but these musty old clothes are too cold to recall.
Anything I want?
I want it all, I said. I want everything and more. Give me your
blood and your breath and your beating heart.
I got hardwood and cold stone and brushed-steel appliances.
Give me your fear, your secrets, your shame and your scars
I'll trade you for every priceless antique I own.
I'll carry hope with you if you give me the chance, but honey,
we have to hold it together.
Honey, he said, I'll bring you the best.
Rob the bees and kill the queen. Take everything, baby, it's
yours.
It's not your fault I misunderstood. You said I could have it all.
But we speak in different tongues and we see with different
eyes.
Where I see the rolling hills, you see obstacles imposing on
your scenic view
Where I see the great blue and golden sky, you see the great
emptiness of space and the inadequacies of man
Where I see the moment, you see the time
Sand dwindling in the glass.
And where I see the bustling hive and the buzzing bees swirl-
ing about in wild blooms
You see the pollen, the stingers, and honey

Don't get me wrong, it's admirable, the way you dream.

The fights you've fought. This life you've bought.

But I wonder where your dreaming ends. To where do all your roads lead?

And how long will the journey be?

Dream big, little love, just don't sleep this all away.

It had been eighteen months since he had last seen Gretchen. The last time had been at his attorney's office, a twelfth-floor high-rise in the city. She was staring out the window watching two pigeons warble at each other from high above the concrete and congested city streets and sidewalks. The whole day she had looked so forlorn; the expression on her face hadn't changed once until she saw those pigeons. Not upon greeting him, not during the final reading of the divorce settlement, not when she signed the papers, or just before then, when Henry had tried one last time to plead with her to stay.

"Gretchen," he said after the agreement had been read aloud by his attorney but before either one of them had taken up the pen. "What if this is a mistake? What if you regret it?"

"Whether or not I regret it will depend only on what I do from here, but I am certain this isn't a mistake," she said, somber and resolute.

"But how? How can you be so sure?"

"Because it took us getting here for you to ask me this. When the ink is already on the paper and the damage has been quantified. When the battle is over and you can tally your dead as I walk away. Only when a man is looking his losses in the face can he come to understand the risks he's taken. That's the difference between you and me, Foss. You were always willing to take the risk, but never willing to accept the conse-quence. But here I sit, accepting the consequences of the risks I took."

"What fucking risks did you take?" he said, almost snarling.

"Mr. Foster, we have to advise—" his attorney began to interject.

"Oh, shut up. The deal is done, it's not getting any worse. You're not needed anymore, so you can leave if you have a problem, but if this is the last time I'm going to talk to my wife then I want some god damn answers."

"You should listen to your attorney, Foss. It's what you pay him for," Gretchen said, staring out the window down onto the city below. "But no one knows better than you, do they?"

"Fuck you, Gretchen."

"I think we're ready to sign, no?"

Henry didn't speak another word. He picked up the packet of papers off the table between him and Gretchen and he flipped one page at a time, initialing and signing wherever indicated.

From the moment she told him she would be filing for divorce, in the fall of 2020, she had asked of him only two things:

1. That they remain civil, regardless of how either of them felt. She said she didn't see the need to sully what memories they had, to spoil the chance to look back fondly on these years, or to make it any more difficult than it was already sure to be.
2. That she would be able to keep the car he had bought for her.

During the course of litigation, her lawyers had tried to persuade her to be more aggressive in her demands and to fight for half of all of their assets, as was her right, and to seek alimony until she found full-time employment and was able to support herself with her own income. Despite her attempt to take the spartan route and walk with nothing—whether it had been guided by pride or nobility—in the end, she accepted a settlement of thirty percent of the cash from their savings account and their mutual investment accounts, a handful of stocks, and the car.

Each time her attorneys returned Henry's offers with further negotiations, he would stomp and curse and decry her greed and her gross misrepresentations of herself. *Of course you want more. You always wanted more. It always starts with those doe eyes and empty gestures, all I need is love, all I need is you, all I need is to blow smoke up your ass and take you for everything you have and then turn around and spit on you while I tell you I need more.*

When she moved out of the house, Henry took up drinking as a daily anesthetic, and occasionally in the evening after he had drunk too much he would call her and leave her long voicemails. Sometimes pitiful, sobbing appeals to her heart, replete with acknowledgments and apologies, promises and lovesick entreaties for forgiveness. More often, they were nasty rants, attacks, and indictments of her character.

She never answered the phone and never returned his calls, but after several such calls, she sent him an email:

Henry,

I know how hard this must be for you. I assure you, it's not easy for me either. And yet it is a difficulty we must both endure. I wish we could be more amicable throughout this process, and I will keep that door open if you come to decide you want the same. Until then, I'm sorry, but I have to ask that you stop with these messages. They are causing me great pain, and I would hate to have to remember you this way. To remember us this way, really. I know I told you that all I wanted was the car, and I'm sorry—it turns out my naivete had gotten the best of me. I will try and explain, and hope that you understand.

My legal fees alone are exorbitant, and I underestimated the time it would take to get back to work and to find financial stability. For these reasons I have come to agree with my attorneys that I ask for some compensation in this process. Furthermore, I think I was being too hard on myself, and too concerned about how you would feel. In hindsight I realize that we saved this money together. We invested it together. We spent this time together, and you encouraged me to stay home from work and to work on my craft and to pursue other activities because you said it would be silly for me to work. This has left me in the unfortunate position of having nothing to call my own, and I can't be expected to start my life over again with nothing after all these years. I hope you will understand.

If it helps, I would like to remind you that you are leaving this situation with the majority of our money, our stocks, and sole ownership of the house we built together. I'm taking what I need, rather than what I deserve, because I have felt subjugated by and indebted to you for too long, and I will not carry those feelings with me any longer. It was my choice to leave, and so I will take only what is mine and you will have to live with what is yours.

It is not my intention to threaten you, and I hope you don't receive it that way, but these calls need to stop. From now on, please let all correspondence go through our lawyers, or I will have to take further legal action.

I care about how you feel, but no longer at the expense of how I feel.

If you cannot be respectful when speaking to me, please at least respect my wishes and do not contact me again.

I hope you find peace, Henry.

With love and a heavy heart,

Gretchen

Upon receiving the email, for a moment he felt a pang of guilt, an intuitive sense that he had been deluded by anger and his feelings of betrayal. He considered calling her and apologizing, promising that he would get himself under control. He considered composing a response in which he would take full responsibility for his actions, apologize, and promise to do better. He considered the possibility that if he executed the message with enough finesse he may be able to convince her to reverse her decision and try again to fix the marriage. He even considered the possibility that he had, in fact, been wrong about so much more than just his handling of the divorce—the possibility that he may have been inadvertently or unconsciously responsible for all the faults

126

in their relationship that she had attributed to his selfishness and his inconsiderate nature.

Such thoughts lasted only as long as it took to think them, however. After deliberations on apology and reconciliation came a wild anger, and he braced himself in defense against her unfounded and manipulative accusations. That she could blame him for the decade she spent unemployed and producing nothing; that she could attempt to extort him into surrender by positioning herself as the unwitting victim of his transgressions and thus sidestepping accountability for her own ruthless capriciousness; that she could expect him to sit quietly alone and bear the entire emotional *and* financial burden of her decision to abandon him—these offenses confirmed what he already believed: Gretchen was not only walking out on him, but she was actively trying to destroy him as she went.

Henry, who prized rationality and objectivity over any emotional influences, became righteously determined not to allow Gretchen to get inside his head. He would not allow himself to be emotionally blackmailed into accepting her betrayal as the result of his actions. Her sickness, her insecurities, her selfishness would be her crosses to bear in life, and he refused to assume them as his own.

Yet he loved her still. This confounding paradox of the human psyche, the complex and short-circuiting machine of mind, body, and spirit, would keep him awake night after night as he tried to reconcile what he knew to be true (their marriage was over, and no combination of words and actions would change that) with what he felt in his heart (the pain of her leaving was almost too great to bear at times, and he wished beyond reason that she would come home again) and what he had become convinced of through his many alcohol-and-grief-fueled deductions (Gretchen was attempting to destabilize his sense of reality to avoid addressing the guilt she felt at breaking her vows and thus must be met with only the hostility of the enemy).

In the forty or so days between the email and the final meeting in the lawyer's office, Henry found he was unable to remain consistent in his resolve. He would find himself turning sharply from longing to resentment, from a mighty and indignant fury to a pitiable whimpering sorrow. He would work and he would drink and he would sleep and he would wake and he would struggle to maintain any discipline over his moods, at which he usually fancied himself an expert. His existence would be reduced to routine and the constant attempt to cope with desires and regrets and a whole galaxy of emotions that he could not name or make sense of.

Even as he stood in the elevator on the way to the twelfth floor, he was unsure how he would greet her or treat her when they met. He couldn't tell if he would prefer to kiss her or spit in her face. He attempted to appeal to his wife one last time and was met with her sullen but unwavering confirmation. When he, in turn, shed the sympathies and revealed his temper, she again had been altogether unmoved. So when he heard from her mouth a soft laughter as he was signing away the last rights of their marriage, he felt what he could only describe as horror arise from his chest and grip his throat. He had been right, all along. With his last signature, she could declare victory over him and drop the act of the poor, pitiable wife. And she was laughing now.

He looked up from the papers, his face gray over clenched teeth and his hands shaking, and he saw that she was not even looking in his direction. Instead she had turned her chair toward the window and her bright eyes, wet with tears, were fixed on two pigeons on the sill outside the window, bouncing on top of each other and pecking and making cooing and clucking sounds as they squabbled. She was holding her hand over her mouth and softly chuckling with obvious effort to contain herself, though she could not.

"Do you remember the pigeons in New York?" she said, and then her gaze turned from the birds to meet Henry's wide, shock-frozen eyes. He said nothing.

"Come on, you have to remember. We were eating at that restaurant on the balcony in the Upper West Side, the one that your patient recommended, with the *awful* overpriced wine? And you told them, 'This wouldn't be fit for a box where we're from' and tried to send it back after we had drunk half the bottle?"

Henry was biting the inside of his lip as hard as he could to keep himself from opening his mouth; he feared somewhere in his head lay a great deluge and this was all he could do to contain it. He nodded, slowly, and his eyebrows lifted as the color returned to his face.

"Don't you remember those pigeons? They were bouncing all around the balcony and I was afraid they would attack us for our food and you said, 'No no, these are city pigeons. They know better than to do that. They are just here to scavenge.'" She began to laugh again, and Henry wanted to smile with her, but he didn't know what her point was. He was drawing blood from his lip to hold his face fixed in place.

"And then that one jumped onto the table as you were talking and stole your bread right off your plate and spilled your glass of wine in your lap?" She was laughing uncontrollably now, doubled over and covering her mouth with the whole palm of her hand. "I'm sorry, I'm sorry, oh my god, the look on your face. You had no idea what to do. You were so angry and it was so funny. I could see you trying to figure out if you should laugh or cry, and I didn't know what I should do either! I thought you were going to lose your mind. And when you decided to laugh, I laughed with you, and then the relief that we could just laugh together at the chaos of the whole thing ... I mean, it was really something. Do you remember that?"

Henry's jaw softened. His lip was bleeding into his gums but it couldn't be seen from the outside and he felt no pain but he was sure he wouldn't be able to hold back the tears welling in his eyes any longer. "Yeah. I remember," he said almost inaudibly, as though the words had been caught in his throat and only the sound of the air passing through his moving lips escaped.

They looked at each other for a moment, or a lifetime, and she said, "I'm so sorry, Henry. I wish it had been some other way. I do. Thank you for all the time we spent together." Then she stood up, looked down once more at the pigeons out the window and then back to Henry with a soft and clement smile, and said, "Take care of yourself, okay? Your people need you to hold it together so they can too."

He nodded slowly and she walked out of the room and his life for the last time.

11

Nick and Lia lay in her bed, wet with a mix of shower water and sweat. Lia stared at him and he stared at the ceiling.

"You sure I can't smoke in here?" he said.

"Can you just pretend to be romantic for five seconds?"

"Oh, yeah, haha, I'm sorry, Li. Yeah, I can wait."

But he couldn't. As quickly as they moved from shower to bed, a stifling remorse had crept over him. Her arm over his chest felt heavy and the stickiness of their sweat made him uncomfortable. The smell on her pillowcases pulled his thoughts to all the times before when he had lain in her bed and wished he were somewhere else. He felt the pressure of her eyes upon his face; he didn't know what they were asking of him, but he was certain he would not be able to appease them.

He thought about Alison and wondered where she was right then. He pictured her in bed with James, naked and damp with her leg around his and her arm over his chest, staring at his stupid fucking face, and Nick winced. He thought of the pills in the pocket of his jeans on the bathroom floor and wished he was home alone with them. He imagined himself in jail again, alone with four walls and a toilet, a sink, a bed, and a book. He pictured himself sitting on his cot, content in his austerity, free from social obligation and commitment and the tangled webs that the heart and the body weaved between people. Free from the need to smoke, to get high, to make any choices for himself. He wondered if he had actually enjoyed the freedom that came with confinement. Then he remembered himself crying in bed at night, wishing he were anywhere but there. Right now too he wished he was anywhere but where he was, and he was afraid that now he could never leave again. He thought of asking her if he could smoke once more, now that a moment had passed.

"I'm glad you came over, you know. You're a real idiot, but at least you're consistent," Lia said.

"Yeah, me too."

"So?"

"So what?"

"I don't know, Nick. Do you have anything to say?"

"About what?"

"God, I don't know, *anything*? You're just sitting there not saying anything after all of that. What's going on with you?"

"Nothing. Nothing's going on with me," he said and grinned. "You've cleared my mind entirely. I have no thoughts. My head is empty. My heart is full. I'm just immersing myself in the moment. You should try it."

"Oh god," she said and he felt her body relax next to him. "I thought you were, like, regretting coming here or something. Doing that thing you do where you're here and then you're gone. I was getting ready to strangle you."

"No strangling necessary. I'm right here, right now, with you."

"Good. Me too."

"Good . . . Now can I *please* smoke in here?"

"Oh my god, you're so annoying. Open the door and turn on the fan," she said.

He did as she asked and then went to the bathroom to put on his briefs and get his things from the pocket of his jeans. He checked his phone and saw a notification. A text message from Alison.

> omg I slept until like noon
> and missed class 😣
> what are you doing tonight?
> Pick me up again late night?

He looked over his shoulder to be sure he was alone and texted her back quickly.

132

What a loser. Yeah,

I'll see you at like 11

Then he disabled notifications.

He put on his jeans and tee shirt and went back into the bedroom, but instead of returning to the bed where Lia waited, he leaned against the doorway to the patio and smoked.

"I said you could smoke in bed," Lia said.

"Yeah, I know, but you've got this place so clean it feels wrong to mess it up."

Lia pulled a small orange device from her nightstand and put it to her mouth, breathed deeply, and blew a thick cloud of smoke-like vapor into the air.

"Christ, not you too," said Nick.

"What do you mean 'me too'?"

"Nothing, I mean, you know . . . just everyone is vaping now. Am I the only person who smokes cigarettes anymore?"

"Yeah, probably, and you shouldn't be either. They're gross and they're horrible for you."

"And those aren't?"

"Well, they're not gross. I actually don't know. They're probably not great for you, but they've got to be better than smoking." Lia shrugged and hit her vape again, the grapefruit and vanilla scent blending with the tobacco smell to fill the room with a sweet and noxious air.

"Whatever. It's not like any of us are long for this world anyway," Nick said.

"What's wrong with you, dude?"

"What do you mean?"

"I dunno. You're just acting shady. All of a sudden you're, like, sulking around and being distant and saying ominous shit like that. What's your issue? Are you okay?"

"Yeah, Li, I'm fine. It's like I said, the last couple months were just fucked-up, I'm still, like . . . not totally with it, and then I'm all hungover

133

still. I haven't done shit in months and then I took too much last night and I just haven't been able to shake it off all day."

"You were fine ten minutes ago when you were fucking me though, weren't you?" Lia was impatient now, trading her maternal concern for a frantic agitation.

"Li, calm down—" he started, but she wasn't finished.

"Don't tell me to calm down, Nick. What are you, stupid?"

"Dude, what the fuck? I just mean you're, like, freaking out and acting crazy. I didn't say shit. I'm just standing here."

"I'm not *acting crazy*, Nick. I'm acting like I'm sick of your shit. You can't just play helpless and talk in codes to try and get out of answering questions with me. I'm not stupid like that little blonde thing you were chasing around, okay? Don't forget, I know you."

"Lia. Stop."

"Then answer me."

Lia was sitting upright in the bed, a blanket across her lap but otherwise nude and somehow exhibiting uncompromising confidence despite the ostensible vulnerability of her position. Nick was still standing in the doorway, leaning against the frame, casually aloof and trying to remain so.

"Li, I don't even understand the question. I just said we're all gonna die and you flipped out on me." The sincerity in his delivery was no doubt maddening to the girl on the bed, who could sense his distance but not confirm its significance.

"It's not that. It's your whole vibe. You're off. Something is off, and if you can't tell me what it is then I just have to fill in the blanks myself, and I don't want to do that because it's never good when I do it. So can you just tell me what happened? Are you okay? Are we okay?"

He stared at the floor, perhaps for too long, but she waited for him to speak before pushing him any further. He took a deep breath as if he were preparing to speak, but then he held it in and exhaled only a noisy and wordless gust of air. And again he breathed in, but this time he spoke.

134

"Yeah. I mean, no. Or yes. Well. Yes, you're right. No I'm not okay. Yeah, we're fine. It's all good."

She waited expectantly, eyes wide and unblinking, with all her attention baited on the elaboration that was sure to come any moment. When it did not, she said, "Uh huh. Would you like to elaborate?"

Defeated and supplicating, ready to capitulate, he said, "What do you want me to say?"

"Do you want to be here?"

"Lia, come on—"

"Answer the fucking question, Nick. I don't have time for this shit anymore. Do you want to be here?"

Nick sucked his top lip between his teeth and stared at her. He saw the anguish she carried in her jaw and her brows, the wistful and tired light of her eyes crying not for love or for conflict but only for relief. Her body was trembling but strong. Her skin and the shape of her were like places where he had played as a boy; he knew every surface, every space, and every secret. His first love. His old friend.

"... Sometimes," he said, and though his every reflex tried to pull his eyes to the floor, he fixed them on her.

"Sometimes." She nodded several times, then spoke slowly. "Sometimes is ... something." Her spine released her body from the defensive stiffness it had been maintaining and she let her shoulders hang lower and dropped her chin while she puffed again on her vape. "You're a real asshole, Nick Wagner. But at least you're honest."

"So ... what do you wanna do?" He was sheepish, like a child awaiting the belt or the spoon.

"I don't know. I don't want to do this. This ... is not what I want to do."

"Yeah. Do you want me to leave?"

"Not really. I don't particularly want to cry alone after having sex in the middle of the afternoon either."

Nick walked across the room and sat on the bed next to her. He paused and watched her for a sign, and interpreting no welcome, he opened his arms and all at once she collapsed into him. They fell down into the mattress which received them like water and together they sank.

They lay in her bed, face to face and entwined, and Lia said, "Maybe I should stop asking so many questions all the time."

"That would make things a lot easier. You know I don't know the answers anyway."

"Then why, Nick, why? Why do you say anything at all?"

"I'm doing the best I can, Li. I hope you know that."

"Yeah. I know. I guess I'll have to decide if that's good enough for me."

12

Nick sat on the eave outside his bedroom window underneath stars that blinked and shone and sparkled in a crystal sky of black with edges that glowed silver and blue. Bats soared and fluttered in wild spirals while owls screeched and swooped to pluck small nocturnal rodents from the street to drag back to their nests and devour. A small team of dangerous hooded lurkers wandered the neighborhood looking for would-be targets for their devious crimes. Or maybe they didn't; Nick wouldn't have known either way. The whole neighborhood could have been on fire and he wouldn't have noticed. He sat hunched over, staring at his phone and smoking, oblivious to the world around him. His mother had come home and napped before returning to the hospital to work an overnight shift, and he was home alone again and as high as he could be while still managing to keep his eyes open.

He scrolled steadily with his thumb past photos and infographics, words he couldn't process and ideas he didn't care to invest in—an exercise in observing and ignoring, a perverse meditation of sorts. Beautiful girls in unnatural poses accentuating their offerings and soliciting engagement. Men complaining about something or another, always complaining or defending their positions against phantom attackers. Political strife, reports from the self-appointed pundits on the frontlines of the great culture wars, and a pervasive theme of loathing and self-loathing expressed through humor and lamentation as art.

He felt a dizziness behind his eyes—maybe it was the gears of his mind groaning as they struggled to process the diluvian stream of information coming at him in saturated color, maybe it was just exhaustion from the effort it took to keep his eyes open at all. *Is this just how we all live now? Are we desensitized to it already? The sickness that comes with having every bit of digitized information in the history of the universe beamed into our eyeballs from eight inches in front of our faces? Is the great discontent of the 21st century just data-induced stress melting our brains? What's* the cost of living this way? There's no way this can be good for us. He took a drag off his cigarette and wondered again if he was perhaps too high to process the content on his phone, and then he breathed a single stony chuckle through a wry and impish grin at the irony of his concerns.

None of us are long for this world, I guess. And he continued puffing on his cigarette and scrolling on his phone. It buzzed in his hand.

Hey idiot are we still on?

Yes Idiot we are still on

Excellent idiot, see you soon?

Yes idiot. 11pm

<3 (idiot)

It was 9:55pm and he knew he was in poor condition to drive, let alone be any sort of company to Alison. If he could make it through the next hour without smoking another pill or falling asleep, he figured he would regain at least a passing equilibrium. Out of an abundance of caution, and since he had not done so since he was with Lia, he decided it would be best to shower, change, and more or less reboot himself completely.

He put down his phone and blinked his eyes several times, and just before he looked out onto the neighborhood, the fires sputtered out, the owls and bats retreated, the mice took cover, and the hooded lurkers thought better of their misdeeds and returned to their homes empty-handed and in a hurry. The neighborhood was quiet, still, and lifeless. Soulless, he thought. *Then again, aren't we all.*

Before he went inside it occurred to him to be proactive and, he thought, even considerate. He opened his phone again and composed a short text message to Lia.

Hey you. I'm still feeling wrecked, gonna go to bed soon. Just wanted to say good night. I love you, you know.

138

He felt good about himself, for making the effort to show her she was loved, if nothing else. And as he crawled back in the window the "nothing else" rang in his ears and he wanted to climb under his covers and sleep until his body starved and the blood dried up in his veins. He swallowed hard and pushed the thoughts from his mind, certain there was a degree of revelation in them that he did not have the time to contend with. Alison was expecting him.

Rejuvenated after scrubbing the vice from his body and clearing the fog of fentanyl-pressed bootleg OxyContin from his brain, he pulled on a hooded sweatshirt and strode to his truck with a fresh sense of optimism for the night ahead.

He had driven the route from his house to Alison's in the middle of more nights than he could presume to count. The stops and turns were reflexive at this point, permitting him to watch the sidewalks and the buildings and the town at large pass him by, though nothing much of anything was ever going on at these hours. At night the suburbs posed for a still-life portrait that no one would care to paint or buy. But it was home, and at night it all belonged to him.

He crossed over the defunct railroad tracks where the town's homeless population had established a tent-and-tarp neighborhood of their own and all at once the character of the western district seeped out through peeling paint and cracked sidewalks, potholed roads, graffiti on street signs, and dilapidated fences. A patrol car was stopped outside of a liquor store but the cop was nowhere to be seen. Nick turned off the main road and into Alison's dimly lit neighborhood where the predictable cast of nightcrawlers stood frozen like deer and watched him pass with wide eyes as though they were expecting him, afraid of him, or both.

He pulled out his phone and texted Alison.

> Come outside, your neighbors
> are creeping me out

Leave them alone,
they're just tweakers

Just tweakers? Have
you met a tweaker

It's okay rich boy, don't be
afraid, they are more scared
of you than you are of them

Mhmm. Stop texting and
come outside. I'm here.

Liar.

He turned the last corner and saw Alison standing on the sidewalk, head cocked and eyebrows raised, tapping her fingers on her wrist and mouthing something condemnatory to him that couldn't discern. He pulled up and she opened the door and got in.

"Nickyyyyyyy," she said as she sprawled across the seat to hug him. "Let's fuckin' go, boy!"

"Why are you in such a good mood?" he said flatly as he pulled away.

She bounced back to the passenger seat and kicked her feet up on the dash and said, "And why shouldn't I be?" She put her feet back down on the floor and then rolled down the window, and in a long series of movements and rearrangements she tried to find a position she liked.

"God, look at you, you're practically vibrating. What is your deal, dude?"

"I am not. I'm just vibing, Nick. You should try it once in a while, you might like it. Can we put on some music?"

"Jesus, how much Adderall did you take?" He was laughing now, though concerned.

"Psh. What are you, my mom? Stoopppp judging me Wagnerrrr, you're no saint. And last time I checked, you were a fucking felon! And you do way more drugs than anyone, so just hush already. Where are we going? What do you want to do tonight?"

"I want to do whatever you're doing. I feel like I'm gonna pass out any minute and you're over here bouncing off the god damn walls, glowing in the fucking dark, making it hard to see the road and shit."

"Oh, all of a sudden?"

"Yeah. Now tell me what it is." Nick was looking at her more than he was at the road, confident he could have driven these streets blindfolded.

"You promise you're not gonna flip out?"

"Yeah. Probably."

"Nick. Promise."

"Fine, fine, I promise. Now what the fuck?"

"Okayyyy, you asked for it." She dug into the miniature canvas backpack she carried with her and pulled out a small plastic bag tied off at the corner and filled with white powder. She dangled the baggie between her finger and thumb in front of blue eyes pleading innocence.

"Ahhhhh, shit. I'm gonna fucking kill him when I see him, you know that?" Nick said, unsure of what his reaction was supposed to be. He wasn't joking about his anger, though it was really more fear than disappointment. The fear that she would lose control. The fear that she would find in the drugs all the cause for deceit and amorality that he and so many he knew had found. The fear that she might become someone else. That he might lose the girl he knew. The fear that it would be his fault for introducing her to people like Connor and the joys of the unsober life. However, if he had been asked about these fears, right then and there, he wouldn't have been able to articulate them; he may not have been even fully aware of them.

It did not help that from some other part of his brain came a great swell of anticipation and desire to do the drugs in her hand, and even some sort of excitement at being able to share them with her. Common interests bring people closer together, after all.

None of the thoughts he had were clear enough to make sense of and so he committed to the bit he had started and decided to sort the rest out later: the approach he had made a fundamental *modus operandi* for the totality of his life.

"You said you wouldn't flip out."

"I'm not gonna flip out. On you. But I'm gonna fuck him up, Ali. I told him not to give you anything but addies."

"Oh, I'm sorry, I actually *have* a dad already, and you might remember *he's a fucking asshole*. I'm not on the market for another one, so sorry! Now quit being a buzzkill, Wagner. Where we gonna go do this shit?"

Nick tried to weigh his options, to consider a single reason that he should not acquiesce to the girl in his passenger seat and the drugs in her hand, but he couldn't, so he tried to put on a face like he was mulling over a difficult proposition with great pain.

"Unless . . . you want me to do it with someone else?" she added, pouting, deftly striking him right where she knew he was weakest.

"You wouldn't dare."

She sat up straight and abandoned all pretense. "You're right. That would be gross. I'm just fucking with you, Nicky. But come on, I've never done it before and I already did a little bit by myself. It's fun, but it would be more fun with my bestie?"

"What's gross is calling me 'bestie.'"

"Sorry, would you prefer if I call you my boyfriend?"

"Well, actually—"

"Sorry, I already have one of those too . . . Incidentally, also an asshole."

"True story, bro. But I have an idea, *bestie*."

"Oooh, do tell."

Nick pulled a hard U-turn and Alison fell into the passenger door and then back across the cab and onto his shoulder. For the second and a half that she had been strewn across him, bracing herself on his leg and his ribs, the town around him was beautiful. The houses to his left were quaint and welcoming, not the usual line of vapid reproductions. The high school passing by on his right that he and Alison had both attended looked more like a relic of a halcyon time than the haunted progenitor of so much of his discontent. With the road before him and in his rearview mirror, the feeling of her hands on his body, and her self-effacing laughter in his ear, he knew he was home and that he would never leave this town as long as she was in it.

Alison righted herself and looked around. "Ew, remember that fuckin' place?" She waved her middle finger out the window. "Loser-ssssssss," she yelled. "Um, sir. Where the hell are you taking me?"

"I know a place," he said.

"Oooh, mysterious. Alright, Wagner, that's the spirit. Take us there." Alison recognized the route quickly. "Holy cow, are we going where I think we're going?"

"Yes ma'am," he said, making the final turn into his neighborhood.

"Mama Wagner is gone?"

"Yeah, she's working like five shifts in a row or something crazy. I don't know really, but she's gone for the night at least."

"Oh my god. I'm so excited, you know I've only been in your house like twice?"

"Yeah, well. Let's make it three times, shall we?"

He pulled his truck up to the curb in front of his house and they made for the door.

"God, your neighborhood is so much nicer than mine. It's crazy," Alison said, her head spinning around in circles and her eyes big enough to swallow the whole scene.

Nick opened the front door and directed her up the stairs to his room.

"Ahhh, I get to see your *bedroom*? What does it look like? Are there, like, spiderwebs and iron chains and old melting candles on those ... those gothy candle things everywhere?"

"Candelabras?"

"Yeah! Those."

He stopped in front of his bedroom door and turned to her, an incredulous look on his face. "Good lord, how high are you? Is that what you think of me? After all this time?"

"Honestly? No. There's probably, like, stuffed animals and pictures of horses or something on your walls. Do you sleep in a little racecar bed?"

"Jesus Christ, shut up and go inside, would you?" Nick pushed open his bedroom door and ushered her in. His bedroom was tidy, partly due to luck but mostly because he had only been home for two days. He had a vintage Germs tour poster on one of his otherwise bare walls. His bed was unmade; black sheets and a gray comforter had been tossed this way and that, piled and bunching and dangling off the edge. He had a particle-board dresser with a black faux-wood finish, a matching shelving unit full of books, and a desk in one corner with a laptop and a small office chair.

Alison looked around. "Ooh, it's nice in here. You need to do something with this décor, though. One poster? Nick, it's not even framed. How do you live in here? You need to feng shui this place, this is, like, your space, you know?"

"Uh huh. I don't know. I just sleep in here, pretty much. I don't even know how long I'm gonna be here."

"Why? Where are you going?"

"I don't know, I just . . . Somewhere that isn't my mom's house?"

"What's the rush? It's nice here. You should stay as long as she'll let you. Do you even have a job? What are you gonna do for money?"

"Money's not really a problem right now, actually. I'll be okay for a while."

"Why? What do you mean?"

"Jesus, you ask a lot of questions, you know that?" Nick sat down in his office chair and Alison sat on his bed, then quickly sprung back to her feet.

"Stop being grouchy. God, you are such a downer right now. I need you to match my energy, Wagner. We need to get you upper. Way upper." She pulled the baggie from her pocket and held it out in the palm of her hand.

He sighed and said, "Way upper." He took the bag from her hand. "God. James is gonna fucking kill me if he hears about this."

"Stop worrying about James so much. He's harmless, you're fine."

"That's what you say, at least."

The bag opened and powder spilled out in a small pile on his desk. He did as she asked and forced a healthy dose up his nose and down his throat, offered her the same, and then repeated the process. She demanded music and he obliged, and for the first time since waking up

144

that afternoon Nick felt like he could comfortably place himself in time and space while processing all of the lights and sounds around him.

All day he had been living as a monochrome character in a technicolor world, overwhelmed and out of place, squinting to see and struggling to pass for living at all. Now his wit quickened and he felt the blood flushing in his head and arms, warming him and galvanizing him back to life.

They took turns putting their faces to the desk and they choked on their laughter and they filled the whole room with words and words until their words were bursting out the window and spilling onto the eave through smoke and vape clouds, cascading from the roof in torrents and flooding the otherwise quiet street below.

An hour or three, or maybe only half of one, passed and they sat together on his windowsill and he watched her talking through waving hands and a gritted-teeth smile and her eyes fixed on his with unbroken intensity. He wanted to take in every word she said, to treasure it and to let her know what each one meant to him. He wanted to listen to her forever. He wanted her to know what he wanted but he didn't dare risk it, so he sat and he listened and he talked and he smoked and he held his fists clenched tight as if the fleeting moment could be salvaged and preserved for as long as he refused to let it go and the sweat in his palms was pruning his fingers and his nails were digging graves in his skin where he buried the desire to reach out and touch her cheek and kiss her face.

Once before, he had allowed his repressed infatuation with her to boil over and out of his stupid blathering mouth in the most vulgar of ways, and it hadn't exactly gone well. After the fight that night in 2020 which led him back to Lia, he and Alison hadn't spoken for over a year. He and Lia lived something like a steady relationship for that time, free of much of the chaos that defined their earlier years. Nick likely never would have reached out to Alison again; he would have been content in his self-pity and his regret and his shame—qualities which only fueled his self-loathing and permitted his self-destruction. Yet Alison had not been so keen to let it end that way, and so on a Wednesday night in

December at 9:42pm, after thirteen months of silence, he received a text from her while he was alone in his room.

> You know what's the
> real difference between
> you and James?

He tried to think of a response but the shock of her outreach had stunned him, and before he could calibrate himself she had already followed up.

> When he treats me like
> shit, he always ends up
> begging me to forgive him.

Still he could muster nothing.

> Not you though. You just
> disappear, don't you?

Finally, uncertain of how to proceed but certain that he must, he responded.

> > I knew that guy had
> > something I didn't.
> > It's the begging.

> Still salty as ever.
> Tell me why that's
> refreshing to me?

> > Because you're unwell,
> > Alison. Did you forget?

> You really are something,
> you know that?

                                        Tell me about it.

Are you gonna
apologize or what?

                                        Does that usually come before
                                        or after the begging?

Actually ... Now that
you mention it, he does
a lot of begging, but not
much apologizing.
It's usually just like
Please don't leave please I'll be
a good boy and then 10 minutes
later he's telling me how it was
my fault in the first place and
how I can avoid creating such
a problem for him in the future.

                                        That sounds like a lot of work.
                                        Can I just say I'm sorry instead?

I'm waiting.

                                        Ali, I'm sorry.

Not good enough.

                                        I'm really sorry?

I need to see your face to know
you mean it. Wyd tonight?

                                        Oh I'm sorry – I'm actually
                                        slammed tonight. I mean ...
                                        I could kick these girls out
                                        and tell everyone else who
                                        is waiting on me that they'll
                                        have to reschedule ...

Oh my god shut up.
You're alone in your room
smoking and thinking about

how cruel and unfair the
world is and how you're the
smartest person who has
ever lived, am I right?

        Sorry, I can't hear you over
        all the girls vying for my
        attention right now.

Shut up and come get me.
You're not off the hook yet.

        I'll see what I can do.

He cleaned himself up and got dressed with a shameless haste, his head spinning amid thoughts of *Why* and *For what* and *What does it all mean* and *What the fuck*. He intended to develop a plan, a speech, or some clever spin to excuse his behavior from their last meeting, but before he had fleshed out anything worth saying he was pulling up to her house and she was getting in his truck. Before she could speak he began, but before he could finish she interrupted.

"Stop. It's fine," she said.

"What?"

"It's fine. Look. Let's just go somewhere nice. Like High Creek or Sleepover Beach or somewhere like that. Somewhere far away, I want to drive for a while." She buckled her seatbelt and looked out the window, then added, "Nick . . . Thanks for coming."

Nick drove west, heading for the coast. The night was overcast but the full moon imbued the cloud cover with its silver-white light and the whole sky glowed bright as a grey winter sunrise and the December-midnight cold rapped at the windows and the doors of the truck. They drove for some time with only the sounds of music playing low beneath the wind and the truck heater blowing.

"You got a smoke, Nicky?"

"Nope, I quit," he said.

"Seriously?!"

"Fuck no. Here," he said and she rolled her eyes as he gave her one and he took one for himself. They cracked the windows and braved the cold together in the name of commitment to the desire.

"So," he said with some trepidation, "who's gonna go first?"

"I will . . . But Nick, I just need you to shut up for once. Can you do that? I know it's really hard for you to just shut up and listen, but I need you to. Okay?"

It stung, but he didn't feel that he was in any position to complain. "Yeah. Sure. Zipped tight. What's up?"

"You really hurt my feelings, you know—"

"I know I did, I know and it—"

"Jesus, you couldn't make it ten seconds, could you?"

"Fuck."

"Yeah, fuck. Now can I talk?"

Nick pantomimed turning a key to lock his lips shut.

"Incorrigible, Wagner. I swear." She looked out the window and thought for a moment before speaking again.

"So look, this stuff isn't easy to say. Just try and keep that in mind if you can and like . . . listen. You hurt my feelings. And you were an asshole, and you do owe me an apology. But I've thought about it a lot, like *why* it hurt so bad, and I think I figured it out and it isn't totally your fault."

"Ali, it is—" he tried to say, but she shot him a wordless stare that was as cold as the wind whipping through the cracked windows, so he stopped.

"It's not. I haven't exactly been fair to you. And I was trying to live out some fantasy in my head that was just never going to be realistic and I dragged you along for so long, just hoping that maybe something would change. And it's not going to, I don't think. And I'm not sure what to do now. Nick, you're the best friend I've ever had. I mean that. Like, ever.

"Even when I was younger, all the girls I got close to were always so . . . two-faced and nasty. Even me. It's just how we were. Like I felt like I had to be in competition with my best friends all the time to earn the right to stay there. You know? Girls can be so fucking . . . just brutal, really. And I probably wasn't any better, now that I've thought about it some. We just didn't know how to support each other, how to build each other up. I think we were too busy fighting to make ourselves feel valid and worthy and loveable and we all got caught up in each other's insecurities and became scapegoats and liabilities for each other. Like you know how they say, like, you don't have to be faster than the bear, you just have to be faster than the slowest person running from the bear? I think being a girl was like that for a lot of us. It was hard, and it was ugly. And I haven't recovered from growing up like that. I don't even talk to the girls I was friends with in middle school or high school anymore. Everyone fucked each other's boyfriends or got caught talking shit behind someone else's back or was stuck in the middle of drama that wasn't theirs and we all just stopped talking to each other, I guess.

"And we didn't have anyone to blame but ourselves, or each other. Like we could try and be mad at the boys, but it never really got us any-where. They wouldn't hear us when we talked, they would just dismiss us or move on to someone less needy, less dramatic. We were expend-able. We were expendable to them, to each other, and, like, honestly it felt like we were walking a tightrope to stay relevant in the world at all. If you weren't gorgeous and skinny you had to be a genius or really good at music or sports or *anything* to fall back on. And if you were gorgeous and skinny, well, congratulations, that's your currency now and you'll never have enough of it. Nothing else you do will even matter, no one will notice, no one will give you credit. And if you couldn't be any of those things, you'd better be fucking funny, because you'll need a sense of humor to survive as an undesirable girl.

"This shit soaked into us, you know? And like . . . I wish I had been nicer to some of those girls, more understanding. I wish they had done the same. I wonder what it would have been like if we supported each other—if we talked about this kind of shit instead of just playing the game and buying into the competition. God, the amount of time we spent lying around talking about who wants to fuck who and who is prettier and what to say and what not to say and how to swallow who we are as people and present something else completely to get guys to like us and how to be better in bed so they would want to fuck us again. It makes me sick. Like, I feel guilty for buying into it all. Which is even more fucked-up if you think about it, that I should feel guilt or shame for doing exactly what was expected of me. But I do. I feel like I betrayed myself, betrayed my friends. Like I sold out and caved in instead of standing up for myself. And that part pisses me off most of all.

"And so then when I met you . . . things just changed. All of a sudden there was this person I could talk to who wasn't like . . . one of the boys, but wasn't one of the girls either. You were this outsider. Just like this lonely little mystery boy who everyone said was dangerous or crazy or whatever, but like, you're just different. And it made me realize that I think I'm different too. Or maybe that none of us are different, that we're really all the same . . . insecure, mistrustful, afraid of each other, but you didn't make the effort everyone else made to cover it up. You didn't try and pretend like you weren't scared. Or that you gave a shit about things that you didn't give a shit about. Like, you barely even came to school half the time and you were always high and didn't even try to hide it. Like you were the first person who was, like, as fucked-up as I feel, but not trying to pretend you weren't. Even those other people you hung out with were so, like . . . in your face about it. It just felt fake sometimes, like they were still trying to be something. But you just were straight-up about who you were, even if no one liked it.

"And you never tried to hide that you had a crush on me, but you always accepted the fact that I have a boyfriend and respected it and showed up like a friend anyway. You showed up like a friend for so long, even if it meant you weren't going to get your way. And in some weird way I've never felt more, like, loved, or appreciated just for who I am, because of you.

"I know it hurt you too. I've always known. But I'm selfish, and I needed you. I needed you then, I needed you this past year, and I need you now. I need someone who sees me and who loves me and who isn't just trying to own me or control me or fuck me. And I've been really good at just ignoring how that must make you feel. I just do my best to love you back, in my own way. And it's been weird. It's been hard. Because I do love you too, you know. Do you know that?"

Nick said nothing.

"I do. And it's confusing. Sometimes I don't know what I want from you either. Like ... do you know that James has cheated on me with two different girls, like ... multiple times? Why would you? You wouldn't know that, because even though I tell you *everything*, I don't tell you that. Because I don't want you to know. I don't want you to judge me for taking him back. I don't want to hear what you think about it, because I know you'd tell me to leave, and you'd be right. But I just ... don't. We've been together since eighth grade. And like, he's a boy. You know? Boys do stupid shit. But he knows he fucked up, always. It doesn't like ... *mean* anything. He just thinks with his dick and some-day he'll grow out of it, and I know he loves me, he's just an idiot and he's immature. Oh my god, it sounds so fucking stupid ... This is why I don't talk about it.

"Anyway. So last year, you said that shit about always going back and fucking him when he treats me like shit and that I should just fuck you instead, and it just destroyed me in every possible way. Like imagine this. All at once, with, like, one sentence, you shattered all of my illusions. Because I *do* go back to him and he *is* an asshole. And I should leave him and move on. And then you did the same thing every other guy does: You just reduced how I love to who I fuck. And it hurt, because you're supposed to be the one person who sees more than that in me. And so I was pissed, but then I thought about it more and like ... I'd been fuck-ing with you just the same. Like, I knew you loved me and that you'd drop anything for me and that you'd be there, like you're here right now on zero notice after not talking to me for a whole year. And I've always taken that for granted. And I do love you. I want to love you like that."
She stopped abruptly.

Nick thought she might have been crying, but he was committed to giving her the space she'd demanded at the outset and so he continued to drive, his eyes forward, tracking the headlights which were lost in the fog that was converging on the coastal road, and despite all that he wanted to say or to scream at her, he kept his mouth closed.

"But how can I? Nick, like . . . I'm not a kid anymore. Maybe it could've worked when we were younger, before everything mattered so much. When nothing mattered at all except the way it all felt. When we were just filled up and bursting with all the possibilities, and everything was forever and always and infinite, like living in one wild dream without end . . . But it did end. It does end. And all that possibility actually becomes just some *thing*, they all do. It became what it is. You became how you are and I became this and we became us, instead of that other *us*. And it can't work now. I've thought about it, believe me, I've thought about it. But we're just going different places. Like. I'm trying to get out of my parents' house. I need to get out of that neighborhood, out of this town. D'you know that neighborhood used to be nice when I was a kid? Or at least it was better. I don't know what happened. It was like one day there were suddenly drugs everywhere. All of a sudden you looked around and the families were gone to nicer places and the police started coming around more and more. It's like the price of being alive just went up one day and everyone who couldn't keep up got put there and got forgotten about. Then the homeless camps went up on the tracks, and now it's like a completely different place than I remember it. Maybe it was always that way and I'm just old enough to see it now, but either way . . . I can't stand it there. I mean, that's not your problem, sorry, I'm just saying I'm going to do whatever I have to do to get out of there.

"And James isn't really going to be the one. I know that. But I know he'll come with me. He is more lost without me than I am without him. But you . . . I don't know where you're going. You used to talk about stuff at least. Like getting out, like what you wanted to do. Music and writing or going to school and teaching high school and trying to make it suck less for the next generation, remember? But you don't do any of that anymore. You graduated a year and a half ago, Nick. And you don't even have a job. Where do you see this going? Not even just with us, but like ... for yourself? What's your fuckin' plan, man? Because you're not a kid anymore either and you're just getting high and I know you and Connor are selling drugs—"

"I don't sell drugs. That's not true."

"Well. I don't know. Whatever you're doing. I know you're making money somehow. And I think about leaving with you. I think about how we could go to a different city, down to San Diego, get away from the cold and take out student loans or something, get jobs serving tables and go to community college and just do our own thing ... But every time I really think about it, I picture you calling me from prison or something. Dying. Or wandering the sidewalks like the people on the west side do. And like ... James might not be the one, but I know I'll never have to see him like that.

"So what, you know? What am I supposed to do? What are we supposed to do? There's no way forward for me that works out with either of you. And I don't want to do it alone. That's just my truth. Maybe it's selfish. Maybe it's shortsighted. But it's true. I'm not ready to do it alone. And you're my best friend in the world, but you're just not a safe bet. I can't watch you die. And when you said that shit to me last year all of this came up for me, and I ignored it for as long as I could but I can't pretend it's not real anymore."

Nick had pulled into a gravel turnout overlooking a small public beach, though they couldn't see anything around them. The fog had swallowed them whole. Through the cracked windows of the truck they could hear the thunderous ocean like a great beast from hell crying out deep tortured hisses and wails with each breaking swell.

"Do you mind if we just stay in the truck? It feels cozier in here," Alison said.

"Yeah. We'd probably fall off a cliff if we tried to walk around outside right now. It's freezing out there anyway."

Nick wanted to say so many things. He wanted to defend himself.

He wanted to deny what she had said. He wanted to apologize. He wanted to take back his words. To undo what had been done. To promise things that weren't his to promise; promises he couldn't keep. But he said nothing.

He felt claustrophobic in the fog, in the truck, backed into a corner at the edge of the world with the raging sea below. He felt like the only thing left to say was goodbye. *But then why did she bring me all the way out here?* For a moment he thought he should hate her. But he knew he would stay here, isolated in the fog and protected by the night, in this secret place where they had always thrived. Where they were sheltered from reality, insulated from the obstacles that made their relationship so impractical in the light of day and in the presence of other people.

Here, he would stay all night if she wanted. Here, he would black out the windows of the truck, create a permanent shelter. He would learn to hunt and fish and treat disease. Here, he would draw borders and defend the land against encroaching tribes and he would fight to his last breath to protect the space where she felt safe. Here, he would die. He would stay here forever before he said goodbye.

"What do you want me to do, Ali? I don't even know what to say," he said.

"I don't know, but I'm cold. Can I come over there?"

He lifted his arms and she leaned across the cab, lying in his lap and bundling herself in her sweater. He reached into the backseat, got the comforter he kept for nights like this, and lay it on top of her with the care of a mother tucking in her child.

"I just want you to tell me if I'm wrong, I think," she said after settling into her new position.

"You are."

"How can you be sure?"

"Because I am. Because I know."

"How do you know?"

"Can I talk now?"

"Yes. Thank you."

"I know, because it's the only thing that makes sense. You and me. I know, because all I've ever done is look for a reason. Just a reason to stay, to fight, to remain interested. You know? Just . . . Nothing in this life so far has really offered any convincing justification for the cost. Like. The cost of everything is always *so high*, and for what? Really, for what? All the time to chase a career, and then all the time spent working. For rationed-out vacations and some free time on weekends and evenings? We are extorted by this idea of freedom into believing that it means the freedom to work to own whatever we want. Like, hey, if you want it bad enough, you are *free* to sacrifice your life to get a speedboat or a motorcycle or buy a house, except we will never pay you enough to actually *buy* the house, we'll just pay you enough to convince a bank to let you borrow the money, and now your freedom has just cost you your freedom because you're shackled to this mortgage payment forever.

"And I know there has to be more to life than this, but I can't figure out how to get around this one part and see what else there is. You know? It's like there's no alternative except to suffer long and die poor. Or, like, convince yourself that a life of scraping by in wage slavery is actually by choice and that happiness is independent of financial security and, okay, cool. Maybe it is. I don't know, I'm not that advanced. But the point is, no matter how you look at it, the price of this life is unreasonably high.

"And don't get me wrong, you are going to do great. I know you are. You'll get all of that stuff. You'll graduate college and you'll make money and you'll probably raise a family, and you'll be able to enjoy it all, because you aren't as ungrateful and petulant as me. You'll be grateful for the life you have and I'll be somewhere just trying my best to enjoy myself."

"That's bullshit, you know. You aren't that special, Nick. And besides, what the fuck are you even talking about?"

"I'm talking about us. Kind of. Look. I'm saying that I've never been able to find any good reason to spend my time kowtowing to the status quo. I've always figured I'd just rather enjoy myself and figure it out day

156

by day and then eventually I'll die but at least I would have had a good time. Kind of. Kind of a good time. I don't know though, I mean. At least I did whatever I wanted, did it on my terms, you know?"

"Yeah, that's kind of my point. Don't you get it? Like. You can't expect me to be impressed by that. It's not realistic. And how can you say that you think we'll work at all, then? Don't you want more than that for me?"

"Yes. That's what I'm saying."

". . . Is it?"

"Well it would be, if you would let me finish."

"Well, maybe if it didn't take you an hour of talking about nonsense to get to your point, Wagner," she said and smirked in self-satisfaction.

"Excuse me Miss Just-talked-for-twenty-minutes-straight-with-a-fucking-gag-order-on-you, I'm so sorry to beat around the bush."

"It's different, you do this all the time, this is just *how* you talk," she said, both of them holding back laughter.

"Fuuuuuck youuuuuu, will you just shut up and let me finish?"

She pantomimed the same locked-mouth gesture he had made earlier and then opened her eyes wide and bobbled her head around as if she were cursing him behind her locked lips.

"That's how I've always been. I'd rather be high than bored. I'd rather be enjoying the moment than depressed about the constant. Focused on a point in time rather than the continuum. It's how I've stayed sane so far. But then I met you. And out of nowhere I saw it, you know? It's love. I know, I know, it sounds so fucking lame, but it's true. It's love, it's the only reason any of this is worth doing. And it really only made me more angry at the way things are. Because I started looking around and I realized that everyone is going through the motions and doing the same stuff. Committing themselves to the system and playing the game and trading their lives for their salaries and their 401ks, and they aren't even doing it for love. They are all so devoid of love they can't even look at each other when they pass each other on the sidewalk. Everyone just builds walls around their possessions and their lives and they neglect their lovers and are frustrated by their children and people divorce and grow apart and live in resentment and everyone I've ever known is so full of hatred for something or someone and to even try and talk about love is like the stuff of delusional idealogues. It offends people, deeply.

"And so now I'm here and I feel like I know the answer to all of it and I have no one to share it with because you have James and, you know ... Lia ... like ... Well, you know about Lia, that's another story. But all I really want is you, and you're somewhere else. But if you were here ... Ali ... If you were here, I'd be here."

"Nick ... That is the gayest shit I've ever heard in my life."

"Yeah. I know it is," he said, looking out the window at the wall of white fog.

"And it's incredibly sweet. But are you honestly saying that you'd change it all?"

"Change it all to be with you?"

"Yeah. Like. You'd stop with the pills, clean up your life, stop doing whatever it is you're doing for money?"

"Yes."

"Nick, stop it. I've seen it. I've seen my dad promise my mom he was going to stop drinking a thousand times. Shit gets bad, he gets a DUI or disappears or rages out, and then she threatens to leave and then he makes all these promises—"

"Yeah, I know. I remember when he got out of rehab last time. But he's a fucking alcoholic, Ali."

"Yeah. He is. But he loves my mom. She is his reason. She's the only reason he keeps going back. The reason he keeps trying, or else he'd have drank himself to death by now. If that's what it looks like to be someone's reason ... that's not what I want. I can't do it."

Nick cracked the window again and lit a cigarette. The cold flooded the cab like water rushing in and Alison pulled the blanket tight around her body and put her arms under his hoodie and his warm belly met her icy skin and he flinched but she didn't retreat and they both were content for the time, dreading the passing of the moment.

Moments passed. Minutes came and went. The cigarette burned out. The tide swelled higher on the shore and the waves licked the cliffside, reaching their tendrils ever closer to the truck. The moon moved across the sky behind the veil of dense fog to find a new vantage point, but they remained still, in hiding, unobservable—frozen and unwilling to move in any direction lest they never be able to return to this time again.

Nick wrestled with himself. Shame and self-doubt clashed with optimism and determination. He told himself they could disappear together, but he was already acutely aware of the distance between here and the pills he had left at home. Some unwelcome voice nagged that he should have brought them with him, that all of this would have been easier if he had them. Some other part of him said she would fix him. That he would never need to get high again if he had her. None of the other voices believed it; some scoffed and derided his foolishness. He tried to find the courage to lie. To fake it. To put his code to the highest test, to promise the world today and figure out how to cash the check tomorrow. His psyche collapsed like a toddler after a tantrum and he resigned himself to self-pity and he hated himself.

With this, he spoke at last. "What if I get clean? Change everything and show you? What if I just show you I can do it first, so it's not on you? I mean, if things were different, you would wanna be with me, right? That's what you're saying—I'm not just dreaming, right?"

"You'd dream of being with a girl like me, Wagner?"

"I do it all the time, you idiot. So . . . What then?"

"Well. If you do that, I guess we'll talk. I'm not going anywhere. You're my best friend. That isn't going to change, I mean, unless you, like, hate me after tonight."

"I can't hate you. Believe me, I've tried."

"Well then. We've got time. Maybe you're right. Maybe you can show me that you want more from this life than to sit around and smoke pills and chase girls and talk shit about all the sheep out there. Maybe we'll get the chance."

"And until then, what about this? What about us?"

"Until then . . . only in dreams, I guess."

Nick sat, chewing on his lip, trying to keep the wetness in his eyes contained before they spawned tears and spilled down his cheeks and fell onto her face.

"I love you, you know," Alison said, staring up at him.

"Yeah, Ali . . . I love you too."

‡

NW: What good does it do to sit around and talk about, like, my hopes and dreams and fears or whatever?

HF: Well, it helps you to practice getting in touch with yourself. Being able to analyze and articulate our ideas, our attitudes, our desires—all of it opens the door to ourselves. Opens a channel of identification from the heart to the mind, and then from your mind to mine. We develop rapport, we develop trust, we explore ideas. And then, ideally, we want to get to a place where you are comfortable acknowledging and discussing your feelings so that we may process them, confront them, and work through them, so that you can live a life unencumbered by emotional repression and other psychological ailments, tricks of the mind. This comes quicker for some than others, of course, but it is the ultimate goal: this ability to effectively deal with our feelings, by feeling them instead of running from them.

NW: Gross.

HF: Do you know what my dad told me the last time I talked to him?

NW: What's that?

HF: He said—mind you, I'm sixteen years old and he's quite literally dying in a hospital bed before me—"Stop crying, who is ever gonna to take you seriously if you carry on like that? Shit happens, crying about it doesn't help. Just makes you look like a pussy."

NW: Well . . . explains why you're such an asshole, I guess.

HF: I'm sure it's a start, yes. But my point is that, in some form or another, this is how so many of us try to treat our emotional responses to life. People spend their whole lives at war with their emotions. Fighting them, repressing them, trying to conquer them by burying them somewhere out of sight and out of mind. Pretending like they aren't happening. And it only ever prolongs

161

their suffering. There is no fighting against them, Nick. There is only delaying the inevitable.

NW: And what's that?

HF: When they break free from wherever we've tried to bury them and they try to bury us instead.

NW: You're real fuckin' dramatic sometimes, you know that?

HF: You and my ex-wife would really get along, I swear.

NW: If you gave her half the cryptic double-talk and stupid riddles you give me, no wonder it didn't work out.

HF: Maybe you're right, again.

NW: So, did you love her?

HF: My wife? Of course I did. In my own way.

NW: In your own way. I've heard that one before. Not a fan.

HF: Yeah, well. Love is a complex thing, you know. Have you been in love?

...

HF: Ah. With your friend, the girl ... Alison?

...

HF: It's not easy, I know. Being in love like that can be a wretched, pitiful place to be.

NW: Yeah. It can. So, what's the point?

HF: For a nihilist, you spend a lot of time looking for the point of things.

NW: I'm not a nihilist. That's why I'm looking for the god damn point.

HF: Right, of course.

NW: Seriously, though. You know, on that note, I honestly used to think that it *was* the point. Love. You know? That love was the one thing. That it mattered even when nothing else did. For a minute there, even though things were fucked-up, I thought it would be love that would change it. That it would set me free from the sad and lonely feeling of being alive. I started to think that love would drive the march of progress, that it would put an

162

end to wars, that it would fill in the empty spaces and heal all the wounds, that it would solve the problems of the world. I thought it fucking mattered. But now it's like ... How can it? How can it, when it doesn't even exist? It's like putting all your faith in God or something. Some invisible force that can't be quantified or proved and waiting for it to make itself known in the world and come to save your soul.

HF: You don't believe in love?

NW: It's bullshit. It's a delusion. A hormonal rush. A survival mechanism. It's a chemical reaction, a misunderstood impulse in the brain that we assign value to and then hold up like a banner until it becomes too much of a burden and we move on to something else. Show me one instance in this world where love isn't conditional. Where it isn't fleeting and fickle and sold to the highest bidder. Where it isn't just cast aside by one party or the other the moment it becomes inconvenient. You can't. It doesn't exist. We talk about it. We shout it from the rooftops and plaster it on bumper stickers and plead with each other to practice it, but it's just that: It's a nice idea. It's a lofty goal. It's a fantasy. It's a dream. And that's where it stays, in fucking dreams. Even if someone is lucky enough to catch it, it just doesn't last. It can't last. Look at you. Look at me. Look at, like ... everyone, really. Who has anything like lasting love? And yet ... we still fall for it. The arrogance. To think that somehow *this* love will be different. Yeah. Hah, fuckin' newsflash, it's not. Nothing lasts forever and that's the rules. So. Why should love be any different? It's bullshit. And it fucking kills me.

. . .

NW: What, no argument? No reframe, no new perspective?

HF: I, uh. I'm sorry. [coughs] I think that what you're feeling is valid. And I can relate to the sentiment more than I would care to admit, actually. But I would be remiss if I allowed you to walk out of here without reminding you that you're young. That what you're describing is such a formative point in a young person's life—that feeling of finding something like love for the first time only to have it slip through your fingers. It's tragic. But those early broken hearts are what give us the ability to soldier on through life. It's how we learn to survive. How we learn that we *can* survive. How we learn at all. How we grow. How we become well-rounded, resilient, and mature people. It's something everyone deals with at some point or another. Whether it's a breakup or our first brushes with loss. Time will pass, and it will bring healing and perspective that I can't offer you right now. You wouldn't even hear it if I tried. But you'll just have to trust me.

NW: Do I? Did it pass for you? Are you telling me that right now while you're sitting around wallowing in your divorce and doing free therapy with a fucking drug addict to make yourself feel better, you still believe that love is the answer?

HF: I never said love was the answer. You said that.

NW: Wait . . . then what's the fucking answer?

HF: Perseverance. Experience. Triumph. Wisdom.

NW: What?

HF: If you spend your life expecting other people to be the answer for you, you will live a disappointing and often painful life. Love can't be the answer, Nick. It never was. Love is a great attitude with which to approach the world; it's a good thing to carry with you and to share wherever possible. But it can't be the answer, because, as you said, most people aren't interested. All you can do is persevere. Live through the pain you're experiencing right now, survive it. Learn about yourself and the world. And find continued growth and freedom from the things that have held you back. Love isn't the answer. You, your life, your experiences, your successes, your failures, all of your victories to come . . . those are all you ever have.

NW: Well . . .

. . .

NW: Well, what's the point of any of that? Who wants to sit and enjoy the spoils alone? It's like . . . the tree-in-a-forest shit. If you don't have anyone to share it with, what fucking good is it? There's no god damn way you can tell me we have to do this alone.

HF: It's all we ever are, Nick. Born alone, die alone. No one can truly take this journey with you. And so you must live for yourself.

NW: That's such bullshit.

HF: So then, which is it? Do you still believe in love?

NW: I . . .

 . . .

NW: I don't think I know what I believe.

WEDNESDAY

13

From a distant place a dog barked so loudly that Henry thought it was in his own house. He woke with a start, disoriented and afraid. His surroundings were alien and dark—a glow from the television screen offered the little light that was in the room. He must have fallen asleep on the couch. He had drunk more than he meant to and passed out while waiting for his food. He checked the time on his phone: 3:36am.

His brain felt swollen in his skull and his stomach turned and threatened his throat with the taste of bile. He wanted to move to his bed but he felt like he was bound to the couch, heavy with slumber, somewhere between drunk and hungover. He thought of sleeping the next few hours where he lay. *A drink would help.*

He weighed his options and watched the heads on the screen—a blonde woman with her hair pulled back tightly and the impossibly rigid posture of a King's Guard was waving her finger like a despot while a stubby, oafish man with sweat on his brow rolled his eyes and shouted back at her. A bar across the bottom of the screen read:

The Last Chance for Our Souls: Keeping the Devil Out of Our House

The dog barked again. His porch light went on and his phone rang all at once. He looked at the phone, afraid but with no good reason to be. The number on the screen was unfamiliar, but he answered it anyway.

"Hello?" he said, barely sputtering the syllables out through his dry throat, congested and paralyzed by sleep.

"He—o Is this—R—Os—r?" It was a woman's voice on the other end, but the connection was poor; the sound cut in and out and shifted to a digitized, almost robotic tone in transmission.

"What's that? I can't hear you? Who is this?" He tried to hide the panic in his voice, but that only made it sound angry instead.

"I'm—orry. Doctor F—ter. Do—r Henry Fos—r? Is this you?"

"Yes. This is Henry Foster. Who is this?"

"Henry, thank god. Can you hear me?" Suddenly she spoke clearly. The voice seemed almost familiar now, but he couldn't place it.

"Yes. That's better. I'm sorry, it's three-thirty in the morning. Who is this?"

"Henry, it's me, An—. I'm s—y. I know it's b———"

"Who? I can't hear you. Can you call back some other time, is this an emergency?"

"NO!" the caller shrieked with a gravelly rage, and the marrow in Henry's bones turned cold, goosebumps rising his arms so abruptly it almost hurt.

"No. I need to talk to you," she said, and the familiar voice returned.

The timer on the porch light expired. The dog continued barking.

"Okay, okay. I'm here. Who is this, I'm sorry. I couldn't hear you. What can I do for you?"

"Tell me why," she said.

"Why? Tell you why *what*?"

"Tell me why you did this to me. Why you haven't come back for me?"

"I'm sorry, who is this?"

"IT'S ANNA, HENRY. DID YOU FORGET?" She was shouting into the phone, her rage unbound and forcing the breath from Henry's lungs. The dog barked louder than it ever had; he could hear the seething anger and long strings of saliva pouring from its tongue and teeth. He looked up at the TV and the woman on the screen was pounding one fist into her other hand, her eyes mad with condemnation, and the chair where the sweaty man had been was empty. The bar across the bottom of the screen read:

The Last Chance for Your Soul: Expel the Devil from Your House

He dropped the phone and tried to get up to look for the remote control. His body felt too heavy, as if gravity were acting upon him alone with special care. The woman on the phone continued to shriek and howl so loudly he could hear her from the phone lying on the floor. The dog was at the foot of the couch now, growling and drooling on his bare feet, and Henry could see in the eyes of the beast that he intended to tear him limb from limb and drag Henry back to the same hell from which he came. Henry tried to kick and scream, but he could only close his eyes and breathe so hard and so fast that he thought he might be able to stop his own heart from beating in his chest before the dog could devour him.

Damp with sweat and gasping for air, Henry opened his eyes to the sun creeping through the closed blinds of his front window. He looked to his phone and wondered if he had really received the call from his dream. That voice, which he had not heard in years, still echoed in his head, and he wondered where she was now, and if he should call her. The television was on, the same woman from the TV in his dream was shaking her fist and emphatically imploring the viewer to do or believe or buy something. A graphic in the top corner showed a picture of Jesus's face emblazoned on a color image of a NASA satellite image of a gas formation in space. The bar on the bottom of the screen read:

The Last Chance for America: Keeping God's Word in the Statehouse

He lay flat on his back and tried to close his eyes, but he kept finding himself staring at the ceiling, thinking, *Fuck. Fuck me. Not again. I can't.*

His stomach was a vacuum, twisting up and crumpling in on itself, and despite his heavy head, there was a hum behind his eyes that wouldn't let him even pretend that he would be able to sleep any longer. He was beyond hungry; he was sick with hunger. And he felt like he would piss himself if he didn't get to the bathroom quickly.

He used the toilet and then splashed water on his face. On his way back to the front door he put eyes on the coffee pot to confirm that it was hot and ready. Outside the door, sitting neatly on the porch, he found a plastic bag with his Chinese delivery. Hot coffee, cold noodles, and the unrelenting dread of a moment that never seemed to end. The noodles made it one of his better breakfasts in recent memory.

The headache made further demands of him, with which he complied by pouring a large glass of water, drinking it down with three Ibuprofen, and then downing a second glass for good measure.

"You should always have a full glass of water first thing in the morning, Foss, before your coffee or anything else. It's what gets the system moving, flushes out the toxins, gets your body ready to fight another day," Gretchen would remind him from time to time as he sat before the coffee pot, waiting for the first cup to be ready.

Then, the mornings were easier. Awful too, but with the clarity of loneliness he mostly remembered them as easier. They would wake up together in the morning and argue about who should bring whom coffee in bed. Mornings which followed nights where finally they had come together at the end of whatever melees the day had brought and in silence and surrender they had taken comfort in each other under the covers of their bed. That was when she was there and he still felt a reason to be anything at all in life.

He ate cold noodles and nursed his headache and felt for a moment like he had destroyed the one thing in his life that had ever been truly good. As he felt inclined to collapse into self-loathing, he heard his father's voice in his head spitting and choking and shrieking at him for being so weak, and he felt trapped between his sorrow and his pride.

I have an idea. What if you weren't such a pathetic piece of shit for five minutes and you at least acted like a man with some fucking dignity?

He gritted his teeth and spat curses at himself and his house and the sweat in his clothes and the clothes themselves which stuck to his body, which he also cursed in its aching frailty and betrayal. *Fuck all of this. I'm done. Done with this shit. Today we move on.*

(I'll believe it when I see it, you fucking coward. Why don't you just pour yourself a drink and call out sick? We both know that's how this ends.)

I said I'm done. Fuck you.

He worked his way back to the bathroom and turned on the hot water, but a great spirit of defiance overtook him and he turned the knob back toward cold. He took off his clothes and got in the shower.

(Things don't change that easily. You've always been a miserable prick. You can't blame her for that. This is who you are. Stop fighting it. Give up.)

Shock. Resistance. He backed out and tried to catch his breath. *Stop being a pussy. Look at yourself. Are you sick of this shit yet? It's fucking embarrassing. You are embarrassing yourself.* Clenched teeth, tight fists, a deep breath in through the nose, then he immersed himself in the streams of cold water. His heart beat faster and he could feel synapses in his brain firing in places they had not in months, maybe years. He was alive.

The white marble of the bathroom walls emanated a heavenly glow as the sunlight poured in through the window over the shower. The blood pumping in his veins was hot and the cold water beaded and ran down his body and his muscles tensed and his skin took on the quality of stone and he thought of all the time he had left in this world. All the women he hadn't met. All the places he hadn't been. All the things he had ever dreamed of doing that he hadn't yet done. Jump from an airplane. Hike to Machu Picchu. Write a book about his experience as a psychiatrist during the pharmaceutical revolution. In one month, it would be a new year. Gretchen was only a chapter in that book, and in the cold water he resolved once more to turn the page on her and take back his own life.

From there, he conducted the rites of morning with zeal. He sang the hook to some pop song that had been stuck in his head for a decade; strutted from closet to bedroom, to kitchen and back. Before leaving the house, he refilled his coffee and then, using a blend of freezer-burned greens and berries he had watched gather ice for years, he blended a smoothie and added protein powder. He listened to music on his drive to work. He yielded to pedestrians and aggressive drivers. He nodded his head and smiled at a cop in a passing vehicle. He drove for a time paralleling a vehicle occupied by a pair of twenty-something girls, and when they looked at him and smiled, he thought about fucking them both. He whistled the whole way up the stairs to his office.

Just as Henry was about to sit in his chair, Will appeared in the doorway like the curious neighbor in an ancient TV sitcom.

"What in the name of Selena Gomez is going on in here?" Will said, then sashayed into the office, sat in the big armchair, and kicked his feet onto the ottoman. "Did you finally get laid or something? What was his name? Tell me everything."

"Why are you so obsessed with me, Will? What did I do? Is it my boyish good looks? My money? Or do you actually respect my character, my intellect?"

"I just love a girl who needs fixing, Foss, you know that. Keeps it interesting."

"Don't we all."

"Seriously though, what's up? Man, you've been like a ghost in here lately. I have to get out the thermal equipment and set fuckin'... booby traps and listening devices to catch you most days."

The accuracy of Will's accusation stung Henry, and for a moment he wanted to push back, to defend, deny, and argue that Will was being dramatic. That Henry was busy. That psychiatry wasn't like finance. That his job carried weight and responsibility and he didn't have time during the day to *bullshit with the neighbors because I have real fucking work to do, you pencil-pushing spreadsheet-jockey frat-boy motherfucker.* But he had taken a cold shower. He had drunk some water. He had made a green juice. He had sworn off his miseries. He was okay now.

"Ehh. You know. I, uh. Man, Will ... " *What do you know about my problems, you naive pretentious fuck?* "It's been a rough go ... You know it. I haven't handled the divorce great, you know. I've really just buried myself in work and just trying to take care of myself, get my head right, you know?"

"Yeah, bury yourself in a fuckin' bottle, man. Been worried about you. Walkin' through here looking like a fuckin' skeleton. Not eating, eyes all sunken, nose all red and shit. You've been a mess, man."

174

Henry imagined lunging across the room and grabbing his friend by the collar with both hands, tackling Will to the ground and pummeling his face with fists until his mouth was too full of blood to breathe, let alone speak.

"Yeah," Henry started, and then with the poise and precision of a politician being interviewed on prime-time television, he continued, "I mean . . . You're right, I've definitely had a few drinks here and there. Certainly more than I used to. But I'm taking a break from all that. I think it helped me stay calm through this whole thing. It really was more of a boon than a burden. Sometimes we need to take the edge off, you know? But it's all been part of my process. And I've turned a corner, you know? I'm taking care of myself now. Eating healthy. I'm going to hit the gym after work. Gotta put some weight back on, you know. Get ready for the next chapter. It's just . . . it's time. You know?"

Will sat, looking studious and nodding slowly. He clicked his teeth with his tongue and then gave the office an unseeing look. "Yeah, man. That's great. Really. I mean, I'm glad to hear it. Good to know you're coming out the other side. I knew you would, man. Was just a matter of time, really. Hey, so you didn't forget about the party tonight, Maddie's thing? You're not gonna bail on me, right?"

"I don't know. You sure you want to go out with a drunken wreck like me? I might scare all your CPA friends with my ghoulishness."

"Foss, I didn't mean like—"

"I'm fucking with you. Now get out of my office. I have a patient coming soon."

"Heyyyy, he got jokes now too. Cool. See you tonight, pick me up at six."

"Goodbye, Will."

Get the fuck out of here, you ignorant little twit.

Will departed and Henry leaned back in his lounger, filled with pride at his restraint, his discipline, his growth. He was healing. He opened his phone to the News app and scrolled through headlines to try to download the happenings of the day.

POTUS Blames Contingent of Subterranean Mole-People for Conspiring to Steal National Secrets; Nation Divided on Veracity of Claims

Nation divided? How is that even possible?

Second-Amendment Activists Protest Gun-Control Talks by Rallying with Rifles Outside the Elementary School where Last Month 27 People Were Gunned Down in Mass Shooting

At least they stay classy.

AI Chatbot to Be the First Non-Human to Be Nominated for Public Office in California, Not Explicitly Prohibited by State Constitution

This actually ... might not be the worst idea. Which is officially the worst thought I've ever thought.

150 Dead in Mass Suicide After One Man Claims to Have Decoded Message from the "Voice of God" Nebula

You've got to be kidding me. It is the 21st century, people.

Henry clicked the last one and read:

DECEMBER 7: First responders in a rural area outside of Reading, PA encountered a grisly scene early Wednesday morning as at least 150 people were found dead in an apparent mass suicide. Police arrived on the scene to investigate after receiving several calls from concerned friends and relatives of people they believe to be part of a cult formed in recent weeks after the discovery of a

176

strange radio transmission from a distant nebula that has come to be known as the "Voice of God."

The alleged leader of the cult, Barry Watkins of Reading, was a local pastor who claimed on Tuesday afternoon to have decoded the transmission from the Nebula NGC-8032. Despite scientists around the world racing to make sense of the linguistic pattern of the transmissions, Watkins claimed to have cracked the code in under a day. The contents of the message, he said in emails now being made public, were of dire importance and not to be ignored.

Many members of Watkins' congregation reported receiving emails and phone calls urging them to report to Watkins' rural property northeast of the City of Reading for an emergency evening sermon. Police have not released further details.

Some members have responded to our request for comment, with many reporting a great sense of relief at having avoided the tragedy. Others have shared their fears that Watkins' message is legitimate. When asked their thoughts on the actions of Watkins and the others, many have offered only prayers for their souls.

In his emails, Watkins implored humanity to put their ultimate faith in God by "turning away from the sinful allure of the mortal body, and returning to God in purity of spirit." He claimed that "the message from God is our last chance to repent and return to God before we are thrust into the End Times."

Elizabeth Kelly, a theologian and biblical scholar from Boston University, has refuted Watkins' claims. Kelly emphasized the danger of trusting any person reckless enough to claim to know the will of God, urging even the most faithful to remain calm and resist the temptation to follow in his footsteps. When asked if Kelly believes the Voice of God nebula is, in fact, the voice of God, she replied, "Isn't everything?"

Officials are warning citizens everywhere to disregard the contents of Watkins' message, which is already going viral across the internet (read it here). Scientists are rushing to point to inconsistencies in the pattern of the transmissions and Watkins' supposed translation, adding that there is still no reason to believe the transmissions are the work of any sentient designer. Still, scientists have come to no consensus as to the interpretation or significance of the anomalous interstellar transmission.

Henry clicked the link to the pastor's translation of the signal, which took him to a Twitter post with a text-image that read:

The people living in darkness have seen a great light; on those living in the land of the shadow of death a light has dawned.

Those who are wicked will fear the light. They will deny it. Those who speak with forked tongues, the liars, the charlatans and false prophets will come to be exposed for the wretched fiends they are. By this light, let them be seen.

Adherents of those who would deny me will be cast into the eternal fire. Lifetimes of suffering without end. Only Now is The Chance for Redemption.

By this Light, Let them be Saved.

And there will be those, the victims of the Ancient Deceiver of the Whole World, those whose faith pales before their greed and their cowardice. Those who would kneel before the Devil himself rather than stand in the Storm and await the Light of my coming, and their Salvation.

By this light, let Me be seen.

So Return to me, NOW! Otherwise I will come shortly and wage war against them with the sword of My mouth.

Return to me, Now.

Henry shook his head and returned to the News app. He skimmed past stories of politicians caught in scandals. *Liars.* Proxy wars for global military powers taking place in developing countries. *Criminals.* A new diet trend that will help you shed pounds and add years to your life (behind a paywall). *Thieves.* The sheer selection of bad news on any given day was suddenly staggering, and he felt an existential fear take shape and harden behind his sternum where before there had been a supercilious indifference.

Something nagged at him. The article on Pastor Watkins and the Reading 150 had piqued his interest. Henry considered—as a matter of curiosity, an experiment—the possibility that the radio transmission was definitive proof of God. Scientists around the world were reeling, after all. *And what do we know, really? We can be so sure of ourselves, but what if we're wrong?*

What would it mean if God revealed themself before its creation? How would the account of humankind fare under the scrutiny of the Almighty? And how would his own, he wondered. If God themself sat down before Henry Foster and asked him to make one great sacrifice to demonstrate his repentance for a life of material whim and pleasure, would he be able to drink the cyanide, to thrust the blade, to take the leap?

Was it a tragic show of gullibility, spinelessness, or an admirable display of unparalleled faith that led the Reading 150 to take the word of old Pastor Watkins and sacrifice their bodies before their creator? Did they truly believe God had come back for them?

Why haven't you come back for me?

The voice from the phone call in his dream rang out in his ears.

Clear as if she were speaking to him now.

Anna.

The thoughts of God and repentance evaporated and all he could see was Anna's face. Calamitous images sparked and shuffled rapidly in the eye of his mind. Anna's face in his office, her deep red hair and green eyes full of misbehavior. Her brow sullen and her lips pursed, cursing him and every man she'd ever known. Her eyes closed and her mouth opened wide in delight with her neck fully extended, her throat stretched long, face up across the pillow. Her childlike sweetness. Her discontent. His name falling from her lips like dead leaves in October.

Anna Dempsey had been a patient of his several years prior. She had come to him on the recommendation of another young woman whose name he could not remember. Anna had walked into his office, twenty-eight years old and coming to terms with what he helped her to realize was a lifetime of untreated mental-health issues.

At the time of their first meeting, she was caught in a love triangle between her husband and a young man that she had been introduced to by a friend. Though she had not yet been explicitly unfaithful to her husband with this particular man, she had been unfaithful with others since being married, and felt as though she were trapped in a pattern she was doomed to repeat. Her concern was that if she didn't address this behavior, it would lead her to a life of unending deceit and suffering, and eventually to harming her husband, herself, and others in the process.

In spite of the troubling nature of what she had shared, Henry couldn't help but find her charming; she spoke in a manner that captivated him to the point that he nearly lost sight of his professionalism and began to take a personal and almost unrighteous interest in her. She was magnetic, even as she spoke of her torment. The juxtaposition made it all the more fascinating to him.

After she had shared her history and her current predicament with him, he shook off improper thoughts and attempted to regain his composure, redirecting the stories of her extramarital affairs back to the topic of her mental health.

"I do want to remind you, though I am willing to assist you in any way that you need, that my specialty is more in treating mental health. I am happy to counsel you on matters of your relationship, with your husband and whomever else, of course, but you could find many people, or even close friends, to do that at a much lower price. So, that being said, I'd like to be sure I'm clear on how you want to proceed here with your treatment?"

"Oh, of course, sorry, how silly of me. Probably boring you with all this drama, aren't I?" she said, blushing slightly but retaining the same pageant confidence in her voice. Henry marveled at the grace with which she expressed even her embarrassment.

"No, not at all, not at all. I just want to be sure you get what you've come for."

"Right. Yeah. What I've come for. Well . . . I guess that's just it. I'm not sure what I've come for. My friend told me that she was going through a lot and really struggling, and that she came to see you and you prescribed her something that changed her life. So. I guess I was thinking maybe it's the same for me. I guess . . . that maybe I need some help, you know? I really feel like it's all too much, all of this. I feel like I'm just going to explode one day if things keep up like this."

"Of course, well. You know, I am the doctor, but you are the expert on you. If that's the course you'd like to follow, we can certainly do that. Things like depression, anxiety, even compulsive behaviors can make it difficult or even impossible to make positive choices for ourselves, leading to inaction or consolidation of poor habits, which then in turn contribute to the depression, anxiety, or shame, and so it continues. Breaking out of these cycles can be the most difficult part of recovery and treatment, and for a lot of people, meds can be the catalyst that helps us break free and start to make some of those positive changes. With me so far?"

"Yes sir," she said, straightening her back and lifting her chin with a playfulness that disarmed Henry and gave him brief pause.

"Right. Alright, good. Ahem," he started. "Well. Yes, so, I guess the question now is: Do you believe that your . . . proclivities are the result of this sort of compulsive action? Meaning, do you feel that they are well-intended, thought-out, and deliberate choices you're making? Perhaps you're not addressing some underlying dissatisfaction in your marriage and you're acting out rather than confronting them? Or do you think it's possible that they come from a place of impulsivity, distraction, or even self-destruction?"

She gave him a hard stare that seemed to contain her full answer to the question, as though it should be so obvious as to not need further comment, or maybe the look simply illustrated disdain for the question itself and an obstinate refusal to answer it.

"The reason I ask is that it can be quite common for people to attempt to treat feelings of unhappiness or dissatisfaction by acting out in ways that feel contrary to the source of their unhappiness, often with no success and a further compounding of the problem. In these cases, we would want to address the behaviors and identify the root of your unhappiness, and then work ourselves to a place where you become willing to deal with it head-on. Whereas on the other hand, such behaviors can sometimes result from an even deeper place in a person's neurodevelopment. Maladaptive coping mechanisms, emotional dysregulation, even mood or personality disorders. These can be more difficult to identify and complex to treat, but both absolutely *can* be managed, and with ongoing treatment, people can find themselves living happy, productive lives again. So, either way, we're going to get it all sorted out, so long as you're ready to do so. We just need to know where to begin. Does any of this sound like it might fit your experience?"

Anna stared at him, still as stone except for blinking eyelids. "Doctor, are you suggesting that my drive to experience pleasure and happiness instead of living in a state of constant dissatisfaction is actually a pathological *disorder*?"

Henry pulled his lips between his teeth and squinted at her, uncertain how best to respond.

Anna's eyes were wide as quarters and a Cheshire grin curled at the corners of her mouth. Then she burst into laughter. "Hahahahaha, oh my god, you should see your face! You look like you're regretting all of your life choices right now. Like you wish you'd never even met me. Hah, yes, doctor. Honestly, all of it sounds quite plausible to me. The behavior, the distraction, the disorder. I'll take it all, ring me up." She continued to laugh, unfazed by the talk of emotional disorders and the long process of recovery, as though such things were to be regarded with the same concern as the question of what one should have for lunch. "The question I have," she said, through eyes that spoke volumes in a mystical language and didn't break their hold on him, "is can you fix me?"

He allowed a diffident smile and a few snorts of almost-laughter to escape him. He was embarrassed, but not nearly as much as he was transfixed. This cavalier young woman with the laughter of the siren and the eyes of the sea was about to take up residence in his head and he felt helpless to stop her.

"'Fix' is a heavy word. Let's start with 'help' and see if we can't work our way from there," he said, calm and composed as if he didn't contain a rising and tempestuous tide of desire within him.

"Sounds very reasonable, doctor. Let's see what you've got," she said and nodded her head in approval.

Henry saw Anna weekly for three months, during which time their talks veered either side of the line between the personal and the intimate. Henry began to reciprocate her tales of marital strife with those of his own. They began to console each other through the travails of long-term monogamy, and even though she was being treated with antidepressants to help combat her impulsivity and though she had broken off her relationship with her most recent paramour, they would often commiserate their shared frustration at the boundless potential for sexual exploration that they had denied themselves by committing to one partner until deaths did them part.

It was only a matter of time before Henry found himself smothered by the weight of her body in his lounger, his tongue in her mouth and her legs straddling his waist. All of their best intentions left to wither and die, unattended outside the locked office door.

Months passed. Assignations in the office lounge chair became parking-garage backseat trysts, hotel beds in the light of the afternoon, "long workday" dinner dates out of town where being recognized was of no concern. Where once their conversation hinged on a mutual despair, an unquenched longing for gratification, now they could exchange fevered and vaporous declarations of love for one another between the thrusts of their hips and the paranoid glances over their shoulders.

This continued until Anna's husband followed her to a hotel on a Thursday afternoon and all but witnessed her adultery firsthand. Though the identity of her lover was not discovered by her husband, the revelation of her infidelity was all he needed, and their marriage was dissolved. Anna sought refuge in Henry as the only person who knew her deeply, but he recoiled for fear that she would misconstrue the nature of their relationship and push for something more now that she was unmarried.

The next time she arrived for a scheduled professional appointment, he insisted that she see another doctor.

He lived for a time in fear that she would appear at the front door of his home, find his wife, and divulge their affair to her. He stopped answering her calls altogether, sometimes reading her texts but never responding. The final time he heard from her was a text message on a Tuesday morning at 11:30am, one month after he had told her to find a new doctor.

Imagine living in a place where the desire to feel alive and happy was not considered a trait of the disordered and maladapted. What a wonderful place that must be. Thanks for everything, Henry. We really had something for a minute there. Take care of yourself.

He did not respond.

Four years passed and Anna Dempsey vacated her residency in his mind, a relief which he did not permit himself to acknowledge for fear of thinking about her again at all. He had moved her to a basement room in his psyche, compartmentalized her in a closet where she would

184

only be heard from time to time in his dreams and in the darkest of his drunken nights.

Anna Dempsey.

Her voice from his dream had resurrected visceral memories of her and had aroused suddenly a desperate curiosity in him. He wondered what it would be like to have her in his own bed, in complete privacy and unrestrained by the bonds of secrecy. It was not impossible that, after this much time, she had forgiven his handling of their parting; that she was still as inclined to promiscuity as ever; that reconciliation and a continuation from where they had left off was possible, realistic, even. Her green eyes condemned him in his imagination and he was as taken with her as if she had been there with him, the way he was taken with her on that first day.

He resolved to call her, but he wouldn't have time now. His first patient would be arriving any moment and he couldn't risk rushing the call with her. It would require his full attention and as much tact as he could muster. His impatience, masked as prudence, suggested he send a text to break the ice and inform her of his intentions.

> Hey Anna, I'm sorry it's been
> so long. I'd love the chance to
> make it up to you. Would you
> mind if I gave you a call later
> today, see if we can't catch up?

He returned to the News app and opened an article cataloging the twenty-one best wardrobe malfunctions of the 21st century, and a response notification from Anna appeared on his screen. He opened the message so quickly that the reflex may have preceded the notification itself, but found only a red exclamation point icon and a "failure to deliver" notice. *Dammit. Still blocked, after all this time, Anna?*

He was frustrated, but he could hear footsteps echoing in the hallway outside his office.

14

Paul Wassel appeared to be worn down under the weight of resentment. He was relatively young still—thirty-five or so—but his back hunched such that his head seemed to protrude his chest, jutting upwards at an awkward angle. His shoulders were crunched up to his ears and everything about his presentation was tense, sullen. He sat down in the chair across from Henry and slouched into himself from every angle, except for his head, which he managed to hold upright, though it looked uncomfortable.

"That bad, eh?" Henry said with a soothing half-smile.

"I can't do it, man. I'm gonna fuckin' strangle her, I swear to god," Paul said, waving his arms out to his sides and not quite seething because he was smiling, but not quite smiling because he was seething.

"... If she doesn't strangle you first, that is," Henry said, eliciting an actual laugh from Paul, who rubbed his head vigorously with both hands and then sat back in the chair.

"Yeah, sure. If she doesn't do that. Man, whose fuckin' side are you on anyway?"

"I don't take sides, you know that. But I am invested in seeing *you* overcome yourself and find happiness and good health. Preferably with your family intact ... You know, no one strangled or in prison."

"Man, someone's gettin' choked out if this shit keeps up."

"It would be so much simpler if they just shut up and did as we wanted, wouldn't it?" Henry was being sarcastic, but not enough for Paul to notice.

"Fuckin' A, it would," Paul said and looked out the window in a picturesque show of man in contemplation. Henry wondered to himself, *What could this neanderthal possibly be thinking about so deeply?*

"And yet, they do not. And we're grateful for this, no?" Henry wasn't in the mood to indulge the bit any further.

"I dunno. Are we? It's drivin' me fuckin' crazy. Ya know, I don't wanna get a divorce, but I can't deal with this shit forever, and the way it's goin' I just don't know if we're gonna make it."

Henry could see that the man's distress was real, that in spite of his boorish instincts, Paul did possess a warm, beating heart and contained all the sensitivities of an adult human being. The trouble for Henry had always been in trying to introduce men like Paul to that part of themselves. It was one of the reasons he abhorred psychotherapy with this particular breed of man.

Paul had been admitted to Willow View Hospital three years prior by his wife, Jennifer, when he attempted to kill himself by overdosing on heroin upon learning that Jennifer was pregnant. To this day, Paul denied that it was a suicide attempt, maintaining that it was just a means for his wife to exert control over him before the baby was born by making his drug use a matter of public record. The truth, of course, was somewhere in the middle.

Henry presumed it went something more like: *Young man is abusing heroin with reckless abandon while pregnant wife fears for the security of her unborn child and safety of her beloved husband. Wife finds psych admission more befitting than calling the police or threatening to leave* (both of which she had done previously, Henry would learn over the course of his work with Paul). However, Henry never spoke with Jennifer after Paul's release from the Willows, so he had to flesh out the blurry edges of Paul's stories with his own intuition.

Henry had prescribed Paul buprenorphine as a replacement therapy for his opioid addiction, and though the first few months came with a series of relapses, leading to an arrest for heroin possession, Paul eventually struck the perfect balance between an exasperated wife, the pressures of a brand-new baby girl, a buprenorphine prescription, and a probation officer, and he had been able to stay off the heroin for the last two and a half years. In that time, Paul maintained a reluctance to participate in any form of drug treatment beyond his brief monthly check-ins with Henry to have his buprenorphine prescription refilled.

"I think there's a ways to go before you two need to worry about divorce, Paul. Divorce is a big commitment. I can't help but think it's easier to figure out how to stay married than it is to learn how to be divorced. And you have your daughter, which is a whole other matter to consider," Henry said.

You fucking moron. After all you've put her through, you have the gall to talk about leaving her, because, what? What? What could she have possibly done, you ungrateful, cretinous leech? "Tell me what's going on at home. I'm certain I can help you work through whatever it is," he said. Warm. Affable. Compassionate.

Paul nodded. "Yeah, I mean. Arright, so, I'm gettin' off probation in a couple months, ya know, and she just keeps gettin' on my case, constantly naggin' about where I'm goin' and what I'm doin', and whenever I tell her to calm down she fuckin' snaps and yells at me about, like, what I useta do and what I'm gonna do when I get off and whatever. And I'm just, like, it's not fuckin' fair. Ya know? You can't just get pissed about shit that isn't fuckin' even real, you know? And I try and tell her, you know, 'Hey, fuckin' knock it off. You're acting crazy and like, the shit yer thinkin' about isn't even fuckin' happenin' and then she just loses it. I swear, we spend more fuckin' time fightin' about shit that isn't even fuckin' real and I don't even know what to do with it. It's like fightin' with ghosts or something. I can't see 'em, they ain't botherin' nobody, but she swears they're there."

"What do you think those ghosts are to her, Paul?"

"They're like all her fuckin' feelings, you know? Always. I know that. And I try to tell her, like, 'You can't be mad at me because you have feelings. I didn't make you feel that way. I didn't even do shit.' And like, if you wanna tell me about how you're feeling, that's cool, but, like, don't come at me all sideways like I did something wrong."

"Is it cool, though?"

"Is what cool?"

"If she told you about her feelings?"

Paul made the face of a dog trying to understand if its owner was saying something about food or not. "I mean. Yeah. As long as she isn't blaming me for having them, then it would be fine. She's a fuckin' girl, ya know? She's gonna have feelings, I know that. I ain't fuckin' stupid. But she knows it too, so I just don't get why she acts fuckin' surprised every time she has a feeling and like someone needs to be punished for it."

"Well, hold on, let's back up." Henry held his hand up and then pulled it back and pushed his index finger to his lips as if he were actually holding back his words while he determined how deep he was willing to go with Paul on this matter.

The malicious intolerance that was his own self-critic crept up his throat like acid reflux and took further aim at Paul. Harsh words burned on his tongue but didn't seep from his mouth. The homunculus responsible for restraint offered instead the reminder of Henry's professional duty, his credo, and his profound need to be the voice of reason everywhere he went. He swallowed his reproval and opted to give Paul the benefit of the doubt. For the good of the kid, the wife, for the good of the challenge. *You're lucky to have me, you fucking child.*

"What does it look like when she blames you for her feelings? Can you give me an example of something she says?"

Paul made that thinking-dog face again, and then did his best to answer the question. "Yeah. I mean, she like. Walks around just, like, sulkin' and fuckin' bein' real bitchy you know? And I'll ask her, like, 'What's yer fuckin' problem?' or 'What's wrong with you?' like that, but like nice, ya know? And she'll just say, 'I'm stressed out' or 'I'm just having a hard time' or whatever. And so I'll ask her, you know, like, 'About what?' Like what do you have to be stressed about, you know? I'm workin', the bills are paid, the kid's healthy, and you don't have shit to worry about. And she'll just out of nowhere start layin' into me. Sayin' she's scared I'm gonna start using again, or that I'm lyin' to her, or that I'm cheatin' on her. Or that I'm gonna fuckin' leave her and the baby, ya know? Crazy fuckin' shit, when I'm just, like, tryin' to eat dinner or whatever." Paul scoffed and shook his head, incredulous.

"Paul ... Can I ask you some questions that might make you uncomfortable?"

"Not gonna make me uncomfortable, man."

"Have you cheated on her in the past?"

"Well, yeah. I mean, you know that, she knows that, we've talked about it."

"Have you promised her you'd stay clean, and then ended up using again?"

"Haha, shit, man, only like a hundred times."

"And have you lied to her, to her face? Made promises right to her face that in that very moment you already knew weren't true, or that you were going to break?"

"I mean, yeah. Yeah, of course I have. But I ain't doin' any of that shit right now. Fuck me, you sound like her, you know that?" Paul was getting more animated, squirming in his seat.

"Yeah, I know, but remember, I'm here for you. You've got to trust me, okay?"

Paul's dumb face tilted slightly, and then he nodded. "Yeah. Yeah, of course. I'm with you."

"Good." *Because if you don't listen up, she will end up taking your daughter, your money, your house, and you will go back to shooting heroin in whatever dingy shithole will have you until you go face down in a toilet and no one bothers to call 911 for you.* "That's good. So, one thing about relationships, especially the intimate ones—family, spouses, and our closest friends—is that we find ourselves *obligated* to consider the feelings and needs of the other person. Even when their feelings and needs may differ from our own, and even when we don't understand or agree with them."

"Hold on though, that's bullshit, there. That's like. Manipulation. Just because you're feelin' something, I've gotta change up my whole shit because you say so? That's not right."

Manipulation, that's a big word.

"Well, okay. I think there are cases where that could be true, sure. But generally, I think it's best if we give the people we love the benefit of the doubt that they aren't trying to manipulate us, that maybe they are just sharing their feelings."

"She doesn't give *me* the benefit of the doubt," Paul said like a lawyer who just caught a witness in a lie.

"Ah . . . but that's because you haven't *earned* it. And that's one thing you will have to understand and come to accept if you want to move forward here. She gave you the benefit of the doubt, for years. And if we're being honest, she still is, because she chooses to trust you and she's still here. Isn't she?"

"Yeah, I guess, yeah, she is."

"So you have to try and put yourself in her shoes. Imagine that she had been cheating on you for years, and you caught her and she swore she'd never do it again. Would you be able to operate on faith every time she took a phone call in another room? Or left the house without explicitly telling you where she was going and when she would return?"

"She would never fuckin' do that. And no, if she cheated on me and shit there's no way, I'd never trust her again. That would be the end of it. No fuckin' chance I'd take her back."

"Aha. Do you see the contradiction there?"

Paul froze while the software in his brain loaded the next thought.

Too impatient to wait, Henry continued, "That is a perfect example of how you are *different*. You say you wouldn't be willing to forgive her, and she has made it abundantly clear that she is *absolutely* willing. In that way, you are different people. Right? So, part of her process of coming to forgive you is navigating the feelings of betrayal, dishonesty, insecurity, doubt, resentment, and anger that she has. You say you haven't done anything to make her feel that way, but I say maybe you *have*."

"So I just havta eat shit for the rest of our lives because of some shit I did in the past?"

"No, not at all. Eventually, the past will become the past, and you will have to eat shit for all of the new things that she has feelings about."

"What does that mean?"

Whoops. "I'm sorry, a bit of a joke. What I mean is that she will *always* have feelings. And she will always express them, however she does, and sooner or later it will be up to you whether you are going to provide her a safe place to process and express those feelings, or if you are going to take them personally and respond with hostility and defensiveness."

"Look, I don't know about all that. Safe spaces and processin' and all that bullshit. I wasn't raised like that, you know? You had a feeling, you fuckin' dealt with that shit and you didn't fuckin' cry about it to anyone else, because no one has time for that."

"And yet, here you find yourself, married and raising a child with a woman who was raised differently. And who is begging you to hold some space for how she feels. How do you want your daughter to be raised? The way you were, or in a way where she feels safe to express herself?"

The rancor fueling Paul's defensive posture leaked out of him and he slouched back in the chair again. "So, what the fuck do I do then? I can't keep doing this shit, man. Going round and round with her. 'Are you cheatin?' 'Are you usin'?' 'I'm fuckin' scared.' Yada yada yada. Havin' to tell her a hundred times a day that I'm not, fightin' with her all day about how she feels one way and it's just not the fuckin' truth. What do I do? What can I do?"

"Put the gloves down. Stop fighting, Paul," Henry said. "Just listen to her. Ask her how she feels. Ask her what you can do to help, and then just listen. If you stop fighting, you'll stop fighting."

"'If you *stop fighting*, you'll *stop fighting*.' I can't believe you just said that," Paul said, stunned. "... Man, your wife must suck your dick every night, she must be so fuckin' happy with you."

"Hah, good. I'm glad you enjoy that. Now, go home. Try it out yourself. I can't wait to hear how it all works out. And I'll call in your script today. You're doing great, keep it up Paul."

When Paul just smiled and thanked him before leaving the office, Henry breathed a great sigh of relief. After time in this line of work, a person came to realize that there are only so many types of people in the world. And with each type of person, there are only so many potential life circumstances that can occur. With each replicating circumstance, there are only a specific number of relevant discussions to be had. And repeating the tenets of basic emotional intelligence to emotionally repressed adult men had been among the first to lose its appeal for Henry. Yet, the same problem with a different face continued to pour steadily in through the revolving door of his care. Since the divorce, however, such sessions had become less mundane and more annoying.

His impatience with Paul and with every other man of his ilk stoked the flames beneath his simmering anger toward Gretchen. That she could leave him over such pettiness as their communication problems and her lack of fulfillment in her own life, her jealousy of him, and her paranoia—it infuriated him. Men around the country were practically neglecting and abusing their wives by way of emotional ineptitude and Henry had only, what? Made her feel lonely while he was out earning a living? One that afforded her the luxury to remain unemployed, completely free to pursue her passions and her every whim! Shopping, traveling, decorating, socializing, writing her incomprehensible poetry and bitching endlessly in her stupid fucking journal about her victimhood. It was preposterous.

He sat unmoving after Paul's departure, and again turned over the final years of his and Gretchen's marriage, the conversations that had repeated themselves and escalated and culminated in divorce. The simmer turned to a boil. He began to shake and chew on his molars like a hound on rawhide. He wanted to call her. To remind her that, with him, she had everything she could have ever wanted. Women like Jennifer Wassel would scrape the crumbs from Gretchen's shoes if it would have given them just a taste of the life she had trampled on.

He opened his phone and tried to compose a text message to Gretchen.

I hope you're fucking happy
I hope you're fucking happ
I hope you're fucking hap
I hope you're fucking ha
I hope you're fucking
I hope you're fuck
I hope you're

I hope
I hope you're fucking
happy, god knows I'm not.
maybe that's what yo
I hope you're fucking happy,
god knows I'm not. maybe
I hope you're fucking
happy, god knows I
I hope you're fucking
happy, god
FUCK YOU
FUCK YO
FUCK Y
FUCK
You left your diary at the house.
Good thing you never wrote
that book, it would've sucked
You left your diary at the
house. Good thing you
never wrote that book,
You left your diary at the
house. Good thing you never
You left your diary at
the house. Come get it
sometime if you want?
You left your diary at the house.
Come get it sometime, it'll be
the pile of ashes outside
You left your diary at the house.
Come get it sometime, it'll be t
You left your diary at the
house. Come get it some

194

You left your diary at the
house. Come get it
You left your diary at
the house. Come
You left your diary at the house.
You left your diary
You left
FUCK
FUCK you fuck you fuck you
fuck you fuck you fuck you fuck
you fuck you fuck you fuck you
fuck you fuck you fuck you fuck
you fuck you fuck you fuck
you fuck you fuck you fuck you
fuck you fuck you fuck you fuck
you fuck you fuck you fuck you
fuck you fuck you fuck you

What happened to all that integrity talk? I told you it wouldn't last. You're a fucking asshole and you'll die alone. Why fight it? Why pretend?

You can't save yourself any more than you can save any of the idiots you shill these pills to. Give up. If you stop fighting, you'll stop fighting.

Go have a drink. It was a valiant effort, but you're just not ready yet.

You're too much of a pussy.

Henry, who, by his own spurious estimation, had never considered himself to be a man who felt much of anything at all, now for the first time ever felt like if he didn't scream he would simply explode.

His feet on the floor and his face in his hands, he squeezed his eyes as tightly as he could and breathed hard through his nose, trying to wrest control of his mind back from the horrible sequence of images that were intruding into his every thought with great thunderous claps and long lingering gnawing sounds of scraping silverware on porcelain plates. Gretchen smiled and laughed and she screamed at him through tears running down her face and she lay naked on the bed with lust in her eyes and she rolled onto her belly and looked over her shoulder at him and then the bed was another man's and Henry was sitting in his own piss on the couch in the middle of the night, an old man missing teeth and shouting obscenities at the TV screen. Anna Dempsey was in tears and Gretchen was consoling her and his college girlfriend Megan hadn't aged a day and she pointed at him and laughed in wonderful and violent vindication.

His teeth felt like they might splinter and break into pieces from the pressure in his jaw and the bottle of Xanax in his desk drawer beckoned him like the warmth from a fire in an otherwise cold, dark house and his resolutions from the morning had all but crumbled, so the internal negotiations began.

I'm having a fucking panic attack. I need a Xanax.

(You're a coward. What happened to pulling yourself together?)

It's not a drink. Xanax is a legitimate prescription medication used around the world to treat anxiety, a condition from which I am clearly suffering.

(Good point, doctor. And why stop there? You might as well take two. Fuck it, call out the rest of the day and get a bottle. You know that's how this ends.)

It might if I don't take something.

(When was the last time you went a day without a drink, again?)

Oh, fuck off. It can't be that bad. It's been a week ... or ... I don't know, maybe a few months? Either way, all the more reason to take the Xanax, really. Alcohol withdrawal can be dangerous.

(Good point. After all, you are a drunken piece of shit, can't even go a day without a drink or poor baby might go into withdrawals.)

I am a hypocrite. I am a charlatan. The liar, the thief, the deceiver of men.

(Yes, you are. Eat the Xanax. Eat the whole bottle, if it pleases you. No one will miss you.)

(Eat the Xanax before you kill yourself over a panic attack. Over a woman.)

((No, take a deep breath and look around. This will pass. Everything will be okay.))

WHEN?!

(Kill yourself you fucking loser.)

((Everything will be okay.))

(Nothing will ever be okay again.)

SHUT THE FUCK UP!

DO SOMETHING

NOW

BEFORE YOU DROP DEAD FROM ALL OF IT

Henry stood up and waddled on wobbling knees to his desk and pulled the bottle from his drawer. He pried his jaw loose and forced the pill between his teeth, chewed it to dust, and swallowed what he could while the rest coated his gums and his tongue and dissolved into his bloodstream. Even immediate relief would not have come fast enough.

He reclined in his lounger and breathed deeply into his nose and out his mouth, again and again and again for some time until quiet became the schism. He checked the clock: 10:30. He had no appointments until one o'clock and he thought that he felt almost comfortable, that maybe he could even sleep for a while. The night before had not brought rest, nor had any in recent memory, and the invitation to sleep felt like a welcome and needed relief.

His eyes closed but faces still flickered to life in his mind and the sight of Gretchen was like fingernails scratching at a wound that hadn't healed over yet. *Who is she fucking now?* The thought made him sick and he breathed in again through the nose and out through the mouth and thought of sleep. *Who is she with?* In through the nose and he wanted to vomit and sleep.

Where is Anna Dempsey? Her green eyes replaced every thought he had. Cleopatra's eyes endured for thousands of years. Helen of Troy's launched a thousand ships. Anna Dempsey's eyes could speak a thousand words without a flutter of a lash. He knew she held the key to his liberation from this obsession. If he could not forget Gretchen so easily, he could perhaps find Anna. He rolled the thoughts of her around in his skull until he was able to muster the wherewithal to open his eyes again.

He lifted his phone to his face and squinted until the screen came into focus. He opened Facebook and searched her name. Dozens of Anna Dempseys, but none of them were his. He switched to the browser and searched "Anna Dempsey California" and awaited the results.

Obituary for Anna Dempsey, 30, Santa Lucia, CA

The office was silent. No ticking clocks, no beating heart. No passing cars, no footsteps in the hall. No voices in the walls, no dull hum of day. No quibbling with himself. No vitriol. No rage. No need for drink, no hunger or desire for sleep. Not even shock or disbelief. He didn't have to click the link or search for confirmation; he had no doubt what had happened. He knew. But he clicked it anyway.

Anna Kristine Dempsey, 30, of Santa Lucia, passed away on Friday night, after surrendering in a long battle with mental illness.

Anna lived her life like a wildfire, burning bright and touching as many people and places as she could with her intensity, her warmth, and her light.

Unfortunately, the conditions of this world are not always suitable for the sensitive souls.

The sensitive are the quickest to love, and love deeply they do.

They bathe in mirth and radiate joy; they carry sorrows that cannot be abated.

They invite the world to share their delight and their despair, for neither one can they contain.

Anna Dempsey is survived by her sister, her mother and father, and her cat, Kitty Scherbatsky.

Anna passed peacefully in her bed, and left the following note, which the family is choosing to share with the public. Whether or not Anna intended it to be shared, the family hopes it will be of use to others struggling with mental illness and their loved ones:

Mom, Dad, Lily, (and Kitty),
If anyone ever asks, please
Tell them there was something they could have done.
If they had tried harder, been better, cared more.
If they had called daily, stopped by, taken me out.
If they had made promises and kept them, if they
had declared their undying love for me and no one else.
If they had forgiven me,
If they had the chance to say goodbye,
If they had known what I was thinking,
If they had only known what I might do.
Please let them all know that if they had
only handled things differently
They would feel so much better about themselves
when they hear the news of what I have done.
I love you, please tell Kitty I'm sorry.
Take care,

> *"Herr God, Herr Lucifer*
> *Beware*
> *Beware.*
> *Out of the ash*
> *I rise with my red hair*
> *And I eat men like air."* *

(PS. Please don't have a sappy funeral for me.
Do it somewhere cool like that place we used to play mini golf
when I was a kid, and play some good f***ing music.)

---

* Plath, Sylvia. "Lady Lazarus." Ariel. Faber & Faber, 1965.

A celebration of Anna's life will be held at 6pm on Saturday, October 17th at the Santa Lucia Family Fun Center. All are welcome to attend.

Henry wasn't sure how to take the information, and so he took it like he was a distant stranger hearing the news thirdhand through a friend of a friend. He nodded gravely and clicked his tongue against his teeth. *The poor girl*, he thought. *She must have felt so alone.*

He was grateful that the family had published her note. He felt that so often victims of suicide and mental illness were swept away like embarrassments and whispered about or denied like taboos. *It was a great service they did her, and others who are struggling, to cast the light of truth on her situation.*

(You mean it was a great service they did you! Exempting you from your responsibility.)

Henry knew he had no responsibility. She had said it herself, there was nothing anyone could have done.

(You were her fucking PSYCHIATRIST.)

He was not so narcissistic as to put on himself the sole burden of her loneliness, especially after she had explicitly said otherwise with her parting words.

*(If you hadn't treated her the same way everyone else had, **maybe some**—)*

Henry shouted an unintelligible imprecation into the empty room and stood up so quickly that the blood rushed from his head and he felt dizzy. The office turned on its side and everything went dark.

15

Dull ache in the skull around his brow. The taste of vomit in his mouth. Antagonized by the unwelcome sunlight coming in from his oversized office windows. He felt like he could sleep where he was with his face on the hardwood floor for the rest of the day and night. But as the awareness of time came back to him, he panicked. What time was it? He couldn't let his next appointment see him like this. Was his office door open? Had anyone passed by and seen him? Surely not, he thought, or they would have stopped and checked on him or called for help. *Fuck, what if Will saw me? That nosy fuck would probably have taken me to rehab or something ludicrous like that.*

He thought of Anna Dempsey's green eyes pleading, for help or for affection or to be fucked and he couldn't tell the difference and he cursed himself for the person he was. He finally gathered the nerve to sit up and then he located his phone and reached for it. It was 12:01. He tried to recall the last ninety minutes, but he couldn't be sure how much of it had been spent in the lounger drinking in the relief from the Xanax and how much of it he had spent unconscious on the floor. Where his head had been there was a small puddle of vomit with chewed carrot and noodle chunks.

That's it.

Henry composed an email notifying the recipient that he had come down with an illness and would be canceling his appointments for the day. He BCC'd the names of his scheduled afternoon patients and sent the email. He pocketed his phone and walked to the door, stopped, turned back to his desk, pocketed the bottle of Xanax, and then left the office and locked the door. He left the vomit on the floor to be dealt with at a later time.

He hurried through the building with his head down, moving steadily and jolting around corners and down the stairs as though he were being chased by something, though the halls were quiet and empty. He made it to his car and once inside he relaxed his head back and breathed deeply and quickly for a moment before starting the ignition and peeling away from the parking lot with a long screech from the tires.

He stopped at the grocery store but didn't remember driving there or deciding that he would stop. He hadn't noticed the red light he treated like a stop sign, the woman in the car who had barely stopped before hitting his car broadside. He didn't see the young children in a passing van who tried to get his attention by pulling their mouths open wide and wagging their tongues at him. He hadn't been aware of the police vehicle that followed him for several blocks before diverging at a stop sign. He didn't remember walking into the grocery store even as he was sitting in his driver's seat with a fifth of Glenlivet in his hand and a liter of ginger ale and a banana on the passenger seat. He didn't know if he had paid or why he had a banana. He took two quick drinks before starting his car and then he walked into his house.

He lay on his couch with his whiskey and his banana, the ginger ale out of reach but offering moral support from the coffee table. The grandfather clock over his head chimed its dirge and rang out twice. He must have fallen asleep again. He sat upright and looked around. The TV was still on, muted. A panel of buttoned-down white people were taking turns speaking from within their own little squares on the TV. A bar across the bottom of the screen read:

Voice of God: More Deaths Today in Copycat Incidents around the Country.

He noticed for the first time how messy his house was, and he made a mental note to call a housecleaner and then applauded the demonstration of his progress and his recovery.

He had the ability to think about essentials like the mess in his house because for a moment he couldn't remember Anna's eyes or the words from her obituary or even what it felt like to be inclined to have sex with anyone. He couldn't remember so many things, or he chose not to

202

remember them: Gretchen's incredible smile that was always hidden from view; the price he had put on his soul that exchanged his psychiatric revolution for palliative care and a kick out the door; the cost of his insatiable wants and shortsightedness; the shame of his failings as a husband and a human being. He had forgotten shame itself. Pride too, and the feeling of desire. The obsession with anything that could make the mind feel alive. The anger at himself and everyone around him. All of it was drowned out and traded in for a head so heavy he had to hold it up with his hands and a room that rocked and spun slowly around him.

He even thought for a moment that if he could get his wits about him, Will's stupid fucking dinner party might be kind of fun. He would need to brew coffee and get some food in his belly. The clock chimed three times and he stood up and walked to the kitchen as though he had been alert and at the ready instead of drooling into his couch cushions with his eyes closed.

He prepared a pot of coffee and ate a few bites of tepid, stale noodles that had been on his counter since the morning. Being upright still felt too treacherous, so he brought the noodles back to the couch to wait for the coffee to brew. He saw the bottle of scotch on the couch but made the wise decision to set it on the coffee table and drink the ginger ale instead. He grinned as he poured the ginger ale through his teeth— *Another healthy choice.*

He dropped his head and rubbed his eyes, assessing whether or not he should nap once more before trying to get ready. He had to pick Will up in a few hours, and he would need time to clean up and refresh himself. He blinked several times and finally opened his eyes to see Gretchen's journal on the floor beside the couch where he had dropped it the previous night before passing out in a drunken stupor.

Fuck you, woman. No one cares what you think. We're moving on.

He glowed with pride at his remarkable resolve.

Then he picked up the journal and flipped through it until he found the blank pages toward the back. He turned back several pages until he found her scrawling ink covering a page.

It's what lovers do, god dammit.

In the dawn of romance when everything is hope, we're so quick to forgive. We temper the moods, sweetly. Softly. Everything is understandable. Everything excused.

Eventually, we must fight. We must stand up and contend with the moods; with words as our weapons we fight. To be heard. To be understood. We fight and we fought and then we moved on and forgot. We lived to fight another day.

At the end, we resign to each other. The misunderstandings and the tense mornings after. All our little moods.

I forgive you because I cannot fight you anymore.

Because, god dammit, this is what lovers do.

You can't be bothered to fight, you never really could.

Easy come or easy go, I know you and I always have. And I forgive you.

Because it's what we do.

I forgive you for what you believe, and what you do not know.

The fear you feel when you see the world spinning out of your hands and when you're still so unwilling to accept it, I forgive you for the way you fight to hold on to something that was never yours.

The words pour forth from your mouth in desperate attempts to make sense of it all but for all your little words somehow you can't find the one thing that you actually mean to say.

I forgive you for being afraid, and for all that you don't know.

I remember when we used to fight, I would have traded it all to have my way.

And I still miss her every day

But your words, your words, they just never stop

Your Malthusian rants, your diatribes on lifeboats and ethics, population control, the delusion of biological imperative

I forgive you for convincing me you weren't ready.

You were right, after all. It would have been a crime to bring her
into a world where she would be resented by her father
My only child, my little girl. For you I surrendered the fight.
And if it's the only kindness I ever do, then I'll surely be counted as
a decent mother.
Sometimes we must be so cruel, but it's what love would have us do.

The coffee pot let out a long shrill beep but Henry was already sober. He didn't possess the skills necessary to effectively digest what he had just read, and so every mental machination that drives a human being came to a halt in Henry Foster's brain. He breathed, he blinked, his heart beat. The room may as well have collapsed. The walls of the house could have turned to dust and blown away. The couch beneath him could have evaporated and he would have sat still, frozen in his pose with the book in his hand like a stone statue: *Man in Suspended Animation*.

The language was clear enough, even for her attempts at poetic device. There had been a child. A little girl. But Henry knew that there had been no child, no little girl. For all the years of quibbling and fighting and retreating and strategizing and broaching and approaching and resisting and arguing about the topic of whether or not to have children, there had never actually been a pregnancy. Not one that Henry knew of. In the years preceding their divorce, the talk of children had become so sparse that Henry believed his reasoning had finally registered with Gretchen and that she had thought better of the whole idea, or perhaps simply aged out of it.

He had never wanted children, but as the revelation of the journal began to sink in, Henry—to his own incredulity—was more angry than he had ever been in his life. He sat still on the sofa with the book in his hands, but in his mind he was rampaging through the house. Kicking over furniture, ripping the TV from the wall and throwing it through the living-room window. He saw himself picking up his phone and dialing her number, submerging his face in the screen and coming out the other end so he could yell directly in her face and spit on her and shame her for her crime. The clandestine murder of his unborn child. The secrecy of it all told him she knew it was a criminally despicable, heinous violation against him and against the sanctity of life, the sanctity of marriage, of their vows to one another, and their honor as human beings.

The clock chimed five times and he hadn't moved, or he had fallen asleep again. But in his mind, he finally broke the *Man in Suspended Animation* pose only to reach to the coffee table and take a drink from the Glenlivet bottle. Then he stood, calculated and deliberate, slowly and with the steadiness of a ballerina, and walked to the coffee pot to pour himself a cup of coffee. He added cream, sugar, and a splash of scotch and retreated to the bathroom where he would shower and get himself cleaned up for the dinner party.

16

Nick woke up multiple times during the day, only ever long enough to note the intensity of the sunlight and to try to gauge the time before surrendering again to sleep. He and Alison had talked until the sun came up about things that had seemed so important, so intimate, so crucial at the time, but now that the moment had passed, neither of them would ever remember what they had been. He had driven her home around 6:30, trying to get her there before her parents were up and about so that she wouldn't have to greet them from behind pupils like plates and a jaw locked tight.

He had chased tracks in the foil trying to catch sleep and eventually did around 9am. Before he did, his mother got home from work and came to check on him, but he had heard her coming and pretended to be sleeping when she came in, so she said nothing and let him be.

She had come into his room again before she left for work at 6pm, during one of his brief moments of lucidity. He again decided to feign sleep; he knew she would be troubled to find him still sleeping, yet relieved that he was home safe and still breathing instead of anywhere else and not. She urged him to get up, asked him if he was feeling alright, and told him that he couldn't expect to live like this forever if he wanted to stay at the house. He groaned acknowledgments and forced out, "I'm not feeling great," upon which she shut the door and left for work without another word. She texted him from the car in the driveway: "I love you, Nicky. I hope you feel better."

It was dark outside when the craving for a cigarette and the need to pee coalesced to a force strong enough to get him out of bed. He checked the time when he returned from the bathroom; it was 10:12pm. He crawled out his window and sat in the warm dark of the summer evening and jostled his hair with his fingers and rubbed his face. The world had left him behind again. A whole day had lapped him while he lay motionless in bed. There would be no reclaiming of this Wednesday in August, no redemption, no value at all. He had lived for the night, though; perhaps that was enough.

He had sat where he sat now with a girl whom he loved; he had listened intently as she told him stories from her childhood and about her ambitions and her benign little secrets. He had shared with her his home, his childhood bedroom, his secret eave, his attention. Being awake for the day was overrated, he thought. He would have traded any day, any progress, any life for a night with that girl. He was going to trade the drugs too. Any day now.

He had tried before he went to jail, but their hooks were too deep in him. That time, he had sworn he didn't need them—they had only been a proxy for a happy life, after all. Last December, Alison had offered him something real, and he meant to follow through. He would stop for a day but with the night would come the sweats, the aches, and the racing thoughts. The cravings would come by way of insidious voices and expert bargaining, bullying thoughts, empty promises, and procrastination. *We'll get clean. Just slowly. Gotta do it safe. Smart. Take some tonight. Take less next week.*

The weeks passed and Nick and Alison continued to see each other as they always had. There were no further talks of romance or the cessation of his drug use. Sometimes they would drink together, and once or twice he would bring her to Connor's place to pick up Adderall at her request. Mostly they smoked and stayed up late; she would complain about James's shortcomings, and he in turn would complain about the instability and unpredictability of his relationship with Lia.

Eventually, he stopped trying to try stopping. It wasn't deliberate; rather, it faded out of his consciousness like fog from the late morning sky. He knew the time to stop would come when it was right. Something would eventually give. And it did, earlier this year, in the spring.

For the year prior, Connor had been driving into the city and buying pills, cocaine, and Fentanyl from a small-time drug supplier named Chivo, né Kyle. After Kyle was arrested and was rumored to be cooperating with authorities to identify the local drug dealers and suppliers he knew, Connor cut ties with the city drug scene and had to find a new connection.

Connor began to order drugs in bulk from suppliers around the world via the dark web, believing it to be a foolproof method of acquiring product. The only vulnerability was in the physical retrieval of the packages from the mail. Connor rented several PO boxes at post offices around town and alternated deliveries between them for a while, until he felt he was becoming too recognizable, his trips too frequent. He began to offer cash to a few of the kids around town who bought drugs from him regularly for their assistance in picking up packages from the PO boxes.

Nick started running packages for Connor, sometimes several times a month. Connor paid him between twenty-five cents to a dollar per pill, or a comparable purse depending on the contents of the package, and Nick was plenty happy with the arrangement. It proved to be mutually beneficial, and since a healthy portion of Nick's earnings would be spent with Connor anyway, Connor was happy to continue the arrangement as long as he could. But all things pass, in time.

Nick was arrested on a rainy April afternoon after coming out of the Second Street post office with a sealed package containing 150 30mg bootleg oxys in his backpack. He was able to convince the arresting officer that he had ordered the pills online for his own personal use and he had no cash or distribution accoutrements on his person, so he was only charged with a series of felonies pertaining to possession and the illegal mailing of illicit substances.

Before the relentless anxiety and turmoil of the bulk of his time in jail were the first four days. Nick was thrust into a small cell in the infirmary wing of the county jail and left to exorcize the opioid habit in his own sweat, filth, and writhing pain until further notice.

He hadn't been able to consider the ramifications of his arrest. He hadn't been concerned with food, routine, or the duration of his stay. He didn't know what he was being charged with and it wouldn't have made a difference anyway. The goliath he was facing was the only concern he had and it alone was unassailable, galactic in size and scope, omnipresent and immutable. There was no avoiding it.

First came the restlessness, and with it the foul temper of desperation. He shouted out his window at any passing guards and jail personnel. He begged to see a doctor and called them rats and pigs and scum-sucking leeches when they ignored him. He tried to sleep, but his misfiring nervous system sent spasmodic shocks through his spine and into his joints and the deepest parts of his bones. He would stand and pace and scheme up plans to escape or to con the med staff into giving him pills until fatigue neutralized him and he would have to return to his bed until that too became unbearable.

Next came the delusions. With all of the systems of his body malfunctioning, his inability to sleep was joined by an aversion to food or drink. The sleepless nights, dehydration, and lack of food compounded the symptoms of withdrawal, and his brain began to wander to peculiar places and down grotesque and bizarre thought paths. In some worlds he conjured, his madness would never cease. There he was doomed to become one of the wide-eyed wanderers of the night like the people in the homeless camps outside of Alison's neighborhood, straddling two dimensions, with his body here on Earth and his mind inhabiting some other hell. In other dreams he found his predicament to be the highest demonstration of a nearly divine expiation which would earn him forgiveness and redemption in the eyes of his mother and even more so in Alison's.

He thought of her to no end. He cried huge, sopping tears of contrition at his inability to stop using when she had challenged him to do so. He paced in the middle of the night and laughed in manic hallucinations at how pleased she would be to see him when he came home clean and ready to usurp James's place next to her in bed. In short, erratic bouts of fitful sleep he would dream of her body on his, and he would wake up overstimulated and wet in his pants, filled with shame, and scream out at the absurdity of the whole scene.

Finally, after several nights, came the migraine and the dull ache of depression as the intensity of withdrawal waned and the reality of his situation began to emerge. He was forlorn and taken with a general antipathy of greater magnitude than he had ever felt, even at the most angst-ridden points in his adolescence. On the final day before he was transferred from the infirmary to the general-population module, he lay in his bed and thought of suicide. It was the first comfort he felt in days.

Over the course of the next four months, he spent an inordinate proportion of his waking hours preoccupied with drug-related fantasies. Persistent cravings and anticipation contributed to his claustrophobia and the severe time-distortion he experienced, but he fought against the obsession instead of surrendering to it. All along he maintained a belief that upon his release he would return to the world clear-eyed and free of the habits which had previously defined his lifestyle. He would return home with the strength and clarity of the sober; he would rise to meet himself in the life he was meant to live; he would be a man deserving and capable of loving and being loved. He would finally make good on those promises he had made to himself which he broke and then discarded and forgot about.

The first day out was an exception, he told himself. The months of incarceration had frayed his psyche and he needed respite, recalibration, a fucking break. He hadn't intended to use for more than that first night while he settled back into life at home and figured out how to move forward from there. But those things which troubled him before were still at home, unresolved and awaiting his return.

His hometown still felt like a foreign land in which he was a visitor, tolerated by some but ignored by most. Participation in the economy, the pressure to conform to the standard path of career development, and basic self-sufficiency still required compromises which he was unwilling to make and, frankly, was overwhelmed by. The time, the energy, the risk, the commitment necessary to survive all seemed to dwarf the paltry return he saw, and the dilemma only incited ire and obstinacy in him. He had some money saved from his endeavors with Connor and so he didn't feel immediately compelled to work, but he was not so senseless as to attempt to derive any future stock from the small sum he had today.

And lastly, Alison was still with James and had carried on in conversation with an unwavering opacity, and he was unsure if she even knew what she wanted or was doing. After the first night, all of the collected reasons to use or not to use for one more day favored heavily the idea that nothing much would be affected if he strung it out a little longer. He committed to buying a few days' worth of pills from Connor and using them without compunction until they were gone. And then he would be ready to say goodbye to them, forever.

He sat on the eave, smoking and trying to catch himself up to the night at the end of a day he hadn't even begun yet. His left hand was in the pocket of his sweatshirt, his index finger and thumb pressing around the small baggie of pills in his pocket, pinching each one, feeling for the edges and indentations of each, and counting as he went. *One. Two. Three. Four.* Each time he hoped for a fifth even though he knew it wasn't there—maybe he had miscounted or not seen one. He repeated the process almost unconsciously time and again.

He didn't think of wildfires. No burning stars or great floods. No life nor death, nor any season in-between. His thoughts were confined to the space between his thumb and his forefinger. He didn't wonder what Alison was doing. There was no time, no number, no life after *Four.* Only *one* again.

The short vibration in his pocket broke the spell and reminded him that he hadn't even checked his phone other than to look at the time. *Ahh, fuck.* For all the various bugaboos in jail, he hadn't missed the phone. The digital leash. It was a drain to his energy, the 24/7 call to *Answer me* and *Look at me* and *Give me your time your attention your soul* that came along with a device that hyperlinked the user to the world and every other person in their network, and he had been truly surprised at how much more stamina (and time) one had to fret and brood and pine without the constant compulsion to pick the phone back up again.

With the buzz came a full-body reaction. A hundred thoughts at once came to mind, each of them more urgently catastrophic than the last. *What could it be? Who? Why? Fuck.* The consciousness of time and space and money and obligations erupted from the placid surface of the liminal mind, and then his hackles rose and his shoulders tightened. He was sick with uncertainty, and there was almost no good news to be had.

It could be his mother, asking him for the nth time today if he was alright, to whom he would tell a lie that was convincing to neither of them. It could be Lia in a full-on tantrum, either enraged and sending a text-message assault or in despair and hurling snares of guilt and demanding that he soothe her suffering—also meriting a response of lies which would be convincing to neither of them. It could be Alison, though, which only turned his stomach back the other direction and intensified the visceral discomfort of the anticipation brought on by a single buzz from the phone.

He let loose a heavy sigh and pulled out his phone. There were only two missed notifications, and both were texts from Lia.

2:29pm: Heyy ... good morning?
10:30pm: It's one thing to be a
flakey POS but to just ignore
me all the time is fucking
rude. I'm sick of this bullshit.

Like diving into icy waters instead of wading in slowly, the stress of the messages was gone as quickly as he processed them. Lia being upset was nothing new; no worlds would end tonight. With no expression of sentimentality or penitence, he swiped the text thread away and opened Instagram. In seconds the content from the app crescendoed in an ear-splitting discordant rabble. The world was racing ahead at tremendous speed and he knew he would be left behind for good. The climate would deteriorate and become uninhabitable and the activists would use the last of the viable oxygen to take in breaths and scream *I told you so* in triumph. The chasm between political factions would no doubt bring forth a civil war which would be fought exclusively from computer keyboards and recorded in the court of public opinion, and everyone would be too afraid to go outside or look another human in the eye for fear they would let on in the wrong manner and find their reputations hoisted upon the petard of war and displayed as the Ultimate Price. Elsewhere the jesters and content creators of the internet tried to make light of the situation, and laughter poured from the gallows' spectators while the masses carried on and whistled as though none of it were happening at all.

Offended but ultimately ambivalent, Nick put his phone away and went back in his room to get high and try to sleep a little longer.

‡

Session transcript from patient files of Dr. Henry Foster
Patient: Wagner, Nicholas
10/31/22

HF: Wow, look at you. Jesus, you look awful.

NW: Professional and courteous as always, doc.

HF: I'm sorry, I just ... Wow, you ... are you okay?

NW: Yeah. Great. Hey, you look like shit too, what's your deal?

HF: I'm sure I do, thank you. What happened to you?

NW: Nah, fuck that. You go first this time.

HF: I'm sorry?

NW: I always go first. But we both know now that you're just as alone and fucked-up as I am, and you look like you got hit by a fuckin' bus. So you go.

HF: I think you've got the wrong idea of what we're doing here.

NW: I think you're full of shit, don't go acting all professional on me now. Don't forget, I know how you really are.

HF: I'm glad to see you're as confident as ever ... even in your current ... condition.

NW: Yeah, I get it, I'm fucked-up. Can we move on?

HF: You're not going to tell me what happened?

NW: Nothing. Just fuckin' James, Alison's boyfriend, or ex-boyfriend, I guess. I'm not sure what he is. But him and his neanderthal friends happened to drive past me in the liquor-store parking lot last night. They doubled back and jumped me like a bunch of pussies. Called me junkie and shit. Said I went too far this time and I deserve whatever is coming to me, and then they just stomped me out. It's fine, though. I'm fine. It's over. Wish they had just fucking killed me, but you can't win 'em all.

HF: I'm sorry, Nick.

NW: Don't be. It's my fault. I knew better.

HF: I—

NW: Don't. I don't want to talk about it anymore. I fucked up, they jumped me, it's over. Now. What's your issue?

HF: Well ...

NW: Mutual respect, doc. Reciprocity, you know? Quid pro quo, and shit like that.

HF: Hah. Alright. Fair. I may have had too much to drink this weekend. It's been a long, exhausting day and I'm about ready for it to be over.

NW: Funny.

HF: What's that?

NW: I don't know. The guy who's supposed to, like ... be helping me figure my shit out or whatever ... He's got the same problem as me.

HF: I'm sorry? How do you figure?

NW: Drugs.

HF: I assure you I don't have a drug problem.

NW: Yeah, but you do. See? You said you were divorced, you've been depressed, and all that shit. And now you're telling me you've been drinking too much. Drinking to make the pain stop. That's the same shit I do, just different substance. Isn't it?

HF: It's not exactly the same thing. First off, I'm not a drug addict.

NW: Denial isn't just a river in Egypt, doc.

HF: Cute. You know, though, you're probably right. I guess I do appreciate the insight. I have been indulging a little too much lately and it's definitely taking its toll on me.

NW: So? How's that different from me?

HF: Well, the difference between us is that I am aware of the negative consequences, and I will change my behavior as a result.

NW: And you don't think I will?

HF: Will you?

NW: Stop using drugs?

HF: Yes.

NW: Sure.

HF: When?

NW: I always figured that when it starts to hurt more on the drugs than it does off of them, then I'd think about stopping.

HF: And so ... how are you feeling now?

NW: Come on, man. You know I hate that fucking question.

17

Come outside
Better hurry, before I
change my mind.

It was 7:05pm and Henry was sitting in his car outside Will's house. He wore nice shoes with dark-blue jeans, a black tee shirt, and a button-down long sleeve with a black-and-navy-blue twill pattern. He believed that he could wash away the inebriation from the afternoon if he only showered long enough, so the hot water ran out before he had time to shave. Still, aside from his overgrown and unmanicured facial hair, his sallow skin, and bloodshot eyes, he actually had done a fine job of cleaning himself up from the state he had been in earlier that day. He was fortified by a blend of coffee and Glenlivet, measured out to what he believed to be the perfect ratio to keep him upright and socially lubricated.

Will emerged from the house and turned back to lock the door, and as he strolled to the car with that contagious charismatic grin of his, Henry smiled back and uttered atrocious words through his clenched teeth. He didn't want to be here, and he wasn't entirely sure why he hadn't been able to say no to Will at the outset or cancel on him at any point since. He felt that Will's assessment of him this evening could validate his state of mind, and he had been sick with the pressure of it for hours.

Who fucking cares what Will thinks? He's a single CPA at a low-level firm in a small suburb of a big city. He's nobody.

But Henry did care, and it infuriated him. Rather than stomp and piss and moan, he rose to the challenge and here he sat, in his car, half-drunk and full of all the rage of the fires of hell and smiling to his friend as he descended the driveway and approached the car.

"The illustrious Dr. Foster," Will said as he sat in the passenger seat and fixed his seatbelt. "Thanks for the lift. You ready to partay?"

"Do me a favor, don't ever say *partay* like that again, and then I'll do whatever you want me to do, deal? Besides, it's a party with all your friends from the firm at a chain bar and grill, right? Not exactly Studio 54, Will, calm down."

Will turned his head slightly and flared his nostrils twice, then squinted and looked around the car. "Jesus, Foss, you fuckin' drunk already?"

"Oh, Christ, don't start that shit with me. Who appointed you my fucking keeper, huh?"

"It's not that man, it's just . . . You want me to drive, maybe?"

"Not necessary, thank you. I'm fine, I had a quick pregame. A little Irish coffee to calm my nerves and give me some get-up-and-go. You're lucky too. I almost bailed on the whole thing."

Will nodded and sucked in his lower lip, then smacked his lips loudly and said, "Yeah, alright. Whatever you gotta do, man. I'm just glad you're outta the fuckin' house for once. This is gonna be good for you."

Will prattled about his day and the dynamics of his office, catching Henry up on politics and preparing him for who would be in attendance that night. Henry had intended to listen but couldn't find a place to anchor his interest; his thoughts were repeatedly pulled back to Gretchen and their daughter who never was.

After everything, all the nights, the months, the years I suffered . . . how could you?

To his mind, the foundation of his suffering all this time had been his struggle to make peace with and heal from his guilt. Gretchen had never known of his infidelity, and so that could not be counted as a factor in their divorce. Still, he knew he could have been a better husband. He knew that she wanted from him things that he had been unwilling or unable to give. She wanted his undying affection and the attention of his every moment, which he would have been willing to give had the conditions of life been different.

He had been obligated to earn a living, to work and to toil and to plan and to trudge from morning until night to be sure that she had a comfortable life, that their mortgage was paid and that she could spend her time in leisure and without having to carry the burden of worrying about money the way that he did. He had given her freedom, but she still wanted more.

He would come home in the evenings sometimes and find her despondent, writing in her journal or scrolling on her phone with languid eyes, offering a listless greeting without looking up to meet him. She mourned her loneliness and decried the distance between them. She would go on about how, even when Henry was home from work, in his mind he was somewhere else; in turn he found her thirst for his time avaricious.

Once or a dozen times, he couldn't recall, she had pleaded with him through tears that he should take some time off work so the two of them could travel somewhere uninterrupted and rekindle their romance.

"We spend every day together, Gretchen. Every night, I'm right here. Every morning, I wake up next to you. I don't know what more you can ask for aside from my every waking moment. And that's too much to ask, you'll never have that. It's absurd, you see that, don't you?"

And once or a hundred times, he couldn't be sure, she had retorted in disconsolation and contempt that it pained her to be told that her feelings were absurd.

"It's not your feelings, dear, it's your grasp on reality. You're just not being reasonable. I've given you all I can, and someday we'll have more time, but for now, we just have to be grateful for what we've got."

He suggested she find hobbies or friends, or work on her novel. He suggested she see a professional: a therapist, a psychiatrist. He recommended she get on antidepressants, try yoga, or exercise. He told her to be patient, to be grateful, to be rational. All of which she did.

And every single day since she moved out of the house, voices would chirp and war with each other, some certain that he had been inconsiderate, selfish. That he had been to blame for her unhappiness all along; that maybe there was something more he could have done. He drank himself through a hundred nights and a couple hundred more trying to make sense of just how he could have failed so badly to provide for her, despite his confidence that he had been doing exactly that.

And now, to find after all that she had harbored a secret so grave ... There was no doubt in his mind that the strain that her deception put on their trust and intimacy was the undoing of their life together. His guilt had drained from him like the last of the whiskey from every bottle he had known, and in its place he felt only scorn, and a righteous scorn at that. Tonight, Henry Foster was free from the suffocating penitence that Gretchen had placed on his head, and he would for the first time be uninhibited by shame.

Will was right, he thought, *this is going to be good for me.*

18

Nick's phone buzzed on the windowsill over his bed, again and again and again. He reached up to silence it, and within a minute the ringing began again. The incessant noise interrupted his sleep every time he dozed off, taunting him to the point that he sat up, ready to throw the phone out the window. He held it in his hand and strained his eyes to adjust to the vibrant light that collided with his endless sleep and opiate haze, and he tried to make sense of the commotion.

It was 11:49pm, still dark, and even at the coolest part of the night the air was warm and clear. He had six missed calls, all from Alison, and he couldn't be sure if he was awake or dreaming.

The phone rang again in his hand and a photo of Alison lit up his screen. The vibration continued and he stared at the photo. She was sticking her tongue out with a snarl on her lip and one eye closed, and he watched like an observer of his own life, staring at the phone until he was reminded that he was the actor and not the audience. He answered the phone, slowly. Skeptically.

"Hello?" He spoke as though he were greeting a stranger in the dark.

"Nick? Finally! Wakeup I needju to come get me, now," Alison said, but her voice was off. Her words came in lapses of emphasis at odd intervals and sounded obstructed, like she was under water, not whispering and not slurring but speaking quickly and quietly.

"Ali? What's up, are you okay?" he said, concerned but still not certain any of this was happening.

"No I'nnot okay, come gemme I'll texx you the address. Hurry up okay?"

"What happened? What's going on?" His senses were sharpening and his tone did in kind.

"Juss come. I sent you the address. Hurry up I needa getoutta here."

Nick looked out the window, again at the phone, and back. He tried to find something out of place, some anachronism or incongruity that would peel back the curtain on the dream or the hallucination he was experiencing. But around him everything seemed mundane and perfectly appropriate. He picked up his phone and his sweatshirt and made for his truck.

He followed his navigation to the address she had texted him. It was on the east side of town, in one of the neighborhoods that wound around the hills overlooking downtown. Nick didn't recognise the address, but he had driven in these neighborhoods plenty growing up. He had smoked weed where dead-end streets met the precipice under cover of night and high above prying eyes. In high school he had attended a few parties somewhere up here as well, but he couldn't remember exactly where.

He made his way up a street that rode along a crest of the hill and his navigation alerted him to an upcoming left turn down into the cul-de-sac where he would find his destination. He looked up from his phone and saw a figure in his headlights. Both of his feet pressed on the brake pedal; for a moment he thought he was about to collide with a pedestrian and the blood from every extremity rushed to his heart to keep it from stopping from the shock. The figure in the road had stepped safely onto the curb, and once the vehicle stopped she ran to his passenger door and climbed into the truck.

"Jesus *FUCKING* Christ, Ali, I thought I was about to kill you," Nick said between breaths so deep his jaw dropped wide open to inhale and his cheeks puffed out with each exhale.

"Well, good thing you didn't," she said dismissively, sounding annoyed. "Now drive, let's go."

Nick turned the truck around and started driving back the way he had come. "Where do you want to go?"

"Can we go to your house? Is your mom home?"

"No. I mean, yeah. Yeah, we can go there. No, she isn't."

"Thank god. Let's go."

He wanted to ask her a general *What the fuck*? but she was restless, fidgety, and looking back over her shoulder, and he didn't want to agitate her further. Plus, his golden-retriever allegiance to her was satisfied to have her by his side, and so he waited for her to fill him in on her own time.

19

Henry was seated at a table of nine in a chain bar and grill he had never been to before. Their table was in an annexed corner room at the back of the house. Out front were tables of families and college students positioned in a horseshoe around a central bar where a litany of flatscreen TVs broadcast various sports and news stations. The whole place was noisy, but not so loud as to impede on conversation at the table.

Henry had been introduced to everyone before he and Will took their seats. He knew the other CPAs in Will's office—peripherally, anyway—from sharing a building for so many years. There were the two brothers, Tyler and Todd, the titular *Sons* of Morgan and Sons CPAs, both conventionally handsome and unremarkable in their conventionality. Then there was Tyler's wife, Ashleigh, a woman who felt she must speak twice as loudly as anyone else in any given conversation lest she not be heard at all. She may have been right, though, for she was rumored to be a prodigious accountant as well as number one in client acquisitions at the company, and yet her name was not on the door. *Morgan and Sons and Ashleigh Too; Morgan and Co.; Morgan, Morgan, Morgan, and Morgan;* perhaps they just hadn't yet found the one that rolled off the tongue.

Maddie, the guest of honor, was seated in the center of the broad side of the table opposite Henry. She was Mr. Morgan's younger son Todd's fiancée—the soon-to-be Madison Morgan. Maddie worked reception in the Morgan office and Henry had had occasion to speak with her somewhat regularly in the few years that she had been around. The young woman presented meekly, but in the breakroom over coffee, while her lunch was in the microwave, Henry had been offered short glimpses into her mind via brief discussions of the day's news or other contemporary matters, and he found her to be oddly erudite, perhaps especially so, considering her modest station and reticent demeanor. He often wondered how she could possibly maintain any kind of intelligent conversation with Todd, whom Henry deemed to be intellectually analogous to a chimpanzee who happened to be proficient with a ten-key.

Next to Maddie were her two closest friends, Marlow and Truce. Marlow was a young-looking woman, likely with some Black ancestry, Henry figured. Her tight curls were cut into a bob that poofed out into a wide triangle framing her head and looked almost orange in the light of the bar. Maybe it had been bleached by the sun; he couldn't tell, but he thought it beautiful. Truce was Marlow's partner, a handsome young person of olive complexion with short, shaggy-by-design hair and baggy clothes. Had Henry been listening in the car he would have known that Truce was non-binary, but he had not been, and so he spent some time trying to discern their gender and wondering whether asking would be offensive or if it would be looked upon as proactive and considerate. He ultimately decided to say nothing and move on.

Seated at the corner adjacent to Truce was a stern-looking dark-skinned woman named Maya with a bald head and uncommonly good posture whom Henry immediately judged to be some kind of militant leftist type. He made a note to try to avoid saying anything that could be perceived as insensitive in front of her in case he should incite her ire and find himself the subject of privilege-shaming or some other such censure. When Henry shook her hand he found her comportment warm and welcoming, her smile wide, and her voice soothing and friendly. He felt a pang of shame at his initial assessment of her but remained wary regardless.

An excitable, talkative young man was taking drink orders around the table and Henry watched with a mounting and unreasonable apprehension as it neared his turn to order. The drink-order-taker had exchanged a pleasantry or compliment with every person at the table.

"Oh, are you two married? You're a lucky man," he said to Tyler and Ashleigh, and then held his hand over half of his mouth and loudly mock-whispered, "She's way out of your league," to Tyler, at which everyone laughed.

"You must be the birthday girl! Oh my god, aren't you adorable? We need to get you drunk, PRONTO!" he said to Maddie, and everyone cheered and laughed again.

He commented on Marlow's stunning hair and immaculate skin and everyone oohed and ahhed. Henry began to fidget with his fingers while the muscles tightened in his body.

Truce's top was gorgeous, and "Oh my god, you made it yourself. Look at you, little DIY wizard on our hands." Everyone at the table who had just learned of Truce's tailoring abilities marveled in awe. Henry thought the top looked like a white shirt that had met with dyes and scissors, but he had never been one for fashion. He swallowed hard and looked at the menu while the young man said something like "Okay, Jada!" before Maya ordered only sparkling water.

"And how about for gruff zaddy over there?"

What the fuck did you call me? He didn't look up from the menu and said, "Yeah, I, uh, scotch and soda, please? Top shelf. And don't be shy, I'll pay for doubles."

"All business. Doubles from the top shelf. Yessir." Then the young man saluted like a soldier while the table laughed again.

"Don't mind Henry, he's been going through a divorce and he's forgotten how to have any fun," said Will before ordering a vodka-cranberry and thanking the server for being so kind to them.

"Oh no, Henry, that's awful, I'm so sorry," said Truce, dripping with a genuine sympathy that made Henry uncomfortable.

"It's alright, you'll all get your turns soon enough. Except Will, the only one smart enough to play the field forever."

Glances were exchanged around the table followed by a reluctant laughter.

"Not us," Ashleigh said, leaning onto Tyler's shoulder and grabbing his jaw with her hand. "I'll kill him before I let him divorce me." Riotous laughter. Henry regretted ordering soda in his scotch, but he was grateful he had pushed for a double.

Through a series of interchanging micro-conversations and collective small talk, the table familiarized themselves with the newcomers, of which it turned out Henry was not the only one. Neither Maya nor Truce had met anyone else at the table besides Maddie, and Will and Marlow had never met, either. Henry participated, politely and as little as possible, and ordered a second drink before the dinner order was taken, at which time he ordered a third.

After everyone had ordered food, Todd looked down from one of the bar TV screens and said, "Have you all been watching this 'Voice of God' thing?"

Several people exclaimed or groaned in affirmation, and Marlow and Truce looked confused. "We don't watch TV, what is it about?"

"You two are so *fucking* cute," Ashleigh said in her booming voice and a mother of two children from a table in the main room looked up in disapproval.

"It's not a TV show, it's like an actual thing," said Todd, and then Todd and Tyler explained the situation in a rapid-fire back-and-forth.

"These astronomers picked up a signal from some star," said Todd.

"A nebula—a star-forming nebula, they think it is," said Tyler.

"Right, whatever, and it's broadcasting in like this morse-code type of pattern that repeats but is too complicated to not be by intelligent design," said Todd.

"Basically, a lot of stars and things in space can transmit electromagnetic signals, but usually they are very basic pulses and things like that. But this thing is sending out a full-on coded message, they think, and no one can figure out what it means," said Tyler.

"So, what is it, like, aliens?" said Truce.

"Maybe," said Todd.

"Of course it's aliens," Ashleigh shouted.

"Well, not necessarily. It could be a lot of things. It could be one of our own signals reflected back at us from the edge of space, or it could be totally random, something we just haven't discovered yet," said Todd.

"Do you listen to yourself when you talk?" said Tyler. "Do you have any idea how long it would take for one of our radio signals to reach the 'edge of space'—whatever that means—and come back to us? It would take billions of years."

"Not if it just, like, hit another planet or something. Sound reverberates off of surfaces. I heard them talking about it on a podcast yesterday. It's totally possible," Todd said. Some people laughed, but no one knew enough about space or sound to argue any further.

"Whatever you say, Einstein," Tyler said. "Either way, the crazy part is that people across the world have started calling it the Voice of God. They think that this star-forming region is actually the kingdom of God or something, and that we have picked up on an actual transmission from God himself."

"I'm sorry—what?" said Marlow, extending her neck out over her placemat and shaking her head in disbelief.

"No, seriously," said Todd. "There's, like, whole cults forming. Thousands of people have already done a suicide pact because this pastor from Pennsylvania claimed to decode the message and found these bible verses telling people to kill themselves and return to Godhead or something like that. It's crazy!"

"Wait, there's bible verses in the message? Is that true?" asked Truce, sitting upright and looking concerned.

"Well, no one has proved it, but the pastor says there are, and all kinds of people believe him," said Tyler.

"What do they say?" asked Truce.

"Basically something like, 'Armageddon is coming and this is your chance to get taken up in the rapture and return to me.' And he took it to mean 'by killing yourself,'" said Todd.

"Well, he claimed the bible verses were in there, but he also, like . . . retranslated them. He said . . . dammit, what was it?" said Tyler.

Todd jumped back in quickly. "He said that the bible verses use the word 'repent,' but that the Hebrew word for 'repent' was . . . umm, 'teshuvah,' I think, *actually* means to 'return' and that we've been mistranslating it all along."

"Okay, but still, what part of that means to kill yourself?" asked Marlow.

"They are talking about the spirit," said Maya, calmly, interjecting for the first time. "They believe that by killing the physical body, they are rejecting the temptation of the material world and thereby setting their spirit free. A spirit which they believe will be welcomed by God into his kingdom."

"Yeah, exactly, thank you, Maya!" Todd exclaimed.

"It's bullshit," said Henry, and the table became silent as everyone looked at him.

"Which part?" said Truce, leaning forward to rest their chin on their upright fist.

"All of it," Henry said.

"Oh god, here we go," said Will, rolling his eyes and his whole head. "Buckle up, everyone, Captain Buzzkill is here to shit on your sandwiches." Henry looked at Will and raised his palms from the table in surrender.

"Never mind," he said.

"No, go ahead, let's hear what the good doctor has to say about it," said Maya.

Henry—self-conscious, aware of how much he had been drinking, and still just present enough to be concerned about offending Will's friends—looked at Will, who stretched his mouth upwards and nodded in approval, and then he began. "All of it. First of all, signals come from space all the time and we don't know what a lot of them are. We blame pulsars or black holes or exploded stars, but even when the frequencies and patterns don't fit what we would expect to see from such things, we still assign it to a neutron star or just call it a mystery from a distant galaxy and move on. This is just another bizarre phenomenon they are using to fill the news cycle and sell ad space."

"Don't you think they would offer a correction once people started killing themselves though?" asked Marlow.

"Is that a joke?" Henry said sharply and scoffed. Marlow flinched, almost imperceptibly, but the most observant would have detected that her posture shifted backwards in her chair and her expression soured slightly. "The western media and information conglomerate has to have more blood on its hands than any military force or organization in history. It's been complicit in worldwide genocides, wars, crusades, and unspeakable hoaxes on the public since its inception.

"But beyond that," Henry continued, unfazed and not looking at anyone in particular, just moving his eyes from point to point on the table as though he were addressing subjects that no one but him could see, "the whole 'repent/return' thing is asinine and demonstrates just how fucking stupid people behave as soon as God gets involved. The verses he supposedly *translated*—by the way, he didn't translate anything, he *divined* them, AKA made 'em up. Anyways, that verse about *repenting* was from the Book of Revelation, which was written hundreds of years after the Hebrew Old Testament, and so it was written in *Greek*, not Hebrew, which he would know if he even studied the religion that he just died for. So this business about mistranslations is just a fabrication, a phantom, a red herring of sorts. Some detail so obscure that it makes him seem credible, but he's just a fucking narcissistic loony with a messiah complex who wanted to go down in history like the rest of them. Jim Jones, David Koresh, Shoko Asahara, Marshall Applewhite, Jesus fucking Christ, and any other demented, suicidal cult leader in history.

"And finally, all of that should go without saying, because the big, gigantic fucking elephant in the room that no one wants to acknowledge, not even the 'scientists who remain baffled,' is that there *is. no. fucking. God.*" Henry let out a long, hearty laugh and finished the last of his third double scotch and soda. Then he reached up and snapped his fingers, looking around for the waiter. When the excitable server boy saw him, he nodded from across the room and raced into action to put in another drink order.

"Alright, thank you for coming to Dr. Foster's TED Talk everyone, you can exit through the gift shop," said Will as he put his hands on Henry's shoulders and rubbed his neck a little too hard.

"You don't believe in God?" asked Maya, altogether unmoved.

230

Henry looked up at her and snorted. "What, you do?"

"Sure," she said.

"You're kidding."

"Why is that so odd to you?"

"Well, forgive me for saying so but ... isn't it a little ... ironic? I mean ... do you think your ancestors were worshiping the Father and the Son and the Holy Ghost before the white man arrived on their shores with his big empty boats and brought them out west for re-education?"

"Whoa, Jesus, Henry, easy, easy," Will interrupted, with a nervous laugh.

"It's alright, Will, we're just talking, you don't need to take it personally," Maya said.

"Yeah, *Will*, the adults are talking. About *adult* things." Henry was slouching with his elbows resting on the table now; he was beginning to slur.

"You're not wrong, doctor, in some senses. I do question your choice of words, but I understand what you mean. The problem as I see it— and it's so common among people of Western European descent—is that you're confusing the concept of God with what you've been shown by Christian fanatics in the west and, rightfully so, you're repulsed by what you've seen, yes? And so now you've closed your mind to anything resembling a God concept. Anything close to the divine. Probably to anything beyond your own reasoning, is that right?" Maya said, her face still warm and her shoulders straight.

"There is nothing *beyond* reasoning. Reasoning is the means by which we get anywhere else. There is no *beyond* that," Henry said.

The rest of the table was silent. Tyler and Todd looked like they were being interrogated by the police about some crime that they almost certainly committed. Ashleigh wore her eyebrows high on her face and an open-mouthed smile, frozen in place. Will was looking down, massaging the bridge of his nose with two fingers.

Maya smiled and said, "But our reasoning is limited by the capacity of the human brain itself. A three-pound slab of gray matter and nerves. And you, in your best judgment, would bet the whole of eternity that this ball of meat in your head is capable of infallible reasoning? That it could begin to comprehend the scope of the infinite, the timeless, the face of the formless, the invisible, the will and the why of the incomprehensible life force of everything?" Maya asked, then continued, "This is the unfortunate state of the world these days, I suppose. So many of us are so certain that our opinions, our beliefs, are sacrosanct. Paramount to the exclusion of all others. In this great big world, full of colors and experiences and ideas and all sorts of perfectly reasonable theories for questions which we have yet to find definitive answers, we are still so guilty of believing that what we think we know is enough to dismiss the significance of all that we don't. It's sad . . . It's such a limiting way to live. Don't you think?" Maya looked around the table, and everyone nodded. Truce and Marlow clapped their hands and cheered and then looked at each other and laughed at their spontaneous synchronicity.

"The fallibility of belief and the presumption of *God* are not the same thing." Henry squeezed his eyes, shook his head back and forth, and continued, "You know, that's not even an argument, what you said. You more-or-less just said 'Hey, what if? Wouldn't that be *grand?!*'"

Henry threw his hands up and knocked over a glass of water which spilled onto Will's lap. Will jumped up out of his chair and cried, "Jesus, Foss, get it together!"

Maya just looked at Henry, and when he finally looked back at her, she spoke with a wistful smile and her brown eyes softly shining with wonder. "But Henry, look at you. Angered to tears at even the prospect of something bigger than you. If this is what being right looks like . . . then I have to ask: What if you *are* wrong? *Wouldn't that be grand?*"

The server arrived at that moment with the first trays of food and Henry's drink, and that conversation was interrupted, not to be resumed. The party ate and returned to smaller discussions among seatmates, and an overall sense of relief at having avoided near disaster washed over the table.

Henry poked at his food through dinner and involved himself in no discussions but smiled politely from time to time when he would meet the eyes of someone else at the table. He continued drinking.

After dinner was complete, the waitstaff brought out a custom cake for Maddie that Truce and Marlow had brought for dessert. The gathered party sang "Happy Birthday" and commended Maddie and offered well-wishes while cake was cut and served.

Marlow cleared her throat and beckoned everyone's attention and the table obliged. "Everyone, I don't want to take away from lovely Miss Madison's party, but ... Truce and I have an announcement." She grinned nervously and looked down at Truce whose face shone a smile as bright as all the lights in the restaurant. Several gasps were heard around the table, as if everyone knew already.

"Truce is PREGNANT!" Marlow exclaimed. The table cheered and applauded and Maddie held her hand to her chest and her eyes filled with tears. Around the table people stood and offered handshakes and hugs and congratulations, except Henry, who sat still in his chair. As the guests returned to their seats, Henry was heard to mutter, "Poor fucking kid, Jesus."

"What was that, Henry?" said Truce.

Will's nostrils and eyes were wide and he looked like he might slap Henry on the back of the head, but he just said, "Don't listen to him. He's wasted. Poor bastard doesn't even know what he's saying. I should probably get him a ride home, actually—"

"I don't need a ride home, and I'm not wasted, yet. Thanks, Dad," Henry said. The guests at the table sat, again taken aback with shock, uncertain as to how to proceed. They looked to Truce and Marlow for guidance, or for action.

"Do you have a problem with people having babies too?" asked Marlow, her words strung together on a taut thread of impatience.

"I do. And you ... You of all people should know better," said Henry.

"What the fuck does that mean?" Marlow asked.

"Henry, let's go, enough of this shit. You've had enough, no one wants to hear your bullshit." Will grabbed Henry under the armpit but Henry shook him off quickly.

"No, Will, let's fucking hear this. It's gonna be good, I'm sure," said Marlow.

Will sat back in his chair and closed his eyes, likely replaying all the chances Henry had given Will to disinvite him and wishing he had taken any one of them instead of being so insistent that Henry come.

"I don't mean anything by it, you've got the wrong idea," said Henry. "It's just that I thought you queer folks were supposed to be at the forefront of progress. Shattering the paradigm and all that. You're the last people I would expect to succumb to the basest of biological imperatives." Tyler and Todd looked at each other nervously and sat bolt upright and went even whiter than they already were. Ashleigh continued to look as amused as ever and Maya just shook her head slowly, her eyes fixed on Henry.

"What does being queer have to do with having kids, Henry?" Marlow asked.

"Fuck that, babe, we don't have to listen to this bullshit," said Truce.

"You have the wrong idea!" Henry said. "I don't mean to disparage you. I support the community, I'm down for the cause and all that. Believe me, I voted against Prop Eight, I can't stand what you people have had to endure at the hands of the fascists and puritans running amok in this country. I just mean to say that . . . Well, I thought you knew better. I thought you wouldn't be blinded by biology. I mean, forgive me if I'm wrong, but there isn't a penis between the two of you, is there?"

"HENRY!" shouted Will.

"Shut the fuck up, Will, we got this," said Truce, holding their hand up to silence Will. "No, neither of us have a fucking dick, Henry, what's your point?"

"It's just that! You haven't let biology dictate your gender and you haven't let society dictate your lifestyle. Why would you let them influence you to procreate? Why? I can only imagine how much trouble you must have gone to. Without the male reproductive system, it couldn't have been easy—it's like taking two negative numbers and making a positive number out of them."

"That's how math works, *doctor*," said Truce, who then grimaced and stuck out their tongue.

"No . . . that's only in multiplication, actually," said Todd, finally contributing something.

"Yeah, but isn't reproduction like multiplying?" said Tyler.

"Not really, I think it's just addition. Like adding two people together, not multiplying them," said Todd, squinting his brow and looking down at his hands.

"No way, you idiot, then it would be like one plus one equals two, but it doesn't. Mom plus dad equals baby, so it's three. Which means it's exponential. Definitely multiplying," said Tyler.

"Is that right?" Truce looked to Maddie, who sighed heavily and shook her head, looking around the table.

"Well, no. It's more complicated than that, really. It's not a direct sum of added parts, and—sorry, Tyler—but it's definitely not exponential. Because the same two parents can increase the size of their family incrementally by repeating the procreative process. Right? So, I guess one and one could equal any number, depending on the variables of existing family size and number of offspring conceived in a single pregnancy. So then, it would require an algorithm—more like a polynomial recursive equation where each iteration in the sequence would be contingent on the solution to the previous equation *and* another variable, which could change every time: it could be one, or two for twins, or three for triplets and so on." Maddie laughed timidly and looked back at Truce. "But, that's not really the point, I guess." Everyone was silent.

"Well, god dammit," Truce said, blinking at Maddie repeatedly before looking back across the table. "Anyway, fuck you, Henry, whatever the fuck you're talking about. One plus one or negative pa-la-mo-nial shits, it doesn't matter. Me and my wife are having a fucking *baby* no matter what you think about our biology, is that alright with you?" Truce said and slapped both of their hands on the table.

"It's not about your biology. I don't care about your biology. I only meant to say that I was surprised. I'm sorry, maybe Will's right, maybe I am too drunk for this type of thing." Henry paused to assess the trajectory of his speech and whether or not he should continue, but before he could make a determination, he found himself continuing in a grave and measured tone. "The world is dying. We are killing it. We are killing each other and we are killing ourselves, and the worst part, my dear, is that we can't even agree that it is actually happening. World governments and political factions are warring about whether or not climate change is even real. The gulf between factions is growing so wide that reconciliation doesn't seem feasible to even the most optimistic mind. There is no way we will survive this mess we've created. People think God is telling them to commit suicide in morse code, and they are doing it. People are in the streets with assault rifles and dynamite hunting subterranean mole-people because a president told them to. Accusing radical factions of aligning with actual *mole-people* to steal secrets and influence government affairs. And all the while, multinational corporations are raping the planet and then telling us to drive less and watch our consumption while keeping us at each other's throat about ... gods and wild conspiracies and disputes over how people should be allowed to express their gender or, or, or their sexuality, and other such relics from the dark ages. This is my point! The Voice of God people *are* right. The end times are here. But not because God willed it. We've done it to ourselves. We've doomed *ourselves*. And bringing a child into this world at this time is nothing short of ... cruelty!"

Henry's red eyes stared off to some place that was miles and miles or entire worlds away from the table at the restaurant and tears ran down his face. His heart was gripped with the pain of thousands of such arguments with Gretchen over the years. Arguments which always ended in her crying and him breathing heavily, panting like a dog on the front porch while he tried to compose himself enough to earn his way back into her favor.

"I just don't understand why everyone is so hung up on this *need* to have a fucking *child* of their own. It's the height of narcissism, of delusional grandeur, of egotism!"

Sometimes we must be so cruel, he thought, and he looked across the table at Truce, wondering if they too would cry or if they would spit on him or perhaps pummel him into the ground. He welcomed any outcome.

The rest of the assembled party looked horrified and supremely uncomfortable. Some scowled in disgust, and some seemed to pity Henry's state. Marlow sat at the ready, looking like she might strike at him from across the table. Will was sitting as low as the arms of his chair and looking up and away from the table, defeated.

Truce looked at Henry's sunken, bloodshot eyes and shook their head. "Dude. You are seriously fucked-up." Then, after a moment, they laughed. The table commenced to laugh behind them—whether it was from the awkwardness of it all or because they saw any humor was unclear. If nothing else, they seemed to be grateful for the break in the tension.

"Imagine just giving up ... " Truce said after the laughter died, their lips pulled up one side of their face in an incredulous sort of smirk. "Imagine if we just gave up. Like ... yeah. The world is fucked-up. It's scary, man. People out there are calling for ... eradication of trans folks. It's totally cool to just hate Muslims, cops are still killing black people in the streets like it's Jim Crow, fuckin' Nazis are running wild. We got trillions for wars that ain't even our business, but we can't feed babies here at home? Or provide, like ... basic fuckin' health care to our own people? And yeah, everyone *is* fucked-up. This country just beats it out of us, it seems like. Like we're fighting for our lives, all of us. We're all fucked-up. Man, you're fucked-up, look at you. But still ... imagine if we just gave up?

"Dude ... Life only *comes* from life. All this ... anger you have, all this anger without any hope—it just perpetuates anger. Perpetuates pain. So, which side do you want to be on? Because me and my wife, and my people? We're fighting this motherfucker until the end. We're not giving up. Shit, your generation didn't save the world. Ours probably won't either. But maybe we're learning, you know? Maybe my kid will be smarter than me. Smarter than you. Maybe their kids will actually be able to figure it out. And you . . . you just wanna give up, because, what? You can't handle it? How can you possibly look around and say everyone else is so fucked-up and all that, when you're just gonna sit there and drink yourself stupid and fuckin' . . . just bitch the whole time?

"I'm sorry, man. But . . . you need help. I hope you get it, I do. You ain't stupid. You're an asshole. But hey, you voted. Thanks for that, I guess."

Henry sat, his cheeks wet. The restaurant began to spin. No one said anything for a good while.

‡

"And how's everyone doing over here? Can I get y'all any more drinks?" To everyone's relief, the excitable server could not read a room.

Will sat up and said, "Thanks, everyone, for having us. Happy birthday, Maddie, I'll see you tomorrow, okay? I'm gonna take him home. Sorry. Just . . . sorry." He stood up and added, "Come on, Foss, gimme your keys."

Henry reached in his pocket and handed Will the keys to his car, downed the remnants in the glass in front of him, and rose to leave the restaurant.

They didn't speak a word on the drive to Henry's house. When they arrived, Will said, "My Uber will be here in a minute. Go inside, get some sleep."

"Will . . . I'm sor—"

"Don't be. It doesn't matter. Get some sleep, Foss."

Henry walked slowly to the front door and patted his pockets for his keys. Will reached around from behind him and unlocked the door, startling Henry so badly he nearly fell over. Will only shook his head, then turned to walk away.

Another 2mg tablet and a shot of Glenlivet and Henry couldn't remember the events of the evening, the day before, or anything at all about his life. He lay in his bed fully clothed and he felt nothing at all but tired.

A wonderful night, indeed.

THURSDAY

20

"Can I borrow a sweater and some comfy pants?"

"Yeah, hold on," Nick said and went to find what she needed. He returned with a pair of black sweatpants and a hoodie, perfect to fend off the post-midnight summer chill. She stood up and pulled her tee shirt over her head and removed her jeans. Nick had never seen Alison with her clothes off, and under other circumstances he might have enjoyed it more. However, under these circumstances, he only felt an impatient concern, and a little self-conscious at the non-negligible bit of gratification at the fact that she had so casually undressed before him. She was comfortable with him. Trusted him. This mattered. It mattered more than the way her thumbs squeezed the waistband of her jeans to pry them from her body, exposing the black lace-trimmed cotton briefs beneath, though he did notice—and then looked away.

She dressed and moved back to the bed, crawled across to the corner, and tried to untangle the sheets and blankets.

"Why are boys so chaotic? Jesus, Wagner, how do you sleep like this?"

"Why are girls such princesses?" He put on a high-pitched voice and said, "Ooh, Nicky, I can't be comfy if the blanket isn't just right."

"Oh my god, shut up. You are the weird one here."

After seeing she was comfortable, Nick slid open the window and moved to get a cigarette.

"Don't go out there. Come here, sit with me."

He made a convincing show of looking inconvenienced as he shut the window and moved next to her in the bed. He sat with his back against the wall and she laid her head in his lap. It was usually difficult for him to resist looking past these gestures—the closeness, the affection—to try to find some promise of something deeper between them than the friendship they shared. But as she lay on him tonight, he felt at peace. Maybe there was no further to go. This could be his entire life from here on out and he would be alright with that. Happy, even.

She could share her body with other men; they could take it, for all he cared. All he wanted was her time, her heart, her trust. He knew secrets of her childhood that she would never tell James in a hundred lifetimes. He knew all the ways that other men had let her down. Romances would come and go; the fickle, fleeting whims of the heart and compulsive cravings of sexual chemistry would wane upon their consummation, eventually declining into monotonous repetition and leading to a need for something new, and under midnight cover, when their lovers had returned to their homes, Nick and Alison would seek refuge in each other and find a timeless and durable love that would not age or tire or decay but grow inward and outward, spreading its roots deep and its reach wide until it was a furtive glen of solace that they both could call home forever.

He did not need to possess her, and she would not be possessed. He knew she needed him, and they needed each other. This had to be worth more than the rest of it. But the doubt nagged.

Maybe this was the consolation of a loser, he thought.

But it wasn't what he felt.

"You gonna tell me what happened tonight?" he asked, quietly but without whispering.

"Yeah," she said, motionless.

"... Well, then?"

"I just don't want you to flip out."

"Why would I flip out on you?"

"No, not on me. Well, also on me, but I just need you to be calm and be here with me, and not do that thing where you flip out."

"Ali, I'm not gonna flip out."

"Promise?"

"I promise."

She turned her body over to her other side so she was looking up at him now and nodded, then began.

"I slept, like, all day today. I got home and made a drink and smoked a little bit so I could sleep, and I just passed out. James called me, like, a million times. He was so pissed when I woke up and called him back—he

244

was just being a fucking psycho. So he says, 'I'm coming to pick you up,' and I'm like, 'Okay,' and he comes and we go back to his house and whatever. But he's being all sketchy and asking me all these questions and he can tell I'm fucked-up so I just told him what he wanted to know, you know? I was like, 'Yeah, I did some coke last night and I'm out of it,' and whatever and he asks who I did it with and where I got it and I told him it was Marcie, this girl from class, and he seemed like it was cool and we moved on.

"And then he starts being all nice and sweet, and he makes me food and asks me if I want a shot and so I take one and we put on a movie and it's all good. But then I fell asleep and he went in my fucking phone and opened all of our texts and he just wakes me up, like, *furious*.

"He's like, 'Are you fucking him? Are you fucking him?' and that's all he kept saying. I thought he was, like, mad about the drugs, but he just kept trying to get me to admit that I'm cheating on him with you and I tried to explain how we aren't but he just wouldn't believe me. And he asks me like, 'Did you get all coked out and fuck him?' but, like, really aggressively and he starts, like ... I don't know, Nick. Like being fucking creepy.

"And so he says, 'Do you wanna get coked out and fuck me?' and he's dead serious all of a sudden. And I don't even know what to say I'm so ... just, like, done with all of it, and I'm like, 'What the fuck is your problem?' but he starts pushing. Saying how it's only fair and that I owe him that much, and calling me a whore and a coke fiend and telling me that if I'll just do it with anyone then I had better do it with him."

Alison slowed and Nick could see tears pooling in the corners of her eyes, but she sniffled and shuddered a little and wiped her face and continued.

"And he starts like. Sitting on me. And I tell him to get off but he doesn't, he just says, 'If you love me, you need to show me. If you want this to work then you need to prove it,' and I start, like, freaking out and he grabs my wrists and holds me down and just won't stop talking. I freaked out, Nick. I kicked him in the dick, told him to get the fuck

245

off me, and he spit on my face and told me to get out of his house. I got up and grabbed my shit and just ran. I just ran, Nick, and I didn't know what else to do."

Her composure dissolved into loud, heart-wrenching cries and the tears poured forth from her face and pooled in expanding wet spots on Nick's tee shirt.

"I didn't know what to do. I didn't think he was going to let me leave," she moaned, her words getting choked up and caught between wails and whimpers and sniffles and hiccups.

Nick held his fingers in her hair and bit down on his own tongue until it bled. His mind was a montage of violence and love. Thoughts of murder and shelter, soft places to hide, protection and nurture and torture. It was hard to make sense of what should be done, but he had promised to do nothing, so he sat and caught her tears and snot in his tee shirt, and he ran his fingers through her hair now dampening with sweat and thought he might cry too.

"You're okay," he said. "You're okay. But I'm gonna fucking kill him."

She sat upright and wiped her eyes. "You said you weren't going to flip out. You promised."

"Who's flipping out? I'm not flipping out. I just might kill that fucking piece of shit—"

"Nick. Stop it. I don't need you to avenge me! Please, just come here. Just be here and be quiet. God, you're so dumb! How many times do I have to tell you to just be quiet before you get it?"

"Probably at least one or two more times."

"Ughhhhh, I could kill you, I swear to god."

She reached out her arms and fell onto him and they lay together for a time. The bedroom was hot. The August night rapped at the window and their bodies were close together after the frenzy of tears and emotions and in the friction of feelings they weren't equipped to contend with but felt nonetheless and they rested in the warmth of the other.

"He asked me if I liked you," she said after some time. "Before he totally flipped out. He said, 'Do you like that fucking guy or something?'"

She breathed a short laugh. "I said, 'No, of course not.'"

She sat up and looked Nick in the eye and he could feel the breaths from her nose on his mouth and his chin and he could smell the remnants of the soap she used to wash her face and the musk of the sweat in her hair. "I said, 'He's just a friend.' And I think he was right . . . I think I was lying."

It was unclear who did what next or how, but their lips met and sunk into each other's, and their breathing was calm and synchronized. His fervor was tempered by his fear of offending, of pushing too far and betraying her trust, but she guided his hands, a conductor keeping pace, and directed him carefully through movements. *Allegro! Let's go! . . . Now slowly,* she said with her hands. *Adagio, Adagio, move slowly,* she said. He followed instruction and then her hips picked up time and for a moment he gave in but then he backed up and said, "Ali, what are you doing?"

"Just shh. Nick, please."

"Are you sure?"

"Wagner, I swear to god if you don't shut up."

So he did. And there in wrinkled bedsheets, sweat-damp and tearful, with no plan for the future or presence of mind, the two surrendered to something unreasonable together. They gasped and they giggled and they struggled and paused, and they looked at each other for whole minutes at a time before resuming, and they both did their best, given their condition, and though neither quite got there they both were fulfilled.

They shared something like love, if love could contain within its embrace a space with no promises and nothing certain but fear and the feeling that they might die alone any second if they didn't make the most of this moment together.

They shared something like love, but neither knew what love was, or what it was that they shared. It was something, though, so it might as well have been love.

21

Henry stood in the night under street lamps. He was furious and had been shouting, but he couldn't remember at whom. A dog was barking, but he couldn't tell from where. This street looked unfamiliar, and he couldn't see his house. He looked up and down the street and then back at Gretchen, who stood in front of him with her arms out at her sides, saying something over and over, but he couldn't make out the words.

He shook his head like a dog drying itself and wanted to return to the point he had been trying to make, but he felt as though he had been thrust into an argument that he couldn't remember starting.

There were several dogs barking now. *They're surrounding me*, he thought. *These fucking hounds will rip me apart if I stay.*

You need to leave, Henry.

Please, leave.

You need to go.

"I know, I know! I fucking know, alright? They'll kill me if I don't get out of here," he growled.

Henry, you need to leave.

Leave!

Please! Why are you here?

Why am I here?

Gretchen was crying now, pleading with him; over and over this ghost from his past would not let him rest without shrieking at his face and crying out at him.

Henry! LEAVE!

"When did you do it, Gretchen?" he said, but the words sank in his chest like wet cement and he had to force them up with all his strength from the bottom of his throat.

What?

What are you doing? What the fuck are you doing here?

"WHEN DID YOU DO IT?" he shouted. "When did you get the abortion, Gretchen? Were you ever going to tell me?"

It's none of your business, Henry.

You're scaring me.

"WHEN?"

I called the police. They'll be here any second.

The dogs encircled him and he could hear them closing in. He knew he would feel the hot grip of their jaws on his legs and hands any moment. This was his last chance to get the answers he needed.

"Gretchen. I know about the baby. I know. I'm sorry. I'm sorry, I'm sorry, Gretchen. But please, I need to know. Did you do it before or after you decided to leave?"

A shrill sound from the distance, sirens maybe. The dogs barked. Henry fell to his knees and surrendered to the beasts. Gretchen looked down at him as he prostrated himself on the asphalt and wept, and with compassion and pity, she spoke.

It's already forgiven. I did it for you. For me. For her.

Henry, I spared you the burden of making the choice.

I did it for all of us so you didn't have to.

And I live with it every day so you don't have to too.

The shrill, wretched siren was so loud now it agitated dogs from every angle and the sky lit up all different colors and Henry felt canine teeth bite down on his wrists and he tried to scream.

22

Nick and Alison sat on the roof, naked under the comforter they had dragged from the bed, exchanging punctuated laughter and sharing a cigarette.

"So what do we do now?" Nick asked.

"Sleep, baby. Sleep."

"I slept all fucking day and then slept more until you called me. I feel wired now."

"Yeah, me too, actually."

Nick nudged her with his shoulder and made a dubious face. "So what should we do, then?"

"Hah, don't push it, Wagner. Do you have any weed or anything? I wanna, like ... get high and watch a movie and maybe we'll fall asleep. Doesn't that sound nice?"

It did.

"Yeah ... it does. I don't have anything, though. I think my mom has some vodka or some shit downstairs?"

"Bullshit."

"What?"

"You don't have anything but your mom's vodka? I call bullshit."

"I mean ... I don't have any weed or anything. Nothing you'd like."

"Oh, come on, don't hold out on me now. There's no more secrets between us, Nicky."

She looked over at him and her blue eyes caught a glint of the white street lamp and for a moment her eyes sparkled like the clear summer night's sky.

He saw the impossible violence of all the stars in the sky reflected in the calm and hopeful eyes of a single young girl, and for a moment he thought that he finally understood what the sky had been saying to him all along; that he saw in her eyes what it meant to be alive.

"Come on, what do you have?" she said again.

Confounded in the moment, he squinted as though he thought he might be able to look past her words and into her intentions, or maybe into the future for some sign that it would be alright. He wanted to get high too, but all he had to offer were the same pills from whose grip he had been working to extricate himself. He tried to consider all the ways it could go wrong and whether he even had the resolve to resist her now when he had never been able to resist her before.

He saw years unfold before them. He saw them sharing an apartment in San Diego like they had talked about so long ago. In one vision she sat on a couch and tried to focus on schoolwork while he pestered her repeatedly for attention and they laughed and kissed and she shoved him back to his side of the sofa. In another they were old, gaunt and lifeless, shivering and shuffling down the streets of Western Santa Lucia, avoiding the eyes of the drivers of passing cars and arguing about who would get the last hit. He saw her shaking on a jailhouse cot, gutted and alone, as he had been. He saw them in bed together, smiling and drifting off to sleep. He saw James coming toward him, red-faced and sadistic. He saw her waking to a mundane morning and quietly returning home, and another year of pretending like a night between them had never happened at all.

"You do have something, don't you? I can't believe you're actually trying to hold out on me! Don't you want to just cuddle up and get high and go to sleep?"

Her eyes kicked out sparks that lit him aflame and in that heat all his attempts at consideration melted to soft puddles of inconsequence. "Yeah, I mean, I have some pills, but they aren't the kind you like," he said.

"How do we know I don't like them if I've never tried?"

"I guess I can't argue with that. But Ali, if we do this, it's only going to be this once, okay? I mean, I'm quitting once these last few are gone anyway. So that's it. For both of us. Tonight. Deal?"

"God, you're always so dramatic, aren't you? It'll be fine. Trust me, I have no desire to sit around and get high all day. One and done, captain. Promise," she said and gave him a Scout's salute.

"Alright, well," he said, and took one long drag from the cigarette before flicking it off the roof with conviction. "Come on, then."

They crawled in the window and she went to the bed while he dug around for his pills and then went to his desk to retrieve foil and an empty pen tube.

"Can I see them?" she asked, her voice soft with curiosity and trembling slightly.

He tossed the small baggie of pills onto the bed and she picked it up and inspected them closely.

"What are they?" she asked.

"Oxys. I think. I don't know, they come from China because you can't get them here anymore. They might be bootleg but they're good either way."

"So this is the shit that you'd rather do than run away with me, huh? Better be good, Nicky, or I might get my feelings hurt."

He froze and looked at her, stung, and she erupted in laughter.

"You're such an asshole," he said.

"You love me."

"Yeah ... I do."

"So what do we do?" she asked, looking up over the bag and into his face as he sat beside her on the bed with all the tools in his hands.

"I'll show you, come on. Come sit on the floor, though, I don't smoke in bed. I don't like it when my sheets get all sooty."

She nodded and scrambled across the bed, and they sat next to each other on the floor. In silence and with focus he tore off a piece of foil and folded it just enough to create a small valley for the pill to run down as it burned. He took a blue pill from the baggie and set it on one side of the foil. Alison watched closely and didn't make a sound. He put the pen tube in his mouth and held it just above the pill with the lighter just beneath the foil, but he paused before he lit the flame. He looked up at Alison one more time to be sure she was okay. He nodded with questioning eyes, and she nodded back in reassurance.

Together they smoked and for a while neither spoke. Nick cautiously observed Alison's reactions and behaviors, but after a few hits from the foil did not bring the sky crashing down, his tension released and he let himself enjoy the moment. At some point the silence of the room was broken by a series of soft, syncopated giggles from Alison's mouth. She leaned back against the bed and looked around the room with heavy eyelids until her eyes met Nick's, and she laughed again.

"Okay, Nicky, okay," she said all breathy and thick, "I see you. I see you. Oh my god, is this the perfect night, or what? Mmm. I am ready. *For. Bed.*"

Nick watched her with some relief. She was enjoying herself; she was calm. She was happy. He became aware that this was the first time in years that he could remember getting high with someone other than Connor. And even then, usually when he got high he was alone and ashamed and trying hard to hide it. He thought to himself that there might be some divine beauty in sharing his last time getting high with the girl he loved. He decided that he would finish the bag that night, and in doing so he would set himself up for the perfect transition from his old life to his new one. He would wake up with no drugs, and instead with her, and together they could begin *Day One* of the life for which he believed they both had been waiting.

"Yeah," he said, "I'm almost ready too. Why don't you go lie down, I'm gonna just finish up real quick and I'll be right there."

She laughed and agreed, but stayed seated, smiling, and peacefully hummed something he recognized but couldn't identify. He put the last two pills on the foil at once and smoked them with a hunger. He held his breath and watched her face as he blew out smoke, and he repeated this again and again until the tracks on the foil were a crisp black ash and produced no smoke when he burned them.

He sat back against the bed and listened to her humming. It was so familiar, but the fact that the words to the song or even the name of it escaped him created a surreal effect and the tune became something like the soundtrack to a dream. In every moment the answer seemed right on the tip of his tongue, but when he tried to speak a word of the lyrics he couldn't recall what should come next.

She rested her head on his shoulder and continued to hum, and he closed his eyes and thought that if ever there were a moment that he wished he could bottle up and hoard and drink in sips of for eternity then this would be it. Naked and intimate, warm and entranced, sitting together atop the crumbled wreckage of the walls they had always maintained between them; he thought that this might be the perfect night. Soon, only the sound of her humming and the tranquil darkness of the night remained. His thoughts were reduced to a whisper, barely perceptible at all.

There is no light. No tunnel. No end in sight.

Whatever color once existed, now there is just absence. Here it's only dark.

There is no sound, no hum, no beating heart.

No fear. No feeling. No sense at all.

But there is something familiar. A longing, a memory, an ache. Now I am forgetting it again.

There is no light. No color. No place, only ~~everywhere~~, ~~now~~here. I am lost and I am tired.

I remember something.

Once everything was moving so fast, I remember now. There were voices gnawing, lingering resentment, hostility and panic. There was anticipation, disappointment. Secrets were weapons and the rest of it just routine naive compromises. Tools for coping. Try again. Learn your lesson. Grow from this. All things pass in time. It was exhausting.

Though there was something sweet, I can't remember—too tired now to care.

There is ~~nothing~~ here.

I remember there was sweetness. There was soft skin. Tongues touched. Electricity in our bones and we could not keep anything to ourselves.

Later salt drops wetted cracked lips and hard words fell in domino trainwrecks. There was love, and there was fear.

I don't recognize this place. I don't see you here. I've never seen you before.

I remember almost nothing. Nothing but hope. Less than hope, if we are honest. Dumb, blind optimism without the option to opt out for fear of losing touch with the one thing that brought us home safely each night: the will to survive. The breath and the blood. The automaticity of existence and the unsolicited impulse to wake up just one more time. The discomfort and disappointment. Impatience and despair. I feel only their absence and cannot identify the void they filled.

Still, there are fragmented reflections in the folds of this expanse.

This starless sky.

This tepid vacuum of space.

Unrecognizable, but familiar. Instead of finding meaning in any of this, I find relief. I have forgotten so many things and I am too tired to care.

There is so much here. There is nothing here. I don't remember skin. I don't remember soft. I don't know what I've forgotten anymore, and I am tired of fighting.

There is no light
no beginning
no end
There is no me.
no earth and no you
no suffering
no joy
no hope
no hunger
no disappointment.

Only abstract—only tired now—only relief. These things don't matter anymore. They mean nothing. I don't know that they ever meant anything at all.

I have forgotten again. This is all we are.

There is no light. There is nothing.

I'm sorry, I don't remember you as you were. I don't know you as you are.

And I,

I am comfortable now.

PART II

23

Marion lay flat on her back atop the covers of her bed. Outside, the sun was setting, but inside her small apartment the day's heat still lingered. Her clothes were damp with sweat and she couldn't remember when she had last eaten anything. In the next room, her son was crying, long and loud. He was too young to speak, but his cries could not have expressed his desperation more articulately had they been in perfect English. *Mama, please don't leave me here, I'm scared! Come back!*

She held her hands over her face and clenched her eyes tight. She wanted so badly to appreciate a moment of rest, but the cries of her son reverberated through her spine and every web and tendril of her nervous system. His pain was hers. His fear was hers. She felt guilty and cruel, and she considered going back into his room and taking him up in her arms. She had to put an end to this. She dropped a hand from her face and looked at the clock beside her bed: 7:03. It had only been two minutes.

Her son was eight months old. He had been sleeping on her breast in bed with her since the day he was born, and now it was time the boy learned to sleep on his own. But two minutes in and Marion doubted whether she would be able to follow through with it.

She swore she heard him call her name so clearly it unsettled her. He cried for her, all pleas and apologies. *Mama, I promise I'll be good, please don't leave me here all alone, PLEASE come back for me! I'm sorry!* She began to weep with him. Her eyes pooled and heavy tears dropped down the sides of her head and into her ears and her hair. She wondered again if she was doing the right thing. She had asked her doctors in advance about the potential for lasting trauma in letting him cry himself to sleep all alone and they had assured her that it was in the best interest of the boy to learn to soothe himself. *Quacks. What do they know? My baby is suffering.*

She had planned to give him ten minutes before she would return to his room and offer him reassurance that she had not abandoned him.

She planned to hold him and let him nurse until he was calm, and then she would try again to lay him down and let him find sleep on his own. The clock read 7:04pm; she hadn't even made it halfway yet.

The draw to answer his cries was hypnotic. She had to actively fight the instinct to move toward him. She felt like she was failing as a mother, that she shouldn't be able to stand by while he suffered. And she felt like if she did go to him, she would disrupt the process and inhibit his development. She knew she would be failing him either way, and the shame of the dilemma filled her lungs like water with every breath. She was a moment from breaking when she heard the front door open. He was home, thank god.

Marion sat up, wet-faced and distraught, and waited for her fiancé to come to her.

"Mar?" Joel called from down the hall.

"I'm in here!" she said in return, responding before Joel had even closed his mouth.

She heard his footsteps moving through the apartment toward her. Still the child cried. Joel stopped in the doorway and looked at her, concerned.

"What's going on, Mar?" he asked.

"I—" she began, but the attempt to explain brought with it the full force of her feelings and she choked on the words, throwing up her hands in a shrug and bringing them to her face again. She shook her head back and forth quickly, as if to express her inability to speak, and more tears pooled in her eyes and spilled out over her cheeks. Still the boy cried.

Joel moved into the room and sat on the bed next to her. Immediately she fell into him and began to sob. He held his arms around her while she leaned into him and then asked again, "What's happening? Why is everyone crying?"

She breathed deep and was able to find composure enough to speak. "Trying to get him to sleep in his room, but I don't think I can do it—it's the hardest thing I've ever done."

Joel laughed.

"It's not funny!" she said and began to weep again.

"It's not funny, you're right. It's ridiculous," Joel said.

Marion stopped crying, embarrassed and confused. Her sniffling ceased and the room went silent, save for the shrieks of the baby through the walls. She sat up and looked at Joel, imploring him with her expression to elaborate.

Joel sighed and shook his head.

"You coddle him. I keep telling you, it's not healthy. You let him sleep in our bed for months even though I told you not to, and now you're telling me he's in his crib and you can't handle it? What's the problem here? You said you were going to do this."

"Joel, listen to him, he's in pain!" she said, now pleading on behalf of her child to his father.

"He's a baby. They cry. It's not a big deal, Mar. Come here, it's okay." He reached his arms out and invited her to return to his lap. She leaned back into him and let him hold her. The tears had stopped, but she wasn't sure if they were assuaged by comfort or surprise.

Was he right? Maybe she was being dramatic. Maybe the baby was just being a baby and she was making this whole process more painful than it had to be. She knew there was no path she could take where she could do right as a mother. She couldn't see the clock from the foot of the bed, but she wondered how much time had passed, if it had been minutes or an hour, and still the boy cried.

"I don't know how you just sit here and listen to that, no wonder you're upset," Joel said. "You should go watch TV or something. It's grating on *my* nerves already and I just got home. Did you cook anything?"

She sat up again and looked at her fiancé with no expression on her face, and then looked at the clock: 7:09. Only two more minutes and they could be reunited. She looked back at Joel.

"No, I, uh—no, sorry. I haven't eaten either, actually. Haven't had time."

"Yeah. It's alright, I'm getting used to it," he said and looked down at the floor.

Mama, where are you? Please don't leave me here, please come back, Mama, I'm sorry!

The boy cried harder than he had yet; she knew he was trying to reach her.

"Well, you do what you want, but I can't listen to that all night. I'm going to go out and get us some dinner," Joel said, patting his hands on his knees and bracing himself to stand up.

She thought for a moment about asking him to stay and letting her go to pick the food up, but the thought became complicated when something within her objected to the idea. Maybe she was afraid he would say no if she asked. Maybe she didn't trust Joel to provide adequate consolation to the boy. Maybe she wanted to go back to her child as badly as he wanted her to return. She recognized the first two thoughts and dismissed them quickly in favor of the third.

"Well, yeah, you had better go. I have to go back in there and try and calm him down," she said, her hesitation too subtle for Joel to concern himself with.

"I don't know why you don't just leave him there. He'll figure it out. They said he needs to do it on his own," he said, standing up and moving toward the door. "You're just dragging it out and making it harder on everyone."

Marion said nothing. She was too stressed to think clearly, so she was not sure if Joel was being supportive or critical, but either way it stung. She watched him from the foot of the bed as he walked out of the room. Listened to him pick up his keys, open the door, and close it behind him. Then she stood up and walked straight to the baby's room, opened the door, and picked the crying child up out of his crib.

He didn't stop crying immediately, but he pulled at his mother and pressed his head against her, embracing her with desperation and relief. She hummed a lullaby and rocked him against her chest. The weight of the child's tiny body was immense to her, as if she could feel the gravity of his entire life within him. The years ahead, all of his potential, every possible event and outcome that could spring from this child was in him like a tree inside of a seed and she had never held anything more precious, more magnificent, or more fragile in her life.

She felt like they were two parts of one body. She was the shell; he was the beating heart. She was the sustenance; he was the warmth. She was the actor; he was the script. She was the movement; he was the reason.

She rubbed his back with her hand and continued to hum. His crying softened into periodic whimpers and hiccups, and his body sank into her. She could feel his spine, his tiny waist, his chest expanding with each breath, and the contractions in his abdomen from the post-crying sniffles.

Eventually the boy fell asleep, and Marion placed him back in his crib. She noted the time, 8:21pm, and became aware of her stomach twisting up with hunger. She called Joel, but he didn't answer.

24

Marion called Joel a dozen times over the next hour. At 9:30 she called the hospital and asked if a Joel Shepherd had been admitted to the emergency department, but he had not. She tried the police, and the jail, and then took a deep breath before calling Joel's mother to ask if she had heard from him. She knew in her bones that she would not see him again that night.

Marion wouldn't speak to Joel again for almost two weeks. She wouldn't see him again for nearly six, when he came by the apartment to gather his clothes and belongings. He came by in the evening; Marion presumed it was to avoid seeing the boy. She had already bagged up his clothes and other effects so that he wouldn't need to stay long. And though she was afraid of raising the child on her own—afraid how the world would perceive her now she was her late twenties, alone, and with a child; afraid that she may be undesirable to other men and destined to be lonely forever—she couldn't bring herself to try to persuade him to stay.

Marion had been raising the boy more or less alone since his birth and she knew nothing would change with Joel's absence. It didn't matter anyway; she would never be alone again. She abandoned the sleep training and allowed her son to sleep in bed with her again. He would sleep in her bed until he was three years old. Even after that time, many a midnight would bring him into her room in tears, trembling from nightmares or strange sounds in the walls or the occasional California thunderstorm, and she would console him through fitful sleeps until he found rest.

In conversations with friends over coffee or phone calls with her sister in New Mexico, they would ask her about her romantic prospects and she would casually dismiss the notion. "I don't have the time to date," she would say, "and I'm not sure I even want to."

Joel had agreed to pay Marion a quarter of his salary in child support—though "agreed" of course means "complied with a court order and followed through on his obligation." She was able to use the extra income to pay for childcare so that she could finish nursing school. Between her schooling and a part-time job serving tables at a twenty-four-hour diner on the night shift, she had no desire to complicate her life further by inviting the temperamental energy of a man into her life.

As the boy grew older, he provided her with as many hours of exhausting one-sided conversation as any man she had ever been with before. Aside from the cravings that came periodically on lonely midnights after her son had gone to bed—cravings which could be easily satisfied on her own—she rarely thought of men. Still, her friends and her sister would pester.

When the boy began to attend junior high, a distance started to grow between them. Marion was working twelve-hour shifts at the hospital and picking up as much overtime as she could to pay the mortgage on the nice three-bedroom tract home she had purchased on the east side of Santa Lucia, where the new subdivisions were going up. The boy had taken to skateboarding after school with his friends, staying out late at the movies or the bowling alley, and sitting around doing whatever clandestine activities teenage boys did when they assembled at night.

They began to pass each other at strange hours of the day, a habit which would continue for years. When she arrived home from work in the mornings, she would wake him up and cook breakfast for him before seeing him off to school. She would wake in the evening from naps after long graveyard shifts and check his room immediately to see if he had made it home safely. She got him a smartphone when he turned thirteen and it eased her worries whenever she couldn't find him at home. She wondered how people ever raised kids without phones.

There was a new loneliness in her life, or perhaps an old loneliness that had now risen again in the increasing absence of her son. On the recommendation of her friends, she downloaded a dating app and began a series of short-lived flings with people she met online.

First there had been Damian, a long and thin man with blond hair and a cool rasp that emanated from a throat that was almost all Adam's apple. He didn't speak much, which Marion liked at first, but after they had slept together twice he stopped speaking at all, and Marion came to understand that talking had never been his interest. But he had been decent in bed and he had gone quietly without any drama, so Marion didn't count the exchange as a loss.

Next was a man named Orlando, whose obsession with the gym appeared to Marion to border on body dysmorphia or some kind of obsessive-compulsive disorder. When he wasn't at the gym, he was talking about the gym. Always measuring everything: his weight, his size, his food rations, the number of pounds he could press or squat or jerk and the number of times he could jerk or squat or press them. Marion was bored by Orlando, and she found his physique deceptive, because he had no idea how to use the body he had worked so hard to perfect. Orlando didn't last beyond two dates.

She dated Marco, a sweet man who brought flowers to their first date and read her poetry that he claimed to have written, though it sounded familiar—she later looked up the words online and found nearly identical poems attributed to Neruda. Though she was embarrassed for him, she found herself almost impressed by the level of boorish confidence it must have taken to presume no one had ever read a poem before, or that no one would question it, so she allowed him a second date, but she grew bored with his impotent talk.

There was Terry, who said all the right things, only too fast and too soon and too perfectly executed. He could not be trusted. Jeremy, who must have spoken nonstop through the entire first date without asking her a single question about herself, and then before dropping her off had the audacity to say, "I like you, Marion, I'd like to do this again sometime."

She and her son would pass days sometimes without seeing each other's faces. Their relationship was reduced to text messages and phone calls; check-ins and follow-ups. Sometimes she would wake up in the evening before going to work and she would check his room to find it empty. She would lie in his bed and look around at the little piles of clutter here and there and she would smell his hair on his pillow and small tears would escape her eyes and her thoughts would turn to self-criticism and fear.

My baby, am I letting you down? I hope you're okay out there, Nicholas. Everything I've ever done has been for you. Everything. This life was all for you.

She would send him texts as often as possible.

How are you?

And

Do you need anything?

And

You know I love you,
right baby?

His responses were always simple, short.

Fine mom

And

Nope I'm good thank you

And

Yes mom, I know. I love
you too, you know

If anything had been wrong, if he had been struggling, or suffering, he would have told her, surely. All she had been doing was working, paying the bills, and ensuring he had food and a nice place to live. She had saved money so he could go to college; she had paused her entire life so that he could begin his. If anything was wrong, she would know it.

Still something gnawed at her. Every time she checked his room to find it empty, or to find him sleeping at odd hours, she felt a fear rise up from her stomach like smoke wisping from a smoldering fire in the seat of her intuition, and she would cough and sniffle and do her best to swallow it. When she should have been sleeping, she was kept up with thoughts that she tried to explain away as missing her son, as loneliness, or even as guilt about not being more physically present with him. But she knew better.

25

Marion's fears were confirmed late on a Thursday morning in autumn. She was awoken shortly after getting to sleep by a phone call from Nick's school. He had been taken to the hospital to treat an apparent overdose. The walls of her house became distorted funhouse mirrors, cracked from floor to ceiling, revealing the gray sky behind them as her lungs froze over and she tried frantically to find her breath. Her heart rate increased to three thousand beats per minute, her entire chest vibrating.

That drive to the hospital was the longest of her life, and still when she approached the doctor standing outside Nick's room, she felt as though she had been asleep in her bed only seconds ago and was not yet prepared to speak to another human.

"Miss Wagner, it's alright. He's alright," said the doctor, whose name escaped her though she knew they had worked together in the past, and Marion was able to take a breath for the first time in twenty minutes.

"What happened? Where is he?" she asked and continued to walk through, frantic and hyperventilating.

"Miss Wagner, he's sleeping, but he's fine, I assure you. It was a minor overdose. From what the school faculty found in his bag, it looks like he got his hands on some of your Vicodin and a bottle of vodka, and the combined depressive effects slowed his breathing and he went unconscious in class. He's fine. We'll observe him for a few hours but he'll be okay."

The doctor was unreasonably cavalier about the whole thing, by Marion's estimation. She hounded him for answers, explanations, guidance, but he offered only his sympathies and a recommendation that she enroll her son in a juvenile outpatient drug treatment program before the problem got out of hand.

Marion waited by Nick's bedside until the doctor cleared him for discharge. She drove him home and he slept in the passenger seat while she cried and tried to concentrate on the road, one eye focused on making sure he was breathing. She called out sick for the shift she was scheduled to work that night. The managing nurse had already heard the story through the rumor mill of the hospital and offered petty sympathies which offended Marion, though she took them gracefully.

Marion lay in bed with Nick while he slept all afternoon and into the evening. She got up only to use the restroom and she raced back to his bedside every time to be sure that he hadn't stopped breathing in her absence.

When he woke up, she thought to herself that she had never seen eyes more beautiful in her whole life, and though she tried to keep it together for his sake, her eyeballs churned out salty drops of water over and over and over again, but she didn't make a sound.

"I'm sorry, Mom," Nick said, finally.

"It's okay, baby, it's okay. I'm just glad you're okay," she whispered, and she hugged him and tousled his hair and inhaled him. Underneath the pubescent sweat and the scent of hospital and sleep, she smelled her infant son—her baby boy—and she missed him more than she ever had before.

She sat up and asked if he was hungry, to which he replied he was not. She asked if he needed anything and he said he did not. She gathered her strength and she swallowed her fear and she asked him, "Nicholas, can we talk about what happened today?"

"Nothing happened, Mom, I just messed up," he said, avoiding her eyes.

"Nick, you ended up in the hospital. You can't call that nothing."

"I just took some pills I hadn't taken before and was drinking with some friends and I didn't know it would do all that," he said, as though he were describing a spilled beverage or something equally mundane.

"Baby, what are you doing taking pills? Drinking? Doing drugs? I thought you knew better than that? What are you thinking?"

"Mom, it's not a big deal. Everyone does it. It's not like I'm smoking crack or something. I just accidentally took too much."

270

"Nick! You were at school, it was eleven o'clock in the morning! This wasn't some house party, this is a problem!"

"I know! I know. Jesus, that's why it messed me up so bad. Can't you see that? I don't do this all the time, I don't even know what I'm doing, obviously. It was just a fluke, Mom, don't worry. I just made a mistake, it's not a problem. I'm not gonna do it again," he said, and she couldn't find any reason to doubt him except for that smoldering pit sending smoke signals up from her belly and crying that she should challenge him further. But she couldn't. Not without acknowledging that something was terribly wrong.

"Good," she said. "That's good. But we can't just let this slide. You almost died today, honey. The doctors want you to attend this class at the hospital. It's only two hours a day, Monday through Thursday. I want you to start going."

"Mom! I don't need a program! I'm not a fucking drug addict!"

"Good. Then it won't be a problem if you go for a little while. Please, for me?"

26

Over the next several months, the apparent urgency of that day would subside and be forgotten as so many painful emotions are with time. Marion would keep a wary eye on Nick's health. She looked for signs— bloodshot eyes, dilated pupils, weight loss, anything she could to try to measure how he was doing and give herself peace of mind.

One morning she came home from work to find that Nick was not alone in his bed. She froze in the doorway of his room. Her first instinct was to withdraw quietly and give him privacy, but she couldn't resist being a bit nosy. She was a mother, after all; it was her job.

The girl in his bed was tall—she lay nearly as long as him in bed with her neck bent down and her head on his shoulder. Her chestnut complexion contrasted with her hair dyed red like feathers from the wings of a phoenix, and Marion couldn't help but stare at her. Her very presence in this room had to be a sign that Nick was doing alright. A *beautiful young girl like this,* she thought. *She wouldn't waste her time otherwise.* She closed the door and backed out of the room, filled with pride and relief.

The girl would become a fixture in their lives, and Marion adored her. Whenever Nick was home, which was far more often these days, Lia was there. When Nick was gone, he would always respond to texts with a simple, "At Lia's, all good," and Marion found herself able to relax for the first time in a great while, knowing her son was safe at the home of a girl instead of out in the streets doing god-knows-what.

The peace would be short lived, however. In the fall of the next year, she received word from the school that Nick was failing all of his classes, and again the fears she had been able to placate broke loose from their resting places and jarred her into near dysfunction.

She was waiting in the living room when Nick and Lia walked in the front door that evening and wasted no time confronting him.

"Nicholas, what is going on at school?"

"Nothing, Mom, they're just being dramatic," he said, breathing with disdain.

"Dramatic? Nick, they say you might not graduate!"

"That's not even true, I just have to take some extra classes next year. It'll be fine," he said.

"Okay, but that's not the point. What is going on, Nick? Is it drugs? I thought we were past all this?"

"It's not drugs! I'm not on drugs, Jesus!"

"Nicholas, don't lie to me!"

"I'm not lying!"

"What is it then?"

Nick withdrew into himself and looked at the floor. Lia had been standing by, observing but offering only silent respect for the situation between mother and son.

"Mom, can we do this later?" he said without looking up, softly gesturing in Lia's direction with his head.

"No, Nicholas. We can't. If you're grown up enough to be sleeping with this young lady, you're grown up enough to talk in front of her. Now tell me, what the hell is going on?"

"Mom, this is so embarrassing."

"It's okay, Nick, it's not a big deal." Lia took Nick's hand and commanded his eyes to hers with just her voice. "Just talk to her, she's worried about you."

"Listen to her, honey. We're just talking. What's going on? Do you need to go back to the treatment program?"

"It's not. Fucking. Drugs," he said, then looked back to Lia, then back to the floor. "I just haven't been paying attention in school. I missed some classes this year. I've just been . . . busy."

"Busy with what? You're sixteen years old!"

"With Lia . . . I guess," he said so softly that Marion could barely hear him.

"What was that?"

"I've been with Lia, Mom. That's all." He looked her in the eyes now and she saw him do his best to look like a man, but she only saw her baby boy in front of her, squared up and feigning confidence.

"Honey, you need to finish school, or else what are you going to have to offer Lia? You think she wants a husband who failed out of high school? You don't want that, do you, Lia?"

"No, Ms. Wagner, but I don't think he will. He's just been goofing off too much this year."

Lia looked to Nick, who looked back at her. She nodded with her eyebrows in Marion's direction and Nick sighed.

"Yeah, Mom. She's right. I'll do better. It's just hard."

"It's high school, honey, and you're anything but stupid. What's so hard about it?"

He thought for a moment, and then walked all the way into the living room and sat down on the couch. Lia paused, then followed him. Marion was in the adjacent loveseat.

"It just feels like such bullshit. Like, I already know everything they teach us that matters, and everything else just doesn't matter. It's like a holding chamber for kids, like we are just incubating and being kept busy. It's stupid. And then, on the other hand, there's Lia and . . . God, this is fucking embarrassing—"

"Language, Nick, come on," Marion said. Lia laughed and the sweetness and confidence in her laughter was reassuring to Marion. Maybe it wasn't all so bad. Nick was a smart kid. So what if he had struggled in school? He was a teenager. Maybe she had been overreacting again.

"Sorry, Mom. I just mean, this is embarrassing to do with her right here."

"We're all family, Nick, just tell her. It's okay, I won't hold it against you," Lia said, taking Nick's hand again from next to him on the couch.

"It's like every day I'm given a choice between two things. One of them doesn't matter at all, school. It's this arbitrary system of merits and demerits based on how well you can follow directions to . . . what? Prepare us to be good little workers? Who cares?

"And on the other hand, I have the opportunity to spend my time with someone who is the complete opposite. Someone who matters. To, like ... talk, and share, and learn and laugh and enjoy my life and get to spend time with a person who loves me back. And every night I think, tomorrow I'll go to school, but then every day when I know she's out of school, I just can't bring myself to waste another minute of my day at school, not with her."

Lia's eyes swelled with adoration and Marion was conflicted between a deep, romantic admiration for his perspective and a sense of maternal concern for the choices he was making. The conversation carried on for another hour, and the three of them got takeout dinner and ate together.

Lia sided with Marion and promised to hold Nick accountable and encourage him to keep his priorities in order. Marion's fears were assuaged again and she spent several months in the belief that Lia might be the best thing that had happened for Nick, and she was grateful to have her in their lives.

27

Another year passed, and Lia's presence at the house became less frequent. Nick's routine was different; he was out late at night and gone from home more often than he was there. His grades were good, so Marion didn't allow herself to indulge her worries further. Nick was nearly an adult, and it seemed that the worst of his teenage indiscretions were behind him.

On a spring night, she was cut from work early and arrived home from around midnight to find Nick sitting in his truck outside the house with a girl whom she had never seen before. By the time she parked and exited her vehicle, Nick had started the truck and was pulling away. He leaned out the window to say, "I'm taking her home, I'll be back later."

Later came and went and Nick didn't come home. It wasn't until the sun was coming up that Marion heard his truck pulling up to the house. She cut him off in the living room and asked about the young blonde girl that had been with him.

"That's Alison, she's a friend," he said.

"What does Lia think about Alison?"

"God, Mom, you need to get over Lia. She's not as great as you think she is."

Marion was concerned, again. But she only asked, "What do you mean, honey? I thought you and Lia had a really good thing?"

"Yeah, well, maybe we did. But it ran its course, okay?"

"Sure, okay. Well, tell me about Alison."

"She's ... she's just a friend. But I don't know. She's different, she's not like Lia and me."

"What do you mean, 'not like Lia and me'?"

"I mean, she's a good kid. Like, you know Lia and I met in that drug program right? I bet you didn't even know that, did you?"

Marion's heart sank. "I didn't ... "

"Yeah, and like . . . I tried, but she just can't hold it together. It's always just something crazy with her and I couldn't do it anymore. But anyway, Alison is, like, going to college next year and stuff. She doesn't do drugs or anything like that. She's a good girl, Mom, you'd like her."

"I'm sure I will, then. You should bring her around sometime, you know, not at midnight. Maybe I'll get the chance to get to know her."

"Yeah, maybe I will," he said. But he never did.

28

"Yeah, and like," I tried but she just can't and it's together. It's alm just something crazy with her and I couldn't do it anymore, but anyway, Alison is like going to college next year and stuff. She doesn't do drugs

Years passed. Nick graduated high school and began to make money doing some job for the mail service or something; Marion didn't understand what it was exactly but Nick was taking care of himself, and so she gave him space to do so. She didn't inquire into his moods, activities, love life, or health. He was an adult, and she sat by passively like a mother in name only. Though her heart still ached to protect him like she had when he was an infant, she had to reckon with the passing of time and the fact that he no longer needed her in that way, and never would again.

He lived in the house, but she never saw him. They texted regularly, but never talked. She felt the loneliness of her life creeping out from behind photographs on the walls and memories of men she had loved before. She spoke to her sister on the phone and made plans to visit her in New Mexico. She considered selling the house and moving out there to be near her only other family—starting over. Nick could come with her, but she knew he wouldn't, and so she made excuses to delay her trip to New Mexico every time it came up in conversation. She would say, "Things are too busy at work right now," or "Money is tight this month, property taxes due," or "Oh, I'd rather come when the weather is a bit nicer, maybe in a couple months," but if she were being honest she would have said, "I'm afraid if I put that many miles between my son and me, I will never see him again."

She received a phone call from an unknown number at 8:49pm on a Saturday as she was drinking coffee in the breakroom at work.

"Hello?" she said.

A robot voice spoke over a cracking line. "Hello. You have a collect call from"—and here she heard her son's voice, distant and blurry, mumble out his name—"at the Santa Lucia County Jail. Do you accept the charges?"

In the moments between accepting the charges and hearing his voice, entire years scrolled through her mind like microfiche scrolling rapidly on a projector. His absence, his moodiness, his sleep schedule, his distance, his lies, his politician's smile, his inconsistency. She was angry and she was terrified and she hung her head in sorrow and she was weeping before Nick even said a word. *How did I let this happen? How did I not see it?*

"Hey, Mom," he said.

"Nicholas, what happened?"

"I don't know, Mom, I just . . . It was just a stupid thing. Can you come bail me out? I'll tell you all about it."

"How much is it?" she asked, ready to spend any amount to bring him home.

"It's a hundred grand, but the bondsman says he can get me out for ten. Please, Mom?"

The smoldering coals in the pit of her stomach that had been ignored and neglected for so long now roared to life with a fire that she couldn't deny, and she thought she might throw up. In her mind she said, *Of course, honey. Anything for you. I'll be there in fifteen minutes and we'll get you out of there and we'll get you home safe.* But for the first time in twenty years, she couldn't give him what he wanted.

"Nicky, honey," she said, "I don't know what happened. And I wish I could. I wish I could get you out of there. I wish I could fix this for you. But, I can't. I just can't. I didn't put you there. I'm sorry, love, you're just going to have to do this on your own. You got yourself in there, now you have to wait until they let you out."

He pleaded and she cried, but she did her best not to let him hear the weakness in her voice. She apologized and offered him all of her love and told him she would be there for him, but that maybe this would be good for him. He grew angry and hung up the phone without saying goodbye and she was afraid she would never hear from him again. She told the managing nurse that she needed to leave work for an emergency, then she went home and cried into her pillow until she fell asleep. It felt like all the blood in her veins was pumping in the wrong direction, and several times she had to stop herself from driving to the bondsman or to the jailhouse.

29

Months passed and Marion made peace with her decision. It had not come easily or without help from her sister, who had three children of her own. Her sister could speak about children in such a crass and vulgar way, which was a healthy counterbalance to the extreme sentimentality Marion felt about her own son.

"Kids are their own people, Mar. What do you expect? Honestly, you've done great as it is. That rat bastard walked out on you and left you to raise that boy all by yourself and you've done great. So what, he gets high? He graduated school! That's more than I can say for Mikey. He dropped out and joined the union as soon as they would have him! But he's doing alright. You know, I worried about him for a while, but now he's got two babies of his own and that sweet little wife of his and it's fine. You remember when Mikey went to juvie? When he and his friends stole that car? Oh god, I thought I might die! But it passes and you realize they have their own lives and they're resilient little things, these kids. Nicky'll be fine. You did the right thing. If you'da bailed him out he wouldn't have learned a thing and he'd be right back in there. Don't be so hard on yourself, Mar. You're doing great. You gotta lighten up, trust me, he'll be fine."

Marion appreciated her sister's words during the day. But at night she imagined Nick behind bars, and she remembered him as an infant the week Joel left, screaming from his crib before he could even speak, and somehow he cried to her now as he cried to her then.

MAMA! Please come get me. I'm sorry. I'll be good, I promise. I didn't mean to be a bad kid. Please come get me and I swear I'll be good. She wept some nights like she had wept back then.

But the truth was that after several weeks Marion realized that she was sleeping well again for the first time in years. Knowing that Nick was somewhere safe afforded her the luxury of relaxing in a way she hadn't been able to since Nick first met Lia years prior in High School.

Nick came home and she was ecstatic to see how he had filled out. He had meat on his bones, color in his cheeks, and he looked well rested, well fed, and well preserved. But he was different. The first few days of his homecoming had been strange; his moods were unpredictable and he slept almost constantly. She was never at home without him sleeping. She woke him up on the second morning and even managed to coax a smile and some laughter from him, and so she left for work and told herself he was just acclimating. *Everything is fine*, she thought. She thought of her sister's words and she decided to not be overbearing. But she couldn't help it. With every text message he ignored, she felt more anxious. She came home from work on her lunch break to see that he was there, and though she would find him still sleeping, she was just relieved to find him at all.

Three times she came into his room and reluctantly held her finger under his nose to feel for breath. When she did, she breathed a large sigh of relief and immediately felt dirty, as though she had indulged some unspeakable notion, then she would shudder and leave the room quickly.

Thursday morning she left work at 7am. She hadn't heard a word from Nick since the night before, when all he had said was "I'm not feeling great" from his bed, and she had a feeling inside of her like she had swallowed a stone.

She pulled up to the house and saw Nick's truck parked outside. Some relief came with that.

She walked inside and heard voices from upstairs. As she walked up the stairs, she realized the voices were coming from the television.

She knocked on Nick's bedroom door and was unsurprised to get no response. She hadn't had a response to her knocks since he had come home on Monday.

"Nick, honey, are you up?" she said through the door, loudly enough to be heard over the TV he was watching. There was no answer. She knocked again, forcefully this time, loud, with an angst that she had been suppressing and didn't even mean to let out.

"Nick? I'm coming in, okay?"

She pushed open the door and almost apologized to the young lady sitting on the floor, naked and leaning against the bed.

And then she screamed.

Nick was lying on the floor next to her, in a fetal position with no shirt on and a large piece of tin foil smudged with black ash in his hand. She screamed and ran to him and turned him onto his back, shaking him by the shoulders and crying a blind fit.

"NICK! NICHOLAS! NICHOLAS, WHAT HAVE YOU DONE?"

She had gathered her thoughts just enough to try some chest compressions, when he coughed twice and drew in a deep breath.

"What, Mom, what? Jesus, what?" he said with his eyes closed, smacking his lips and breathing heavily.

"NICHOLAS, WHAT THE HELL IS GOING ON?"

"Nothing, Mom, I'm just sleeping, Jesus, calm down," he said and then all at once his eyes opened and he pulled the foil under the blanket.

"Sleeping? Smoking dope is more like it! And you, honey, what the *hell* are you doing? Are you mixed up in all this too?"

Marion turned her attention to the girl slumped on the floor. She noticed the purple-tinged pallor of her pouted lips. She noticed the stillness of stone in her awkward repose. Then she screamed from a place so deep in her belly that she could have split mountains and parted seas were she near them. Instead, she was at home in the suburbs on a warm August morning and the screams only reverberated through the house and escaped through open windows to be heard by every neighbor on the block.

The ambulance arrived four minutes after she called 911, two police patrol cars in tow. Alison Taylor was pronounced *dead on arrival*, and Marion observed herself watch the EMTs cart her into the ambulance as if it were all happening on screen and she was viewing it remotely.

She didn't have the chance to say goodbye to Nick before the police took him into custody. He didn't look up as they put him in the car and drove off down the street; he only stared off into some dimension that she couldn't see, and it was probably for the best. She too was still in that other place, only watching, and she couldn't have offered him any consolation had he looked for it.

‡

Session transcript from patient files of Dr. Henry Foster
Patient: Wagner, Nicholas
8/29/22

HF: Nicholas, do you know where you are?

NW: FUCK YOU.

HF: Nicholas—

NW: Don't call me Nicholas or I'll rip your fucking tongue out.

HF: Nick, I know you're hurting, but I need to know that you are lucid.

NW: FUCK YOU, GET THE FUCK OUT OF HERE NOW.

HF: [muffled] Nurse, can you unlock the door?

‡

Session transcript from patient files of Dr. Henry Foster
Patient: Wagner, Nicholas
9/05/22

HF: Good evening, Nick.

NW: Fuck you.

HF: Still on that, are we?

NW: Let me out of here.

HF: Nick, I can't let you go anywhere until I know you'll be safe.

NW: Who cares what I do? It doesn't matter. It doesn't fucking matter. [crying]

HF: Nick, it—

NW: LET ME THE FUCK OUT OF HERE!

‡

Session transcript from patient files of Dr. Henry Foster
Patient: Wagner, Nicholas
9/12/22

HF: Nick, do you know where you are?

NW: Yes.

HF: Can you tell me?

NW: I'm at the psych hospital.

HF: Do you remember how you got here?

NW: Yeah. The police brought me.

HF: That's right. Do you remember why?

NW: Yeah...

...

NW: [crying] Because... [screams]

HF: It's okay, Nick, it's okay.

NW: It's not fucking okay! It's not! [indecipherable] I can't do it, I can't.

HF: Nick, I can't let you go home as long as you talk like that.

NW: I don't care. I don't want to go home. I can't. Just send me back to jail, alright? Send me back, I'll deal with it from there.

HF: Nick, I know—

NW: STOP IT. YOU DON'T KNOW. YOU DON'T KNOW SHIT. SEND ME BACK OR FUCKING LET ME GO DO IT MYSELF.

‡

Session transcript from patient files of Dr. Henry Foster
Patient: Wagner, Nicholas
9/19/22

HF: How are you feeling today, Nick?

NW: Fine.

HF: Fine? Well, that's good. An improvement.

NW: Yup.

HF: Are you willing to talk to me for a little bit?

NW: Do I have a choice?

HF: You always have a choice, Nick.

NW: Then no.

HF: I can't let you out if you won't—

NW: I don't care. Leave me alone.

‡

Session transcript from patient files of Dr. Henry Foster
Patient: Wagner, Nicholas
9/26/22

HF: How are you feeling today, Nick?

NW: Fine.

HF: That's good.

NW: Mhmm.

HF: I hear you've been participating in groups this week. How's that going?

NW: Like shit.

HF: Why's that?

NW: These people are fucking crazy, dude.

HF: Hah. Yeah, well, this isn't the Ritz, you know.

NW: Why am I here?

HF: You don't know?

NW: No, I mean. I know why I *was* here. But why am I *still* here?

HF: Nick, we've been over this. I'm not comfortable granting your release until I feel you are no longer a danger to yourself or anyone else.

NW: Do I look dangerous?

286

HF: That's not the point. I need to know that you aren't going to hurt yourself, and frankly, I don't feel confident in that right now.

NW: What do you care?

HF: Pardon me?

NW: Why would you? No one would. I mean. My own fucking mom would probably be relieved. Not having to worry about this shit anymore. I can tell you a long list of people who would probably celebrate if they found out. I bet you if I don't kill myself, at least two other people will find me first and kill me for what I've done. So what the fuck do you care?

HF: Is that what you think? That you've done something wrong?

NW: HELLO, AREN'T YOU THE DOCTOR IN THE ROOM?

HF: Nick, you have survived an awful, awful tragedy. But you're not alone. This thing . . . it's an epidemic. It's a national health emergency. This fentanyl is getting stronger and stronger, and it's in everything. You can't blame yourself. This thing is beyond you. You're lucky to be alive, and what happened to your girlfriend—

NW: She wasn't my girlfriend, she was just . . . [crying]

HF: Nick . . .

NW: [crying]

HF: Nick, listen.

NW: No. You listen. [crying] Let me out or send me back to my room. I don't care which, but I'm done.

‡

Session transcript from patient files of Dr. Henry Foster
Patient: Wagner, Nicholas
10/03/22

HF: How are you feeling today, Nick?

NW: Fine.

HF: Just fine again?

NW: What do you expect? Do you want me to be ... fuckin' ... peachy? I'm peachy, doc, just fucking swell.

HF: No, I don't expect you to be peachy. I do hope that you're taking this seriously, though. I would like to let you out of here one of these days. Maybe see you return home and start to put the pieces back together again.

NW: Hah. Back together.

HF: That's funny?

NW: Depends on how you define funny, I guess. It's just, "back together" implies that there is something to go back to, something that fell apart. There's nothing to put back together.

HF: Surely that's not true. I understand how you feel that way but—

NW: Do you? Do you understand? Do you have any idea what it's like to lose the one thing that gave you any hope? The one thing that made everything else feel like it kind of had a purpose? Because I do. I mean, I was hanging on by a thread before, sure. But I had one friend, one person, one fucking thing in my life that kept me from really just going completely off the rails and probably dying or disappearing into oblivion. I had one person, doc. She was my best fucking friend and she made my life better, but me? I just ruined hers. And then I fucking ... and then I did this. And now, for some fucking reason, I'm still here. Me. I didn't want to be here in the first place, even. I have just pissed and moaned and squandered my entire fucking life just looking for all the ways to shut it off, tune it out, just to end it but being too much of a fucking coward to actually do it. And she had ... she wanted it. She wanted to feel it all. To do it all. She wanted to have all of the experiences she could have and she loved it. She fucking loved it, and she made my life better because she loved hers and in maybe the sickest joke in all of history, I am here talking to some community-college therapist about how I'm feeling sad and alone and the best person I've ever known is dead because of me. So. You understand how I feel? No. You don't. Because if you did, there's no fucking way you'd be at work right now. No way you'd be sober. No way you'd be asking me these stupid fucking questions. You'd be sitting where I am, or worse. If you knew how I felt.

30

Nick was released from jail that August day without any charges pressed, into the care of the psychiatric hospital across town. He remained there for almost two months. Marion took an extended leave of absence on an emergency basis and she used that time to finally take the trip to New Mexico.

Her sister met her at the airport and immediately began talking too much for Marion to tolerate. Marion asked politely if she could give her some time and some space, and then thanked her for understanding and allowing her to stay.

Her sister's neighborhood seemed to have been dropped in the middle of a desert in the shadow of a small mountain range. A single road provided the only way in or out of the neighborhood, to and from the highway which led to Albuquerque or Santa Fe. The small subdivision was surrounded by miles of low, barren flatlands spotted with shrubs and small flowered succulents which provided shelter to lizards and the little round mice scurrying from bush to bush.

Marion wandered in the desert most days, taking in the isolation but ignoring the scenery. Some days she wept and some days her face was the picture of stoic resolve. She took phone calls from the resident psychiatrist at the hospital every week and he updated her on Nick's progress, of which most weeks there was little to speak.

She retired to her bed early at night, though she couldn't sleep, and she stayed in bed long into the morning. She skipped meals and she only bathed four times during her stay of five weeks. She had no time for physical maintenance, given the war she was fighting in her mind.

She resolved to call Joel for the first time in nearly twenty years to tell him about the fate of his son, to tell him that the boy might have some use for a father now more than ever. But she thought better of it; Joel wasn't the man Nick needed now. Marion didn't know what he needed.

She wrestled with thoughts of *If only* and *How could I?* Slowly, over the course of her despondent wanderings and restless nights, she was able to find some clarity, even if peace eluded her.

The doctor called to let her know that Nick would likely be released within the next week, assuming nothing unexpected should occur, and Marion made plans to return to California. She hugged her sister tightly but briefly and thanked her for her hospitality and for giving her the space she needed to process her grief and prepare to return to life.

31

Nick's homecoming was met with no celebration. He got into his mother's car at the hospital silently and not a word was spoken on the drive home. That whole first day contained only the most necessary of interactions between them.

Over the next few weeks, Nick rarely left the house. He went out on Monday evenings to meet with the psychiatrist and follow up on his treatment plan. He ran small errands and went out to get cigarettes, but he managed to move so stealthily that she often only knew he had left when she heard him running up the stairs and shutting the door to his room on his return.

In the middle of the night, Marion often woke to awful sounds and Nick in her bed, crying out in his sleep. He would shriek and curse and mutter incoherent expletives, and the pain in his voice called forth hot tears from Marion's eyes. She would hold him and say, "Don't worry, honey. It's okay, you're home. It's okay," and with time he would calm and return to a more peaceful sleep.

Thanksgiving came to pass, and they shared light conversation over dinner. Nick expressed a desire to go back to school and Marion had to work hard to contain her enthusiasm. Whether it was to protect herself from disappointment or to avoid making him uncomfortable at her surprise, she wasn't sure. Maybe it was both.

Marion had quietly saved a healthy sum of money for Nick in a trust which he would have access to when he turned twenty-one the coming January. She had feared for some time now that setting up the trust had been a mistake, and she had occasionally looked for means of revoking his access, but some enfeeblement intrinsic to motherhood always overtook her, and the effort was put off to another time. Hearing him talk of returning to school breathed life into the dim and flickering flame of hope that still burned in her heart, and so she finally resolved to tell him about his trust. She thought that perhaps it would fortify his desire to go back to school, and even then she doubted her judgment.

There was no Christmas tree in December, but they did get each other gifts and planned to exchange them on Christmas morning. She bought Nick a nice backpack and a button-down shirt, as well as a book—a collected anthology of great essays by philosophers throughout history. It was bound in leather with gold-foil lettering and had a burgundy silk ribbon to mark one's page.

On Christmas Eve, Nick went out to see some friends, he said. When he returned home, later than expected and looking sallow and out of sorts, Marion couldn't contain herself.

"Where have you been, Nicholas?" she asked, and then she screamed, "What are you doing?!"

"Nothing, Mom, I'm just tired. We smoked a little weed and I haven't been high in a while—" But she had no patience left.

She was a woman at the end of a twenty-one-year rope, having been let down and lied to and abandoned and betrayed and taken for granted, and she had held her ground and bent with the winds all this time, but that night, on Christmas Eve, she looked her only son in the face and she said what she was thinking for once. "Nicholas. Enough with the bullshit. I can't do it anymore. I can't watch you do this. After everything, that girl, that poor girl, all your time in jail and hospitals—this has been going on for years. I don't know if you're sick of it, but I sure as hell am. So, it's now or never, Nick. This is your chance. Either you stay here with me, and we do this together, like we talked about. Or you take your little drugs and you leave. But you can't have it both ways, not anymore."

Nick snorted and stood still in the living room, aghast and indignant. He shook his head several times and then he laughed and said, "Merry Christmas, Mom. Thanks a lot." Then he turned and walked out the front door.

Marion stayed home through the end of the year. She tried to resist looking out the window or watching her phone for replies to her many calls and texts. But again and again she found herself sitting on the couch just so with the television on in the background as she watched out the front window.

He didn't respond, and he didn't come home.

In mid-January, she got the nerve to open the present he had gotten for her, which was still sitting on the living-room floor in a corner next to a potted fern and the gifts she had bought for him, also still unopened. It was a vintage pressing of Louis Armstrong's *What a Wonderful World* on vinyl and a card with a picture of a cartoon beetle wearing a Santa hat and looking grumpy while a second beetle smiled wide and strung colorful lights on a decorated Christmas tree. The inside read *I'd be a Bah Hum-Bug if not for you*, under which Nick had written, *I love you Mom, Merry Christmas. PS, I'm sorry for everything.*

She listened to the record late into the night and lost track of the time in her tears.

Months passed.

She thought she would never rest again.

32

January 19, 2023

To: Henry Foster

Re: Pending Review of Medical License

From: CA State Board of Medicine, License Review Committee

Mr. Foster,

After careful analysis of your recent criminal 'convictions', to wit:

1. M: Trespassing
2. M: Disorderly Conduct
3. M: Drunk in Public
4. M: Menacing
5. F: Driving Under the Influence
6. F: Possession of a Controlled Substance Without a
    Prescription

We at the CMB License Review Committee have determined that you are not currently fit to practice medicine. Your license will be revoked, permanently and completely, effective immediately.

If you choose to appeal this decision, you have 90 days from today's date to state your intent to do so.

Kind regards,

Della Peters

Chair of the License Review Board

Henry dropped the letter onto his coffee table and picked up the bottle again. Several weeks or maybe months had passed since his arrest outside of Gretchen's house that night. His license had been suspended within days of his arrest, and now after his conviction the final hammer had fallen.

He had been lucky to avoid jail time. The bulky, indestructible band around his ankle kept him bound to his house except to attend probation meetings and the grocery store and other essential errands from a pre-approved list he had been given by his supervising officer at the county building.

He continued to pay the lease on his office, not yet ready to pack up and move his furniture out, but he fantasized about burning the whole building to the ground.

No one came to visit.

The house became his entire world. The place where all of his devils and ghosts gathered in the evening and whooped and hollered in his ear through the night and held his nose in his sleep until he woke up gasping for breath and then hyperventilating until only drink could get him back to sleep. Where the morning came on like a fever, with shivers and sweats and hallucinatory sensations, and he confused his life for a nightmare and all of his nightmares for his life.

He dreamed of falling bombs, of being swept up in the blast as he ran for his life; of people with demented faces, their open mouths drooling and tongues wagging and their skin discolored or missing, and they were all grasping at his hands and clothes, begging him for help, but they frightened him and so he ran with feet like concrete blocks until they climbed all over him; of his father, coughing up blood and shouting, *This world will bleed you dry, this world will fucking bleed you! You'll never make it, kid—you're just too fucking soft for it!* and then choking and spitting at him.

He dreamed of a little girl. Her eyes were bright as the sun reflecting on snow-covered ground and she smiled like someone he thought he used to know. She played hide-and-seek and snuck up behind him and covered his eyes and laughed and laughed. Once she hugged him and her hair smelled of cotton and fresh lavender and when she pulled away he was crying and she said, "Don't cry, Daddy, it's okay. Everything will be okay."

He would wake in the night and sleep through the morning and drink from noon to midnight. He refused to sleep in the quiet, haunted bedroom and so he lived on the couch. He would watch the news of the world on twenty-four-hour cycles. The television became his company, his comfort, his work. The world, his only patient. He empathized and grieved and pained with the people of Earth and he diagnosed their problems and criticized their failings and he offered many solutions, but no one listened.

He watched ballistic missiles fire across the borders of countries whose names all sounded the same to him. People marched in the streets to protest people marching on the other side of the street, who protested back at them. Young people turned up dead by the thousands from every conceivable cause except nature. Suicides and mass murders were commonplace headlines, and Henry drank and cried for their fates.

Sometimes at night, in quiet moments, he would hear whispers, a voice from outside his mind—spirits in the walls or transmissions from God or something beamed from the distant cosmos.

They would tell him that all of this had been his own doing. That it could be his to undo, as well. That it wasn't too late to turn back. He heard soft-spoken pleas for his penance, that he might alter the course of his life still.

You haven't gone too far yet.

There's time to appeal.

You're still young, and well off.

Just put down the drink, Henry.

Come back.

Come home.

There's a light at the end of this tunnel.

But with each passing day the volume of his sorrows compounded until they drowned those voices of hope. The sorrows screamed so loudly he would cry out into empty rooms, "SHUT UP! SHUT UP!" and the only relief he found was in compounding his drink and his pills in kind.

All the voices, from the stars to the walls, from the television to his mind, tried to offer a light in his dark, something to guide him out from the prison of grief he had built for himself. He drank and he chewed on pills and listened for that distant light promised by the Voice of God.

He drooled and he choked and he sputtered with chest heavy and heart beating slow, and finally, as his old grandfather clock tolled twelve times, he took too much and found himself in a dreamless sleep, and to his horror and relief his final thought echoed and faded and repeated again and again:

There is no light.

33

"Why don't you tell me what brought you here today, Nick?"

Nick looked up from the floor he had been staring at absently for some time. His gaze met the doctor's, and though he tried to maintain resolve in his stare, his eyes betrayed him. His lids and lenses quivered and pulsed, and water only barely refused to spill out over his face, which looked tired and drawn.

For weeks, or a month or more—he'd lost track—Nick had been staying in a motel in the city. He had abandoned any routine of sleeping, waking, or eating and instead adhered only to bodily compulsions and the demands of his cravings. He would wake and take pills and powders and smoke cigarettes until he slept again. From time to time, he would venture out into the cold and wet winter nights or mornings or mid-afternoons and get cash from the corner-store ATM to buy a carton of cigarettes and a fresh bag of whatever the boys on the corner were selling that day. Then he would retreat to his room and repeat the cycle of consumption until he ran out of wares again.

Earlier in the winter, on Christmas Eve, he had been overcome by his loneliness and his remorse, and he tried to treat it in a way which had always worked before. He left his mother's house and arrived on Lia's doorstep late in the evening. She came outside to meet him on the porch, holding a mug of hot cider in one hand and pulling the door closed behind her with the other. She stood with her arms folded over her puffed-out chest, obstructing the door by trying to make herself seem bigger than she was.

"What are you doing here, Nick?" she asked frostily.

"I just . . . I don't know, Li . . . I missed you. I wanted to see you." He couldn't look her in her eyes so he kept his fixed on the ground. "To see someone. You know? It's been fucked."

"Yeah, well. I bet it has. But I'm not the one, Nick. Not anymore," Lia said. Nick didn't detect the space in her tone that he had always found.

It was as if there was no question to answer, no invitation to discern. He didn't have the energy to press and so he surrendered before putting up a fight.

"Yeah. I get it. Well. I don't know. I'm sorry, I guess. I'm really sorry, that's all I wanted to say," he said, and he looked at her face one more time with a dying hope that something would give, that her eyes would look on him with that old maternal concern, that pity that so often welcomed him back to her. He found only coldness. Cold eyes, cold everything. She stood still like a soldier and guarded the entrance to her palace, and he felt smaller and more reviled than he had before he arrived.

"Sorry? You're fucking sorry, Nick? Are you?" She didn't flinch or bend or move as she spoke, but somehow seemed to become even more imposing, bigger; less forgiving.

"Yeah, Li . . . Of course I'm sorry—"

"Yeah. Of course you're fucking sorry, Nick. All you ever are is sorry. It's all you've ever been. It's like sorry is the only thing you know how to be, and I don't want to hear it. I don't care. Go away. Good luck with your sorries, or whatever it is you're doing," she said, and then a sound of some commotion came from inside. She broke her posture to look back over her shoulder.

"What was that? What . . . what are you looking at? Do you have someone in there?" Nick asked, suddenly exchanging the soft whimper and sunken shoulders for squinted eyes and a sneer in Lia's direction.

"It's none of your business what I'm doing in here. Now leave me alone, Nick." She almost shouted the words, but held just enough of her composure that it was unequivocally clear to Nick that he should leave, at once.

What had been a pit of sadness—a black hole of desperation reaching outward from his center, spreading its tendrils in search of something to consume, some comfort or solace to fill its emptiness—now collapsed in on itself like a dead star, and a raging fire exploded within him.

"Yeah. I get it. Well, I guess you can just call me when he gets bored with you, or something. I might still be around, you never know." Nick smirked like a demon and let loose a snort that could have spit sparks and black fumes from his nostrils before he turned to walk away.

He heard the sound of something hitting the back of his head and the world flashed white for an instant, but it wasn't until the mug had shattered on the ground at his feet and he smelled the hot cider soaking into the hood of his sweatshirt that he realized what had happened. He thought of turning back to her, of shouting, of calling her a whore and lecturing her for abandoning him in the time he needed her most, especially after all the years she had spent trying to win back his affections. He thought of charging through the front door and finding the man inside and holding one hand on his throat while he pummeled him with the other until he was choking on his blood and his teeth and the regret of his choice to be there that night.

But he didn't turn around.

He walked without interruption, grimacing as the pain from the back of his skull radiated down through his jaw and into his ears, eyes, and neck. He got into his truck and he clenched his jaw and tensed all the other muscles in his face to try to stop the tears that were pooling in his eyes. After a few deep breaths, he punched his steering wheel hard enough that he winced from the pain, and then started the truck and drove toward the apartment of the one person he knew would be there for him.

On the drive to Connor's apartment, he tried to recount the events of the previous months, to surmise how long it had been since he'd been out of his house. How long it had been since that night. He figured it must have been at least three months, but if someone told him a year had passed, he wouldn't be able to argue against it with confidence. He hadn't been high in a long time, either way. He gripped the steering wheel as tightly as he could to neutralize the nervous shakes in his hands. The anticipation and apprehension at the thought of getting high were dueling electric currents in the conduits of his blood, bones, and nerves. His teeth chattered so hard they exacerbated the ache in his skull from where the mug had hit him.

There were several times along the way that he considered turning back, going home. His thoughts cut and spliced like bad film edits with rapid, frenetic energy. The metallic sounds of rusted machinery screeched with each transition from one thought to the next. One minute he thought he should go back to Lia, to admit the full depth of his shame and his failure and plead and promise the world one last time so he wouldn't have to be alone. He thought maybe he meant it. He thought of going home to his mom and asking her if she wanted to stay up late and watch a Christmas movie together. He thought maybe he could still fix everything, and he believed it.

His vision flashed bright like lightning and that metal sound shrieked and all he could see was Alison holding the pen tube in her mouth and breathing in smoke and in the next frame she was blue and his chest froze until he was choking to breathe in again. He couldn't go home; he might not survive the drive. There was no fixing anything. There was no going back. Not tonight, anyway. His shaking calmed and he lit a cigarette and drove on to Connor's apartment.

Nick knocked on the door and waited. Connor opened the door just enough to push his head out and he looked around nervously in every direction.

"Why didn't you call first?" he asked, sharply.

"Good to see you too, dickhead. Can I come in?" said Nick.

"Um. What's up? What do you need?" Connor continued from where he stood in the cracked-open doorway, talking quickly in a hushed voice.

"I need to come in, man. Jesus, why is everyone acting like this right now? I haven't seen you all in months. No one calls, no one checks in, and then you all act like I have the fucking plague when I show up. Let me in, Jesus fucking Christ, Connor."

"Okay, okay, man, just be quiet, Jesus!" Connor pulled the door open a little further and ushered Nick inside. "You can't make a scene dude, god damn."

Nick walked in and began pacing back and forth in the front room.

Connor closed the door but stood with his hand on the knob, looking at Nick with a nervous inquisition.

"Are you gonna sit down or what?" Nick snarled.

"Man, you can't be here long. Just tell me what you need."

"What? What the fuck do you mean I can't be here?" Nick stopped pacing and looked up into Connor's eyes with a swirl of malice and grief.

"Nick . . ." Connor held his hands up like he was trying to calm a stray dog barking at his feet.

"Nick what? What the fuck do you mean?"

"Nick. That girl is dead, bro," Connor said.

Nick almost lunged at him but instead snarled back, "You think I don't fucking know that, Connor? What's your point?"

"Dude, I can't let anyone see you here. They all know who you are. If the cops drive by and see your truck at my place, man, I just, I can't have that!"

"Are you serious, Connor? You fucking coward. After all I've done. I've been arrested, twice,"—he held up two fingers and thrust the gesture inches from Connor's face—"TWICE, for your stupid ass. And I haven't said shit. You think they didn't ask me? You think they didn't say 'Hey tell us where the pills are coming from and we'll cut you a break?'"

"Well, how do I know you didn't?" Connor said.

"HAVE THEY FUCKING BEEN HERE, CONNOR? Have you seen any cops? It's been months, you idiot. I kept my fucking mouth shut and I did my time. More than you would do, I'm sure. You fucking chickenshit motherfucker. How dare you." Nick wasn't sure that he wasn't going to punch Connor in the face, but some sense of self-preservation reminded him that it wouldn't be productive, and so he just stood before him, seething and panting heavily until Connor spoke.

"Yeah. Yeah, man, I know. You're right. I'm sorry. Can we just sit down for one minute? This is stressing me out."

"Suit yourself. Just get out that fucking box of yours. I need it," Nick said, and he backed up to make room for Connor to pass him.

"Nick . . . I can't sell you any dope, man, that's crazy—you're way too hot. Are you sure you even want to? Haven't you been, like, clean this whole time?"

"Connor. Shut the fuck up."

Connor sat on the couch and Nick looked to the lockbox sitting in plain sight on the coffee table.

"Nick, I'm not kidding, man. Look, I know you've been through a lot and I can't imagine ... how you're feeling or whatever, but I can't sell you anything, man. If you get caught out there ... I can't do it." Connor said these last words with unflinching conviction, the same way Lia had told him to leave, and he realized that Connor wasn't open to negotiating the matter.

"Well," Nick said, and he nodded his head slowly and looked toward the door, "Good thing you never keep that thing locked, you fucking idiot." Before either of them drew another breath Nick had taken two quick strides from the entryway to the coffee table and snatched the box up into his hands. Connor sat, shock seeming to delay any reaction, and by the time he stood up, Nick had opened the box and pulled out a baggie full of blue pills, a wad of foil and a small folded stack of mixed bills rubber-banded tightly together.

"Nick, what the fuck! What the fuck are you doing, man?" Connor tried to step towards Nick, but his shin hit the coffee table and he stumbled. Nick threw the metal lockbox at Connor's head and the remainder of its contents scattered about the room as Connor fell to his knees on the floor, nursing his head with one hand.

Nick opened the door and walked quickly through the complex toward the parking lot. He heard Connor shout behind him, "Nick! Come back here, what the fuck are you doing? Are you serious?"

Nick didn't slow down and started shouting, "This guy sells drugs, everyone! This guy is a drug dealer!" It was dark and quiet in the complex, but it wasn't so late to presume that anyone was asleep. Nick yelled up to windows lit by Christmas lights and flickering television screens and Connor didn't give chase. He only shouted words of disbelief which Nick ignored as he got further away from his friend's front door.

The route from Connor's house was determined one juncture at a time. Nick didn't know where he was going and hadn't processed what he had done. He drove through town looking up and down the streets and in his rearview mirror, half-expecting someone to be pursuing him, but there was no one to be seen. The streets were desolate. Most people were probably inside with their families, celebrating the holidays together. Still, he felt uneasy in town and wanted to find somewhere more secluded where he could smoke in peace and put the obnoxious and incessant jackhammer pace of his heart to some rest.

He drove west until the roads started to wind, and even though he had driven through here more times than he would ever be able to recall, he felt like the surrounding terrain had become foreign to him. It no longer held any spirit or life. Only dirt and pine needles and dreary trees and cracked asphalt. There was no romance or nostalgia, no familiarity or sense of home. He hated every scene that was caught in his headlights and wished all of it would drown in a rain without end or find itself engulfed in the same kind of raging fire he felt burning in the bottom of his stomach.

Finally, he came to a turnout he knew well and pulled off the road. He wasn't concerned with the place or any memories it held. He didn't even look out his windows or turn off the engine. Expressionless, mechanical, he moved through the necessary preparations. He fished out an old hollow pen casing from the driver's door pocket and held it between his teeth. He pulled a pill from the bag and put it on a freshly torn piece of foil, and for what was probably no time but felt like an hour, he pictured Alison as she was the last time they had been in this parking lot. He smelled the lotion on her skin and the oils in her hair. He felt the weight of her head on his chest and he wanted to cry.

He thought he might still throw the pills out the window and return home to his mother. He thought about Doctor Foster and the doctor's story about his father who had told him he was too weak for this world. He thought about his own father, who chose to forsake his family the moment he found himself inconvenienced by the consequences of his own actions. *You can't depend on anyone else for your happiness*, he thought.

He flicked the lighter and breathed deeply while every thought he had crackled and melted and ran down the foil and disappeared into the smoke that filled his lungs.

‡

Nick stared at the doctor through hot, bleary eyes and tried to find some combination of words that would answer her question.

"I . . . I don't know where else to go," he said.

"Alright, that's alright," she said, her air professional but not at all sterile. She was friendly without being patronizing. Concerned without condescension. "And where is it that you came from?"

"You mean now? Here, in the city. Downtown. A motel," he said, gathering himself somewhat in response to the doctor's invitation, "but I can't go back there."

"Of course not. We don't want that. And what about before that, where were you? Where is home for you?"

"Home?" he asked, as if she had spoken a word in a language he didn't understand. "I can't go back there either. That's just it. I have nowhere to go. I can't stay where I've been, and I can never go home again."

He held her stare for as long as he could, until the sadness in his eyes overflowed into hers, and when he saw that she carried it too he felt shame at the burden he brought with him. He cried out and went limp and nearly hit the ground with the great weight of all of his grief, but she caught him in her arms and held him while he wept.

"Honey, it's going to be okay," she said. Another member of the staff, maybe a nurse or some administrator, came over and Nick heard the doctor tell the woman, "It's okay, he just needs a minute. It's alright."

"I'm sorry," he cried, "I'm sorry. I'm sorry. I thought I could do it. I thought I could do it on my own and all I ever did was make everything worse for everyone. I ruined everything. I ruined everything. I'm so sorry! I'm sorry!" He shouted until he trailed off into loud, uncontrollable sobs.

After some time, the doctor helped him return to the chair and she took the seat next to him. They sat in silence; she gave him space to breathe, but kept her eyes fixed softly on him.

Eventually, she spoke.

"Listen to me. There is nothing you have done that you can't come back from. You're here now, so there's hope. And you're so young, look at you."

"You don't understand," he said. He was defeated, but still he wanted to plead with her to stop being so kind to him. He wanted to tell her what a monster he had been, what unforgiveable crimes he had committed. He wanted her to look at him with revulsion and tell him that it was too late. He wanted her to tell him that there was no hope for him, that it was over. He wanted her to give him permission to give up.

"Whatever it is, I'm certain I do. You may have been around the block a few times, but I've been here a while myself. I promise you, there's nothing you can tell me that I haven't heard before. You're just gonna have to trust me on that for now, okay? You're here now, honey. That's what matters. Let's worry about the rest later. How does that sound?"

Worry about the rest later, he thought. He took a deep breath and looked back at the doctor. "Yeah," he said, "Okay. Yeah, that sounds alright. I'm sorry, I can't believe I'm acting like this—"

"Hush. Don't take it back now. I bet it's been a while since you've let yourself have a good cry."

"Yeah," he said. He sat back in the chair and wiped his face. He looked around at the walls of the intake office and read the platitudes from the framed wall-hangings with some contempt and some relief.

One Day at a Time one read, and he could have laughed at the irony of it all. The axiom he had adhered to all along, repackaged and sold as the solution to the very problems it had created. One day at a time, figure out the rest later. To figure it out later was all he had ever planned to do.

"So," the doctor began again, "shall we try again?"

Nick looked at her and pushed his lips together. He thought about what it meant to try again, and if such a thing were even possible. He thought about Alison, and how she would laugh at him if she could see him this way. *It's always all about you, isn't it, Wagner. God, a girl can't even get the credit for dying without your help, can she?* He nearly did laugh at the thought of her, but as quickly as it came, she was blue in his head again and he was consumed with a sickness in his heart.

He thought of his mother. He wondered if his absence was a burden or a relief, but he believed that it must be at least some part of each. He wondered how long it would take her to heal from all the pain he had caused. He wondered if he ever would, or if he deserved to.

He thought of the stars that he saw reflected in Alison's eyes that night. Of all the impossible millions of light years some dust had traveled from those stars to the earth to become him, to become her, to become them. From eons of nothingness, it all had exploded into being and would expand ever outward, sprawling and burning and yawning forever. Gases were breathed into life that decayed and died as it traveled through time and through space and it would again be reborn to breathe in some new way. He thought of her that night, on the roof from where he had so often looked to the sky for an anchor to a home that no one truly remembers; where he had always felt more alone than "alone" could begin to describe.

But once in a while, he'd find himself in the back of his truck with her head on his shoulder, staring at those same baffling stars sitting alone, unfathomable distance between them. Yet they all hung together, illuminating the vast expanse of empty space to form something so much bigger and more breathtaking than each piece of the whole ever could on its own.

He thought that even though this would all come to pass, again and again, that for just one moment, if one looked at it just right, that no one—not the people with their fences, their locked doors, their phony projections and all their fears; not his mother with all her worry and work; not that ass Doctor Foster with all of his troubles; not Lia, with her poor desperate heart, full of love—that no one was ever as alone as it seemed.

He thought that maybe somewhere, light years away, in a distant part of space and time, there could be a light out there that burned for him still, even if he hadn't couldn't see it just yet. He thought maybe he had seen that light in her eyes. He thought that there had to be some justice in all of it, some grand picture he couldn't yet see. He thought there had to be some way to make it mean anything at all. He thought that he had no choice left but to try.

"Yeah, okay, let's try again," he said, and nodded his head.

"That's great. Wonderful, really. I'm so glad to hear it," she said, and smiled. "So, Nick, what brings you here today?"

ABOUT THE AUTHOR

From the California suburbs, through the depths of the heroin crisis throughout the Golden State, and to the edge of an all-too-real hell and back, **Sean J. Gebhardt** wonders every day why he's still alive when so many have been lost to the opioid epidemic. But, for better or worse, he lives—writing late into the night, trying to silence that question through storytelling.

By day, he goes to work, pretending his job matters exactly as much as he needs to so he and his wife—who is absurdly out of his league—can provide for their strange and bewitching young daughter.

Everything Will Be Okay is his debut novel, a poignant, scathing reflection on broken lives and the elusive promise of healing.